Midnight Gate-opener

Enhanced Edition

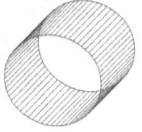

Author's Books
(As of June 20, 2020)[*]

Non-fiction

Fiction

---

[*]12 older books are Enhanced Editions and printed in 2020. They were resubmitted to the Library and Archives Canada Cataloguing as well. If a book's 'print date' on the copyright page is older, the newest version is available at Amazon and bookstores.

MIDNIGHT
GATE-OPENER

A Novel

Enhanced Edition

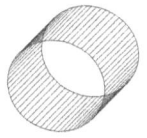

Tom Omidi, Ph.D.

Omidi, Tom, 1945-
Midnight gate-opener / Tom Omidi.—Second Edition.

ISBN 978-988351-10-0 (paperback)

I. Title.

Old edition at
Library and Archives Canada Cataloguing in Publication
PS8629.M53M53 2016   C813'.6   C2016-902398-2

Published by Eros Books,
Vancouver, British Columbia
Canada

erosbooks2020@gmail.com

Front Cover: Designed by Tom Omidi

Enhanced and Printed in 2020

Table of Contents

Dedicated to the memory
of my dear, weird parents.

"I cannot cite any childish need that is as
strong as the need for paternal protection."
Sigmund Freud

"You said it!"

Kian Noori

PROLOGUE
My Morbid Mission

Kian Noori happened to be a rather easy Persian name for *lucky* foreigners to pronounce and remember. In fact, it sounds rather musical, like Keanu Reeves! So, my parents deserve a big round of applause for doing at least this one thing right for me despite their own long, difficult names. As you can see, I'm desperate, but also eager, to find any funny reason to praise my dear parents and acknowledge their importance to me. I would also like to apologize in advance for my possible cheekiness in the following pages and divulging some of their secrets and sins merely for improving my health.

Yes, my health! I'm told that the best way to avoid a nervous breakdown or heart attack is to muse over those old memories in my loaded head and jot them down, as a sort of self-therapy. This distraction may also ease my stress from work and family issues. Anyway, there's no other way. I must just recount those haunting old stories and drag my parents into this messy account of my pitiful past. And no amount of apology would probably wash out my seeming badmouthing of their lifestyle, either.

Aside from a daunting family history, it is hard to imagine that a childish infatuation for a gypsy could map out a person's destiny. But that is exactly what happened to me as you will read all about it later. I followed her advice to escape my parents and reshape my fortune in some foreign lands. Still, all those risky adventures couldn't relieve my growing-up traumas, despite my relative success on many grounds later. I guess when destiny sets a crooked course for your life, nothing you can do to avoid it, although I admit to making many bad decisions, too—so wrong to exonerate even my ill fate! Marrying a witch can all by itself end one's life. Just one mistake! Though, I doubt my misfortunes relate to my stupidity alone. My kids' apathy and cockiness these days cannot be my fault, too, can it? They hate my guts even for my rarest fatherly advice when they're about to dive into an abyss. Then, of course, they still expect us be ready to bail them out at whatever cost and personal pain. You curse God's wisdom when the malice of people you love so much hurts so deeply.

Now I feel for my own parents bearing my youthful mischief on top of their endless marital rows, retaliations, freaky secrets, entrenched personal grief, and baffling dilemmas. Still, life was far easier then, as family affairs were simpler and more defined. Honestly, there is no contest, judging by kids' arrogance and neediness nowadays, though we cannot blame them, either. Life feels less fun and meaningful for every generation facing more setbacks with their parents, spouses, children, and friends, not to mention the rising social chaos and climate threats. What is left to be happy or proud about then? Staying hopeful becomes a tough daily chore all by itself when living often gets so tiresome and we feel so helpless. Our hopeless, pitiful efforts to indulge everyone take a big toll of our psyche, anyway.

Surely, whining and blaming others is unbecoming and futile as well. Yet we all do it naturally like a kind of self-defence. To be fair, I must blame only my naïve infatuations and dreadful adventures for my agonizing stalemate nowadays, unable to choose my next move. Now, all those endless hopes, dreams, and passion feel so foolish. Asking still the same corny questions about life at my age feels pathetic, I admit with shame. Anyway, you be the judge! Read this funny account of my adventures *with patience,* while many tales and characters come together in Parts II and III and set off daunting events and endings, one blow after another as things get really crazy! Brace yourself.

Kian Noori, M.D. April 1997

PART I

The Gypsy

CHAPTER ONE
Narges and the Gypsy

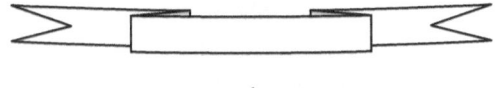

1

The doorbell rang as I rushed into the perfectly cool hall of our house in Tehran and banged the door behind me. It was a dry, hot summer afternoon in 1967 with a mild wind out there blowing a narrow heap of dust in the air now and then. Our manservant, Rahim, appeared out of the kitchen to go answer the door at the far end of our walled garden. Then Narges popped up like a jinn in the corridor above the stairs. She peered over the big hall and frowned when her squinty eyes spotted me.

"Kian, go see who's at the door," she yelled at me with her forefinger pointing south.

Both Rahim and I froze in our tracks.

"But I'm thirsty," I yelled back.

"Go answer the door first," Narges ordered, her forefinger still pointing south, like I didn't know where the door was. She kept glaring at me all along to stop me from arguing. I wasn't going to, anyway, because it would only become a laughing matter for the servants. I only rolled my eyes and turned, pretending that I was going. From the corner of my eye, I saw her return to the master bedroom with a smirk, like proud Genghis Khan marching back to Mongolia, thrilled with all his tyranny for today. She looked a lot like him, too, going by his picture in my history book in grade five that year.

That rotten Rahim just stood there with a grin of his own, so wide you could count all his teeth. After enjoying my frustration enough, he turned on his ugly toes with a swift twist, flinging his fists above his head—like a victory dance. The dirty bastard whispered, 'bye-bye,' to me before rushing back to the kitchen to continue playing with his newlywed young wife, Batool.

Narges was always this way. She liked picking on me for no damn reason, as if my frustration was funny or something. Others got their share of her twisted charm, too. But bugging me seemed to make her day, every day. I really liked to know why! Actually, solving this mystery alone had turned into a holy mission for me, as though I could put the jinn back into the bottle and escape.

Narges Banu was apparently my mother. Everybody said so! But I'd doubted this outrageous claim every other day. I wished I could complain to some authorities about this horrible mistake and end this ridiculous relationship. You'll agree with me soon, I promise. Just wait until you read the stories I'll be telling you about her. For one thing, she made me work like other servants; sometimes more. She enjoyed my labour with some kind of keen malice, like she'd carefully planned to give birth to a slave. It didn't even matter if I'd just returned from school or my friends were calling me from the street to go play with them. Sometimes, I said I had a headache or a lot of homework. She just gazed at me like an angry judge checking out the evidence. I had to defend myself and give her ultra-solid proof while Her Honour nodded with suspicion. She then made a ridiculous ruling like, "Take an aspirin." Or, "Take an hour to finish your homework fast." What killed me the most—more than work itself—was that I never knew who the hell I was in that family: a servant or a nobleman's son. Wasn't my father this wealthy deputy minister in Iran? Wasn't I the only child of this big shot?

I was still standing in the middle of the hall without really knowing why. Except that stalling was often my way of bugging Narges in return. I really got a big kick out of stalling sometimes. So I just watched Rahim and Batool chuckling in the kitchen and peeping at me through the door. They were laughing at me, those stinking peasants. Doing their jobs really sucked, especially when everybody could see them just fooling around instead of working.

To give you an example of my chores, I spent over an hour every week to grind gum tragacanth in a brass mortar. The pestle was so heavy I had to stop every ten seconds to rest my wrist. The goddamn pebbly bits just kept jumping out of the mortar, too, although I held my hand over the opening. I had to collect them and put them back in their places. Every time I said it was ready, Narges checked it fast, and yelled, "Not yet... Continue." After a hundred inspections, she'd finally let me go: "Okay, okay... Just leave it there and go, you lazy lizard." Instead of a simple thank you, she cursed my half-assed effort in front of the servants while they chuckled. I giggled sometimes myself when Narges continued the grinding herself with rage.

When the powder was soft enough, she mixed it with three egg yokes and henna and laid that gross, pasty stuff over her hair for a few hours before taking a shower. It was supposed to boost the roots of her thinning hair, but I'd seen no improvement all those years—zilch. Both my efforts and hens' labour to lay those extra large eggs were going to waste, yet we were all on the hook forever as long as a single strand still lived on Narges's barren head. I wished a judge or jury could review this grinding business at least and rule that this hair therapy wasn't working. "Just wear your wigs, lady, and let those tormented strands die in peace," they'd suggest while tittering. I wished I dared saying that to her myself! This chore alone was driving me nuts, I tell you.

The way she favoured our servants over me was insulting, too. This wasn't my imagination, I swear. For one thing, she kept saying that it was hard to find good help. And she always ordered me, "Be nice to them."

Are you mad!? Do their work and be nice to them, too?

I was tempted many times to tell my teacher that I couldn't do my homework because I had lots of housework to do for Narges. The only reason I never did it in the end was that I was afraid the

teacher may ask who Narges was and I didn't know if I should
say she was my father's wife or my mother! Then she would
probably contact Father to find out about all these housework that
I claimed I was doing and why I called my mother Narges.

I'd thought of two reasons for Narges's nastiness. First,
maybe I was an orphan or something. Several clues rejected this
possibility, though. The main clue came from Narges's circle of
friends whenever I barged in on them. They stopped their gossip
abruptly, as if dying for another chance to review my physique.
My entrance was usually the main trigger reminding them that it
was time *again* for another round of arguments on this very topic.
They sounded like obsessed lunatics insisting that my eyes, nose,
or something resembled Narges's or Father's. My growing nose
raised disagreements the most. Anyway, the way they fought over
my resemblance to my so-called parents probably proved that I
wasn't an orphan, after all. My other conclusion about Narges's
malice toward me, and spoiling our servants instead, was too
harsh and embarrassing. That is, sometimes, I became so cynical
I wondered if she had some wicked thing going with that sleazy
Rahim! *Curiosity kills the cat, ha?*

'Curiosity kills the cat' was something new Narges had
learned and kept telling me often those days when she thought I
was being nosy—'Out of Order,' as Her Honour would yell! I
didn't know exactly what she meant, but it sounded like she was
hinting something about all those cat-killings not being accidents
and that I was being warned. *But I'm not a sloppy cat, witch,* I
whispered to myself anytime she said it. I meant to ask Father if
he knew what exactly she meant and where she had learned it.

2

Narges yelled from the bedroom when the doorbell rang again.

"You're still here, Kian?"

"Why should I go?" I yelled back just for the heck of it. "Why
can't Rahim go?"

"Because it's probably your stupid friends ringing the bell. Just go, you devil!" Narges shouted and the servants chuckled in the kitchen harder more furtively. I guess we'd hired them only to sit there and laugh at us, although the pressure of suffocating their laughter so much all the time seemed torturous enough despite all the joy. If I didn't hate their guts, even I might've felt for them for their dire struggles to conceal so much fun at my expense alone!

"You wanna bet it's not my stupid friends?" I screamed.

"NO, JUST GO, YOU HEAR ME?" Narges shrieked.

Her pitch was so high I was thrown out into the portico while Rahim exploded with a loud laughter in the kitchen this time. I slammed the door behind me, hid in a corner, and gasped. Then I started staggering along the garden path, around 250 feet, hoping that whoever was behind the damn door would go away. I knew it wasn't my friends, since they always shouted for me instead of ringing the doorbell, exactly like I'd told them. I'd also explained it to Narges a million times already. But she refused to believe me, although she could always hear them shouting my name in the street when they came to get me. She complained about their racket now and then, too, but still preferred to forget even this loud, obvious fact just to bug me.

Like a turtle, I really took my time to get to the door, giggling all along. Narges must understand soon that she couldn't trust me to do any job right. A thick ten-feet-high brick wall with a huge wrought-iron gate surrounded our house. Both Rahim and I hated running the long distance in hot summer days or chilly winter nights to open the door for visitors, or the heavy iron-gate for my parents when they honked their car horns from the street. Often Rahim and I stared into each other's eyes, like two poker players, until one of us lost his nerve. Although we each invented great excuses, we didn't know what goddamn lies the other one was cooking up to tell my parents about the delay and whose story they'd believe better. "I didn't hear the car horn," was our richest excuse, which really pissed them off. In return, they honked their car horns longer and faster, and kept complaining, anyway. It was a mortal sin if the majesties were kept waiting, or had to get out of their comfy cars to ring the doorbell. Sometimes, we ran all the way only to discover my parents hadn't been the ones making all that racket. In Iran, people honk their car horns all the time for a million silly reasons. Especially, around our house, the spiteful neighbours did it just to bug my parents. I'll explain the reason later.

Anyhow, I unlocked and pulled the small door built inside the gate's panel. But nobody was there. My stalling had worked like a charm. All I had to do now was to shut the door and report my glorious finding to Narges gladly. I could look into her squinty eyes—if she opened them a little wider please—and enjoy her frustration for trusting me with all these crappy chores all the time. For some mysterious reason, however, I stuck my head out the door and watched the woman who was walking away. I bet the Devil pushed my head, because this one simple mistake changed my life forever.

The woman turned her head and saw me, then walked back toward our house. Now it seemed too late to shut the door and go away. As she got close, I noticed that she was a gypsy. Her exotic garments, dark skin, and glossy black hair had a special charm, although they startled me a bit first. I checked her out from head to toe, where her red shoes stuck out from under her long, baggy, black skirt! *In this heat!?* The colour of her shining blouse and the small scarf around her neck matched the colour of her shoes. All that glossy red burned my retinas, I tell you. The smell of her strong, possibly homemade, perfume tickled my nostrils, but I let it go. I glared at her with tension and big question marks in my eyes. But she stared at me with absolute calm, like I had all the time in the world.

With the tip of her tongue, she licked the length of her meaty lips, then rounded them like a rose bud. Maybe she was showing them off or trying to say something. Maybe she was just dumb, praying, putting a spell on me, or teasing my obvious impatience with all those funny question marks in my eyes. She was really starting to piss me off. If she was a beggar, I'd slam the door in her face so fast her ears would fall off, I swore to God in my head. But, as I gazed at her mouth to speak, my heart banged in my chest. Those lazy lips were so perfect for a big kiss. They had suddenly made me speechless to shout: "What...? What do you want?" Usually I was rude to vagrants to make up for my timidity around others.

My fascination for a gypsy felt weird after my fury a second earlier, but I just couldn't take my eyes off her moist, pinkish lips. They quivered subtly, like a rainforest butterfly flapping its wings to shake off the pesky raindrops. I merely swam in a soothing fantasy with some unusual peace and pleasure. She kept gauging me, too, like she'd forgotten her reason for ringing the doorbell.

At last, she said, "Go ask your mother if she wants me tell her fortune."

Now she was ordering me around too! I almost slammed the door in her face, but quickly realized that she was too pretty for my chronic rudeness. So I raced all the way back into the house and up the stairs to the second floor. Narges was ironing Father's shirts with incredible care. Her attention to the starched collars of his shirts was stunning. But all those desperate attempts to satisfy Father seemed ridiculous when you saw their frequent fights and deep spite. She always cursed him, too, especially behind his back. When I passed on the gypsy's message, she unplugged the iron and dashed toward the stairs. She ordered me to bring the gypsy inside the house. So I charged again toward the gate, this time more enthusiastically, though! With silly hand motions and stutter, panting like a racing hound, I led the gypsy through the garden path toward the house entrance.

"You have a beautiful garden," she said. "Especially those red roses are gorgeous."

I looked around to see what the hell she was talking about now. Everything looked boring like usual, especially this minute, with my mood and all. What was so special about those flowers and shrubs that most people admired right away? Father's fuss around them and arguing with gardeners so passionately felt strange, too. *This gypsy likes anything that is red, anyway,* was my brilliant conclusion. I only peeped at her blankly.

"Smell'm one day," she said, probably thinking I was stupid.

I grasped her last comment even less, but let it go. This time I didn't even peep at her lest she'd think I was indeed stupid or teasing her.

3

Rahim and Batool weren't in the kitchen anymore. Fully charged up after all that fooling around and chuckling, they'd apparently dashed to their detached, private suite to make out again. This show was now repeated a thousand times every day in this circus we called home. And it was getting on my nerves! Maybe I was a bit jealous, but pissed off too. I had to rush around to run Narges's errands while they were screwing in bed and laughing about me. I was surely energizing their sex life a lot! Maybe he was still working hard on the bride's solid virginity. Eavesdropping once, I'd overheard him telling Narges that he had difficulty taking care of the business. He looked desperate and angry, which made my day. This was about two months earlier, during the first week of bringing the bride home. *This cute, tiny Batool is probably extra virgin,* I mused. Was he still struggling? I hoped so. I wished he'd never get through. *Maybe I could help?* What kind of advice was he hoping to get from Narges or she could give, anyway? I tried to imagine some of her *pussyble* suggestions and got mad. Some matters around our household really sucked, I'm telling you.

This crumby Rahim was good-looking, tall, and strong. No wonder! Narges had chosen him after interviewing a bunch of peasants four years before. She often joked with him, too, maybe for making Father angry or jealous. Three months earlier, he went to his village, somewhere near Ghazvin, to marry Batool. She was an attractive shy girl, but getting more comfy now in our house, giggling and enjoying life while Rahim chased her like a horny hound. She teased me on the side, too, with some kind of a sly shyness and grin that only village girls possess. I liked her sneaky peeks at me sometimes, as though she wished to kiss me.

4

The gypsy's soft chatter with Narges, maybe about her psychic power and fee, interrupted my musing. Then they sat behind the big table in the hall, which is a large foyer common in Iranian architecture. It stands at the centre of the house, where the kitchen and all other rooms join through it. But it is also a large space for a dining set, television, and other furniture needed for family and informal gatherings.

I stood near the fridge in the kitchen and gulped one bottle of water fast. I chuckled when I imagined my friends' dried mouths and frustration sitting in the shade behind the wall of our house and waiting for me to bring them water. I wasn't trying to be mean or anything, but their attitude was getting more annoying every day. I'd actually grown a kind of mixed feelings about wasting my time with those fatsoes. I was bored to my bones wandering like dopes around the barren fields with a bunch of losers aimlessly. Well, this is still another sad story I'll explain later. But I'd figured I had to hang out with them sometimes, anyway, before going crazy in my parents' madhouse.

Narges's attention to a peasant gypsy was odd and amusing. But seeing a psychic for the first time had raised my curiosity as well. I wondered about the sanity of any person who claimed psychic power. Even crazier would be the person believing her. But I was myself hypnotized by the gypsy's raw beauty at least. She simply glowed, even without any makeup or fancy outfits.

The gypsy's soft, soothing voice sounded angelic. I could see her profile if I leaned a little, but I was dying to see her full face, especially those gorgeous lips. *How would they really taste?* Narges's pitiful expression ruined my daydream, though. Her anxious attention to the gypsy's gibberish was an appalling and haunting scene, I tell you. Her face showed a heartbreaking mix of gloom, desperation, and hope—as though she'd been waiting, tolerating, and hoping a lifetime for some kind of a miracle. Her deep despair was obvious from not only allowing a gypsy into our house against Father's strict orders, but also relying on a stranger to bring her hope. Her constant nodding to the gypsy's promises looked so pitiful—so unlike her normal personality, which showed only arrogance and anger. Now, suddenly Narges looked like a sombre soul. Relief might be just around the corner, after all. *How can a clever witch like her be so gullible as well?*

I stayed quiet to listen in as long as Narges didn't kick me out. Her gloom today felt even more shocking than her vulgar gossips with her friends, which she always stopped me from hearing. I couldn't help wondering if her misfortunes could be blamed on her homeliness. If yes, then the poor gypsy was really wasting her time. How could she overcome such a huge obstacle and tell her anything positive about her future? I felt both embarrassed and sad. Feeling sorry for her was an odd thing all by itself and a bit scary, too. But I also felt sorry for myself. Why couldn't the gypsy woman have been my mother instead?

Narges probably didn't know I was in the kitchen, but the gypsy turned and peered at me twice. I bet she'd detected my suspicion about her psychic power and manipulation of my poor, glum mother. But my fascination with this whole shenanigan might've also made me grimace. According to Father, I frowned often when listening to people or trying to focus. He'd said it was annoying and maybe even insulting. So I grinned quickly before offending the gorgeous gypsy. She ignored that too, pretending to be very serious about her mystical profession!

Her focus to contact supernatural seemed idiotic but genuine. Still, fooling with poor Narges's shattered soul looked funny, too. Narges's polite stare was even funnier. I wished I had a camera to take her picture and hang it in my room to cherish this historical moment of her deep despair and frailty. It could help me build confidence and rebel against her tyranny soon. Many people tried to snub Narges but always failed. Not even Father or the snooty women in parties could bully her. But now a gypsy had made her look so pitiful just for hearing some lousy messages of hope. I wished I dared telling everything to Father and maybe others.

Narges now looked totally convinced of the gypsy's genius after she predicted that the source of her gloom was 'her man.' As if Narges weren't blaming Father for everything already! Despite the gypsy's correct diagnosis, her messing with Narges's brain was irritating. But her coldness toward me, like Narges's normal apathy, was killing me the most. I was angry, especially when trying so hard not to grimace *merely* for her sake. But what was I hoping to achieve, anyhow? Why was I so anxious to get this wandering peasant's attention? What was I thinking?

My sudden fancy for a gypsy felt really bizarre. She wasn't even as pretty as many gorgeous women around my family. Their glamour and heavy makeup had captivated me for years already, especially at formal gatherings with their embroidered gowns and glittering jewellery, dancing long hours into the night to the Western tunes of tango, samba, mambo, waltz, and cha-cha. I'd enjoyed those plain miracles of nature when I hadn't been too depressed. But this gypsy's effect on me felt different—rather magical, indeed.

5

Then a miracle happened! The gypsy woman turned and glanced at me with a gentle grin that jolted me like a lightning. It just killed me so tenderly. That swift, soft sparkle beaming from the corner of her large black eye for only a moment carved a scar in my heart deeper than any laser ray could have. Her sweet, sneaky glimpse shattered my childhood innocence right there and then.

My friends began shouting for me from outside our house. I ignored them for a minute, but they sounded restless and thirsty. I knew Narges would get mad at me if I didn't stop them. So I ran outside and showered them with some mean curses. I slammed

the door in their astonished faces and sneaked back into the
kitchen. Narges frowned and the gypsy sighed, as if I'd disturbed
her precious concentration. Big deal! I sat behind the small table
used for cooking preparations again. I hid in a corner where only
the gypsy could see me if she turned, though I still worried about
Narges questioning me any second.

I kept hoarding water like a camel, now merely as an excuse
to stick around. Passionate thoughts turned in my hankering head
with colourful images of kissing the gypsy. For a moment, the
idea of loving an older woman felt crazy for a timid boy who
hadn't learned to like even his own mother. Still I couldn't stop
my sexy fantasies. The commotion inside me was mystical, like a
divine inspiration to explore love for an older woman as the most
natural adventure in the world. No more guilty feeling for my
sneaky sensual dreams about those fancy women in Royal Club
and parties. No more shyness, but only a desire to build courage
for getting into those fiery females' hearts.

An abrupt silence in the hall broke my daydream. I bent over
and looked into the hall. Narges was opening her purse to pay the
gypsy. So I decided to sneak out of the kitchen and escape into
the street before Narges could interrogate me for eavesdropping
for an hour.

"Do you want me to tell your fortune, *pesaram*?" the gypsy
asked. Her soothing voice shook my heart again.

Pesaram! Calling me 'son' felt especially fantastic—so odd
but delightful. Besides jolting my heart, her startling sincerity had
surprised my brain, too. I'd never been called *Pesaram* before, let
alone with such tenderness. Mute and dazed, I didn't know what
to do. Was I allowed to accept the gypsy's offer? Then, I also
wondered about my parents' problem all those years to speak soft
like this gypsy, to me and each other.

"Pesaram?" the gypsy called again.

I was numb and dumb, so I staggered to the hall and stared at
her like a drowning idiot. Narges watched the situation in shock,
flustered by the gypsy's gentle tone and generosity. The gypsy's

guts had annoyed her more than it had bemused me. She was quite a rebel! I loved her more every minute. Did she need a son or a lover? She'd already said *pesaram* twice, but who knew what she really wanted to do with me.

I peeped at Narges for a hint, but she appeared powerless for once. She just stood still, looking useless and disgusted, her hand frozen inside her purse, probably still under the gypsy's spell. I gazed at the gypsy's gorgeous black eyes and her kind grin spreading all over her full, naturally pink lips. They were really tempting for a kiss and I wondered again about its feeling and taste. In the movies, actors seemed to enjoy it a lot, going by their quiet long stares into each other's eyes before and after the kiss. So soft and sweet like ice cream, the gypsy's lips looked inviting for a taste right this minute. But I was paralyzed like a gloomy, washed-out actor. She stared at me with a mix of pity and passion before checking out my quivering lips that also seemed unable to utter an audible word.

A time for bravery. I needed courage for loving older women, anyway, I thought, as if reciting my lesson for today! I must rebel and speak for myself. So I gathered my nerve and muttered: "*Bashe...*" Another blow to Narges. She was going nuts with all the rebellions against her in one afternoon, yet probably petrified to peep in fear of the gypsy's curse spoiling the rest of her life. *A psychic intimidating a jinn!* I was having a ball.

"Come sit here, dear," the gypsy said while pulling out the chair next to hers and patting its seat for me.

The word 'dear' made me blush, while I hurried to the pointed chair. Now I was her *dear*!

"What's your name?" she whispered as I sat next to her.

"Kian Noori," I murmured, forcing a smile to prevent my possible sneaky grimace.

She grabbed my left hand and opened my clenched fingers one by one. Her warm forefinger traced the lines crisscrossing my palm. The exotic smell of her breath so near my face rattled all the cells in my body. I moved closer to her and inhaled the air she exhaled. Narges took the money out of her purse at last, put it on the table, and kept watching us. The gypsy's silence and cool indifference finally convinced her to leave us alone.

The gypsy ignored the money too. Her focus on the sneaky lines zigzagging all over my tiny palm was admirable. Then, her sharp gaze turned into a gorgeous grimace, unlike mine. It seemed that omens hidden in my hand were too creepy, perfectly telling my looming life story.

At last she said, "You'll have a long life. Ye see this lifeline?"

I nodded.

"You'll be a successful and rich man." She paused and pressed the skin of my palm harder with both her thumbs, as though digging up the lines. I wondered whether they'd grown into their final forms yet. If not, her predictions were rubbish then. Should there be a minimum age for visiting a fortune-teller? Why were we bothering then? My usual paranoia!

"You'll travel beyond the oceans… You'll go to the new world," she continued. "You'll meet a nice girl… And you'll have four cute children."

Gloom dulled her face, and her eyelids fluttered fast as she peeped at me. Then she smiled, like trying to hide a bad omen.

"Did you see something bad?" I murmured.

She grinned again while clutching both my hands and rubbing them softly with her thumbs. She stared at me for a long time before whispering. "No… nothing too bad…"

"Are you sure? Tell me the truth," I mumbled, yet proud of my courage to question such a powerful and charming woman.

Again, she gazed into my eyes with angst, as if absorbing the horrible information in my palm. Her silence made my future feel gloomier every second. Was her gesture only a gimmick to scare me enough to do something she'd intended from the beginning? At last, my horrified eyes convinced her to say something before I had a heart attack.

"Don't get so alarmed, *pesaram*. But you should remember something important. Can you do that for me?"

I nodded fast, believing she was only testing her spell over me, already guessing I'd do anything for her.

"A mysterious woman will come into your life soon…"

I sighed and stared at her moist eyes. Was she talking about herself? Who could be more mysterious than this gypsy?

"That's before your long journey to the new world."

I just gazed at her with suspicion.

"Be careful with this woman. Promise me…"

I nodded with panic and a ton of curiosity.

"Control your feelings," she continued. "Instead, plan for your travel to the new world. Okay?"

"*Bashe…,*" I said and nodded repeatedly.

Her eyes got sadder and moister as she examined my palm two more minutes without saying a word, as if that final review was none of my business, but only for her personal curiosity! Instead, she leaned over and kissed my cheek, as though paying for her private review of my palm, or maybe for giving me the power to fight the bad omen. I trembled from the touch of those lips, though I would've really preferred them on my own lips. Yet that damp spot on my skin burned from tenderness and lust. I believed she'd read my mind perfectly about my craving for a kiss! Reading people's minds was her job, after all! But, surely, she couldn't have planted that big kiss on my lips. Not today!— with Narges possibly watching us with fury from a corner!

She took Narges's money and asked me to show her out. She seemed in a rush to leave—to avoid my sad eyes and scary palm perhaps. Those lines might've revealed only more bad omens. On the other hand, she had possibly seen my entire future the second she'd laid eyes on me. Her long silence at the gate, while we'd gazed at each other curiously, might've been from her initial shock. And her zeal to read my palm had been only for verifying her original premonition, fill her curiosity, and caution me about this mysterious woman crowding my life soon. Her warning felt like a serious, scary matter! But it also felt like a big adventure I looked forward to. *Or I'm fooled as much as Narges was.*

We strolled down the long garden path. She stopped abruptly
to smell a red rose bud that stuck out from a bush and bobbed to
her reverently in the shallow wind. At the gate, she stroked my
hair and kissed my other cheek, and then left.

6

I stood in awe, watching her walk away without looking back to
meet my anxious gaze. I stared into the horizon for a sign of a
gypsies' caravan or something. I began following her aimlessly,
but kept a good distance from her. I wasn't sure whether I wanted
her to know, but didn't wish to hide myself, either. I decided to
walk as far as necessary to at least learn where she came from.

After five minutes, she stopped at a house and rang the bell.
She talked with somebody, then walked to the next house and did
the same routine. In front of the third house, she spoke longer
with someone. Then she turned, peered at me, smiled and waved
before going inside the house. I waved back at her. Why had she
ignored me until the last moment then? Was this all part of her
plot to lead me into her trap on my own feet? Was I still under her
spell? Did this mean that she wanted me to wait for her? Had she
planned this entire fortunetelling masquerade to kidnap me for
ransom or for herself? So many children had been kidnapped in
Tehran in recent months. Daily papers were full of such stories.
But going with her would be a blessing, anyway, regardless of
her intentions. I cared too much for her to fear her. Actually, I
wished she'd kidnap me. *Maybe I'd better beg her to kidnap me!*

I remembered Father's repeated order to all of us. He said,
"Never bring strangers into the house if they came by and asked
for a glass of water or bread or money. They're spies. They try to
learn about the situation in the house to return at night with
proper preparation to kill and rob us." For a moment, I tried to
imagine the gypsy as a scout for bandits who would attack us at
night. But my heart rejected this ridiculous suggestion quickly.

Anyway, despite Father's advice, under the gypsy's spell or not, I'd go with her to the end of the earth if she wanted me to.

My pissed-off friends were coming fast toward me, but I was still too mesmerized to run away. If they wanted a fight, I'd give them one. My flustered face discouraged them to argue with me, anyway. They only asked what I'd been doing at home and why I looked so pale and miserable. They were also curious why I wanted to hang around that place like a fool. Hashem said I looked like a zombie and I cursed him. But I knew myself that I felt and acted quite weird, even beyond my regular foolishness. I had become a new person—maybe a man. But explaining my astonishing feeling for a gypsy to those bigmouth juveniles was just pointless.

It was getting dark when my friends left. I'd upset them enough for one day, which felt like a good triumph, at last. I had to pee after drinking all that water and holding myself for so long. I rushed to a corner and poured the poison out of my body with incredible relief just in time. My fat friends and pesky piss gone, I could think better about my options. *Should I ask the gypsy to take me with her or only follow her to find out where she lives?*

I considered knocking on the neighbour's door and asking for the gypsy. But I didn't know what to tell her if she came out and stared at me. She might accuse me of breaking her concentration again, too! Maybe I could tell her that I'll wait for her out there. But what if she asked me why? I had no answer if she didn't know, either. So, I just lingered in the empty street, totally hyped up to follow her and then see what happens.

I gasped a deep breath. What a bizarre afternoon! Many deep, odd emotions and questions suddenly bombarded my brain. She had psychic power, after all, contrary to all my initial doubts. The best powerful clue was that she'd inspired me like nobody had ever done before. Now my life and needs felt so much clearer, especially for gaining my freedom away from Narges. Some mystical discoveries had now replaced my childish wonderments with a swift, delightful blow as well. I was no longer a lost child.

Her tenderness had shaken my heart, and her charm had moved my manly urges to a magical sphere. Together, they'd caused an amazing commotion inside me. Merely discovering that human emotions are so fragile and flexible frightened me. But finding that feelings could be expressed so easily, with such soothing sincerity and effect, was a refreshing experience. Facing all these emotions for the first time felt weird. Why discovering such startling feelings only now? From a stranger? Many parents, all over the world, are crude and I was only one of millions of tormented kids. But how many kids ever faced the astonishing magic of meeting a kind gypsy who was so pretty and maybe looking for a boy to love, too? Were many people out there with real psychic power? With a gift to move someone to a new world? To make someone so restless? Her life-saving expertise felt phenomenal! She'd asked me to plan for going to the new world, but I was in a fantastic new world already, right now!

Half an hour later, Father's car stopped behind me. He looked disturbed seeing me ruffled, standing alone in the middle of the road, staring at a house like an undecided burglar. He got even more surprised at my hesitation to get in the car. I didn't know what to do. I almost ran away, but realized that it'd only mean abandoning my post, anyway. Father would follow me in his car or might even call the gendarmerie to find me and the cause of my madness.

"Hurry up, we must get ready to go out," he yelled.

After thinking another ten seconds under Father's anxious eyes, I got in the car. But my mind and heart remained near the house where the gypsy was.

Later that evening, I felt a strong urge to start a diary and record that day's story and everything else about myself and my family. Many events, thoughts, and feelings—mine and others'—overwhelmed me gradually in the months and years after the gypsy's visit. They led to odd adventures during the following years and decades and threw the course of my life on a highly emotional rollercoaster. Writing almost every night about those experiences, especially all the sensual commotions around and inside me, helped me forget my troubles. But more importantly, my diaries have proven quite handy for writing this story. I have in fact copied the exact wording and moods noted in the diaries for this book, especially in the first two parts.

CHAPTER TWO
The Pathetic Bourgeois

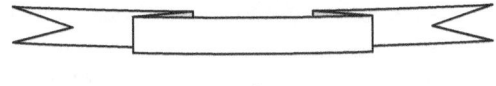

1

Narges was startled when Father and I arrived home together in his car. She glared at me with panic before watching Father with tension, as if expecting him to shout or say something. I knew what was bugging her. She was wondering if I'd told him about the gypsy coming into our house and telling our fortunes. She hadn't had a chance to order me not to. I smirked at her in return, despite my gloom for losing my chance of chasing the gypsy. Teasing her was a hard job this minute with my gloom and all, but I simply couldn't pass up the opportunity of fooling with Narges whenever a marvellous situation like that came up; even if I wasn't in the mood too much. When Father went upstairs without raising hell, she gasped a deep breath and walked away after another nasty glare at me and shaking her head. I thought the way we bugged each other was really funny as well. But she always got upset, which made it so much funnier for me. Her frustration and whining only encouraged me to tease her more often, although she always proved to be a bigger bugger.

We got ready quickly and went to Royal Club—a private gambling house, though it didn't look like a casino. The two gambling floors had about dozen large rooms with few tables for various types of card playing, mostly rummy and poker. With no card-dealers at the tables, gamblers played in their own teams, mostly for gossiping, flirting, business, and political plots. Only seldom they joined a different group when there was no room at their regular tables. They only paid an hourly rate, in addition to the steep membership fee. The Club's director, Mr. Bashiri, tried to arrange the teams based on players' personalities. Still, some gamblers got drunk and rough sometimes. Yet they never fought like the cowboys in American movies I watched those days and wondered about people killing each other left and right, often for just a few dollars! Altogether, Royal Club was a quiet place for a bunch of big shots to wind down, have dinner and drinks, make contacts, flirt, and play cards.

My parents abhorred gambling. This was most likely the only virtue they had in common. But we often hung around Royal Club when they weren't invited to any particular party. More than gambling, they hated spending their evenings alone or together. So we got out of the house most evenings or entertained guests at home. Especially during summers, they often joined their friends at the Club without worrying about my early rise to go to school. The reason I was dragged to these parties and clubs was bizarre all by itself: Father had built a mansion on the outskirts of Tehran, in the middle of nowhere. So my parents had decided that leaving me alone at night, even with the servants around, was unwise.

The Club also had a big hall for dancing, occasionally with a live band in presence. A fancy bar in its far corner offered drinks and snacks, but food was served upstairs in the restaurant or in the garden during the refreshing summer evenings. The huge, colourful garden had a great atmosphere for eating outdoors and socializing. The food was always delicious, especially the chicken kebab that the chef was famous for.

Father behaved like an honorary member since he was Mr. Bashiri's friend. Besides, he took care of Royal Club's frequent violations of city bylaws, including the long hours of operation and the presence of children in the Club, mainly me. Therefore, we enjoyed all the fun in the Club freely. His tab for food and drinks was also erased regularly. It appeared strange when all the couples at our table got a bill, except for Father. He'd probably done Mr. Bashiri another big favour, I imagined. Father also felt free to invite his friends to the Club regularly. The situation looked out of control, especially when a bunch of them showed up uninvited or when we weren't there. At the end, a big group of non-paying members came only for dinner and dancing. Their extravagance at the bar and restaurant stopped Mr. Bashiri from whining too much. He only kept them away from the gambling rooms in the upper floors of the large building.

2

I felt sadder than usual. My normally endless appetite vanished, too, after I finished the big plate that the chef always put together specially for me. I'd lost even my usual craving to watch those pretty women indulging themselves with flirting and gossiping all night. They looked silly tonight with their noisy arguments around the large dining table and their sexy swirling on the dance floor under the dim light. I shunned their sneaky stares, too, as if they may detect my juvenile fancy for the gypsy. Still, I felt some women were teasing my sentimentality about a vagrant who'd passed through the wilderness of our subdivision. Maybe my secret was out, possibly through Narges's big mouth. I used to imagine that mothers could sort of read their children's minds, especially such an obvious one. Maybe she'd overheard the gypsy's words to me and seen her kissing my cheek, too.

Knowing Narges, she could've started a gossip with her nosy friends about me and the gypsy just for fun or something. She might even convince Father that I'd invited the gypsy and begged Narges to let her tell our fortunes. Maybe I was getting cynical a little or a lot. But many experiences in that creepy family justified my paranoia. The incident eight months earlier is an excellent example to give you a crash course about Narges.

Late last autumn, I was in my room when I smelled smoke in the house. Narges was in the bathroom, putting that gross gum tragacanth stuff on her hair. I ran down the stairs and found the table in the middle of the kitchen ablaze. I couldn't get to the sink for water, nor did I have a bucket. So I decided to pull the table out of the kitchen before the fire caught the drapes and spread. I opened the entrance door and began pulling the table's legs from the side where flames had less strength. I hauled it into the hall and toward the portico, all along shouting: "Fire, help…" Flames roared on the top of the table and around the legs on the opposite side of me. I kneeled to hold the lower parts of the legs. Still, my hair caught fire a few times and I brushed it off with my hand.

At last, I brought the burning table out into the portico and pushed it over into the swimming pool. I was out of breath but proud of my bravery. At this point, Rahim and Narges had arrived and watched me in shock, while I waited for their big applause for my bravery, dedication, and quick thinking. Instead, Narges shook her head with anger before charging toward the kitchen, Rahim chasing her with stress. She stood naked with only a towel wrapped around her breasts and upper thighs, and a shower cap over her head. The messy lines of henna and gum tragacanth leaked from the corners of the cap. They dripped on the floor as she moved around and spread the nauseating odour of henna.

"What'd you do?" she yelled at me.

"Saved the house from burning to the ground. Can't you see?"

"But how did you start the fire?" she asked while Rahim watched us from the corner of his guilty eye.

"I smelled smoke and when I got to the kitchen the table was on fire. I'm sure Rahim had put the heater near the table and the tablecloth caught fire. He just leaves the heater on and goes away to his room."

Rahim looked on like a sleazy mouse. Narges peeped at him furtively, until she took his silence as a sign of his guilt. Then she began to control the situation.

"Rahim, go pull the table and everything else out of the pool, hurry up," she shouted as we followed her back to the portico.

Rahim pulled the half-burnt table, tablecloth, and debris with a rake out of the pool and tossed them over the garden wall into the wasteland surrounding our house. We went back inside again. Narges looked around the kitchen with tension. Debris and black smoke were all over the kitchen and the hall. She ordered Rahim to clean the kitchen. I started toward my room.

"Where do you think you're going?" she shrieked.

"To my room!"

"Go get a rag and clean the smoke off the walls. Hurry up."

"But why me? It's not my fault that Rahim put our house on fire and made this mess."

"Stop nagging, Kian. We must clean everything before your father gets home."

"Do I have to?"

"Yes, hurry up. Get going. Clean everything carefully. And nobody says anything about the fire to your father. Understood?"

Rahim nodded.

"Why not?" I barked.

"Because we don't know what happened or who did it."

"Rahim did it, of course. Why don't you believe me when I say I was in my room? Rahim pulls the electric heater too close to the table to keep his feet warm. You understand?!" I cried.

"I don't care, Kian. Just keep your mouth shut. Is that clear?" she yelled.

"Umm," I mumbled and then whispered, "No..."

"What...?"

"Nothing..."

"Go get a rag and start cleaning the walls."

As I turned, she called me back. "Let me look at you."

She examined my hair and face and then said, "You've burnt your hair and eyebrows."

"How bad?" I asked and ran to the washroom mirror. It was bad. A few parts of my hair had burnt and my eyebrows were singed a bit as well.

"We must shave your head," she said.

"Shave? Can't you just trim it?" I asked with anger. I really loved my long, brown hair in the Beatles' style.

"No, I'm not a barber. Go get the shaver."

I considered arguing with her, stalling, or running out to the street and hiding there until Father got home, but I knew it would have serious consequences for me for many months to come. So, I staggered to the bathroom upstairs and brought the shaver. I felt like a captured soldier in a prisoners' camp who is asked to go get the shovel and pick to dig his own grave before they shot him in the head. She made me sit on a stool in the middle of the kitchen, wrapped a sheet around my neck, and shaved my gorgeous hair in two minutes. She trimmed my eyebrows too. I was forced to clean all that silky hair and chuck it in the garbage. Then I rushed to the mirror again. I looked like an ugly scarecrow with those trimmed eyebrows, big nose, and a shaved head dangling over my bony body.

Narges smirked with gloat at the anguished scarecrow she'd created, threw a rag at me, and ordered me to wipe the smoke's smudges off the walls. Then she helped Rahim carry a small table from another room and put it in the middle of the kitchen. All along, she just walked around in semi-nude without shame and ordered us, like Tarzan training a couple of dumb monkeys. She stretched her arms and legs to spread a tablecloth over the table. She reached up to open the windows to let out the rest of the smoke and smell. I was afraid the towel might drop any second if the damn knot loosened. She just made me madder every minute with her casual view of her appearance and her carelessness about a possible catastrophe.

"Clean the walls in the hall, too, before taking a shower," she ordered me.

She then burnt some wild rue on the oven to kill the smell of fire. After she thought that Rahim and I could clean up the mess in and around the kitchen, she returned to the bathroom to wash the mess on her hair and face. I cursed Rahim, and that asshole only laughed with a loud roar to imitate Dracula. I thought I should've let the house burn down instead of cleaning so many walls as a reward.

By the time Father arrived, the kitchen and the hall showed no trace of the fire. The first thing Father noticed was my shaved head, of course. He asked me why I did it and I said Narges had asked me to do it for the summer. He didn't seem eager to buy such bullshit that Narges had cooked up and forced me to repeat like a parrot. He then looked closer at my eyebrows, but didn't say anything. He just stood there, sniffed the air, and then went to the kitchen. Narges chased him everywhere, which surely made Father more suspicious. Rahim got startled and guilt showed all over his face as Father stepped into the kitchen. I bet he preferred to confess and get it over with, too, if Narges would let him. I was really mad about the masquerade Narges had started instead of telling Father the truth. Still, I thought I should stick around to see the ending of this freaky show. I usually enjoyed Father's yelling at, or punching, Narges sometimes. Although it intimidated me, too, it didn't happen frequently enough if you asked me.

"Is this a different table?" Father asked at last.

"No," Narges replied and Rahim shuddered.

"Don't lie to me," Father yelled at her. "This table is smaller than the one that was here before. This house smells like there's been a big fire. What's happened?"

"*Your son* almost burnt the house down," Narges shrieked.

I jumped up and screamed, "I didn't start the fire. I saved the house. I took the burning table out and threw it in the pool."

"But nobody else was in the kitchen, Kian," she said so damn casually I wanted to run over and strangle her on the spot.

"Oh, God...," I screamed and ran to my room.

Besides my humiliation and frustration, the fact that she was absolutely sure about Rahim's guilt was even more maddening. Otherwise, she would've not asked anybody to take the table out of the pool or clean the walls until Father arrived and she blamed me for everything.

These types of incidents always happened in our house. Many times Narges had blamed me in front of Father for her own crappy decisions, blunders, or to protect the servants. Aside from her natural wickedness, she had a loose mouth, too. And then she punished me if some truth slipped my tongue by accident. I hated her goddamn hypocrisy. Then again, I must confess I had had the best times of my life on those few occasions when Father had slapped or punched Narges after another one of her big, tenacious lies had driven him to madness. Alas, it hadn't happened in recent years. In fact, I was thinking seriously if it was now time to give Father a good reason myself to do it again by telling on her about the gypsy. Would that be enough? Would it work?

3

I just lingered in my regular corner on the couch in the far end of the dance hall. I'd ruined an expensive couch by sitting in that spot all the time, for hours so many nights. You could see the mould of my bony ass sunk deep into that poor cushion. I was bored and sad. Still I tried to appear *normal* for Kian—depressed enough like usual, but no grimace! It wasn't an easy job, though, since the gypsy woman's image wouldn't leave me alone. I kept reminiscing about her red shoes and scarf, her soft voice, her kind words, her meaty pink lips, her scary warnings, her nonsense about the red roses, her exotic breath, and certainly those two hot kisses that still tickled my cheeks' skin. A fantastic daydream about kissing her made me blush and a chill jiggled my spine. Narges probably knew that my gloom related to the gypsy's visit and hiding it from Father. He'd be furious if he heard that a likely spy had been in our house. Narges's past retaliations—for telling stuff *without her permission*—had taught me good lessons. I could not even ask her whether she meant to mention the gypsy to Father. Her anguish to answer either "Yes" or "No" would constipate her for a week and, naturally, I'll end up paying a big price for *it*. I was learning plenty of politics early on in my life.

Father had this cute paranoia about spies. He thought they were everywhere spying on him for various reasons. Some were trying to steal the confidential government documents he walked around with all day. He brought them home to read, but hardly got a chance to do so. He had this big safe at home to hide them at night. He usually had some secret papers when he returned from a conference abroad. "They're for the minister's eyes only," he explained, anyway, although nobody ever asked him anything about a bunch of folders in his hand or briefcase. He just wanted to help everybody remember what a big shot he was. He claimed that another group of spies was trying to find dirt regarding his personal life to ruin his reputation and the chance of becoming a minister. He believed he'd already been bypassed a few times for this opportunity because of rumours that spies had spread around about him. He even suspected some of his friends to be spies.

After moving to this new subdivision, another category of spies was invented. They would supposedly come inside our house to learn about the opportunities to rob, and maybe kill, us. Or they might kidnap him, or force him to open the safe—which I assumed might be empty and embarrassing, anyway.

Long story short, Father hit the roof when he suspected that a possible spy had invaded his privacy or even walked too close to our house by accident. His reaction was both irritating and funny. His eyes bulged from apprehension and anger, while giving us long lectures, in a loud, energetic tone, about all those lowlifes having nothing better to do in their miserable lives than plotting against him. He went on for hours and nobody dared to peep lest he restarted or found even more grounds to explain his evidences and suspicions more diligently. The worst part was his whining, afterwards, about our idiotic apathy and inability to really grasp the extent of the conspiracy to destroy him.

Anyhow, I'd decided not to mention the gypsy to Father, not merely out of fear of Narges, but to avoid another one of those comical scenes and Father's possible heart attack. Besides, the gypsy's predictions about my adventures with women and travel to the new world were too embarrassing if the subject was raised, which was a very likely scenario. Narges knew how to bring it up in front of Father for fun or retaliation. She might even blame me for the gypsy's predictions of my future. "Who's the woman that the gypsy was talking about then?" she'd ask me, for example. Thank God, she seemed still chewing on the gypsy's words about her destiny. Whenever she turned like this, she'd just forget about me, as if she'd left this planet. It didn't matter what I did, where I went, or what troubles I got myself into, even if I arrived home with torn clothes and a bloody nose.

I tried to forget the gypsy for a while. So I focused on the hoopla on the dance floor. The hoopla! A lustful theatre put on by this cocky crowd in the Club. What I saw, I saw a bunch of horny old men and women hugging, giggling, and swirling with a lousy harmony. Their hearts pounding from excitement and exhaustion. Their brains pondering wicked plots and sexy adventures. Their bodies and breaths burning with passion. Their eyes glowing with devilish joy. Their hands subtly caressing each other's bare skins with subtle gestures. Their cheeks touching just enough for a taste of an ultimate thrill. Their legs rubbing inside each other's laps. Their saliva moistening their lips, ready for a kiss. Their tender stares hinting deep secrets. Then, worst of all, killing themselves with some crappy dance steps to mask the whole masquerade and their filthy manoeuvres—pretending their sex hormones stayed numb as long as they moved with the music. And a solid promise to separate quickly the instant the music stopped—before those hungry hormones woke up. *Oh boy, what a lot of horny phonies!* They just killed me. In fact, I just wanted to kill myself knowing that this big bunch of gambling, garish officials were in charge of running my godforsaken country. Some earnest revolutionaries could possibly start a coup d'etat just by bombing Royal Club and blowing up so many of those big shots in one place.

Of course, not everybody was having fun in the dance hall. Some just mingled aimlessly and ate their hearts out while their spouses fooled around a few feet away from their eyes. I bet many of them had lost the energy to fight over all those flirting. Some danced only out of boredom or for showing off their noble civility. Many of these rising bourgeois were only trying to adapt

—a small sacrifice for associating with the men of authority. So many favours and secrets were exchanged among the big shots and their followers, I imagined. The bottomline was they were accepting the price of mimicking a modern lifestyle in a hurry with great enthusiasm, despite the humiliation that at least some of them could not hide. The whole shenanigan felt embarrassing and disgraceful to me just watching their frantic faces, never mind being a subject of those silly masquerades!

Loud conversations and phony laughter filled the hall as the lustful crowd tried to cover up the romantic mood of slow dances by fast-talking and cheers. They looked silly hoping to fool their spouses and the audience, pretending that all those touching and twirling were merely playful and innocent. Their sheer arrogance, above their idiocy, made them believe people were collectively too stupid or busy to notice their filthy flirting. Father's piercing, embellished laughter was always distinguishable in the crowd. He was having fun, as usual, dancing and embracing different women, mainly his friends' wives. He believed that some of those friends were spies, anyway. So, flirting with their wives was a fair retaliation in his mind. All along, the gullible husbands pretended that everything was under control. Restricting their wives would only make them more restless, after all. I believed some of those men had become spies due to their frustration with Father. They just had to avenge Father's arrogance somehow, right? It was hard to guess who was retaliating or spying on whom because of what, I tell you. Yet, they all pretended to be good friends! *Oh boy, what a lot of silly hypocrites!* They were dying to embrace the life of the bourgeoisie and outdo modern societies. The middle and upper class Iranians were being spoiled faster than the showy Westerners themselves.

Some women, especially, seemed to be having so much fun quite liberally, as if they lived in Paris. Sometimes they invited me to dance, too, but I always declined shyly. I imagined they felt goddamn sorry for me, the way I looked so lost in that grownup crowd. They surely noticed my fascination with their charm, but also my contempt for their phoniness and shameless flirting. Their tension about my presence and grimace was obvious. But I was forced to be there and I suffered for it, too. On the other hand, watching such beautiful bodies swinging on the dance floor appeased my pain a little. My craving to smell their skins bathed in the latest perfumes from Paris and London competed with the agony of being there—lost amongst a bunch of cocky aristocrats. Pain and pleasure mixed into a foggy picture of life for a young adventurer like me. But the more I enjoyed those pretentious, pretty women, the more Narges's homeliness and hopelessness became evident, which made me sad sometimes. Was my mom the only ugly woman in the world?

Narges looked more like the Hazaras. Instead of a round face, though, hers was a long rectangular. Her eyes were narrow, as if always squinting to find someone's fault or frailty. Her lips were thin with almost no visible lines, as if always biting them out of spite or stress. Her nose was long and narrow with raised nostrils, as if fitted for snubbing people. Her long ears stuck out, as though always ready for eavesdropping. All these thin, narrow features spread over her long face with a vast forehead, which led to some kind of thin hair that I've already told you its story. This narrow face stood on a long neck dangling over her chubby body.

Narges always sat alone at the table and sipped her vodka mixed with Pepsi Cola and tension. She tried to bury her pain of witnessing this charade night after night. Once or twice the whole evening, Father made a gesture to dance with her as well. This, again, appeared to me more like a futile attempt to fake a modern husband's civility. I wondered why she agreed to come to these places, unless she found it useful to stick around at least, instead of letting Father flirt fully out of her sight. Out of courtesy or whatever, some men invited her to dance once in a blue moon as well. But you could see they weren't enjoying it—far from it. She felt their apathy toward her, too, but kept a straight face spiced with sour arrogance. Often she even turned down their requests for a dance just to avoid the final humiliation. Her attempts to hide the sad facts surrounding her life made her look even more pathetic.

Yet, a few men were way more pitiful than Narges. They sat quietly at their tables with long faces all evening. All they did, they just watched their wives' casual flirtation with the big shots or young, handsome guys. They pretended to grasp the norms of this society, but their anguish to bear the charade on the dance floor was clear even to a distracted child like me. These 'rejects' had the patience of Noah, it seemed. Yet, they talked with Narges only sporadically with little patience. They just refilled their whisky glasses and sunk in their misery in silence around the big table, near Narges sometimes, while the others danced for hours. They looked more depressed than those gamblers who came down to the dance hall right after losing their shirts.

Just watching these wretched rejects sit there all night and get drunk depressed me to my bones. How could they keep coming back to this circus so often? How and why would they take all this nonsense? I bet the worst part of it for them was watching me witness their misery from close up. The steaming hidden rage in their dismal stares scared the hell out of me so often. And in turn, my clear apprehension increased their rage, realizing how their demise was evident even to a child and scared the hell out of the poor chap forced to be there. I imagined that their wives dragged them here the same way Father obliged Narges. Anyhow, they all looked pathetic, though the saddest part was witnessing Narges being ignored even by the rejects. Actually, I worried about her, despite her mysterious malice toward me.

Many times, I'd overheard Narges's friends trying to push her nerves, for God knew what personal intentions. They asked her how she could tolerate her husband's open, shameless flirting with women. Her answer was a profound one: "I'd rather share a spoon of honey with my friends than eat a whole barrel of shit alone." She offered a solid argument to cover up her turmoil, but I doubted anybody really bought it. I bet not even she believed in her sound philosophy.

I wondered about all the secrets these people in the dance hall kept. I imagined most of them could write shocking novels full of juicy secrets. Many wild stories were always brewing behind the pretentious civil scene and all those corny dance manoeuvres. My hot imaginations grew from the ongoing furtive stares, whispers, gossips, and rumours around the club, which nobody could miss. Madame Bovary's story would prove too childish compared with some affairs shaping in the Club. Yet, I believed, most of those women had already read and memorized *Madame Bovary*.

4

A particular man in that rowdy crowd, Dr. Hassan Afzali, was extra anxious about my presence and watching his wife, Mina, dance with different men all night. She was quite a sexy and ultra sociable woman. Only once in a while, she also danced with Dr. Afzali, which seemed more like a pity dance to keep him content —like the ones Father wasted on Narges. The rest of the time, he just sat there and observed her charm, which she pretended to be normal and innocent. His pathetic love for her was evident in his restless eyes that chased her round the clock, even when chatting with people, while she mingled energetically. Yet, Mina's casual attention to the poor doctor looked like a merciful gesture at best. Even I'd noticed all those freaky emotions. He kept chatting with other 'rejects' for hours, only killing time, maybe boasting subtly about owning her, pretending that his gorgeous wife was still his in the end, maybe because she hadn't yet asked for a divorce. Sometimes, he looked edgy about people's possible thoughts, especially mine, while he struggled to hide his embarrassment, anguish, and stress. Yet, the rage in his eyes was hard to miss, especially when he glared at me with a frightening mix of anger and humiliation; as if telling me, 'At least you shut up judging me, you little rascal'.

One night, about a month earlier, I overheard a heartbreaking conversation between him and his brother, General Afzali. This guy was a three-star general of the army and came to the Club now and then. That evening I was again snoozing on the couch in the quieter corner of the dance hall. I heard some murmurs from the nearby couch. I recognized Dr. Afzali's voice talking to his brother. They didn't notice me in that dark corner or assumed I was sound asleep. I kept my eyes closed and pretended to be asleep, anyway.

"It's disgraceful, if you ask me," General Afzali whispered.

"I didn't expect you to be so naïve and listen to gossips like a woman," Dr. Afzali replied.

"But I have my own senses. I'm saying all this for your own good. I'm your goddamn brother, for God's sake."

"You don't understand my life," Dr. Afzali replied.

"Why don't you explain it to me then? Maybe I can help."

"I love her, you know? I really love her. Besides, I don't care or believe what people say. These people are a bunch of idiots."

"How can you love someone who's so careless about you?"

"Loving someone takes no logic. I need her even though she's cruel sometimes."

"So you agree that she's cruel to you?"

"Sometimes … But I've come to a major conclusion."

"What's that?"

"Humans are cruel by nature. Women in particular are a bit crueller these days because of the new shitty lifestyles. So it doesn't matter whom I marry. In this modern society, I must pay a price if I want to have a wife."

"But what about your pride and honour? I hate to interfere in your life, but… God… I wish I never was in this position to tell you all this stuff, but I love you, brother."

"Let's not talk about it anymore then. You're probably a bit drunk now," Dr. Afzali said with frustration.

"*Masti-o-Rausti*, you know!"

"Well, if you think you're talking honest since you're drunk, maybe you're too drunk to know what you're talking about."

"Stop denying facts now that I've got the nerve to speak out."

"What facts? What're you trying to say, anyway?"

"All I'm saying," General Afzali continued, "is that there's a line-up to seduce Mina. Here, I said it."

"That's stupid. I hate you for saying this… How dare you?"

"Deep down you know that I'm right. Stop denying it."

"Even if the rumours were true, what do you expect me to do? Divorce her and go wait at the end of the line myself? At least I'm at the front of the line now," Dr. Afzali said with a giggle.

"If you're that open-minded or stupid, then I don't know what else to say," General Afzali said and left.

Dr. Afzali stayed alone on the couch for the rest of the evening deep in his thoughts perhaps. Meanwhile, I agonized pretending to be asleep. I didn't dare open my eyes, thinking they'd show my fear and guilt for hearing such a humiliating conversation. I even considered snoring. I'm pretty much sure I heard Dr. Afzali weeping in that dark corner. But, again, I didn't dare open my eyes to check. In those moments, I hated the whole world and myself for being in the midst of it all.

Behind my closed eyes, I pondered people's philosophies about sharing their spouses with others. Especially, Narges's and Dr. Afzali's theories sounded sensible, despite their absurdity and gloominess. Obviously, they made up their theories only out of desperation. But the irony was that their fake philosophies only made the agony of their depressing marriages more obvious. It also suggested that the only way to deal with marriage nowadays was to somehow adopt the kind of philosophies that I'd heard firsthand from these heartbroken experts—these big losers! It felt too tough to build such a liberal mentality. Yet, one must adopt a similar mindset before falling in love, I thought. Or never fall in love! As though I were not already torn by all the freakish words, glares, and curses between Father and Narges, now Dr. Afzali's life and love felt even weirder and scarier to me. His outrageous chitchat with his brother and weeping like a baby in private was pathetic. I wondered about his pride and options. I also imagined he always wondered about the same thing: his pride and options.

When we went home that night, I cried in my bed for a long time, too, like him, without really knowing why. Was I sad for Dr. Afzali, Narges, other 'rejects,' or only for my struggling spirit desperate to emerge out of these frightening settings and messy sentiments unscathed? Could I save this forgotten child called Kian Noori?

5

I walked to Narges and asked her when we were going home. I often did this useless, nagging routine only out of desperation. Sometimes I did it just for the heck of it—to bug Narges. She said, *Go ask your father*, just to bug both Father and me in return. She knew I wouldn't dare doing such an outrageous thing. He didn't look tired or willing to go home yet, anyway. She just wanted to make Father angry with me. So I went back to the couch. One of the kids who sometimes came to the Club with his parents was sitting on the other side of the couch and watching me return to my usual spot—King Kian's permanent throne. I avoided eye contact while he kept staring at me. I sat on my side of the couch and peered at the dance floor as though I hadn't even noticed him. Sometimes, the gamblers brought their kids to the Club and sent them to the dance hall to play in a corner with cards and board games. If I wasn't too depressed like tonight, I played with them around the hall or in the big garden of the Club.

"Do you wanna play Snake and Ladder?" the boy asked.

I didn't even remember his name. "No, I don't feel like it," I murmured without looking at him.

"You wanna go play in the garden then?" he asked.

The big garden was well-lit and often kids spent hours playing some kind of a silly game out there, usually chasing one another idiotically, making a racket and all.

"Not really," I growled.

The poor guy shut up. He didn't peep for the next couple of hours that we both sat on the opposite corners of the couch. I didn't even bother to ask his name. I never asked anybody's name if I forgot it or they didn't mention it themselves. I didn't know the names of most kids that I'd played with in the Club for months or years. Even when they asked my name, I never cared asking theirs. It was none of my business, I figured.

Bored and edgy, even the idea of playing with that lonely kid felt torturous. I even considered roaming around the Club to get away from him if he bugged me just one more time. Sometimes, I even fled to the gambling rooms on the upper floors to avoid the dancing masquerade and the nosy kids. This was against the city bylaws and Father had warned me against wandering around. Yet, I often either forgot when I was bored or did it on purpose. Besides, I enjoyed watching those gamblers' tense concentration to win and their frustration of losing. They looked really funny. Some of them, as well as the Club's staff, were usually nice to me. They indulged me because of Father and offered me soft drinks. But sometimes some spies reported me to annoy Father or Mr. Bashiri, who received yet another notice from city officials.

I noticed the grownups on the dance floor watching us two kids on the couch and chuckling. The scene was apparently funny to them or something. Two miserable-looking kids sitting on the opposite sides of the couch and not even bothering to speak with each other. We looked dismal for sure, as they pointed us to one another and giggled instead of focusing on their own goddamn dancing and flirting. I tried to ignore those so-called grownups. But watching their silly smirks and pretensions at the Club every night made it hard for me to dismiss their idiocy or stop hating their guts for calling themselves 'the grownups'! That dumb, godforsaken kid sitting on the other side didn't even know we'd become the laughing stock for a big crowd of morons.

Narges turned around to see what the heck people's fuss was all about. I wanted to go yell at them: "What? What's so funny, you horny morons?" Too bad, I didn't have the guts. Narges and I exchanged glances, but she turned her head fast. I wondered what she was thinking at that moment and every night in the bedroom when making love to her naughty husband. How could her brain reconcile such conflicting emotions? Sometimes she looked quite embarrassed for being in the midst of all those commotions. But we both found some relief in the fact that she wasn't the only miserable person there. *Go ask your father,* I giggled, recalling Narges's earlier comment. Oh, gosh, she was really sneaky, too, as soon as she found time to bug me or an opportunity to turn Father against me.

My struggle to read grownups' minds had turned into a big, tiring obsession, I tell you, like a fanatic scientist going cuckoo by repeated failures. When something freaky was going on, people stared at me to see if I'd noticed it, too. Especially when Narges or Dr. Afzali stared at me, I knew they were trying to distract me. So, in fact, I got keener and returned to our table to be closer to the dance floor. I was becoming a wiseass fast despite grownups' efforts to fool me. Narges often said, "Why don't you go rest on the couch or read a book?" Then I knew something was going on for sure. I asked her, "Why?" and opened my eyes wider. It was usually hard to understand what was exactly going on, though. I wished I knew psychology to read people's minds even better, though I thought I was becoming an expert too fast for my touchy nerves, anyway—torturing myself enough already.

I wondered if other kids noticed everything going on in the Club as clearly and cynically as I did! Did they understand all the commotions and flirting that went on in the Club or parties? They were the same age or older than me. So, maybe we could share our ideas about all this vulgarity, instead of playing in the garden and pretending ignorance. They could see the dancing hoopla and all those other clues floating freely; in the ways people murmured in each other's ears, exchanged glances and grins, clinked their liquor glasses with a playful wink, touched when lighting each other's cigarettes, bought liquor for women, spied on one another from the four corners of the dance hall or in private parties. Of course, our naïve, pathetic parents tried to hide their mischief and secrets. Still many rumours reached even our innocent ears. Wild vibes were constantly circling in the air begging for our raving review. Regular rumours also fuelled my conclusions, and not that I were born so cynical. So, other kids probably felt the same way, yet didn't seem sad or even conscious of this masquerade. *Was something wrong with them or only me?*

6

Father's group often held the biggest table in the dance hall. Some gamblers also came for a short rest at the bar or for some dancing. A few handsome, young men always roamed around the dance floor, too, without belonging to any particular group or holding a table. Those gigolos somehow found an excuse to be there. Among them was the chef's son, Nosrat Yaghobi. He danced with Mina Afzali more often than he did with other women. This image alone caused suspicion for Dr. Afzali and everybody else. Yet, nobody dared to make too much fuss about it. Dr. Afzali was a famous surgeon and a physically strong man in addition to his social affluence. He'd been a junior wrestler and won a few international titles before getting into university.

Narges turned to check on me again. That particular night she looked gloomier than usual, maybe because of the gypsy, too—the same way I did. Her frailty had been exposed just for trusting a gypsy to give her some hopes to cling to. Our eye contacts were timid, as if she knew that I realized the sadness of her life and her intention to keep the gypsy's visit a secret. I wished I could tell her somehow that she didn't have to worry about this matter at least. I was guilty, too, for letting the gypsy tell my fortune. This thought triggered my paranoia: Had Narges asked the gypsy to tell my fortune to stop me from telling on her? Compared with her normal tricks, the idea of making the gypsy say a few words to me appeared like a natural plan. If so, I'd been betrayed by the gypsy woman, too. Maybe she had no special affection for me, after all, and her predictions were probably all rubbish as well. Was I going to travel to the new world or not? Was a mysterious woman coming into my life soon or what? Now I had even a bigger motive to find the gypsy woman to clarify my future.

The kid on the other side of the couch started snoring. He'd fallen asleep in an awkward slouch. I got up and walked away to check him out from a distance. He looked utterly pathetic and helpless like an abandoned kid in a busy train station. That was the way those grownups saw me every night, too! Everybody could see how pitiful I looked in my corner, except my parents who didn't see it or cared about it. I decided to go outside and walk in the garden instead of being around that miserable kid. I had to look a bit less pathetic for a while at least. Sitting there and watching a bunch of drunks dancing and laughing like lunatics were already exhausting and embarrassing enough. But, sitting next to that helpless boy was just too much for my pride. So I walked in the garden for over an hour, thinking. I wished Father would get tired so that we could go home, but he wasn't showing any sign of fatigue or giving up anytime soon—*Mashallah!* I wished I were in my bed. I really had to do something about my life. Like what?

CHAPTER THREE
Listing My Family's Secrets

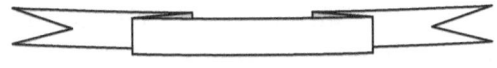

1

Just past midnight, Father finally quit and we left Royal Club. I wondered where he got all that energy! *Mashallah!* I got dizzy only watching him chitchat, laugh, drink, flirt, and dance. We always arrived home past midnight after those agonizing night outs. I usually dozed off in the backseat of the car while Father drove us home. He had this light-blue Chevrolet Impala with long, one-piece seats both in front and back. As we got close to home, I usually woke up from the car's rattling on the gravel road in our subdivision. If the clatters didn't do the job, Narges jumped in herself to wake me and say that we were almost home. I had to use my key to open the gate for the car to get in. It didn't matter what time we arrived home and how sleepy and exhausted I was. They wouldn't honk the car horn for Rahim to come and open the gate that late in the evening. I squinted with pain to avoid the car's intense headlights as Father drove through the gate and parked the car in front of the house. Maybe my grimacing habit, which Father nagged about often, was the outcome of all that late night forced squinting against his car's headlights? I was building my nerve to mention it to him the next time he complained about my grimacing. During winters, especially, this chore of opening the gate was so darn torturous, I tell you. Sometimes the grounds were covered with snow and ice and the gate panels got stuck. I had to shovel the snow out of the way first while the majesties watched me from inside the heated car with impatience. Lifting the gate's frozen handle and pushing the two icy, heavy panels on the slippery path could kill you, especially if you were exhausted, pissed, and sleepy. I couldn't keep my eyes open, yet I had to fight off the car's intense headlights, too, while handling the gate. Then it took me a long time to close the gate and stagger on the snowy path to the house. Often I thought they took me along to all those parties and clubs not out of fear for my safety if I was left alone at home, but only because they needed a gate-opener when they reached home so late most nights. I was merely their midnight gate-opener.

Anyway, this was another crappy chore I was stuck with on the earth—not a topic for discussion or bargaining. Kian was born to do it! Period. Narges's apathy was expected because, to her, this was just another chore—and surely not ladylike to do it herself, even if she weren't wearing those high-heels. By the way, I never understood how she could balance her chubby body on those thin, five-inch high heels and walk, too. Father couldn't go open the gate, either, I imagined, because he was the driver. I didn't stop to think that he could do both if he really cared and was willing to trouble himself a little. But Father seemed to be lost in a fantasy world, anyway, not conscious of all the misery and slavery around him. That's the way he appeared to me at least. I never thought he didn't like me or anything. But he liked so many other people and things, too. He liked the women around him, dancing, photography, and books, as well as his job, music collection, state of the art stereo system, car, garden, friends (even the suspected spies), ties and shoes and fine suits, and of course, most of all, he loved himself very very much. The amount of time he spent to trim his mustache and put beauty cream on his face to keep it young was by itself horrendous. He just really didn't have time to worry about me too much, and not that he was mean or anything. He was only selfish like Narges.

Anyway, I closed the gate that night and ran all the way to my room. Thank God, I was never forced to brush my teeth if I wasn't in the mood too much. I undressed fast and collapsed onto my bed. I thought I'd get a few hours of deep sleep after another eventful but exhausting day. I was hoping to forget the gypsy and

Narges and all the new questions in my head. But I was wrong. It felt like only one minute of sleep before Narges's excitement in the master bedroom woke me up. My bedroom was far away from theirs. Still, with all the doors closed and all, I could hear her careless moaning and satanic blabbering during their moronic sex. This was another weird twist, and pussyble comfort for poor Narges, that they often had great sex when they returned home after those parties. That was her reward, I imagined, for behaving herself and not bugging Father too much at the club and parties. But I could never understand why she talked so much during sex. Didn't she scream enough all day? I'd never heard Father though, not even a peep, although I could only assume that he was the superman entertaining Narges so perfectly that late at night. Was he only humouring her or even suffering like me? I was furious, anyhow, while Narges was dying not merely of joy, but mostly proving to me, herself, and the entire neighbourhood that Father was still wrapped around her finger. What a futile dream! What a torturous show of existence! I hated her vulgar show off.

I covered my ears and tried to ignore them, but she sounded restless for some crooked reasons I abhorred to analyze that late at night. My brain was about to blow up and I couldn't take it anymore. So what I did, I went downstairs quietly to hide in the closed-door kitchen. I could still hear Narges. So I slammed the cabinet door with rage. The loud bang echoed in the hall as I walked to the fridge to find some food. Food always calmed my nerves—for an hour or so. I grabbed the baloney, butter, bread, tomatoes, and pickles—a great mix to make myself a satiating sandwich.

"He's always nibbling like a pregnant woman," Narges often told people for teasing me, "and he's lazy like one too... God knows where all those calories go!"

They only increased my height and appetite—that's where all those calories went. I was too skinny but tall for an almost twelve-year-old boy. I ate lots of rice, lamb, and greasy potato chips, along with any other food that caught my eye all day. All this eating was from stress, I bet. It also related to my incomplete meals—because they were filled with stuff that Narges knew I hated, like carrot, spinach, or egg. She insisted they were good for me to embarrass me in front of Father. Of course, I wasn't feeling too happy about the way I looked like a long stick. But I wasn't dying to look like Narges or the neighbourhood kids, either. The more junk I ate, the chubbier they got. The world seemed to have gone mad when those fatsoes mocked my tall, tiny body. I had a crazy nightmare a few nights earlier that was funny, too: I dreamt Narges had given birth to a fat, ugly baby—about hundred kilos if you could weigh her in my dream. Narges kept hugging and kissing her while ordering me, 'Don't touch my beautiful baby.'

I was stacking up the layers of my sandwich when the kitchen door opened and Father stepped inside.

"What're you doing?" he asked, like he was blind or the lights were off.

"Making a sandwich…!" I answered, pointing to the growing masterpiece in front of his eyes.

"Is something wrong?"

"No."

He just kept peeping around nervously, perhaps trying to find the words making sense in that kind of situation that late at night. He couldn't find any. He looked so helpless and desperate. Then suddenly he got excited, as if he'd just found a cure for cancer.

"Aren't you sleepy?" he asked with a triumphant grin.

"I was… But not any more."

"Are you sure you're okay?"

What did he expect me to say? That I wasn't okay because of them? 'Please keep it down when you're fooling around, so I can sleep'? 'Just take it easy, you two…; will you?'

Instead, I said, "Yes. I'll just eat this and go back to bed."

"Wow… Can you eat all that?" he asked with a smirk.

"I'll try," I replied, spreading another big chunk of butter on the bread for the top of the whole pile without minding him. At that moment, I most likely had the biggest grimace he'd ever seen on my face, but he didn't peep about it as much as I was ready with my answer!

"Okay, goodnight then..."

He left without closing the kitchen door. So I got up and slammed the door, but not as loud as the first big bang. He was probably startled a bit going up the stairs. Good! Anyway, these kinds of haunting experiences at home and the hoopla in the Club and parties had made me anxious about sex besides ruining my brain. But now, after the gypsy's visit, I was suddenly curious about it, too, in a new way.

I blamed Father for certain things, too, but at least he usually was calm and kind if he was around, although his mind was often somewhere else, anyway—probably pondering his job, business, spies, or girlfriends. It made him look mysterious or lost—hard to say which one, though. Sometimes, I wondered how he did his job as deputy minister with so much on his mind on top of so little sleep every night! He was very mindful and critical of the gardeners' work though, which showed his fuss for perfection.

All those years, I didn't know how I really felt about Father. Sometimes, I admired his knack in flirting with women. Other times, I found it disgusting. Sometimes, I felt proud of him as a rich deputy minister. Sometimes, I envied his charisma. Other times, I blamed him for letting women take so much of his time away from me. Sometimes, I felt sorry for him for living with Narges. Once in a blue moon I resented him, too. Overall, my feelings for him were vague and complex, yet always mixed with some kind of love, unlike the way I felt so flat for poor Narges. I only felt sorry and sad for her, especially when she sat pensively at the table in the Club with a scary smirk to dismiss Dr. Afzali and a few other dejected men in her vicinity mourning their own gloomy destinies. It was weird I had some soft feelings, or any compassion at all, for Narges. Yet, those rare touchy moods hardly helped my hatred for all the stuff she did to me, especially her blabbering during sex that only heightened my curiosity about her sanity.

The gigantic sandwich was now ready and my mouth began watering as I admired my voluptuous creation. Its size always showed my stress at the time of making those fat masterpieces. I washed a big bite down with Pepsi Cola. I could hear the muffled voices of the humiliated Romeo and horny Juliet from upstairs arguing about me or something for a while. Then they shut up.

2

While enjoying my late snack and the precious quiet, my rising obsession to figure out my parents' lives and marriage began banging in my head again and agitating me. Hundreds of tough questions and touchy secrets seemed to demand my investigation and I just couldn't let the matter alone anymore.

As a start, I wondered about the way Father's head worked. What was he thinking and feeling about all those pretty women in the dance hall while ignoring Narges? It surely couldn't be easy handling such conflicting emotions and episodes day after day. Also amazing was the way he arrogantly ignored some men's dismal stares, while he flirted with their wives so casually, maybe even as his natural right. How could he laugh so loud and dismiss the fact that his masquerade wasn't fooling anybody, in particular his so-called friends? Did he even bother himself with these silly thoughts? How brave he seemed embracing all those beautiful women so openly, and then coming home and making love to this…, this…, Narges even more courageously? Was it only his sense of duty that made him sleep with her, too? Or was he doing it just to keep her mouth shut a little?

Their relationship was really bizarre, I tell you. Actually, I was dying to know how these two characters had even come together. A major question was, 'Why Father, such a handsome, outgoing person, had decided to marry this homely, nagging, and aloof Narges in the first place?' I had to dig this information out of my grandparents and uncles. It was a big job though, because of the embarrassing nature of my questions. Yet, this mystery had to be solved somehow—as though my sanity depended on it.

If you asked me, Father and the gypsy women would've looked really nice together. I would've surely been proud to walk between them. Just imagine the gypsy with Narges's jewelleries in one of her fancy gowns (after they made it eight sizes smaller, of course). Wow! Father would've never wasted so much time on other women. He'd become prime minister long time ago. On the other hand, I thought Narges and Genghis Khan would've made a perfect couple, too. Together they could've conquered the rest of the world. No problem there at all!

By the way, I hated this Genghis Khan more than all the other kids at school did. Not only his wild personality, but mostly his picture reminding me of Narges, scared the hell out of me. The other thing that bothered me, when I looked at his picture or other pictures of kings and conquerors in history books, was that I just couldn't stop wondering who had painted them with all those fancy, vibrant colours so many centuries ago. There was never any mention of the painter or a date. I asked our teachers a few times whether they knew. The whole class roared with laughter and the teachers thought I was trying to be a clown, so they sent me to the principal's office. But I was not joking at all. I was madly serious, in fact. The principal never believed me, either, and ignored my question, as if they were all conspiring to hide this secret from the rest of the world. I really hated not knowing who had painted those pictures, when, how good a painter he'd been, whether the subjects had posed for him, where he'd found all those permanent pigments, and how much the pictures really matched their owners' faces, especially this jerk Genghis Khan's. Did he really look like Narges? Was she possibly a descendant of him? That jerk had spread his genes in Iran, too, after destroying a good bunch of our cities first.

Psychologists may offer many reasons for Father's temporary insanity to marry a woman like Narges. The mystery was even more puzzling since Father had left the bride on the wedding night to go to a village a hundred kilometres away from Tehran with a bunch of his bachelor friends—sinful boys and girls. He'd returned home to his newlywed wife after a week, as if he'd gone out only to buy a newspaper. This was a bizarre behaviour even by Iran's standards. The way Father had felt about this marriage all along—probably even before his wedding night—made the mystery specially more peculiar and fascinating. But anytime I'd tried to find an explanation even for Father's historical escape on the wedding night, I was put down flat by people who knew a lot about it. This only made me more curious though. I even found the nerve once to ask Narges about it directly. I considered her a reasonably reliable source for investigating this primary mystery. "Why did Father go out of town with his friends for a week on your wedding night?" My rude, direct question startled and then agitated her, even though I avoided using the word 'escape' with a great deal of torture. Narges's hasty answer was, "Because your father is a bad man! He's a jerk. That's why." But Father was a good man in my mind. He was educated, gentle, kind, stylish, and an outgoing, handsome man. He'd always been surrounded by intelligent friends, men at top positions and women of high elegance. So Narges's answer was crooked as usual. I knew I still had a high, steep mountain to climb for finding a useful source and solving this mystery alone.

A big hurdle—a mystery all by itself, in fact—was that neither Father nor Narges liked to discuss their pasts or parents, as though they brought them sad memories or shame. So full of themselves, yet they didn't seem to be proud of anybody else in their families or anything about their youth.

In particular, I could never ask Father these questions. First of all, it would've been impolite and outrageous, especially in the older Iranian culture where fathers held a godly image. But mostly I was worried that asking this particular question would break his heart. He would've been embarrassed to explain his stupidity and realize how his mistake of marrying Narges was obvious even to his own child. How bizarre the situation looked even to a boy who was supposed to be attached to, and protective of, his mother in the most natural way. This ungrateful child knew that his own existence had depended on this marriage and still questioned his father's decision and sanity!

Anyhow, such a stubborn jerk I was, I was dying to discover everything my parents had been hiding from me so religiously. Now, I felt obliged to solve all these mysteries somehow, not merely out of spite for their sly secrecy, but as a sacred mission bestowed upon me by God—probably as a prelude for setting my destiny straight!

Near two in the morning, I wished I'd had the guts to make Father sit down and answer my questions regarding his marriage and other stupid decisions, instead of asking me silly questions about my appetite and sandwich. For one thing, forcing us live in this godforsaken place was the reason for my nightly tortures at the Club or parties. And for being still up this late in the evening with all kinds of crazy thoughts and eating all this baloney. It also forced me to make friends with a bunch of measly kids in the neighbourhood. The mere fact that I went to parties and clubs almost every night depressed the hell out of those poor kids who had nothing to do, especially at night. Actually, this community's existence by itself was the reason that the entire neighbourhood resented my family, which I'd promised to tell you about before. So let me do it now.

3

The whole thing started with Father's brilliant idea to develop a residential subdivision and make a killing. No killing happened, financial or factual. However, this project ruined so many lives, especially mine.

Father created a private consortium of greedy investors about five years earlier. It bought a large land in a barren region outside Tehran at a cheap price. As a pioneer, he built himself a mansion in this ghost town to set an example for conservative families in

Tehran. The idea appeared appealing, anyway: building a large, modern house on a cheap land instead of paying a huge price for a small, smelly, old house in Tehran. However, people had major concerns about security, aside from the limited city services. The water, electricity, and phone services were all locally produced, and nobody liked to collect our garbage. The water was pumped from a well and distributed through private pipelines a few times a week. It gave households a chance to fill their private tanks on their roofs. The electricity was produced by a large generator that consumed a lot of gasoline and often stopped working. Home telephones were operated through a main switchboard fed by five incoming lines. Two amateur male operators, both rotten, worked alone in two shifts, to connect the incoming calls to our home phones. The ugly, heavy telephone sets had no dialling ring. They reminded me of the telephone sets I'd seen in the old war movies. We picked up the receiver and wound the handle a dozen times, until the operator came on line and we asked him *very politely* to connect us to a certain number. If he'd gone to the washroom or was busy with himself, we'd be winding the goddamn handle a million times until he'd decide to pay attention. He was a real jackass, I tell you. Both of them were. He gave us a limited time too. Then His Highness jumped in and ended the call. During a heavy load, he disconnected the line even without warning. He claimed to be giving everybody five or six minutes during those times. But he often disconnected people even when there was no load—just for the heck of it. He was having a ball proving his power over us desperate residents. I believed he also listened to people's conversations, either for fun or deciding about the nature and importance of people's chitchats to disconnect them.

Garbage disposal was another big headache as the authorities refused to provide a regular service. Every household carried their garbage in their cars to a nearby designated lot and dumped it there. The mountain of garbage piled up and the circle spread wider every day until the authorities sent a crew to burn it every few months. The smell of the rotting garbage, mosquitoes and flies, and the smoke when it was burned were the added hassles of this poorly planned suburban living. No regular mail service existed, either. But then an eager mailman showed up out of a blue once every few months—maybe when he had nothing better to do and hoped to collect some tips for bringing the stale mail.

The subdivision was near Karaj Road at about six kilometres west of Mehrabad—Tehran's International Airport then. A few roads were paved in the subdivision to connect to Karaj Road. But most houses were reached by dusty gravel roads loaded with debris and ditches and bumps.

Around dozen humongous Boeing 707s and 727s took off daily at a very low altitude over our houses. Their ear-piercing and jaw-shattering sound froze everybody and we put our fingers in our ears. The windows rattled and the glassware near the edges of the shelves and tables fell down and broke into thousand pieces. Sometimes, those gigantic flying machines were so close over my freaking head it looked as though I could hit them with a pebble. I froze like a statue, forefingers deep inside my ears, sometimes with an idiotic smile if Father was around. He tried to be a cool role model with a pompous grin, pretending that all that torture was only a small nuisance. He even refused to cover his ears just to prove his point and toughness. All the claims about the speed of those engineering marvels were terrible lies, at least during the take-off. They really took their time to pass over our house. Sometimes, the passengers peered out the tiny windows, maybe laughing at my helplessness and panic. Instead of getting angry, though, I only envied them for going away to better places that I'd only read about in geography books. *I'll be doing the same soon,* I thought with delight, if the gypsy's predictions were true! Thank God, only a few flights were scheduled for departure after midnight every week. Father insisted that there was already a plan in place to build a modern airport outside of Tehran for international flights.

Of course, the biggest hurdle for promoting the subdivision was security. Newspapers were full of stories regarding bandits cutting house owners' throats from ear to ear. This happened even in the crowded Tehran, sometimes for a meagre value of furniture and rugs. Anyhow, the consortium had convinced a bunch of fools, including Father, to test this lousy suburban life. When we moved to our new home two years earlier, only a dozen duped families like us lived in the subdivision. Many lots were sold, but only a few of the petite landlords had gathered enough courage to build. Still, more houses were built randomly in scattered manner over a vast barren area. Bandits could easily mix with the regular flow of nearby villagers who carried fresh fruits and vegetables on carts to the centre of Tehran. Many caravans also passed through the desert in the southern part of the subdivision. They camped out there for days, according to Father. Of course, no police, gendarmerie, or private security looked after the safety of the residents. So, I couldn't really blame the neighbours too much for hating Father and his family. Their worst retaliation skim so far for irritating Father was to drive by our house, sometimes by going out of their usual ways quite a bit, just to honk their car horns. Yet, at the end, this gawky gimmick only caused me and Rahim the extra pain of running to open the gate, assuming it was my pissed parents honking their car horns with such tenacity.

4

I returned to my room after eating my entire masterpiece. The house was now sunk in deep silence, but my mind was too busy to go to sleep. So I created a long list of daunting mysteries I had to solve. Some of them had to be handled fast, and some needed careful investigation. I was almost sure now that an odd situation or event had made Father marry Narges. Thank God, it couldn't have been because of me, since I was born ten freaking years after their marriage. At least I wasn't a lame excuse for their huge mistake to join in a bizarre, torturous matrimony. My conscience was clear that I hadn't been a part of this masquerade. And so, it couldn't be the reason that Narges hated me, either.

Of course, I realized that solving my family's freaky mysteries wouldn't change the sad facts ruining my life. But I believed that finding some justifications might help me feel better about my parents and their sanity, and then possibly lighten up a little. Their marriage was an embarrassing mystery in itself, but maybe a key for solving many other mysteries as well, including the reason for Narges's grudge toward me. Therefore, I had to dig deep into my parents' lives before their marriage one way or another. There seemed to be no way around this matter!

I went to bed at last, hoping to unwind by thinking only about the gypsy woman. Many issues she had to clarify for me. For one thing, she had to tell me a bit about the mysterious woman I was supposed to meet before travelling to the new world. Despite her dire warning and my quick promise to be very careful, I was now actually quite anxious to meet this mystery woman. What did her warning really mean?

"Can you *at least* tell me her name or how she looks? Any hints at all, please?" I liked to ask her as soon as I found her. Then I wondered how much details these fortune-tellers can really see or are allowed to reveal!

More importantly, maybe the gypsy woman could in fact help me run away from home and become a gypsy like her.

"If you take me, we don't have to worry about that mysterious woman, either, ha?" I planned to tell her to convince her faster.

All these crucial and delicate deliberations made me edgier, less sleepy, and more determined to find her, as if now bestowed with another holy mission demanding my immediate attention. After I finally dozed off, I had nightmares all night regarding my investigations and haunting discoveries. In my dream, I became a gypsy too, and it felt like a lot of fun being so carefree.

CHAPTER FOUR
Recruiting the Fatsoes

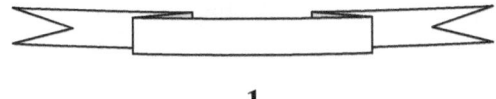

1

The next day, I decided to get my cranky friends help me look for the gypsy. But I couldn't tell them my reasons or about my plan to run away with her because I was sick of going to the clubs and parties. How could I bear their joy after realizing my misery? All those years, their envy about my parents taking me with them everywhere, especially clubs that they had never seen, had elated me a lot. That was the ultimate parental love for those morons. So, confessing my nightly tortures and turning their jealousy into jubilation was too much to pay even for their cooperation, which I needed urgently unfortunately.

Instead, I told them that the gypsy was most likely a spy sent by bandits to check out our neighbourhood for robbing us later. I said I couldn't tell Father about her, because he'd get mad at me and my mom for letting her into our house. "So we must find her ourselves to save the neighbourhood," I insisted like an idiot, as if I were the subdivision's Robin Hood or something now.

I felt awful badmouthing my dear gypsy only to convince those fatsoes who listened to my gibberish blankly with doubts. But what else could I do? I just hoped she'd forgive me if she were watching me in her crystal ball. She was probably happy, though, to see my passion, pain, and plan to find her.

I wasn't lying too much, anyway. All morning, I'd felt rather guilty for hiding the gypsy's visit from Father only in fear of

Narges. What if she'd been a spy and I was under her spell, too, like Narges perhaps? Betraying Father felt risky at the very least. He would've known how to handle the situation, maybe also calling the gendarmerie, if necessary. So, I had to at least find out if some bandits were camping nearby, the way Father always said they might. I had to make up for Narges's timidity around Father and maybe even accusing me of inviting the gypsy to our house. Then again, I knew only my sneaky love hormones were pushing all these silly excuses into my head.

"Do you remember getting mad at me yesterday for sticking around that neighbour's house?" I asked the kids. They nodded.

"You know why?" I asked.

They shook their heads 'no' this time, like those fat Japanese wooden dolls with springy necks and sleepy eyes.

"Because I wanted to follow her and find out where she lived. But my dad showed up and took me home before she got out. Besides," I insisted, "we'll be heroes if we find the bandits."

After my lies pricked their ears enough and their curiosity was picked a bit, at last the kids agreed to help me. At least the chance for some adventure could also beat our boredom in the lifeless subdivision. I felt proud for making a bunch of chubby chaps follow my lead for a change. I was sick and tired of arguing with them about the useless games they always wanted to play. I hoped to show them my leadership, too, while pushing them into adolescence a little faster perhaps.

"But how're we going to find her?" Hashem asked.

"Leave the planning to me," I said. "You just follow me."

I marched fast and serious, exactly like Robin Hood, for about eight minutes toward the last house the gypsy had visited. The kids trailed behind me and stood on the porch with surprise about my sudden boldness and energy. The idea of finding the gypsy had surely made me silly restless, I tell you. I felt my madness too —bothering the neighbours and all. Yet I couldn't help myself. I rang the bell, calmed my nerves, and put on an idiotic grin when a middle-aged woman opened the door. I'd seen her around the neighbourhood. Surely my family knew her better than I did, but I hoped not enough to hear about my intrusion and the lie I was about to tell her. Having a snobbish family had its advantages, I reckoned with delight! I told her Narges wanted to contact the gypsy to tell some of her friends' fortunes. She grinned giddily about snotty Narges finding the gypsy useful as well. She gauged the kids crowding the porch, as if trying to see if she knew any of us. Then she said the gypsy had stayed late to tell the fortunes of half a dozen guests. Although they'd all been impressed by her predictions, nobody had asked her about a way of contacting her. Idiots! The woman asked us whether we were thirsty. We nodded and she vanished toward the kitchen. After a minute, she returned with a pitcher of lemonade and eight cookies. I bet she thought we'd made that entire story just to get some snacks from her.

The fact that the gypsy had stayed in one house for six hours to tell so many fortunes—instead of giving an excuse to leave— sort of proved that she hadn't been a spy. So Father was safe. It was also safe for me to love her. This delicate discovery dawned on me while washing down a large cookie with lemonade. Then I started coughing suddenly and almost choking, as Narges's old joke, "He's always nibbling like a pregnant woman," rolled in my head. *Sometimes her sarcastic sense of humour was funny, I had to admit.* Everybody stared at me and the next cookie in my hand.

I decided not to share my brilliant conclusion about the gypsy with the kids—to avoid sabotaging my plan to find her. Their brains might work eventually to figure out that no point remained to look for a real fortune-teller then. The kids' stupidity so far to catch this point felt good all by itself.

My brave interview, and the sweet rewards of knocking on people's doors, excited us. We giggled all around and decided to visit other households in the neighbourhood, ask them about the gypsy, and also see who gets the most cookies. Giving water and snacks to kids had become sort of customary in our community, but we had now learned a gimmick to abuse this custom more often cleverly—just by knocking on people's doors and asking all kinds of neighbourly questions. Apparently, living in the middle of the desert had revived the neighbours' ancient tribal habits—although our scattered houses didn't look like any tribal setup, either, and most families didn't even socialize with one another. It was hard to say what the heck the nature of our subdivision was.

We chose and assigned twenty-six houses among us, avoiding our own parents or their neighbourhood friends. If necessary, we'd tell them that our mothers wanted to contact the gypsy for fortunetelling. The kids warned me that, if caught, they'd tell their parents that I'd pushed them with the rumours about the gypsy. I agreed quickly, just to prove my courage as a leader. Once we worked out these details, we split.

Interviewing the lucky neighbours chosen was easy. However, covering all the distances between the houses took time. The last guy returned with the record for the fewest interviews in longest time. I'd hoped his delay was at least a sign of good news, but he'd only been goofing around. He'd actually gone to his own home to eat lunch and go to washroom. I wanted to kick his ass, which felt weird in itself. It was just another sign of the devil that the gypsy woman had awakened in me. I stayed cool, though, to keep this lousy gang together as long as possible. Anyhow, no useful information was gathered. Only a few people had seen the gypsy during a period before she'd arrived at my parents' house. But nobody knew anything else about her or how to find her.

At dusk, I told the kids the matter was more serious than we'd initially thought. They didn't seem to grasp my logic and insisted on abandoning the project. So it took me an hour again to make them see the importance of continuing our search the next day.

2

On my way home, I decided to test Narges about making the gypsy tell my fortune. Her silence or a shoddy reply would prove my suspicion. It'd show for the thousandth time that she used me anytime she was in trouble. But if she denied it, I'd double-check it after finding the gypsy and asking her the same question. This was another good reason to look for the gypsy and also a great opening line as soon as I found her. I was actually itching for an excuse to confront Narges, anyway. I was getting myself hyped up for a rebellion.

In the past, Narges had always denied whatever she'd said or asked me to do with such confidence that I'd doubted my sanity. Her gross lies or denials of what she'd said or done only a few days or hours earlier crushed my nerves. I wondered whether my brain, eyes, and ears worked. Maybe I'd only imagined certain words or events? This time, however, I planned to write down her answer on a piece of paper right away before I forgot.

I really liked to know whether Narges was born a liar, or she'd learned all that talent from Ozra Banu—her adoptive mother. Was I becoming a hypocrite, too, from her teachings and genes? I was a big liar myself already! Besides the ones Narges forced me to say, I had to lie for two other reasons: First, telling the truth about my family and events around us were too embarrassing. Second, I tried to invent dazzling stories to impress others, the same way adults always did for making friends.

I found Narges in the kitchen and asked her, "Did you ask the gypsy yesterday to tell my fortune?"

"No," she mumbled, sounding so cool, as though expecting the question all along. *Only a guilty person would prepare herself and react so cool, especially a hyper jinn like her!* Besides, she turned her eyes away from me too fast toward the big pot on the stove to pretend being busy stirring the food she was preparing. *Why all witches always seem to be stirring something in a big iron pot!?* I went closer to look into her eyes, but she only rolled them away. The food smelled horrible, like another one of her recipes loaded with vegetables and vitamins to make her body thin and her hair thick. So I walked away.

"When is Ozra Banu coming over?" I asked.

"What? Why? Since when are you interested in her? What's the matter with you today, asking all these silly questions?"

Narges's surprise was understandable since both Father and I had little patience for Ozra Banu. She usually appeared harmless and helpless. But our indifference toward her looked obvious to the whole world, especially Narges. Maybe we unconsciously blamed her for the way Narges had turned out and tortured us. I was never rude to Ozra Banu because Father wouldn't allow it. Despite his feelings, his respect toward her was sincere. It wasn't even for Narges's sake. She visited us regularly and we treated her like a family member, almost the same way we treated Grandma—Father's mother.

At last, I gathered my nerve to answer Narges's question and hoping my tone of voice was convincing. "I was only wondering why she hasn't come around for such a long time?"

"You talk a lot of nonsense today. How many times must I tell you not to play in the sun? Your brain is cooking finally."

Narges was right. Even I wasn't convinced of the sound of my voice and sudden show of kindness, especially toward Ozra Banu. I could fool Narges only in my dreams. So I just went to my room, agitated and depressed. Then I decided to check the neighbourhood from the roof for a sign of bandits.

I squinted into the horizon from the flat roof of our house, far beyond the barren fields around the scattered houses, for any sign of a caravan camping out there. Then I borrowed Father's strong binoculars from his study away from Narges's eyes. Still nothing unusual in the horizon came into focus other than some dust blowing in the wind as trucks and carts crossed one of the gravel roads. Father often checked the neighbourhood from the same spot on the roof with his binocular, too, making sure everything looked tidy and quiet in the neighbourhood and no spies were getting too close to our house.

Back in my room, I thought Narges's affection toward Ozra Banu was bizarre, considering the likely torture of living under her rule for twenty-two years. For a cruel woman like Narges, protecting Ozra Banu like a saint made the whole thing appear even odder. She prevented Father and me from criticizing even her big mouth and smugness in our house. Yet Ozra Banu always nagged at her and complained about everything. Narges took the abuse and felt sorry for her, too. She probably pitied her for being forced to live such a lousy life in a small suite after such a lavish lifestyle with her husband. Everybody was determined not to tell me what had happened to all that wealth—still another mystery to solve. Why was everybody so secretive about their past lives?

Ozra Banu was a short, stooped, and nagging creature, a true hunchbacked witch. She had about a dozen brown and broken teeth scattered in her big foul mouth, like our subdivision houses. She'd probably visited a dentist only to pull her teeth one at a time when they'd decayed beyond repair. Yet, she could eat food with amazing ease and eagerness by using her strong gums. Her resistance, against Narges's persistence, to build dentures like all the elderly in Father's family showed her startling stubbornness. She avoided eyeglasses too, yet tried hard to read newspapers and books by holding them about ten feet away from her face. Instead, she had this abundant semi-curly black hair with only a few strands of grey near her temples. I bet Narges was envious of her thick hair. According to Narges, she was in her seventies. But she looked more like a thousand years old if you counted the wrinkles on her face. As a whole, Azrael had forgotten Ozra as much as she was scared of him. Still, old-age symptoms hardly affected her energy. She was active, alert, and aggressive for her age. She staggered around the house like Inspector Clouseau, nagging and ordering everyone all day. Her endless study of diet books and following their advice so religiously, as well as her self-loving personality, had kept her healthy. She avoided red meat, salt, and sweets. With a large bony nose and tiny grey eyes behind several layers of wrinkled eyelids, she was so ugly it was hard to believe she'd been even slightly attractive her entire life. Therefore, the stories I'd overheard about her lovers after her rich husband died puzzled me a lot. Who in his sound mind would've wanted to be her lover? Why? Oh boy, the number of mysteries kept growing every day! They all felt important to solve, too.

Narges tolerated Ozra Banu with a mixed sense of duty and pity. I could see both in her eyes. She often scolded my coldness toward Ozra Banu, and she often dragged me to her place after school for a visit. Those visits and bearing Ozra Banu's non-stop nagging were more torturous than Narges's chores. But now I needed her for getting information about Narges's childhood and the circumstances of my parents' meeting and marrying. I had to interview her before Azrael could convince her to give in.

Narges's patience with Ozra Banu also demonstrated her own complex personality and long-forgotten virtues, including a soft heart and respect for the elderly. She was a high school graduate —quite an achievement for any woman in the 1940s. She was an elementary school teacher and assistant to the school principal. She was quite popular with commoners and working class, in contrast to her low standing among her lazy, useless aristocratic friends. She was so generous with money she was always broke despite her good income. She assisted school staff in any way she could. In return, many of them came by our house to help her with various projects and chores. She used everybody and they didn't seem to mind, unlike me. The way they loved her appeared weird as well, compared with the way Father, our aristocratic friends, and I felt about her selfishness and cruelty. Her kindness to some strangers contrasted her nastiness toward her husband and child quite a bit. Father's flashy lifestyle could probably be blamed for Narges's spite for him, but why me? Was it because she knew I loved only Father—and now the gypsy woman, too? But how could I love Narges, like any good son, if she never let me? She spoiled Ozra Banu, Rahim, and her colleagues, and then always bugged me for unknown reasons—, which now I had to waste a lot of time and energy to figure out, too.

Hiding my face in the pillow, running away from this haunted house felt easier than solving all these ominous, dark mysteries begging for the light of day. But I didn't know where to go alone and how to feed myself. Only the gypsy woman could help me elope; or even better, keep me for herself. I really had to find her.

3

The next morning, my friends and I set out again to find the gypsy. We rode our bikes in the barren fields, determined like the explorers of the South Pole—although with a more vital mission: We were looking for a beautiful, hot creature instead of the iciest spot on earth. Then, instead of sticking an ill-fated flag on ice and leaving it alone forever, I was going to stick my lucky self to her warm body and follow her everywhere until eternity.

We started westward to locate a caravan or maybe a nearby village. I recalled seeing a small settlement near our subdivision in the past, when my family had driven to Karaj or the Caspian Sea. The scorching sun shone overhead and sweat ran down our faces as we tried to skip the ditches and rocks on our path. We hadn't even brought water with us. Those days, we knew nothing about dehydration, nor carried water bottles. We drove ourselves to the limits and then tried to find water somewhere, mainly by knocking on people's doors. That was another reason for the neighbours' habit of giving kids water or juice.

Everybody was quiet. Only the sound of ten bicycle wheels clanking on the rough terrain broke the silence. Clink-clank, clink-clank, we pushed forward. Once in a while, somebody bitched about the bumpy terrain. Otherwise, we kept our energy for paddling toward the empty horizon. Every one kilometre or so, I let one of the kids check the horizon in all directions for a caravan camp with Father's binoculars that they loved. Although I believed I'd seen caravans in the past camping around the neighbourhood, today I doubted myself and my memory. Maybe I'd been only brainwashed by Father's repeated stories about caravans passing through those areas like the old times. He said they travelled on their camels on a course from the southern parts of Iran through the desert surrounding the subdivision to migrate to the north-western parts of Iran for a cooler summer.

We rode forty minutes without any sign of a caravan or the settlement I'd believed would be around there. Everybody was getting edgy and thirsty, so began nagging, although I let them use the binoculars more often. Hashem Maleki argued about the silliness of my plan. "It's stupid to look for a caravan on bicycle, anyway," he said and others nodded.

Ahmad Javid asked, "Hey, Kian, what're you gonna ask the bandits, anyway, even if we find them?"

"Hey, Ahmad," I replied with irritation. "I'll ask for the gypsy. I'll say that my mother would like her to come back for telling her friends' fortunes."

"But if they're bandits, they won't like our snooping around."

"Well, that's what we came here to do, isn't it?"

"They'll be dangerous if we get close to them. Besides, you think they'll admit they're bandits instead of gypsies?" he asked.

"We must somehow find out and ask about the gypsy, too."

I tried to act decisive as a leader, but the fatsoes' questions sounded logical. How come they hadn't crossed our petty minds before? Still, I hated to admit missing such crucial points during my diligent planning. So we kept arguing about getting close to the bandits that we couldn't find, anyway. I knew we wouldn't be facing any bandits on account of the gypsy woman, who was already proven not to be a spy after interviewing our neighbour. But I couldn't explain it to the kids without revealing the secret I'd kept to myself all along. On the other hand, we could still face some bandits by sheer accident. They might even keep us as child slaves. Actually, I was suddenly getting anxious myself about facing real bandits by accident. However, finding the gypsy felt far too important for me to worry about any ruthless bandits.

"I think the whole thing sucks," Ahmad said at last.

"No, only you suck," I snapped.

"Yeah, because we listened to you in the first place."

"What do you suggest? Give up and go back already?"

"Yes," Hashem groaned.

"They won't harm us, I promise," I said, feeling quite silly for talking so much nonsense and pretending to be a fearless leader.

"You promise? How?" Ahmad asked.

"I just promise," I said like a desperate lover, which I seemed to have become after meeting the gypsy.

"Let me teach you some logic, stupid," Ahmad said.

"What logic, Einstein?"

"There's no caravan around, right?" he asked and I nodded.

"This means they're gone and didn't mean to harm us," he said and others nodded. Now this biggest fatso wanted to show he had a brain, too.

"Maybe they're hiding somewhere and return in a few days to rob and murder us," I shouted before noticing my utter stupidity today. But Ahmad got it again right away. Now this dumbass in fact proved to have some brain, after all.

"Well, if they're hiding or gone away, we won't find them, anyway. You're really stupid today, more than ever," he said and the kids roared with laughter.

"We may still find them, if we try."

"How, moron?"

"You're an asshole," I snapped back.

I sensed my brain's and leadership's lousiness today! The sun was certainly cooking my head, just as Narges suggested all the time. I was also thirsty and convinced that we couldn't find any caravan today. Yet my plan being attacked infuriated me. Now I was really mad for tolerating those jerks and playing their silly games all the time. Then again, I hoped at least Ahmad and I could square things before going back home with some pride still left for me.

"It's useless searching the desert like lunatics," Ahmed said to the kids. "Let's go back and tell our parents about the gypsy and bandits according to Kian's stupid Dad. They know what to do."

I'd had too much humiliation and arguments for one day. My hopes for finding the gypsy today, or ever, had shattered, too, but I still stalled and hoped to save my face a little. The kids suddenly turned their bikes around. Bastards! Their rebellion agitated me, but being left alone too far out in the middle of the desert felt scary. Besides, I had to stop them from talking to their parents.

Father would hear about it, too, which would result in both my parents punishing me, for different reasons. So I turned my bike around as well.

"Okay, let's stop today," I muttered with a long face. "But don't mention the gypsy to your parents. They'll get upset if they find out we've been chasing bandits. They'll stop us from going around anymore."

At last they agreed after I promised to tell them an awesome new story I'd just finished reading. Then we started toward home.

4

After riding halfway back, we noticed two wild dogs in some distance fooling around in a suspicious way. I rode toward them on a new course and the fatsoes followed me, not as their leader this time, but only because the scene looked weird to them, too. Near the dogs, we got off our bikes to watch their fishy activity, which seemed against our latest knowledge of sex. Two wild male dogs took turns screwing each other like they'd signed a serious pact or been practising this rotten routine since good old puppyhood. Each spent about thirty seconds on top of the other before switching places. They made the best of their limited time to keep the whole affair fair. The routine by itself proved that both dogs favoured a particular role over the other. The only question was which position, how they'd come up with such a complex scheme, and how they kept time for their turns without fighting!

For two minutes, we watched those dogs' idiotic, keen efforts, which also looked too exhausting. Not even our intrusive arrival had made them stop or move an inch. We could almost touch them, if we dared, yet they continued without shame or paying attention to us. At last, I thought I'd seen enough crap and that I had to do something about that nonsense. Maybe I was still upset for not finding the gypsy. So what I did, I looked around, found a sharp rock, and threw it at the horny dogs. It hit the lower one and nothing happened. So, I found a bigger and sharper rock, aimed, and hit the dog on top. It wailed, glared at me, and pushed the both of them away by about five feet while still stuck together. Then they continued all over again. Their determination made us laugh. The kids got excited and began throwing stones at them, too, to test their stubbornness. The kids' following my lead to spoil the dogs' fun made me feel as their leader again.

Our massive attack obviously hurt the dogs' bonny bodies, as they yowled and moaned, but moved away just a bit every time. They threw accusing glares at us, groaned, but never stopped their vital, urgent business. Most likely, they were amazed at our perseverance as much as we were of theirs. Yet they had no time or willpower to stop to rip us apart first, or at least bark a few times. I bet we would've simply fled without our bicycles all the way home if they'd merely growled a bit more seriously. Instead, we chased them until they escaped and hid behind the hills. They seemed quite agitated, but had probably agreed that continuing their business elsewhere was better than wasting time on killing us first and losing their precious moods in the process. We'd proven more stubborn and wilder than they were. We'd won, thanks to my leadership, so we continued our trip with lots of giggling and howling of our own. I wondered why dogs were so different in temperament regardless of their sizes and breeds. Some of them, like the ones we had encountered today, were so timid and gentle despite their big bodies, whereas some tiny ones were too vicious, loud, and showy. That was another big mystery, but not worth adding to my list of pending projects!

When we reached the subdivision, I rode toward home alone. I wondered whether there was a better way of looking for the gypsy woman. Father could probably find her with the help of the gendarmerie. It was a silly idea, however. How could I mention the gypsy to Father? Before reaching home, I remembered it was Tuesday. I hated Tuesdays, since my parents held open house for their friends. This was on top of formal parties they threw on some weekends. Tuesdays was an informal gathering when a big bunch of freeloaders took advantage of my parents' loathing for being alone or together. Often many friends called on Mondays to invite themselves for dinner the following night. Many arrived without prior notice, too, before or after dinner. Yet, there were always enough food and alcohol to serve the unexpected large number of people who showed up.

Narges and our servants hated this so-called *casual* Tuesdays, too, more than I did maybe. They detested all the extra work they had to do every week for no darn reason. Father was the only one enjoying these parties. He showed off his music collection and amused a bunch of pretty women who appreciated his generosity. Most men didn't mind their wives' flirting with Father as long as they got all the free booze and food, and for mingling in the circle of these new aristocrats. After these parties, Father just brushed his teeth, whistled while putting on his pyjamas, and went to bed quickly. He started snoring while Narges and the servants kept on cleaning for another hour or so before going to bed.

Oh, actually, father sometimes yelled at Narges and servants from the bedroom, "Could you people stop making so much noise? I must go to work tomorrow…"

"Don't I have to go to work tomorrow, too?" Narges yelled back from the kitchen.

That particular Tuesday, especially, I wasn't in the mood for all the noise and phony laughter. I didn't want to be among that conceited crowd. Feeling lonely, missing the gypsy woman, and anxious about the unsolved family mysteries, I wished I could at least be left alone in my room. But I knew that both Father and Narges would call on me throughout the party to do small chores for them. What a drag!

CHAPTER FIVE
Interrogating Ozra Banu

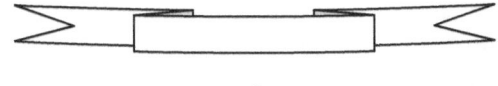

1

The hot summer days grew longer every day while my temper got shorter. Surrounded and tortured by such lousy parents, playmates, servants, and nightly affairs, reading novels non-stop helped me stay sane and get a more natural sense of life, too. It was bizarre that my life during the day had become as spooky as it had been at the Club most evenings. I just tried to adapt myself somehow and get along with the fatsoes the same way I did with the adults at the Club: by just sitting, watching, and keeping my mouth shut. Except that I had to sit on the hard gravel during the day instead of a soft couch in the evenings.

The fatsoes were dying to hear about Royal Club, but I said just some general stuff about it sometimes. Describing the hoopla to them was pointless, even if I knew how to explain my cynical observations. According to Father's *meticulous reminders*, telling people's personal lives was rude, anyway. I knew he was mainly worried about his reputation being sabotaged by his own son, too. I didn't want him to think of me as another spy, either! Besides, my parents' lives were too embarrassing to share with a bunch of bigmouth kids who would certainly repeat everything to their own parents.

They always whined from boredom, yet quit helping me find the gypsy. Ahmad Javid called me a *halloo*—a stupid jerk—for making them ride their bikes in the hot desert to find a caravan or going around to interview the neighbours. "That was the dumbest thing we've ever done," he said. He was their leader now, since everybody enjoyed the way he always mocked me and since he was getting fatter faster than the rest of them, too. Leader of what, I wondered, if there wasn't going to be any adventure?

"But what's the point of chasing the shadows and sitting on the gravel in the shade all day like the lazy hombres in Mexican movies?" I asked.

"Riding in that sun will kill you!" Ahmad kept saying.

"Are you a bat or vampire?" I said with frustration, thinking that this pale dumbass should've been Narges's son, looking so plump and having a grudge against the sun, too, like her!

The gypsy's spell had surely been too deep, as I kept looking for her on my own the rest of the summer. Two or three days every week, I drove my bike in one of the four directions of our house like a haunted lover. I rode in the hot sun amidst the bare fields for hours and watched the horizon with Father's binoculars, too. Then I returned home tired and thirsty. I ran to my room first, under Narges's suspicious stares, to hide the binoculars. Yet she never asked me anything even when she saw my torn shirt and pants a few times. I fell into ditches and creeks frequently while riding my bike in a haze, daydreaming about the gypsy woman or running away solo. I also thought and wrote about her in the privacy of my room anytime I got a chance. She remained my only hope for escape, but also the goddess of my fantasies.

Ten days after the gypsy's visit, I returned home exhausted and frustrated. While staggering up the garden path, I recalled her comment about the roses: "Smell them one day." I stopped near a large rose bush and smelled a few of its flowers. Their riveting fragrance mesmerized me, as if smelling a rose for the first time —an experience too weird for a person living in such a colourful surrounding. We always had a garden full of flowers, especially roses of various colours. Though we never brought them inside the house on account of Father's severe hay fever.

I strolled around the garden and smelled the roses for about half an hour. I went from one bush to another and compared their varied fragrances, as though fulfilling the gypsy woman's order to smell the roses was the best way to break the spell and bring her back to our house. Narges saw me from the window upstairs, probably wondering what new madness made me go around the garden and smell each flower like a busy bee. It felt as though the more I smelled the roses, the more my spirit contacted the gypsy's, and the more I could find beauty in other things besides women. For someone living in such a fancy garden, my deep ignorance about the smell of roses only showed how my mind had been distracted by some kinds of dilemmas or a curse all my childhood.

I studied each flower, amazed at the elegance of their petals and the tidiness of their patterns. Some stems were full of young blossoms, which were tight like a shy bride. On another stem, a few flowers had grown into ripe, open roses ready to be smelled and enjoyed like a young woman. And some roses had withered like a wretched widow. The gardener would soon clip and chuck them out. This thought reminded me of that particular rose bud that the gypsy woman had smelled on her way out. I rushed to the pathway. I found the bush and that special rose that had bobbed to her and was rewarded by her touch. It was no longer a bud as lively as it'd been the day she'd smelled and probably kissed it, too. I stared at it and felt sad that all beautiful things die so soon. A smooth wind made it bob to me, too, the same way it had to the gypsy. I smelled it and then kissed it after making sure Narges wasn't watching me. I gazed at it for another minute and realized that the gardener would clip and toss it soon. So I ran into the house and returned with the scissors. I clipped it and took it with me to my room. Narges glared at me and the dying flower as I went up the stairs, but again she didn't say anything. I reckoned she'd already decided she had a mad son on her hand and nothing she could do to help him! Wandering so much under the sun had surely cracked up her son. After that day, I found a new passion

for fragrances and beauties in nature beyond what I was hoping
to find in a woman—all thanks to the gypsy woman again.

That cherished red rose lay on my desk and withered near my
eyes and nose for the next three days. Then I laid it in the middle
of my big history book to flatten and dry. I made sure it wasn't
the page with the Genghis' picture. Afterward, I kept it in the first
notebook of my diaries. It still lives there so nobly for a dead
flower still stirring such an amazing memory.

2

I still joined the kids some days to waste our lives away together.
But humouring them all the time and wondering why I needed
them were frustrating. We just wandered like phantoms in the
ghostly neighbourhood and hoped that somebody could think of
a way to amuse ourselves. Not even a flat surface existed to play
soccer on, even if those fatsoes agreed to run a little. Ditches and
debris were everywhere. So we just moved from one shaded area
to another as the blazing sun crossed the sky and changed the
shape of the shadows.

In recent weeks, the kids seemed to be resenting me because
of Father, too. Their parents had apparently been cursing Father
quite openly now for encouraging them to build a house in that
wilderness. They could get back only a fraction of their initial
investments, even if they were lucky to find some fools interested
in buying their houses. That was surely a good reason to despise
Father more every day. They probably cursed him while driving
such a long distance to and from the city and when the blasting
planes flew just a touch above their heads. But I felt they hated
him mostly since he could buy a good house anywhere in Tehran
any time he wanted. Father wasn't ruined, relative to those pitiful
petite bourgeois who worried about their big investments. Yet, his
sense of obligation or fear of more hostility probably stopped him
from abandoning the neighbours. He only laughed tensely when
neighbours drove by our house intentionally just to honk their car

horns fiercely as a gimmick for retaliation. He also fought with Narges who kept insisting on moving back to a more suitable location in Tehran. This had been another source of their regular arguments.

The fatsoes' animosity toward me on account of Father was simply another proof of their sheer stupidity. Yet, I also felt sorry for them for being stuck in this ghost town like me. They surely suffered their parents' agony on top of their own. I suffered the most, though, on account of living in a desert, while fighting my angry playmates' rebellion as well. Father refused to move us out of this hellhole and my friends bullied me because of him.

They came by to get me less often. When I complained for ignoring me, they kept silent or said that our house was too far away from theirs, which was true. Their houses were around the proposed shopping area, whereas Father had tried to avoid the commotion of the planned market in the subdivision—a dream that may come true in a thousand years. Only one tiny grocery store had opened so far, which could hardly survive on the odd business of four dozen households, while they mainly used the supermarkets in the city. The poor villager was fooled to open the store with big promises, but was already fed up and threatening to close his shop unless the residents got more serious.

"But our house has always been there," I told the kids. "Why is it too far so suddenly?"

They just stared at me and one another quietly. So I continued, "You're just getting fatter and lazier every day. Now you just sit behind the walls of your own houses."

Blaming their sluggishness was better than complaining about their rebellion. I hid my humiliation of now being snubbed by a bunch of lowlifes, too. Talking about the gypsy was also pointless after Ahmad had called me *halloo* and everybody laughed for ten minutes. I couldn't reason with those fatsoes who preferred to sit in the shade all day and talk nonsense, including the two queer dogs. Why wouldn't they at least read a novel or something, for God's sake! I was glad I hadn't revealed my real story with the

gypsy or the hoopla in Royal Club to a bunch of morons who
would probably never grasp the madness of the grownups' world.

Another smart thing I did, I asked the grocer whether he'd
seen a pretty gypsy with red shoes, scarf, and blouse. He said no.
So I told him to keep his eyes open and tell her that I was looking
for her. I didn't even care if Narges found out about my desperate
search for the gypsy. My mission was now too holy to worry
about Narges. Even if she learned about my plan to run away
with the gypsy, she'd probably be only happy. She never shopped
from this poor grocer, anyway. I asked the kids the same thing I'd
told the grocer. After all, they wandered in the neighbourhood
more than I did nowadays.

All along, I always imagined that the gypsy woman would
show up in the neighbourhood one of these days. I had no doubts.
I also believed I'd be the one opening the door for her again
when she returned to our house with the message from the grocer
or the fatsoes. To Rahim's big surprise, now I always ran to open
the door anytime the bell rang. I'd already decided what to tell
her, too. I'd just tell her to wait only a few minutes so I could pick
up a few personal items and then we'd go away together. I'd be
brave this time and tell her that I want to be a gypsy like her. No
more hesitation or goofing around.

3

I took up smoking just for the heck of it, but also because adults
did it to calm their nerves apparently. Maybe its magical power
could help me, too. The biggest clue was, of course, Dr. Afzali's
tense chain-smoking and drinking whisky at Royal Club, while
suffering Mina's manoeuvres and dancing with vulgar men, in
particular the cook's son. If such a prominent surgeon found
smoking useful for something, I mustn't deprive myself from this
magical cure, either. I'd forgotten the good doctor was probably
trying to commit suicide. Anyway, both the nasty habit and the
smoking gestures distracted my regular gloomy thoughts a bit.

Cigarettes soothed my sense of helplessness and anxiety, while finding the gypsy felt more impossible every day.

Even better, I made the fatsoes smokers, too. It was a genius plan to keep them around me, while I also told them fantastic stories based on Russian novels and short stories I was reading at the time. I took the humiliation of humouring them too much, since I needed a bit of their simpler world—to forget the spooky adults' world I couldn't avoid. Like poor Shahrazad, I kept telling stories one after another to stay alive. I fooled them to come back the next day to hear more. It was sad to know that I needed them. But it was scary to imagine that 'no one would ever understand me.' This sad realization made me wonder about the purpose of my life if I was really a cursed creep. My confusion about who I was or becoming, along with many other kinds of doubts and mysteries, increased my paranoia every day. I realized with pain that the character I was becoming so helplessly would simply be too freakish to bear for anybody, even for myself! Yet, the option of adopting or imitating any other personality nauseated me as much as talking to those people did!

I stole cigarettes from Ozra Banu whenever Narges brought her over. She lived on the opposite side of the city. Narges had to drive a long distance to pick up and return her, so she usually stayed a few days or weeks anytime she came over. She smoked cheap domestic cigarettes, which I had to tolerate as well out of necessity. Father smoked only one Winston every night, while I often tried to linger around him to gulp the grey cloud hanging in midair. I liked its delicious fragrance, but rarely dared to steal a cigarette from the pack in his pocket or on his desk in the study.

On the other hand, Ozra Banu smoked a lot around the house with several open packs left in various places. She roamed from one room to another to watch TV, read a diet book, or whatever. She also read cards a few hours every day, hoping to find any last-minute clue about an improvement in her fortune during the final few years of her boring being. Then, she often called Narges to bring her cigarettes. Narges was also lazy or fed up with Ozra

Banu's orders and her casual smoking around her sparkling household. She grabbed a fresh pack from the refrigerator for her usually, instead of going around and looking for the open ones.

I had lots of money, usually stolen from Narges, but I couldn't buy cigarettes from our conscientious neighbourhood grocer, nor did street vendors come to our subdivision. Alas, all these diligent planning and fussing over the supply put extra pressure on me and raised the demand for even more cigarettes faster. This was now just another pain of living in a desert. So, now I needed Ozra Banu also to steal almost a dozen of her cigarettes every day. I hoarded most of them for later, but shared a few of them with the neighbourhood kids. Once they got hooked, I pushed them to steal cigarettes from their parents and visitors. So we sometimes had American or English cigarettes as well.

I believed Narges knew about my new fabulous habit to steal and smoke Ozra Banu's cigarettes. That she hadn't yet bugged me about it wasn't strange to me, either. She was keeping it for the right time to use against me most dramatically. Or maybe she assumed I needed cigarettes to fight my fate's burdens bravely. Witnessing my turmoil had possibly revived her memories of her own lousy childhood. Yet, she found herself useless to help me in any way, besides letting me smoke and solve my problems on my own. She hardly talked with me anyway. Her odd apathy toward me was as spooky as her addiction to bug me. Yet, it made her appear somewhat open-minded—maybe even as much as Father was. By the way, she neither drank alcohol so much nor smoked. She coped with her endless anxieties and problems by a perfect mix of wisdom and malice. She was a superwoman—at least until the day she'd kept nodding to the gypsy like a fat puppet. On the other hand, I was less scared of Narges now due to that scene—another thanks to the gypsy. What a pity I hadn't been clever enough to at least ask her name, to call it loudly every time I was thinking about her or thanking her for so many things.

4

The hoopla at Royal Club or people's mansions was sometimes a blissful break from my long house confinements and stressful daydreaming about the gypsy. Then writing about those nightly events in my diary the following day occupied a lot of my idle time, too. This lousy hobby and distraction was both calming and educational. Oddly enough, my parents took me to parties even when Ozra Banu was around. She was left to face the bandits alone if they came along. She was considered dispensable like our servants, I reckoned, due to her age perhaps. Then, I laughed my heart out imagining the scene of the hunchbacked Ozra Banu arriving a few steps behind me, both chasing my parents, while they explained to everybody why they'd brought her as well.

Only one time my parents decided to leave me at home with Ozra Banu. The party was formal by a new minister—Father's new boss. He hadn't yet been informed of Father's bizarre reason for taking his son to the parties he and his wife attended together. Anyway, I jumped at the opportunity of interrogating Ozra Banu about Narges. She was both surprised and upset that I followed her everywhere, instead of staying in my room like usual. My chance of success felt even better when she asked me whether I knew where Father kept the liquor—as if I were stupid and couldn't read her old, sneaky mind! Her guilty grin showed how she'd helped herself to the liquor in the cabinet a thousand times when she'd been left alone at home. But, I'd be witnessing her regular snooping around the bar tonight. She was only trying to stop me from telling on her; that's all! Her gimmick reminded me of Narges's tricks to include me in her schemes when she wished to hide something from Father. Now I could see firsthand where Narges had learned all those precious lessons. One small mystery solved already, before asking her even the first question!

I nodded and got off my chair to show her the liquor, which felt really ridiculous when I was absolutely sure she already knew its place. But I let it go, all for the sake of grilling her as soon as she got drunk. My cooperation pleased her, but still she asked me for insurance, "You won't tell anybody about this?"

"No," I said. "But may I have a cigarette?"

She gazed at me awhile, smiled, and pointed toward her pack of cigarettes on the coffee table. I took a cigarette and lit it after plunging onto the chair. I watched her pour half a tall glass of vodka and return to the couch. She swallowed a big gulp and lit a cigarette. We puffed our cigarettes in silence in the smoke-packed room. Surely, I didn't need her permission to steal her cigarettes, but smoking in front of her would make our bond even stronger than she'd intended—a great plot, I thought, to probe her tonight and in the future. She looked pleased with my new attitude, too, and my promising future as a corruptible addict. With a smirk, she watched me inhale the smoke, hold it for a long time, and then release it in bits, like a professional smoker. That was the exact atmosphere I'd hoped to create. Now I only had to wait for her to get just a bit drunk. I waited and waited, but she seemed to take a very long time to warm up, if ever. Suddenly I recalled the incident when she'd gotten really drunk. So, I thought I should attack her from a different angle as a start.

"It was an interesting night at Hariri's villa, ha?" I said with a sarcastic tone, like an adult starting a touchy conversation. The cigarette between my two long fingers and the smoke flowing slowly out of the corner of my mouth completed the scene.

Ozra Banu was startled by my cool, haughty tone, bringing up that peculiar party that had gotten out of hand at the end, near dawn. She burst into coughing, almost choking with her own cigarette smoke. She remained silent for a long while, clearly turning my rude question in her fuzzy head and searching for a sensible answer. Maybe she didn't remember much about that night, anyway, thanks to all the vodka she'd drunk. I remembered everything perfectly, though, because I was the only sober person among that big crowd. I'd watched the hoopla with horror and also participated in some of its commotion with both excitement and astonishment. Its memory was still fresh in my sneaky mind.

5

The party was for men only at Mr. Hariri's resort, a huge garden with two villas on opposite corners. It was in Golab-dareh, then a small village in the northern part of Tehran, past the district of Shemiran. All those areas are now developed and have become parts of the Greater Tehran. Mr. Hariri was a flashy, handsome bachelor, and a member of the parliament. He was a close friend of Father's and the son of a prominent cabinet minister. Almost every weekend, he threw parties for his friends, which entailed all sorts of entertainment, including alcohol, opium, prostitutes or easy women that some guests brought with them. Sometimes they gambled too. Only seldom Father joined them when he gave in to Hariri's pressure, whom he seemed to like a lot as a friend. Still, Father tried to avoid more disrepute and likely spies in those vulgar parties. For example, the guests were expected to drink alcohol recklessly like joining a sacred ritual of self-sacrifice for ultimate drunkenness.

Nobody counted people's number of drinks, yet the contest continued in full force automatically: Everybody was supposed to have vodka, whisky, or similar hard liquor in his glass while in a group and chatting, but disallowed to only sip it. He was pushed to keep drinking and emptying the glass in line with repeated toasts about one silly thing or another. The group ganged up against anybody who tried to cheat. They'd make sure his glass got refilled and emptied in his stomach faster with repeated toasts until he caught up. Mr. Hariri himself mingled, made silly toasts, and supervised the enforcement of rules. People moved around to socialize with everybody. But the minute he entered a different circle of friends, his drinking was controlled by the new group. So cheating was impossible, and nobody dared to cheat in fear of becoming a marked man. There was no point coming to these extravagant parties, anyway, if someone wanted to cheat.

A few times, they'd returned Father home after one of those parties, unconscious and half-dead. They'd just dropped him on the bed, teased Narges about Father's low capacity for alcohol, and fled, leaving the task of reviving Father to furious Narges. It took at least a couple of days before Father fully recovered.

One weekend, about a month earlier, Mr. Hariri and his cousin sort of kidnapped Father when they learned Narges was out of town. They told Father a foolproof plan would be in place to stop excessive drinking—a promise sounding empty even to my ears. Mr. Hariri insisted he needed Father's opinion about a singer's talent attending the party—another nonsense to charge his ego, I reckoned. Father said he couldn't leave me alone, so they pushed him to bring me along. When we arrived, Ozra Banu was already walking in the crowd with a glass of vodka. I knew she was a distant relative of Mr. Hariri. So I wasn't overly surprised to see her there, except that her age and presumed standing didn't match those men and a few whores at the villa. Hariri and his cousins had always treated Ozra Banu like a family member. But in that particular party, she was treated with much higher regard than usual. Later on, I learned more about her background and why she was treated with such high regard. That night, however, the whole situation and her presence looked bizarre to me, although she seemed to know all the guests already, many years before that party. Hariri told Father that Ozra Banu was invited because they hadn't seen her for a long time and that this particular party best suited her taste, as a special night of musical entertainment.

Mr. Hariri introduced Farida to Father. She was an attractive singer who accompanied a group of professional musicians all night. Two guests were from Tehran's main radio station to judge Farida, too. For a good portion of the night, the musicians played some soulful Iranian tunes and she sang along with a delightful voice. Hariri also announced everybody must pay one thousand rials (a large sum of money then) for each drink, instead of the regular free alcohol loading. Ozra Banu would be in charge of the bar and money that would go into her purse.

Ozra Banu pretended to be embarrassed, so the guests led her to the bar and insisted that she accept this mission as a favour to everybody for less drinking. At last, she sat behind the bar and refilled her own glass of vodka first, then began selling drinks and collecting money. With Hariri's hidden intention now clear to the guests, everybody rushed to buy more drinks to support Ozra Banu's business and suck up to Mr. Hariri.

The noise, laughter, and music grew louder in line with the speedy consumption of alcohol. Farida sang along for the drunks who gulped alcohol even faster than previous occasions when drinks had been free. The keen crowd ambushed Ozra Banu, all striving to compete with one another in front of Mr. Hariri. She couldn't keep up with the rush, over sixty men and a few women needing urgent attention, as if seeking medication in a hospital emergency room during a serious epidemic. So she asked me to help her with collecting the money. Hariri handed me a wooden box to use for holding the cash and giving the customers their change. I was excited to be involved and also play with so much cash for the first time. Iranians always carried big bundles of cash with them then, and still do it to some extent even now.

Singing and noise died down near dawn, after it was decided that Farida was a great singer. She'd have her debut on the radio's Friday morning show two weeks later. The drunkards scattered around the villa to find a place to sleep or snoozed in the opium smoking room. Hariri and Father took Farida to the bedroom to explain the details of her upcoming career, I reckoned at first. But then felt the need to sneak behind the door and peep through the big keyhole when I couldn't hear anything. They were taking their turns with her *without talking*. I enjoyed Farida's naked sexy body in dim light, which was ten times more appealing to me than her alleged beautiful voice. The poor girl must've been really exhausted after all that singing! And now this!

Back in the deserted living room, I found a blanket and passed out on a couch. None of those zombies seemed to notice me or care about my sleeping arrangement. Father and Ozra Banu had probably forgotten about me altogether.

I woke up around noon and found the house cold and quiet like an ancient cemetery. It felt too depressing after all the noise and hoopla the night before. For a moment, I thought everybody had forgotten about me and left, but soon I noticed two guys slouched under blankets on the floor. The bastards hadn't been able to find a better place in one of the bedrooms to collapse. There was no sign of Ozra Banu who was stinking drunk near dawn when a few men helped her walk to a bedroom and another man carried the box full of cash for her. She was probably given the best room to recuperate.

6

One month after that memorable night, I was sitting near Ozra Banu once more and watching her get drunk again. She sipped the vodka in her glass and watched me with suspicion, showing no sign of getting drunk still. The atmosphere and crowd's loud crudeness in that party had been quite educational for me, despite my regular study of vulgarities at the Club and private parties. I didn't mention anything about it to Narges, although I believed she had a good idea about the nature of those gatherings.

Ozra Banu parked her cigarette in the ashtray, hurried to the liquor cabinet, and poured another half a glass of vodka, as if knowing the place of the liquor now gave her all the rights to stuff herself. So I lit another one of her cigarettes in return, this time even without asking her. She lurched to the couch and watched me smoke my next cigarette with a Clark Gable gesture. We could hardly see each other, though, with all the smoke filling the room and all the windows closed. I was confident she wouldn't rat on me about my cigarette smoking. Her teasing smirk showed her pleasure to find me so easily corruptible. She also seemed happy about the chance for our alliance after failing to pretend any type of family ties all along. Narges had expected me to view her as a grandmother. But I'd never cared to pretend she'd been one, due to not only the truth, but mainly her rude personality. At her old age, she'd probably realized, too, that she hadn't been even a decent adoptive mother for Narges, let alone a patient grandmother for me.

"Farida is on the radio all the time these days," I said at last.

"Good for her. She has a good voice," she replied.

"And a great body too."

She chuckled. "You're too young to talk like this..."

"Like what?" I asked with giggle.

"Were you only checking her body instead of listening to her, you devil?"

I wished I could brag and tell her everything I'd seen.

"Hariri made her famous, didn't he?" I asked.

"Hasn't Narges thought you to address adults as Mr. or Mrs.?" She blasted. You should say Mr. Hariri and Ms. Farida. Don't you know even these basic rules?"

"Why should only kids do all these extra works?"

"Now I see why Narges complains about you so much..."

"How much you made from selling vodka that night?"

"None of your business," Ozra Banu said with angst, thought for a second, as if worrying about my big mouth and telling on her. "Around 390,000 rials."

"Wow... You kept all the money?" I asked.

"Yes."

"Give me some of it then, will you?"

"What do you need money for? To buy cigarettes, ha?"

"Yeah," I said fast. "But I helped you with collecting money."

"I've already used the money on old debts, kid."

That much money could have covered her living expenses for a couple of years or more. But I believed her, as she was careless with money like Narges, who always came to Father for paying out her debts despite her own good income. So I decided to focus on my mission of dragging some vital information out of her.

"Did you give Narges money when she was a child?"

"No, she never asked for money. She wasn't a brat like you."

"How about dolls? Did you buy her any dolls at least?"

"Dolls? No... Toys weren't customary those days."

"So she never had a doll or any other toys?" I asked in shock.

"No. I guess not."

I didn't remember having many toys myself. I recalled only one small toy car that my grandaunt brought for me when she returned from Hajj. Oh, a soccer ball, too, for one day. It went under a car tire and burst into a million pieces the first day I took it out to play with my friends near a busy street. This was just before we moved to the new subdivision. Those good old days! The poor ball would've been safe in this empty neighbourhood completely, only if we'd moved here a few weeks sooner.

"Was she a good child?" I asked in a mocking tone.

"She was quiet and polite, not like you."

"Why did you adopt her?"

"You ask a lot of questions tonight, kid. I'm drinking the vodka and you're getting drunk!"

"I just want to know."

"We needed a child and I couldn't have one. Is this a tough thing to figure out on your own?"

"How old was she when you took her from the orphanage?"

"One."

"Why did you pick her?" I asked with a giggle.

"Because she looked cute," Ozra Banu replied.

"She looked cute?" I asked with my eyes popping out.

"Yeah... Why?"

"So what happened? What kind of food you gave her then?"

"What do you mean, kid? What the heck is happening to you tonight? Have you drunk vodka too?" Ozra Banu yelled with a grimace, pretending not to understand my question, but then she couldn't control herself and burst into laughter.

"You're really crazy, Kian, aren't you?" she asked with a grin.

"Why?"

She didn't answer, so I continued, "Did you like her at all?"

"Of course... But I'm not very patient with kids, anyway."

"Especially with pesky kids like me?"

"Exactly."

"Why not?"

"Because they're both noisy and nosy, always asking so many silly questions."

"Instead you liked to have lots of parties," I asked with a grin.

"Who told you that?" She got really angry this time but also pensive, as if I'd hit a sore note—maybe recalling the pleasures and consequences of those crazy times.

Poor Ozra Banu was really trying hard to tolerate me, only for keeping my mouth shut about her liberty with Father's booze.

"How about your husband? Did he like Narges?"

"Of course… But he was always busy."

"What was his job?"

"He had a shoe factory. He was Reza Shah's and his family's custom shoe maker as well."

"So he met Reza Shah and his family?"

"Yes, until the last day the Shah abdicated and went to Egypt with a new pair of boots," she said with loud laughter, apparently enjoying her own humour

"Why did he abdicate?"

"He was forced into exile because of his ties with Germany during the Second World War. The Allied Forces occupied Iran and put his son in charge as the new king," Ozra Banu said with impatience and a sign of exhaustion, but no sign of drunkenness still. All that vodka was going to waste for sure. She probably needed five bottles merely to warm up and give me some lousy information instead of being so defensive.

She went to the liquor cabinet and refilled her glass again, and I thought I should jump in and ask the main questions. I'd waited long enough and we were both getting too exhausted already.

"How did my parents meet and marry?"

"Are you okay, kid? What's the meaning of all these silly questions?"

"I just want to know, please," I begged.

"Your grandparents came to our house and asked for your mother and we said okay. That's all."

"That's the way it happened!?" I asked with surprise.

"Yeah, sure... How else do you think it could've happened?"

"Did Narges always call you Ozra Banu?" I asked, trying to give her a break for a minute before raising Narges again.

"Yes…"

"Why?"

"Why what? What's wrong with you tonight? I'm going to bed… I'm tired…" She left with distress after emptying her glass down her throat with rage, perhaps thinking that bearing me was not worth a few more glasses of vodka.

I pondered the fact that Narges had never called anybody 'Mother,' either. I had no idea why I'd been calling her Narges, or Narges Banu, but never 'Mother.' Nobody had told me to call her anything else. It had never felt odd to anyone, either, not even myself, although I'd noticed all other kids calling their mothers by title instead of their first names. Both Father and Narges had also been okay with this formality. I got up and went to bed too.

By the way, some of the most awkward moments of my childhood happened when Narges and I witnessed a mother and her child play or laugh together. We just peeped at each other and wondered what the heck was wrong with them! What was going on? Why were those people so weird? What were they trying to prove? People having such corny emotions and also daring to show them so openly felt bizarre to me and possibly Narges, too. During such peculiar parades, a huge confusion overwhelmed me, but I also felt ashamed for not knowing what the hell was going on out there. Narges looked disturbed and confused, too.

Anyhow, that was all I could gather from Ozra Banu that night and during the rest of the summer—nothing. Nothing useful, at all, for opening even a tiny window to the mystery of my parents' marriage. Yet I hoped to get Ozra Banu really drunk soon and grill her if my parents left us alone again. By the way, whenever

Father went out without Narges, I stayed home with her—as though she could protect me against bandits, or that I might as well die if she was murdered. Their guidelines seemed absurd and arbitrary. Their logic killed me. Actually, their random show of concern felt ridiculous, considering their meagre tenderness toward their only child.

Yet, Father's devotion to protect us, or at least himself, seemed genuine. For one thing, he'd borrowed a puny handgun from a buddy of his who was a colonel in the army. I had no idea how this colonel had himself found the handgun and so many bullets that Father used regularly. It was hard to imagine that he'd borrowed it from the army, because guns and ammunitions were strictly controlled under the Shah's regime. No weapons were sold in the free market, either. So the origin of that tiny handgun remained as another mystery. Father probably knew where it'd come from. But if it were the good colonel's personal handgun, he'd taken a major risk lending it to Father, in return for some favour perhaps! Maybe a pretty whore Father had gifted to the lonely colonel who, in his mid forties, still lived with his mother! How could some people live with their moms for so long after the age of ten or eleven, if that, I wondered with confusion! Then again, here I was myself, almost twelve, still struggling to find a way to run away with the gypsy or some other way.

A few times every month, Father took the handgun from its hiding place, stood in the middle of the garden, and fired half a dozen bullets in the air. Sometimes, he went on the flat roof of the house to fire the shots. He tried to look brave, but the way he held that puny handgun as far away from himself as possible, while turning his head and pressing his eyelid shut before firing a shot, was really funny. Then, after each shot, he looked around and at us to make sure we appreciated his bravery. Oddly, the blasts in fact sounded quite loud for such a meagre handgun. With this charade, Father meant to warn the neighbours and bandits, who might be going around the subdivision undercover, that he had a gun and wouldn't hesitate to use it. He often checked the neighbourhood from up there with his binoculars first—probably counting the number of a few unsuspecting souls that were going about their chores—before deciding it was a good occasion for wasting a few bullets. I remained sceptical about the value of his scheme to scare bandits, spies, or angry neighbours even if they happened to be around and heard the gunshots. Narges was even more cynical about this whole shenanigan. She kept recounting his comical bravery to protect his family everywhere with a great deal of theatrical details in a mocking tone.

Then, one day, Father revealed the secret hiding place of the handgun and bullets to Narges and me. He also showed us how to handle it without explaining his reason for doing all that. I guessed he wanted to prepare us to use it in case of emergency— when he left Narges and me alone at home. Or maybe he was hoping that I'd use it to kill Narges on one of those occasions when she pushed my nerves to the limits.

While Father was killing himself proudly to teach us how to use his gun safely, I was only fantasizing about borrowing it soon secretly and teaching the fatsoes a lesson. It was so easy since they could hardly even run. I'd kill Ahmad Javid at least, then make other kids carry his bullet-ridden body to the garbage site and bury it under the pile of trash. "Let's put this fat trash where it belongs," I'd order them. His body would soon be burned with all the other garbage and no trace of his life would be around to prove my crime. I'd warn the kids to keep their mouths shut or else. I'd tell them I wasn't joking or worried about going to jail and removed from my family, anyway; so I'd kill them as well, before the police could find me. Sadly, Father startled me out of my sweet daydream before I could finish all the killings and burying the corpses. He asked me if his instructions were clear. I nodded, though I wasn't sure at all.

The kids asked me one time about the gunshots they'd heard coming from our house. I said it was Father's and I knew where he kept it. This news alone brought me some instant respect. They asked me with awe whether I could bring the gun out of the house and show it to them. Enjoying my sudden popularity and power, I promised them to do so as soon as I got a chance. I would surely become their leader, I reckoned, when I actually took the gun out of its hiding place one day and waved it near their faces. Only then, I realized that being a leader is so easy without knowing anything about leadership. I'd been going about this matter the wrong way all along!

Anyway, the summer ended without any worthwhile triumph to write in my diaries despite my efforts. I looked forward to start my last year of elementary school. The gypsy woman, and all the questions she'd raised in my mind, still haunted me, though.

Then the night before school, a pleasant surprise gave me a great reason to feel a bit less miserable and more optimistic about life, after all—a sort of sensible purpose to stay alive. It happened when I was taking a warm bath and enjoying my routine sensual thoughts about the nameless, pretty gypsy. I really wished she were there, to take a bath with me. I imagined washing her pretty body and cursing my slow brain for not asking her name at least. My dream proved too potent and I reached puberty in a magical way. This heavenly, novel discovery proved the amazing delicacy of God's mastery in creating nature, wow! He'd known He must give His tortured creatures such an incredibly strong incentive to stay interested in living and playing the game of life that He'd invented with such complicated and frustrating rules.

What wisdom!

Still amazed and restless later in bed, I had some more fun at God's expense, imagining how empty the universe and Nature would've been without sexual lust. God could've sent all sorts of messages and most persuasive prophets to encourage procreation, yet humans would've found the hassles of bearing and raising their kids not worth the tentative joy of parenthood before those brats' arrogance drove them nuts. *It isn't gonna work!* God thinks.

So after a few millenniums of thinking and abhorring the slow procreation, in spite of all the compassion and maternal urges that

He had injected in His early creatures so diligently already, God gathers His angels at last.

"Okay…, enough being a liberal God and fussing about the tyranny of temptations! I'm gonna make these idiots horny to populate Nature," He proclaims. "That seems to be the only way I can make this thing work, especially with this lazy humans that I'm expecting to evolve into something useful eventually…"

So this most potent source of sins—sexual drive—was added to the DNA finally after sixty million years of trials and errors when no other option worked for passing the responsibility for some aspects of Creation to creatures themselves. And now, most of our deeds and thoughts relate to sex, so pathetically, without thinking even about our own welfare, decency, or obligations when lust blinds us. We are now made of tons of desires facing billions of temptations every day!

"Oh, what have I done?" God is probably thinking these days! "How can I now get these humans to stop making too many of themselves—such thoughtless, pathetic beings one generation after another—and causing so much misery for themselves and my beautiful Nature?

"I should've made them a bit more brainy than so horny. How can they fill their beautiful brains with such absurd imaginations and speculations, especially about my designs? And now, tonight, this idiot Kian is trying to divulge my deep secrets, too, not to mention his annoying knack for whining! The only remedy now is probably to just wait and watch their lunacy and spite grow quickly to extinct themselves in a century or so, which is like a second for a patient God Who takes millions and billions of years to get something done. And then these imbeciles still say I did everything in six days!"

Thank God, I fell asleep before insulting Him even more and ruining my fate for good.

God, please forgive me. My blasphemies are all Ozra Banu's fault, as You know, I'm sure…! Or do You want me to explain that, too?!

CHAPTER SIX
Mother-what? Who? Me?

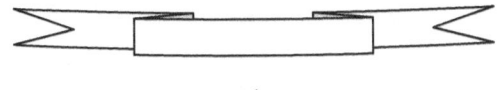

1

Amused on the long drive to school, I mused over my previous night's sensational novel experience, cute imaginations about lust and God, and then such a funny dream. I was a ruthless general conquering the world with my new vastly potent weapon of mass production. Women everywhere cheered as I invaded cities and villages and spread my genes generously with passion.

Regardless of the dream's possible interpretation, international reactions, and its relation to my blasphemous, bizarre thoughts about God before falling asleep, the thrilling symbol of puberty had by itself made me see life and God in a brighter light all of a sudden—still another credit for the gypsy woman, the nameless goddess fuelling my fantasies. I wondered if her appearance and predictions had in itself been the clue that I'd asked from Him—to show me His presence. You see, I've had a special dialogue with God for years, too, which I'll explain gradually.

Anyway, the rosy sign of the fabulous adolescence had really inspired me to start the last year of primary school on a positive note. I felt quite ready to redefine Kian and break new grounds as I sat in the car next to Narges. She drove for 45 minutes to school without either of us saying a single word. All along, I planned to make a bunch of new friends and forget the horrible summer I'd endured in the ghost town with some haunted kids and horny servants. As a start, I'd make them smokers, too, I reckoned.

But soon I realized my foolishness again. I got anxious and angry as we arrived in the school and a few assholes called me mother-boy. *Sons-of-the-bitches!* A mother-boy! Me? Narges? It sounded insulting but mostly gross. Yet, I could neither reason with them, nor change my method of coming to school. Surely, it made sense for me to come along with Narges since she taught grades one and two at the same school, and also because our house was too far away from the civilized world. But, of course, my numbskull classmates couldn't get these simple logics, even if I cared to explain everything to them sixteen times. On the other hand, perhaps being a studious son of such a tough teacher already qualified me as a mother-boy, anyway!

All my plans for having some fun before kicking childhood and also gaining some social skills were spoiled in only a few minutes. From a safer corner of the classroom, I looked around at my classmates acting foolishly and noisily like kindergarteners. They jumped around and made bizarre sounds and gestures like monkeys. They laughed idiotically at silly jokes, shouted their stupid opinions, threw things at one another, and brawled like mountain goats. They set their territories and built their petty gangs to bully others, especially the old geeks and new pupils. They invented phony stories about their adventures during the summer to outdo one another. They arm-wrestled to show off their growing strength, fought over the desk they wanted, and all the rest of it. The same old mockery in the first week of school every year. I was forced to take the last desk nobody wanted, right in front of the teacher's. I was still on the geeks' list even though I tried to participate in their hoopla a few times. They kept teasing me like previous years. Yet I stayed cool, feeling blessed for my big breakaway to manhood relative to those juveniles. They were right about my passivity, though. I only smirked when they pushed me around, instead of smacking at least one of them. Then again, my cocky smirk seems to piss them off even more.

I spent the whole day in a haze, especially during the breaks when the kids let go of all the energy they had restrained during the class. All that suffocation surged in a big blast as soon as the relief bell rang and they got wild again. The way the sound of a bell erupted such an explosion so swiftly was amazing, as if the teacher didn't exist anymore or wasn't in the middle of talking. I wished I could scream the same way, but just couldn't. Where all my restrained energy was going day after day, I wondered.

Instead, I mused like an astonished alien on the weird planet Earth. Those restless kids looked lost like me, too, but somehow could pretend to be happy in their delusional world. Another bunch of carefree, wandering souls. Not that I worried about their wellbeing, but the situation made it awkward for me to fit in and last another school year. I envied their mindlessness for a minute. But, swiftly, I dreamed of bringing Father's handgun to school one day, too, for good use—probably the day after I killed Ahmad Javid. If I murdered one, I might as well relieve a few more lost souls from their miseries.

Anyway, I just sat there the rest of the day, flipped through the new textbooks' pages, and stared at the pictures in the history book. I tried hard to ignore the travesty around me, but it was a tough condition to cope with or avoid. An eerie parallel to what I'd faced the whole summer with fatsos in the neighbourhood. I wished I could go to high school today rather than wrestling with such an absurd situation an entire year.

The funny thing, I believed they bullied me mostly for taking revenge on Narges, anyway. She'd been their teacher at some point, too. So even at school, I was paying for Narges's malice that had bruised the lives of many students as well. This was just a bizarre parallel to the neighbourhood kids picking on me for Father's creation of the subdivision. How bizarre! Still the fact that all the kids in the world detested me because of Father or Narges helped neither my anxiety nor my sense of loneliness. My agony mounted because I had to account for my parents' evils to everybody, even my teachers.

Three years back, when I started grade three, my gloomy life improved a little, as I was no longer Narges's student. Not being controlled by Narges round the clock was a major relief. I liked the new teacher, Mrs. Fateh, who was Narges's good friend and quite aware of her dry personality. Unlike Narges, she was pretty, patient, and passionate toward all her students, especially me. She actually seemed eager to help her students regain their confidence after bearing Narges's tyranny in prior years.

One day, when Mrs. Fateh had just begun her lessons, one of Narges's students came over and told her that Narges needed me for something. Mrs. Fateh looked at me tensely with hesitation. I was unhappy about the intrusion, too, and hoped she'd say no. But, after some thinking, she told me to go.

I followed Narges's messenger to her class, where she gave me money and instructions to go to the pharmacy and buy her a bottle of aspirin. This chore took me around 25 minutes by the time I returned to my own class. Mrs. Fateh asked me what I'd been doing all that time. I told her the story in front of the whole class. She got furious, which I sort of understood. But you know what she did? She told me to go stand in the far end corner of the classroom and face the wall, I swear to God. The class roared with laughter and she yelled at them to shut up. She was really pissed off. I stood there and stared at the white wall for twenty minutes, after all that walking already, until the bell rang and the class was dismissed. My classmates teased me again in many ways, but the worst insult was their senseless corny 'mother-boy' accusation—*bachenaneh, bachenaneh,* they chanted.

I didn't blame Mrs. Fateh too much for causing me so much humiliation besides the punishment. She said I should've come to her and asked for her permission before running out of the school and doing errands for Narges. But she'd never told me to do that. This was the third time Narges had fetched me to go buy a bottle of milk or a snack for her from the grocery shop. This had been a routine when Narges had been my teacher. A hundred times, I'd left the school during the class to buy her stuff. So, her attitude felt normal to her. Only Mrs. Fateh's reaction appeared silly, as far as Narges was concerned. In fact, she was shocked when Mrs.

Fateh had gathered her courage and confronted her in the staff lounge later that day. Narges told me that herself in the car later that afternoon while cursing her, just as a prelude for the main news: that from then on, she'd wait until lunch break with plenty of time for me to run her errands. Mrs. Fateh's fuss had shocked her, maybe more than Mrs. Fateh's resentment of Narges's lack of respect and commonsense. Mrs. Fateh had been wrong, though! Narges at least had enough sense not to abuse her own students for running her errands besides fetching me to do her chores. Their friendship was shaky for six months.

Thank God, at least Narges could not interrupt my education at her pleasure! Still, similar incidents gave students a great deal of ammunition to call me *bachenaneh.*

2

The humiliating way of commuting with Narges annoyed me for other reasons, too, especially when she dragged me after school to do her shopping or visit somebody. I wished I could take the bus or walk to school like all other kids. I hated their guts, but I wanted to prove I wasn't a mother-boy, after all. I wanted to stay after school to play soccer or basketball. I wanted to smoke with them and be included in their mischief around the city. Maybe I could learn to loosen up a little, instead of mocking their stupidity all the time. But taking the bus home had many hassles besides the risk of facing wolves. The only bus stop at the subdivision, near the proposed location for the imaginary shopping centre, was far away from our house. So I was deprived of the simplest joys that even the poorest kids in Tehran took for granted. What was the point of living in a rich family then? How ironical!

The only good thing about returning home with Narges was to watch Rahim shivering in the cold winter nights while opening the gate for us. He knew I hated coming back home with Narges every day, so he tried to mock me with his big smirk, but the car's headlights blinded him. Instead, I enjoyed his agony, while I sat leisurely in the heated car. I always threw a sly smirk at him as Narges drove past the gate.

The fatsoes said the bus always ran almost empty. So, the bus service was just for showing the city official's half-assed efforts for suburban development and supporting Father's project. The fatsoes didn't use the bus, either, even though their houses were much closer to the bus stop. They commuted with their parents, too, resented this neighbourhood, and were getting fatter daily. All Kids suffer someway nowadays. If my brilliant idea comes true—about giving kids the right to sue their parents with proper evidences after legal age—all the courts around the world would collapse from the sheer volume of complaints!

I decided to rebel anyway. I psyched myself up to ignore the long walk and the danger of facing wild dogs and hungry wolves, especially in the dark, freezing winter nights. I thought I must be brave and accept all these risks for the sake of freedom. I just had to pay the price for not being dragged to places, or come home, with Narges after school. The opportunity of being a bit carefree like my classmates felt more tempting every day. But Narges and Father kept rejecting my idea of taking the bus. More than my safety, I believed, they feared the business risks for Father if some wolves ate me whole, but left enough of my bones for evidence.

At last, I forced my parents to let me try the bus for a few days. We had long arguments and I broke a few dishes in anger until they agreed. I walked home alone in one spooky winter night, and that was enough adventure for the rest of my life. The bone-crushing cold and the heartfelt fear of dogs and wolves brought me back to my senses. Hearing the crunchy sound of my feet pounding the snow in the night's silence was frightening enough. But random howling of dogs or wolfs not too far away also felt horrific. Many other freaky noises echoed from several directions as well. I got home pale and panting, so scared and cold I couldn't stop my shaking hands to put the key into the lock and open the door. The bus-ride wasn't for me, I concluded after only one night of bravery. Instead, this experience hurt my sense of manhood some more. The huge gap between my imaginary toughness and the horror I'd endured for about twenty minutes was humiliating. I learned that I still had a long way to go before achieving even the basic elements of manhood; that is, if this manhood thingy wasn't a fantasy altogether. Apparently, puberty had not a damn thing to do with manhood, either.

Another consequence of my humiliating bravery was that now Narges found a new topic to tease me often slyly. She asked me with a serious face every now and then, "So what happened to your plan to take the bus home?" She'd noticed my flustered face when I'd arrived home that night and now she was going to mock me about it forever. "You broke the dishes for what then, *Rostam the Brave*?" I wondered sometimes whether she mocked me just for fun or trying to stir my pride to take the bus again and again until wolves would hopefully eat me!

That sole historical bus ride had only one benefit. I learned that 'freedom' was just another human delusion. The torture of getting home in the cold winter ruined ten folds all the fun and freedom I'd enjoyed earlier with some lousy friends after school. This harsh reality about 'freedom' has been confirmed time and again with similar experiences in too many social circumstances. The price to pay for it would always be too high in all respects for us social creatures.

3

I made it through another depressing school year somehow. Managing my homework with minimum effort gave me a chance to read many Persian translations of Russian novels and short stories. Those characters' horrific dilemmas made my problems feel somewhat paler and tolerable, although I still wondered what would happen to me if I didn't escape soon; but how? I'd run out of options for finding the gypsy. Where would my destiny take me then? Only the gypsy's promise, "You'll travel to the new world," kept me going, while I wished things improved faster.

Hope, even for embracing that illusive freedom soon, helped me get through many restless nights. I hoped entering the gates of high school—not alongside Narges—would bring me a relative independence for now. Yet, all this dreaming, and constant hope for a brighter future, in return, screwed my mind in a different way. I never learned how to live. Nothing was in the present to live for. So my mind only dwelled on the past failures or hoped for better possibilities in the future. I never learned that I couldn't change the past. I never learned that the future would bring only similar miseries. I never learned to control my self-pity and petty notion of running away.

The summer came rather fast with the dusty wind blowing again over the fields around our house. It promised some new adventures, including the return of the gypsy. She'd come back to update her visions according to the force of the new zodiac. I prayed to God: Let the hot wind be a true messenger of Thee. Let its promise about the gypsy's return come true.

The sizzling summer of 1968 also brought me the jubilance of graduation from elementary school. At last, thank God! Three other events that summer affected me in big ways, too.

The first one started with our trip to Mashad, the city where Imam Reza, the eighth descendant of the Prophet Muhammad, is buried. Muslims from around the world, mainly Iran and the neighbouring countries, make pilgrimage to kiss his shrine. They make *nazr* with money and other sacrifices in return for his mercy, to grant them their *niaz. Nazr-o-niaz*—pledges and wishes. The idea of travelling to Mashad came from Father's aunt, whose grandson, the twelve-year-old Jamshid, was very ill with diabetes. She and her daughter (Jamshid's mother) were going to beg for Imam Reza's mercy, to cure Jamshid. Grandma decided to go along with them, then invited Narges, too.

Narges jumped at this opportunity, which showed her rising despair about her own destiny sliding down the hill fast. Maybe Imam Reza could help, since not even the gypsy's premonitions last summer had brought her any relief. Nothing positive seemed to ever happen for her. Father had already taken off for Europe for two months with one of his bachelor buddies—the colonel that had given him the gun, in fact. The guy who still lived with his mom! They were going to buy two Mercedes Benzes, travel all over Europe, and drive back to Tehran. At the bus depot, the scene of Narges's quiet sobbing looked pitiful. She'd come with mixed feelings to see Father off for the journey to West Germany thru Turkey. Narges knew that he'd most likely fool around with women all over the Europe and still had come to see him off.

Narges had almost three months of summer holiday like her students and she hardly went to parties without Father. Living in the big house without Father affected her mood, which in return spoiled ours. In all, the trip to Mashad was handy for pleading to Imam Reza. Except that I wondered about the nature of her plea: To return her unfaithful husband home safe and sound, or kill him to end her guessing and suffering! She always cursed him, especially when they fought. "I hope you burn in hell; never see another good day; become a leper; etc." She liked a particular Iranian song and played its record quite often. The female singer whines so pitifully, "I hope you die, so that I know where you are!" But Narges loved Father like a heroin addict, or because she couldn't find anybody to replace him with. Even then, at my age I mean, I couldn't understand the meaning of love when lovers kept begging God to kill their beloved. What would be the point of that then? Lovers seemed more vengeful than passionate—to love someone just for who they were—I mean if they really must love him or her in the first place.

Of course, I had to go along with Narges to Mashad and she invited Ozra Banu, too, who accepted fast. I wondered why she, a sinful, alcoholic atheist, took the trouble of visiting Imam Reza or dared asking him for anything. From my limited knowledge of Islam, Imam Reza could not humour a blasphemer. She knew these clear rules too well and still hoped to convince the Imam to make an exception! Maybe she'd repent in hopes of salvation?

Maybe she could argue that her parents' neglects or bad genes were behind her sins, blasphemies, and the way she'd treated Narges. Overall, her intention for this trip felt fishy to me!

By the way, my parents weren't religious at all. Narges's case was of course crystal clear, being raised by Ozra Banu and all. Still, she held some minimal faith without practising any Islamic rituals. Father never cared about religion, despite Grandma's pushy fanaticism. Her attempts to inject some sense of Islam in me had gone to waste as well. Instead, Ozra Banu's regular funny blasphemies sounded both radical and rational to me. Her points about God were refreshing, in fact. Grandma got angry when I teased her with Ozra Banu's heretical views and questions. Surely, in this hectic environment, I was confused by both blind beliefs and blasphemies of the role model adults around me.

Besides the dire effects of growing environment, I believed my cynical views about religion and God were Narges's fault as well. Asking God questions regarding Narges had soon turned into questioning Him because of her. She and He had turned into two related mysteries and my doubts about both of them grew deeper every day. As my creators, they both were too insensitive toward me. Still understanding Him was easier, because he didn't nag or bug me every day. On the other hand, the more I could blame God for Narges's crabbiness, the less I needed to hate her. Anyhow, my parents and I weren't so godless like Ozra Banu, although I often understood her normally solid logic and atheism.

Grandma's family looked down on Ozra Banu, because her alcoholism alone was a sin according to Islam. Anytime they happened to be in the same crowd, religious arguments erupted. Grandma was diplomatic and careful not to offend Ozra Banu and Narges. Anyway, Narges asked for Grandma's permission to bring Ozra Banu along to Mashad and she agreed.

On the train to Mashad, we all cooped up in a compartment for twenty hours. We couldn't even take a nap in that crowded, noisy space. Jamshid was resting flat on the three seats on the left-hand side of the compartment. So the rest of us tried to sit randomly on the right three seats. Anytime I sat on the tip of the seats that Jamshid occupied, Narges ordered me not to crowd him. His mother and grandmother walked around frantically to serve him, too. I wondered if it was really necessary, according to Islamic rules, to bring the suffering patient along. Did the good Imam and the patient have to meet in person? Couldn't Jamshid's mother explain his bad condition to Imam Reza and beg Imam's pardon for not bringing Jamshid along for a firsthand visit?

At last, I couldn't hold my big mouth any longer. I asked Grandma whether the patient really had to go to Imam Reza's shrine and plead *personally* for his mercy. Grandma got upset from my clever, supposedly blasphemous, cynicism and snapped: "God forgive your ignorance. Stop talking like a godless idiot."

This wasn't a goddamn straight answer at all. I liked to know my sin for asking a simple, honest question. Anyway, I gathered that probably the answer to my question was, 'Yes.' It was really necessary to bring the patient along—to impress Imam Reza or give him a chance to check out the severity of the patient's case firsthand, I imagined! Maybe I was a bit rude or sarcastic due to the inconvenience I had to put up with in that crammed space. But often I wondered whether I was the only sane person in this family, or too mad to grasp the logic of these blessed people?

All along, Ozra Banu's endless arguments with others caused an added torture, although her heretical questions sounded wise and hilarious like mine. Again, I wondered why she was making this pilgrimage if she insisted to be an atheist and if not planning to repent in Imam Reza's shrine. Her presence on this torturous long trip seemed even more ridiculous than Jamshid's! Unless she'd come along only for the free ride, out of boredom, to argue with those fanatics about religion, or just to annoy and embarrass Narges. I was surprised that nobody asked her the most obvious question: "Why are you going to Mashad then, you godless witch?" I was too scared of Narges to ask this question myself. So I whispered it to Grandma's ear so that she could raise it. But she didn't dare, either, out of fear of Narges, too, I imagined.

My duplicity to agree with Ozra Banu' sacrilege, yet run to conspire with Grandma felt hilarious, but also hideous as a clue about my confused character! *Who am I, anyway?* I wondered.

At one point, I got fed up with all the religious arguments while Narges tortured in silence. She looked angry with herself for inviting Ozra Banu. I walked to the washroom, where many people were waiting. I decided to wait as well, instead of going back and listening to more nonsense from a bunch of possessed, old women. A woman in the crowd held a pretty girl's hand, about five years old. I looked around and at them, too, before staring down at the floor, quite baffled about my derailed destiny on a train to Mashad for no goddamn good reason.

Suddenly the woman stepped forward and slapped me in the face so hard I was thrown from left to right. I looked up at her in absolute shock. Nobody had ever slapped me. Nor was I ever as confused as I was at that moment. Not even Narges had ever slapped or confused me so much. In shock, I just stared at the woman. Then I peered at the bystanders with shame for having been hit by a stranger and not knowing what to do. They were stunned as well. With tearful eyes, I watched the fierce anger of the crazy woman and the amazement of the spectators. *Why was I hit and what must I do?* My mind was numb. Had I possibly done something nasty unknowingly? I checked my pants to see if I'd peed in front of everybody. Everything looked fine and dry.

At last, a man asked her, "Why did you slap him?"

"Because he was going to steal my daughter," she shouted.

Everybody checked me out suspiciously for ten seconds. The terrified look of a tiny boy incapable of stealing even a chicken convinced them that something was wrong with the woman. Her ridiculous accusation had perplexed and paralyzed me even more. I was drowning in a deep sea, while the arguments heated up between the woman and a few of the bystanders. I questioned God's wisdom for bestowing so many types of odd punishments upon me in odder situations every time for the weirdest reasons anybody could imagine. Or was this punishment actually a direct warning from Him for my share of blasphemies all day? I'd fled the awful arguments in the compartment to arrive here right in time for a vicious slap! Then this absurd accusation. And now a new round of gross arguments, all caused by me this time! With a perturbed posture, pain, and pressing pee, I returned to our noisy compartment. Narges noticed my fright right away. Unlike usual, this time she asked me what was wrong and what had happened to me. I said, "Nothing," and charged toward the wide window at the end of the compartment to hide my red face and tears.

I watched the speeding fields and telephone poles. I got dizzy as I focused on the hazy view rushing before my eyes. So, I shook my head and closed my eyes to stop the commotion in my head. I pondered the frailty of my presumed manhood. How helplessly I'd stood there with pain, unable to utter even a word of objection. I should've punched that crazy woman in the face, broken her freaking jaw. I should've smashed her empty skull. Instead, I'd only cried like a little girl. Even the five-year-old girl had watched me with pity. She looked surprised of her mother's baseless assault and accusation, too, while I'd merely frozen like a melting Popsicle and done nothing. She was probably confused as well, mostly about me, but also about her mother's madness. Maybe she wished being kidnapped away from her maniac mother, after all. I hadn't even been able to tell my grievance to the train attendant who'd appeared after the crowd confronted the madwoman. In fact, everybody might've concluded that I was guilty after I'd left without defending myself and, even worse, changing my mind about peeing. A person who can hold his pee is definitely guilty of something! I hadn't even dared to reveal the incident to Narges, partly in fear of causing more chaos around us. But I also imagined she may think I was guilty of something. After years of fooling each other, she might actually assume the worst—that I had a sexual intention for kidnapping that girl. Like any young man with a surging sexual drive, some odd feeling of guilt hit me occasionally, even for a simple sexy scene in my dreams. So, I imagined Narges picturing me the same way my horny father had proven himself to her. Maybe she'd think, 'Like father, like son,' and then tell everybody in town and broadcast it all over the world! Mistrusting your mother is horrible and sad!

I got madder and sadder about my shaky manhood while the train pulled in and out of two stations. I watched passengers buy bread or fruits from the running vendors through train windows as it waited twenty minutes in each station. My face still burned from the madwoman's hard slap and I still had to pee, but I didn't dare go out there. I knew I should learn a lesson from all this pain. What was manhood? Was I a man or a kid still? How could I become a real man then? I must rush to build a strong character and assertiveness, especially around women. But how? Reaching manhood felt too vague and difficult. This sad, severe realization dampened my mood throughout our trip to Mashad. The result of the slap in the face was that it pushed me into a pensive haze and I felt happy to stay there. I was tired of the way things seemed to work in the world, thus preferred to stay in this detached state for now. Like a kind of pleasant numbness. I didn't know how to get rid of it, anyway. Yet it helped me forget the ongoing arguments amongst the four loony ladies that Jamshid and I had to endure.

4

In the end, after a week in Mashad, poor Jamshid couldn't take the mayhem any longer and fell seriously ill. The *nazr* and *niaz* to Imam Reza weren't helping him, either. Like so many other sick people in the shrine, my grandaunt had made Jamshid touch the golden barricade surrounding the Imam's tomb. A few times, she tied a long ribbon from Jamshid's wrist to the railing, like a phone wire, to make the contact more direct! It couldn't be wireless, I supposed. They left Jamshid tied to the railing for hours. Now I understood why the poor patient had to travel all this way and be present in the flesh!

Several doctors visited Jamshid in the hotel room where he lay almost breathless in his bed. His mother and grandmother took turns visiting Imam Reza's shrine a dozen times every day. Our hotel was near the shrine so conveniently. They pleaded more for their *niaz* and pledged a higher *nazr* every time. They took a few of Jamshid's belongings, such as his handkerchief or pyjamas to rub over the tomb's railing and bring them back to rub all over poor Jamshid's head and face. But Jamshid's condition showed no improvement, if not getting worse from all the extra germs brought from the shrine and loaded on him. Imam Reza was perhaps busy with so many other cases! About two hundred ropes and ribbons tied the dying patients on the floor to the railing anytime we went there. So, how could the poor Imam handle so many calls for mercy in a day? *I wonder if they still tie ribbons even in this age of digital and wireless communication!*

Ozra Banu visited Jamshid only once in his room, but stood at a safe distance in case his illness was contagious. What if some other viruses had also infected him on top of his regular diabetes? Then, as she entered the suite she shared with Narges and me, she swore on Imam Reza's honour—whose shrine stood at a stone's throw from our room at that instant—that she was sicker than Jamshid. Narges scolded her for making such an outrageous claim and comparing herself to a dying young boy.

I visited Jamshid often. Staring at him lying on his deathbed, I grasped Einstein's theory of relativity much better for the first time. Father had tried to explain it to me rather vainly one week before his departure to Europe. On the train to Mashad, however, the example he'd used to simplify the theory kept ringing in my head. He said that if I were sitting in a moving train, my position would be static *relative* to the train, but dynamic *relative* to the objects outside the train. He then explained other stuff that I couldn't grasp or remember. They didn't feel important at this moment, anyway. It was mostly important that Einstein had liked trains better than buses or cars, if Father's story held water. I did too—at least before being slapped on a train by a crazy woman.

Watching Jamshid's pitiful anguish was too frightening, but I couldn't turn my face. The relativity theory felt more relevant, in fact, when Jamshid's face showed humans' absolute nothingness in spite of their endless conceit and cruelty. I wished Father was around to explain death to me. But what could he or anybody else say about Azrael, anyway, such a jerk he's always been? Yet, I was mad with God, for letting a bunch of loonies, like Azrael and Satan, pain His allegedly beloved creatures so much? Expecting us to fight these mighty opponents and win, in order to live longer or qualify for heaven, was too much of an expectation on His part, if I may respectfully say so. How could death be such a casual matter to Him, while we poor creatures should struggle so pitifully and painfully to elude Azrael all our lives, and knowing that he'd definitely win eventually.

Handling His game of life and idiotic beings is such a horrific task already without Azrael and Satan always butting in as well. Why create them anyway, especially this jerk Satan? I recalled Ozra Banu challenging Grandma and Grandaunt. "Are you now saying that God created everything except Satan or lost control of him later? Or created him just for testing humans?" Then, she continued, "If you believe Satan created himself or somebody else did it, then we'll have even a bigger mess on our hands." The fanatic duo only rolled their eyes, shook their heads, and cursed her with religious chants. Ozra Banu only smirked and continued, "The problem with you god-loving people is that anytime I find a hole in your divine theories, you accuse me of blasphemy instead of answering my questions."

I couldn't help the gibberish circling in my anxious brain. *Oh, Imam Reza, what is happening to me with all these hideous thoughts?* It all came from watching Jamshid's bleak condition and thinking about the relativity theory. I realized right there and then that I wasn't a man yet. I was only a self-absorbed bastard. I was a wicked boy always bitching about the way my parents had ignored me or the genes they might've passed on to me. Always nagging about the way I was forced to live in a crooked family and environment and all. How silly all my excuses for feeling miserable had been. At that point, observing Jamshid's struggle to survive, dying for just another breath, I was ashamed of occupying a healthy body filled with so much petty fears.

I missed Father and his patient character more than ever those days with all the confusions about manhood and death crippling me. This was the first time he'd been away this long. I missed his encouragements and attempts to explain the tricks of manhood whenever he could. He was a kind man, aware of my turmoil, but also unable, like Narges, to help me. Despite his busy schedule and women, he tried to spend some time with me, too. He always read English books and journals and encouraged me to do the same. He only watched the American Channel on TV, a service for the U.S. Army personnel, which had a base in Iran during the Shah's regime. Many American civilians also lived in Iran during that time. The main shows that Father and I watched together were Perry Mason and Rawhide with Clint Eastwood playing the role of a tough guy even then.

As much as I missed Father then, I was glad he hadn't been around to witness my breakdown. I knew I should really get a grip of myself and stop worrying Father with my sinister views of God's game of life. Still I jotted down a lot of gibberish in my diary every evening in our suite when I had nothing better to do. I always made sure to hide my diaries in a secret place that nobody, especially Father, could find.

5

We stayed about three weeks in Mashad—much longer than planned. But travelling was unwise with Jamshid's condition worsening every day. Ozra Banu complained non-stop for being sicker than Jamshid and being ignored while everybody focused on him. Narges told her bluntly that it was only the fear of death that had crippled her. With a glare, Ozra Banu ignored Narges's accusation, but kept insisting on returning to Tehran, so that she could go visit her doctor. She distrusted the doctors in Mashad, especially since their efforts to help Jamshid weren't working.

But I believed she just wanted to escape an environment reeking of the stench of death. These days Azrael was too close for her comfort. What if he realized that she was a fitter candidate than Jamshid? Narges took the torture of handling Ozra Banu, but also enjoyed the fear of death maddening that old, arrogant woman. I enjoyed the way she'd been teasing Ozra Banu during the whole trip so slyly, despite her deep affection and pity for her.

At last, one evening, when everybody looked distressed and lost already, Azrael stood next door. Oh, you ruthless angel of death, show mercy. Ozra Banu was still swearing how worse her sickness was compared with Jamshid's when Grandma came over and announced that Jamshid had passed away. Imam Reza!

Jamshid's father had arrived in Mashad a few days earlier. He stayed behind to arrange for transferring his body to Tehran after getting a death certificate. He wanted to send the women back to Tehran to rest. Three excruciating weeks with Jamshid's ordeal and Ozra Banu's nagging had exhausted everybody. On the train, however, Ozra Banu felt better as we approached Tehran. She felt quite well as we arrived at our house. By the way, she went to Imam Reza's shrine several times. She'd brought her *chador* to wear when visiting the shrine. Women must wear a long veil to cover themselves from head to toe. For a person who hardly used even a hair scarf, she'd come fully prepared to visit Imam Reza. She often went to the shrine alone, even though others, especially Narges, insisted to go with her. I also begged her to take me with her, but she refused. I was just dying to see what she did in the shrine and what she said to Imam Reza. Did she kiss the railing with all the germs piling up from millions of visitors' kisses? I bet she did. I was sure everybody, especially Narges, was eager to see her begging in the shrine, too. I got mad with my brain later when I realized that I could've followed her secretly and watched her from a distance. My stupid, slow brain!

Still, Ozra Banu resumed her blasphemies during the return trip, anyway. Understanding her motives and everything that went on in her old brain seemed impossible. Were all her new arguments with Grandma and Grandaunt only a front to hide her new frailty after years of youthful arrogance and atheism? *See, I've not changed my mind, and all your prayers to Imam Reza for Jamshid failed, too,* she was probably trying to prove. Yet, enough loneliness and destitute had probably broken even this proud atheist. She was only hoping that Imam Reza would ignore her massive mouth and pretensions about atheism. Hopefully, the generous Imam could at last relieve her from the miserable life she was enduring—at least by granting her a painless death.

Sometimes I thought about all the *nazr* and *niaz* that must've been going on by all the women in our party in Mashad. The main purpose of the trip, to rescue Jamshid, had only led to his death. Narges's *nazr* and *niaz* didn't bear any fruits, either, if she'd wished for Father's reform or his death. When he returned at the end of the summer with a black Mercedes 220, Narges found many pictures of him and the colonel with women all over the Europe. He didn't even try to hide them, which only showed his indifference about being discovered by Narges. Had he been behaving so carelessly all along, from their wedding night? Was he trying to crush Narges's pride? Drive her totally nuts? Make her escape?

I'd made a *nazr* and a *niaz* too. I asked Imam Reza to help me go to the new world and find that special girl the gypsy woman had promised I would find there. I needed the Imam's blessing to fulfil my desires, especially finding a mate to make up for all the love I'd so far not received. I needed a pretty, loyal wife so that I wouldn't have to search for love all my life. I hated the way both Father and Narges had been cursed to seek love forever, outside their marriage, with such desperation, all those freaking years, all in vain.

The childish gibberish I wrote in my diary the night Jamshid died

Grandma keeps saying that everything is only God's plan, anyway.

"It's all part of His wisdom," she often emphasizes with pride.

So, does anybody know why God wants us to die, especially so young, like Jamshid? To go to hell or heaven apparently—according to Grandma and religions—to face the consequence of our actions!

"Because He loves us so much," Grandma also insists.

"Otherwise, He would've not created Azrael and nobody would've died, ha!?" I've challenged her a few times after doubting her religious knowledge. Instead of answering me, Grandma has always only rolled her eyes and told me to go wash my mouth!

So old age and sickness are apparently only for getting our asses over there—to face the music. But this poor Jamshid didn't get even a chance to live a little, let alone sin.

It's great that He writes our destinies, because then we are not logically responsible for anything we do. Our bad genes, luck, and environment are all for carrying out His plans. This notion makes it easier for us to live, maybe even like a bum, without worrying about so many decisions, while we wait for our destiny do its things in due course. So why does He send us to hell on account of the destiny He chooses for us and all the stupid things we do like idiots to make it happen? What's He really thinking? Besides, mustn't He forgive us for our sins and stupidity, anyway, even if we don't repent, going by His alleged generosity and love for His creatures? And since He's created us so weak to begin with, anyway. Isn't He responsible for making us so weak and wicked and then writing a crooked destiny for us, too? Don't all these ~~stories~~ *talks* about His love and wisdom actually make Him look at least a little mixed-up if not vengeful? Why do we have to repent then? And is He so naïve to believe us when we repent just out of fear or hope for heaven? And why is He so secretive about His intentions and all the rest of it, anyway?

On top of all this ~~nonsense~~ wisdom, Grandma also insists that *God almighty could create anything anyway He desired.* So, why not do it the right way from the beginning, or at least not create Azrael. What if no ~~killing~~ deadly diseases existed and we had a choice about dying? Would anybody choose it just on a messenger's shoddy promise of being reborn later? Would anybody choose the chance of going to heaven, instead of living *as is* forever? How many mullahs would gladly quit their religions as a condition for eternal life on earth?

We'd continue to kill each other or commit suicide—don't you worry—but we wouldn't die of oldness or sickness so painfully like that poor Jamshid. Instead, He teases us with the taste of a short life and a scary ending. Why? Worst of all, He makes us feel so pathetic pretending to be brave, while suffering the fear of meeting Azrael all our lives or for losing our dear ones, especially our kids. Watching Jamshid's grieving mother today tore my heart into million pieces.

Oh God, will Father be angry or amused if he hears my ideas? Surely, Grandma will put the final curse on me one of these days.

I was only four years old, just barely feeling alive, when Azrael appeared out of nowhere. In my feverish hallucination and fighting chickenpox, I was playing on a beach at the Caspian Sea, when God suddenly gave me a shocking piece of news—a serious heads-up.

"You're having fun, ha?" He asked rather cynically.

"Thank You for creating me. I like this life," I said ~~thankfully~~ politely with a big bow, my head almost reaching my toes.

"Stop playing with sands and listen. You see this monster? I give you a few minutes head start to escape, hide, eat, and exercise to get strong, but once he catches you, he'll torture you before knocking you out for good. If you're really lucky and he's too busy, he might finish you faster. Got it? Now run!"

"But why? Is that all part of Your wisdom and love too!?"

"No questions… Just run."

"How far? How long?"

"Forever! As long as you like to live…"

Icy blood ran in my veins and my knees trembled as I peeped at Azrael again, wept in confusion, and apparently wet my pants that night, too. I shivered from fear and fever for a week hoping to find an answer or a place to hide. At last, I realized He was quite serious. Feeling helpless and lonely, I kept running. Azrael's image and the promised torture will ~~follow~~ haunt me forever until I can no longer hide or run. Then the final, real torture begins, exactly the kind that wrecked Jamshid bore before my eyes this morning. I wanted to cry watching his agony, but my flimsy manhood stopped me because everybody in the room was staring at me, as if wishing I were in

Jamshid's place. I don't know what I've done to all these people, other than repeating Ozra Banu's words and questions all the time.

Why not at least make death fast and painless like birth? How do His plans about Azrael and Satan match His clever creation of such a huge universe and billions of creatures He loves so much? Then He also gives His favourite species just enough intelligence to suffer not only from Azrael's attitude, but also for wondering about God's mighty wisdom. Why?

We would've learned much better about life and when to call it quits without Azrael, anyway, instead of making so much fuss about life being short, painful, or all the other stuff we imagine about it. This way, the fittest would live longer and the weaker soon commit suicide or get killed by people God creates stronger and prettier to begin with. Overpopulation wouldn't be an issue, either, since we'd lose our interest to live forever, anyway, even if we didn't destroy everything with our obsessions for cruelty and by butchering one another so ruthlessly.

It is all Azrael's fault that we love this miserable life. So maybe creating Azrael had actually been God's only other solution for keeping us interested in living another day—fervour for sex and the fear of Azrael. But are these solutions really fair and fit for us or God? Maybe all these sufferings are because of His tenacity for doing everything all by Himself, without any consultation, which is now causing us pain and confusion. And a chance for a mad boy— this bigmouth Kian Noori—to fill out so many pages of his diary, this late at night, with all these gibberish and blasphemy.

"God forgive you, you godless idiot," Grandma has yelled at me a few million times.

But, honestly, couldn't He have come up with a less painful ~~life~~ design? Looking around, we must admit that He is Almighty alright, but do we really have any proof about His wisdom and kindness, too? Of course, we humans are quite amazing with our brains and imaginations as well, including all the science. But we're also cynical and cruel. So, maybe God did in fact create man in His own image!

Oh God, what am I becoming!? Damn Ozra Banu!

Goodbye Jamshid.

CHAPTER SEVEN
Hanky-panky on the Donkey

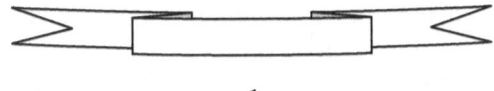

1

Two other events in the summer of 1968 made lasting effects on my life, too. They began right after we returned from Mashad.

Narges brought Ozra Banu to our house to keep an eye on her health. She looked quite energetic to me after two weeks of moaning in Mashad about her presumed near-death condition. The way she loved every second of her meagre life was quite an eye-opener for a restless, suicidal young boy like me. Her fierce fear of death felt so funny, but Narges stopped me from joking about it or teasing her. I asked her how come she could do it but not me, and again she only rolled her eyes and told me to *go away*. Her sense of loyalty toward Ozra Banu, even after all the recent torture Ozra had caused her in Mashad, was admirable. Despite her clashing feelings for Ozra Banu and Father, Narges pampered them passively with pain and patience amid her busy daily affairs. Her tolerance of Father's compulsive infidelity and Ozra Banu's endless demands, while hating both of them, was just amazing. She was an iron lady. Yet, her extreme benevolence toward Ozra Banu felt bizarre to me, in particular.

By the way, anytime Narges told me to go away or get lost, I got keener to make her wish come true by finding the gypsy woman. To save time, when the gypsy woman would be waiting at the door for me to pack and run away, I'd prepared a note for Narges already, **with a copy to Father**: "I'm going away to get

lost as you'd asked me so many times. You sounded very serious
to me, so I'm honouring your wish…!"

*Let's see how happy or horrified Narges would be! But I was
sure Father would beat the hell out of her, anyway—just another
yummy incentive for me to do it—run away fast. Alas, I won't be
around to enjoy watching the scene I'd been missing for so long.*

Narges had another reason for bringing Ozra Banu over, too.
She wanted to avoid many long drives to her suite in case Ozra
was actually sick. She rented the first floor of a house in Fozieh, a
rather cheap neighbourhood. The owners lived in the upper floors
of the house. Since Ozra Banu couldn't afford a private phone,
Mr. Nozari, had placed an extension in the first floor for her for
emergency. So Narges had to go through the Nozaris to speak
with Ozra Banu. She had to listen to their complaints about her
calling on them for help often. That was another big hassle for
Narges when Ozra Banu was staying at her own place.

Narges called Mr. Nozari to say that Ozra Banu was staying
with us awhile and she'd bring the overdue rent in a few days.
Mr. Nozari told Narges that a stranger had come by and asked for
Ozra Banu. He'd left a phone number to contact him. Narges got
the number and called it herself. She spoke on the phone quietly
and strangely for about fifteen minutes and then stood in silence
with a flustered face. She finally regained her composure and
said that the man on the phone claimed to be her brother.

The news amazed Ozra Banu and me, too. I tried to imagine
the outcome of this development. Especially for me, finding a
new uncle and learning something about Narges's past felt quite
intriguing. How would she react toward her real family?

"You know anything about this?" Narges asked Ozra Banu.

"No…"

"He's probably a crook trying to swindle me," Narges said.

"Well, you give money to strangers all the time, anyway."

"I bet he's learned about me from someone."

"Maybe someone in Mashad noticed how you like throwing
money away," Ozra Banu said. "Charlatans live everywhere."

"Do you know anybody like that?" Narges asked, sounding as if suspecting Ozra Banu about all this. It was no secret that she was always broke and often made friends with strangers.

"Are you crazy? How dare you ask me this question?"

"I'm only trying to know if someone's got some information from you about me, that's all."

"No," Ozra Banu snapped.

"All right... Why are you so testy now?"

"Because you always ask stupid questions. What'd he want?"

"Nothing... I told him I don't have any brother."

"Good... So you got rid of him?" Ozra Banu asked.

"I tried, but he kept insisting to meet us. He lives in Isfahan, but will be in Tehran for a few days," she said before sinking into deep thoughts again. We all kept quiet to mull over this matter.

This was another curious story that this guy was adding to the long list of family mysteries. Finding out about his motives would be interesting, too, especially if he was a crook, with or without a connection to Ozra Banu. Contacting Narges during Father's absence made it even more suspicious. Narges might need my assistance, anyway, in case the guy was a crook. I was the man of the house in Father's absence, according to Narges's nosy friends who teased me in front of her any chance they got. They did it often just to agitate her about Father not taking her to Europe with him. Those sneaky women! I felt those women were insulting both of us by implying that I, such a measly child, was the best man Narges could ever have in her life!

With so little time I spent with the fatsoes nowadays, and the task of finding the gypsy woman stalled, the new mystery could amuse me awhile at least. Was this guy acting on the information the gypsy had gathered from Narges last summer?

The awkward silence broke my patience at last.

"So what're you gonna do?" I asked with a giggle.

Narges stared at me tensely, irritated by my excitement. She looked embarrassed for her past history surfacing, yet probably curious to learn a bit about her heartless mother at least.

"I promised to call him in a day or two," Narges replied at last, which was odd all by itself. She seldom answered people's questions, especially mine, especially when she looked pensive. Most teachers often ignored people's questions, anyway, always pretending to be thinking about something more important.

"Why?" Ozra Banu asked tensely.

"To let him come for a visit perhaps."

"You want to let him in this house when your husband isn't around?" Ozra Banu objected.

"Should I stop living because my selfish husband is having fun in Europe?" Narges yelled and we shut up again.

Her deep frustration about Father's lengthy trip showed on her face more than ever. I bet she was hoping that this guy wasn't her brother, but rather a cute, tameable crook she could elope with. In clubs and private parties, sometimes she tried to charm any man to intimidate Father. She also appeared eager to taste the kind of fun other women had with different men so openly. She probably felt too lonely every night amidst all those sinners. How selfishly they denied her the opportunity of being as sinful as the rest of them! I felt sad when other men ignored her like she wasn't even slightly attractive. Her efforts to hide her lasting grief looked even more pathetic. Surely, all those rejections frustrated her, but also made her keener to find a lover, or at least a man to rescue her.

"What's his name?" I asked.

"Mustafa," Narges replied with a grimace, still wrestling with her dilemma—maybe even a chance to see her real mom at last!

Ozra Banu and I glanced at each other. She needed a glass of vodka and I needed at least a smoke. Poor Narges just looked too confused for such a decisive woman. I imagined how difficult it must be for her to discover her real family and past in case this guy was in fact her brother or, even worse, if he was a crook with some information about her real family. Making a right decision appeared troublesome for her. For the next couple of days, she was agitated, which made life more difficult for the rest of us. At last, she decided to call Mustafa and invite him for a short visit.

2

In our casual attires, we sat around the oval table in the hall and waited for Mustafa. Narges didn't think he was important enough to dress up for or receive in our lavish drawing room. Instead, she stressed she wanted to end this meeting quickly.

When the bell rang, I leaped and ran to open the door, while Rahim watched me with surprise and delight about my recent attitude toward this chore. A handsome man, in a stylish beige summer suit and tie, smiled at me.

"*Salam,*" I said.

"*Salam, pesaram,*" he replied and patted my shoulder. That magical word again, except that hearing it only from strangers was getting really too depressing.

A sparkling Chevrolet Impala was parked at the curb. Driving a car similar to Father's made me like him already. Mustafa's looked brand new and white though. On the other hand, Father was going to bring even a newer car, a Mercedes in fact.

I guided Mustafa toward the hall where he greeted Narges and Ozra Banu with excitement, even leaning to kiss their cheeks. But their blank eyes stopped him in time. We were all amazed at his great looks with no resemblance to Narges at all. This striking contrast was already making it hard for us to believe his claim of being Narges's brother. He didn't look like the Hazaras at all. I noticed the subtle shock on Mustafa's face, too, when he saw Narges. He surely wondered if his search had taken a wrong turn somewhere and he was in a wrong house. He'd brought us two elaborate handicrafts and three boxes of tasty *gaz* from Isfahan. Narges offered him a chair at the table. He didn't look bothered for not being received in our formal drawing room.

I watched him drink tea and answer many tricky questions that Narges and Ozra Banu asked him. Then he told the story of his long search for Narges during the last five years after his mother's confession at her deathbed about her abandoned child. After meeting Mustafa's father on a trip to Isfahan, she'd returned

to Tehran and given Narges away for adoption. She'd then gone
back to Isfahan and married Mustafa's father without mentioning
her to anybody ever. Mustafa added that his research hadn't quite
confirmed everything about the manner she had given the child
away, where, and at what age. Then he showed us his mother's
picture. She was really pretty. Narges looked astonished staring at
her mother's picture. Mustafa asked her whether she wanted to
keep it. Narges said no and returned the picture quickly. From
Mustafa's story, I imagined that his mother had probably been
pregnant again, with Mustafa this time, before rushing to marry
Mustafa's father. She'd said nothing about Narges's father. *He'd
probably run away back to Turkmenistan or some place like that.*
My imagination was running faster than Mustafa was talking, but
all those conclusions simply added up. It sounded as though my
beautiful grandma (Narges's alleged mother) had been a slut as
well as a manipulating liar. Period. On the other hand, any young,
pretty mother might've given Narges away, anyway!

We listened to Mustafa's stories and gauged his sincerity.
He'd pursued his father's flourishing trade in carpets. He had a
wife, three daughters, and one son. He looked surprised on two
accounts in particular. First, that I had no siblings. And second,
that Father was travelling in Europe with his friend instead of his
wife. With all the clues he offered, Narges seemed convinced that
he was her half-brother, after all. She asked him to stay for dinner
despite her clear reluctance, as if doing it as a one-time favour.
Maybe she did it only because Mustafa wasn't showing any sign
of leaving anytime soon, anyway. The supper was, however,
served at the same table in the hall. Keeping him for dinner was
already a big concession for Narges without having the supper
served in the formal dinning room as well.

I was fascinated by Mustafa's Isfahani accent and charming
grin, but Narges and Ozra Banu kept their guards against him the
entire evening. Their attitudes sucked, especially since they now
looked convinced about Mustafa's story. Narges, in particular,
was rather nasty with him. She showed no emotions to his sincere

efforts to establish a family relationship. He invited us to meet his family in Isfahan. But Narges replied with only a cool shrug and awkward silence again. He hoped to get a clue from Narges about the possibility of visiting us again in Tehran, perhaps with his family, but Narges ignored his hints. Mustafa remained calm the entire time, though. He refused to be discouraged by Narges's stubbornness to accept him as a half-brother or even a worthy acquaintance.

My Uncle Mustafa stayed until late that evening. At times, Narges looked so tense I was afraid she might ask him to leave. I would've been really embarrassed if she'd kicked him out. I was getting to like and respect Mustafa more, the more he ignored Narges's indifference. He reacted only with his charming jokes and lively stories. He described his teenage kids and their desire to see me and their aunt. He even offered to take me with him to Isfahan to meet his family. He said I could stay with them for two weeks or so. Then he'd bring me back as he often travelled to Tehran on business. I really liked his idea. Maybe I could even find an excuse to stay in Isfahan for good. Maybe this stranger could rescue me from my weird family. I'd lost the chance of running away with the first stranger, my darling gypsy woman. So maybe this time I should act more decisively and ask this new stranger to do something for me.

"Can I please go?" I begged Narges.

"No...," she replied with agitation.

Uncle Mustafa stared at the floor to hide his embarrassment. Yet, he seemed to appreciate that at least one member of this odd family was happy to have known him. At the end of the evening, he appeared to have grasped the seriousness of Narges's marital problems. He asked her whether he could do anything to help her, which sounded crazy to me, as if offering to have Father's ass kicked. Before leaving, he asked us again to contact him if we needed anything, which also again sounded foolish, going by the luxurious furniture surrounding him in that mansion. Maybe he thought we were poor because our house was in such a gloomy place outside Tehran. At the door, he tried once more to hug and kiss Narges, but she stood stiff with a blank face, determined to deny the existence of her half-brother, or any real family history. She was already too absorbed in her present mess of lost identity to welcome other options and relationships.

I followed Mustafa outside the house. He sat behind the wheel in his impeccable Impala and turned on the engine. He smiled at me again, then called me to the driver's window and whispered, "Call me any time you need anything... Anything at all... You understand?"

I nodded, wondering why he was so nice, so unlike his nutty half-sister. I also wondered what I would possibly need from him. Six years later, I remembered this scene and Mustafa's words in a quite different situation when I happened to need his help.

3

The most wonderful event of the summer started the following week when Narges accepted an invitation for a four-day trip to Damavand—a cosy village at the foot of the glorious Mount Damavand, only fifty kilometres from Tehran. Some of our close friends had planned this last family outing for the summer. They invited Narges after ignoring her most of the summer. Our lengthy travel to Mashad could be their excuse, of course. Yet my cynical brain insisted that those hypocrites were merely trying to minimize the chance of Narges badmouthing them to Father for ignoring her in his absence. Father might've cared or not, but why risk. I bet they'd hoped she'd turn down their invitation, anyway, the way she usually did.

We left Ozra Banu alone in our house even though she sent a million clues about her desire to go with us. But Narges had learned a good lesson. Her memory of Ozra Banu's bitching in Mashad was still too fresh to make another mistake so fast. In fact, she'd probably accepted the invitation just to get away from Ozra Banu for a few days at least.

"You'd better rest a few days…," she told Ozra Banu anytime she hinted an interest to tag along. "I would've asked you to come with us, but I'm sure you'll get tired and sick again."

Ozra Banu could read Narges's mind, though, and only stared at her with despise. They read each other's sneaky words and minds better than best psychiatrists, since they were so similar.

Narges followed the caravan of six cars loaded with family members, while we stuck to our protocol silence the whole time. She looked lost in her world, while I pondered my regular idiotic thoughts and imagined Ozra Banu taking her revenge on Father's vast supply of liquor. She'd enjoy the open bar and get really drunk this time, now that I wasn't around to judge or interrogate her. She'd blame Narges for all the liquor bottles emptied, too, simply for leaving her alone and depressed. I bet Narges had the same thoughts! I'd begged Narges to leave me with her, in vain. Losing such an excellent opportunity to break Ozra Banu was frustrating. Maybe I could even start drinking vodka with her while smoking lots of cigarettes. Instead, I was being dragged again to another gathering of conceited, pretentious adults and their cocky kids—for four freaking days.

Soon I dismissed Ozra Banu and vodka to mix with a big bunch of brats—what a drag. They had their own usual hesitation too. Bastards! This third group of kids probably resented me for my weird personality somewhat, too, but mostly because of my parents again—like the kids at school and in the neighbourhood. I bet they were totally confused and angry about my parents' roles in their families. They'd surely heard their parents' remarks and quarrels about Father and Narges, besides witnessing the regular vulgarities and gossips in the parties. Their mothers had surely badmouthed Narges's snobbish attitude as well as her spite, which naturally related to Narges's hostility towards those women's mere flirting, or full affairs, with Father. And those kids' fathers had certainly badmouthed Father plenty of times for being a womanizer and flirting non-stop with their wives.

Still those kids tried to include me in their games, although only because their parents had told them so, I reckoned; just out of etiquette and for keeping the appearances like usual. Anyway, we all did our best. I took part in their mindless games awhile before hiding in a quiet corner. Even if they meant to bear me somehow, my cynicism about their sincerity and sanity stopped my enthusiasm in record time. Again, I proved to be a useless, stiff playmate, alienating people everywhere—at school, in the neighbourhood, at the Club, and in family outings. Usually, being around adults felt more natural and easier to me, although I hated their guts, too. It was getting harder for me every day to decide whose guts I hated more: the kids' or adults'. Both groups were difficult for me to get along with or understand no matter how much I pushed myself to be a bit more realistic and natural like all other human beings.

At the end, it seemed easier to bear the adults, though. I hardly participated in their conversations, although they often sought my opinion, as if they knew about my *secret* views of them. Their sly efforts to drag the truth out of my hardened brain were funny but stressful. I usually only smiled with a short answer, since I knew they wouldn't be thrilled to hear the truth, which could escape my mouth if I opened it more than a second. A good thing about the kids was that at least they didn't give a damn about who I was. But with the adults, that was a different story. In fact, the adults' apparent frustration, dying to figure me out, was quite amusing for me when I tried to read their minds: Was I a repressed child, a snub bastard, or a shy freak? Was I an evil, too, like my dad or mom? More like which one?

Even my supposedly child-expert teachers had had difficulty figuring me out, let alone those snobbish good-for-nothing adults. You'd think at least teachers grasp the youths' turmoil and mind. But they were the most impatient and testy people. What did I expect? Narges proved how any weird personality could become a teacher! My teachers often got upset as I focused to absorb their lectures—unlike any normal student. Instead of taking my efforts as a habit of a diligent pupil, they assumed I was judging them like a snotty provincial inspector, or a smutty spy for Narges—the assistant principal. Or like I was only mocking their teaching technique. Their attitude was really bizarre while I tried to be a grateful student. They refused to take my grin as my gratitude, and also trying to avoid any possible grimace. Instead, they asked me what I was thinking. When I replied, "Nothing," with another grin, they got angrier. Their persistence to mistake my grin for a smirk was frustrating. I was really trying to pay attention, impress them, and do less studying at home, to read more novels instead. I hated myself, too, for not knowing what else to do now that both my grin and grimace were offending people.

My inability to correct people's impression of me made the matter worse, as my frustration showed on my face eventually. So, in the end, they were right about their views of my attitude: They made me the way they judged me correctly only at the end. Narges's glares and comments hinted that many teachers had complained about my smirks.

"I don't know what else to do with him! He always does it with me, too," she'd probably told them, instead of defending me or thinking that perhaps my grimace and smirk were her own bloody presents to me. "He's learned all these gimmicks from his stupid father," she would insist instead. Yeah, I was sure Narges had already badmouthed Father at school around her colleagues as well, the same way she always did it around her friends and Ozra Banu. The way her colleagues stared at Father with despise, whenever they came around to help Narges with a project or something, showed Narges's success in brainwashing them, too. They all appeared tense and confused for both hating Father and admiring his easygoing and charm maybe!

My teachers might've also imagined that my smirks related to my good grades, Narges's position at school, or my judgment of Narges abusing them, while they depended on her generosity so often, too. How could a student be so good in all subjects—except for physical education?

Anyway, the first two days in Damavand proved absolutely freakish and frustrating, exactly as I'd predicted, which made me proud of my growing psychic power!

4

On the third day, however, a miracle happened! It started when the families decided to have some fun riding donkeys to a nearby almond orchard. The idea was to pick and eat fresh almonds peeled out of their soft green shells. Also, each family would fill their large sacks with unshelled almonds to carry back and dry in Tehran. Narges refused to go on account of being afraid to ride a donkey. Instead, she volunteered to mind a few toddlers unsuited for this venture. She was probably planning to chat some more with the sturdy peasant busy trimming the shrubs as well. Like a natural communist, she drew commoners as effortlessly as she agitated the aristocrats. On this particular matter, I wished I were at least like her, instead of hating humans equally, communists or capitalists!

I was excited about riding a donkey for the first time, until they announced kids must ride with their mothers or another woman for safety. Initially, I believed I'd be exempt from this embarrassing proposition, on account of my long legs at least. I was man enough to handle a donkey myself, I insisted. Actually, I imagined it could be a good exercise to restore my manhood after being slapped on the train to Mashad and feeling so helpless to defend myself. But the adults kept fussing about my safety. I got quite upset, but then the scene of those kids clinging tight to their mothers on the donkeys made me appreciate at least my amazing luck for Narges's refusal to go with us. Just imagine riding with her and rolling my arms around her waist for safety. I would've surely fallen off the donkey and died that day.

During the adults' serious conversations leading to a decision about the kids, the men's selfish excuse for not taking them had sounded like a decent reason to me after watching those sickly donkeys lining up before us with watery, sad eyes, and trembling legs. They looked terribly concerned about carrying those chubby men on their backs on a trip that was absolutely useless for them —the donkeys, I mean! Besides, kids couldn't roll their tiny arms around those men's huge bellies for safety. Yet, my cynical mind still suggested that the men's refusal had only a selfish motive: Riding with the kids would reduce their fun to push the donkeys and race one another. They proved me right, right away. Poor donkeys! The animals, I mean again!

Anyhow, as though I hadn't been lucky enough already, soon I realized God really loved me. In fact, I reckoned I'd been the luckiest bastard on earth that particular day beyond belief, after all. Amazingly, the adults' splendid decisions that glorious day must be highlighted in the history of humanity concerning Kian. For all those brilliant ideas, that day happened to be the one when heaven opened its gate to me!

I was told to ride with Mehri Mahjar, a thirty-year-old woman whose young kids were left under Narges's supervision. Actually, the Mahjars were my parents' closest friends. So, it was only natural for me to ride on the donkey privileged to carry Mehri's full curvy buttocks. Wow... luck after luck! Sitting right behind this gorgeous Mehri instead of that gross Narges was indeed the universe's biggest miracle that day. It was just marvellous! Mrs. Mahjar—my precious Mehri—was the prettiest creature you'd ever seen. She was the sexiest woman alive.

Her husband, Mr. Amir Mahjar, personally put me behind his wife and made sure I clutched her waist tightly lest I might fall off the donkey. What a nice, concerned gentleman! I wanted to kiss his hands for settling me in such a divine position with such care and concern.

Still, I felt quite insulted too... What was going on here? Hey, everybody! I looked like a man. I felt like a man. But apparently, nobody could still see my long legs, cottony beard, and chronic melancholy. Being taken only as a boy was humiliating and it showed in my big grimace, especially to Mr. Mahjar. But deep down, God knew, I was now only pretending. I was now in total peace with myself and all the suddenly nice and wise adults around me. Now, I loved them all! The idea of embracing Mehri had made me speechless, anyway. Maybe my blush and grimace had saddened Mr. Mahjar, too, for putting this shy boy in this embarrassing position. But there was no other choice. Sorry! So I decided to cooperate! In fact, I was almost sure that if I whined one more time, they'd find me a private donkey. So I shut up.

I rolled my long, tiny arms around Mehri's narrow waist. Wow! Heaven! I felt her warmth and her paralyzing body scent. How wonderful life can really be, oh my dear creator! I had never imagined it could be like this! How could it be so marvellous?! The ecstasy of holding Mehri in my arms and laying my cheek on her spine made me quiver. *Thank you God! Please forgive my stupid blasphemies in Mashad when I was watching the dying Jamshid. I'll learn to do my prayers five times a day, if only Thou make this experience last a few hours! I'll worship Thee forever, my amazing Creator. I'll cherish your body, my precious Mehri, if you just let me be your slave.* His special love for me was proven today once and for all. This experience alone should've made me stop doubting God forever, if I were a normal person.

Out of the blue, however, the humiliating scene on the train to Mashad ruined my concentration. The image of the woman's fierce, ugly eyes after slapping me for no reason at all shattered my tender sentiments with a dire fear. That rough memory made the idea of clasping such a gorgeous body feel like suicide. She'd simply push me off the donkey to my death. Terror competed with thrill. I tried to tell my cowardly brain that I was doing only what I was told. But it was in no mood for any logic again. Would Mahjars forgive me if some kind of obscenity happened by accident?

My nerves calmed down a bit as our donkey began staggering along the trail behind others. The devoted husbands had already raced out of our sight. I recalled my thoughts next to the window in the train compartment: cursing my frail manhood. I'd run away from the madwoman who'd hit me. She'd made me feel like a guilty moron. I should've slapped that maniac five times for attacking me. I should've killed her for making me sad and feeling guilty for nothing. Instead, I'd peered through the big window in the train, with a numb brain, in a deadly static domain, like a bronze statue. I'd been stiffer than the 'man on the train' in the relativity theory example—but I'd worried also about peeing in my pants, *which probably made this tough relativity concept even more tricky and complex than what Einstein had imagined! Surely, I couldn't stand completely still!* I'd wondered how much longer I could hold it, while watching the outside world pass by my tearful eyes at the horrific speed of the train, only the sunlight racing faster to emit the fainting rays of the day.

Now, sitting behind this goddess, who let me hold her with passion, why not behave like a man? Why fear the possibility of insulting her or her husband? When and how was I going to test my manhood then, if not when I had a big chance like right now? It was time to prove myself instead of being only a defenceless boy forever. All these brilliant justifications were the works of my sneaky hormones, I bet, talking inside me, pushing me around, and building all the wicked courage I needed. I felt too horny and helpless. I let my hands touch her breasts when the donkey made a quick jump over a ditch or something and I lost my balance for a moment. Then I placed my hands right back beneath her breasts to enjoy their sexy wobbling in harmony with the donkey's slow galloping. She didn't object or try to correct my hands' positions. She could've, but didn't—wow! Nice woman! Excellent.

Thinking that she might tolerate my dirty deeds excited me even more. I imagined in some glorious moments that she was even encouraging me. My manhood moved a little and I didn't try to tame it by negative thoughts and earlier fears that had tried to ruin my day. Instead, I pushed it when it lined up with the heavenly crack between her buttocks. She was wearing a thin summer dress that hung over the big bloated belly of the donkey. The wind had flapped parts of it, on both sides, over my bare legs

sticking out of my tiny, loose shorts. They touched hers now and
then, although I decided to do it more often without raising her
suspicion too much. It felt so delicious. With every jerky stride of
the donkey and my finer imaginations, our sly touching became
more precise and riveting.

The warmth hovering near my manhood wasn't summer's
fault. Damavand is a cool country and we were riding in shades
along the treed trails. The tender heat came from her heaven, just
making me shiver and believe that it was my goddamn natural
right to approach and knock at its gate. I was invited and had to
accept out of etiquette. She showed no sign that my thoughts and
deeds were crooked. Her generosity boosted my nerve to protect
my position and pursue my purpose. In a moment, I felt she'd
become fully aware of my intentions. Next moment, I imagined
her putting me in my place. Yet I couldn't help myself anymore.
Now, it was too late! Now, I was absolutely ready for any damn
consequence. I was ready for her objection or screaming. I was
ready for Mr. Mahjar kicking me in the guts. I was ready to die
for Mehri. I really was. Now, so suddenly, I could feel the devil
inside me, so careless about the whole world, people, and the
consequence of every desire running in his mad, malicious mind.
In such a moment of dire urgency, I also giggled subtly when my
idiotic rumination some months earlier regarding God calling His
Angels to announce His desperate, final act to invent lust and
ecstasy to populate His kingdom rolled in my horny head. *He'd
surely made it too powerful, I must give it to Him! Maybe He'd
lost control of the dosage and now we must pay for His mistake!*
Now, most of humans' thoughts, energy, spirit, and actions are
devoted to, and wasted on, lust and sex directly or indirectly. Our
struggles for power, greed and even wars revolve around lust.

Apparently, Mehri felt my eternal devotion to her and decided
to have pity on me! She began welcoming my bravery with her
open mind and legs, willing to cooperate for whatever the heck I
was hoping to achieve. For a second, I imagined she was in fact
pushing backward toward me, as if trying to sit more firmly on

me. But soon I realized I wasn't imagining anything; everything was real. She was no longer cooperating, but rather coordinating. Actually, she seemed eager to smash my arrogant manhood with the squeezing pressure of her ass—as a fair revenge for my rude intrusion of her privacy perhaps! Though, she would've been merely silly to think I would've minded her type of vengeance. In that instant, my manhood was the last thing I would've minded being shattered into a thousand pieces. Each piece would've found a vigorous life of its own, like alien creatures in movies multiplying with every bullet hitting them.

I became braver and learned how manhood arrogance grew. I put my hands on her breasts for a second, then did it again and again, each time allowing it to linger a bit longer. I made sure other riders didn't see my gallantry. The next time I grabbed her breasts she leaned forward a bit, toward the neck of the donkey. I thought she was trying to free herself from my overreaching hands. But soon I realized my silly mistake again. While bending forward, she began rubbing *herself*, very softly, over my proud manhood. Its very tip was now sticking out of my shorts next to her pussy. I pressed her breasts gently. And she swirled her sticky genital over my hungry organ artfully, as though seriously hoping it'd find its way to her heaven any second.

We kept silent, hardly caring even to breathe. We could hear some riders chatting and joking along the path. But we two had nothing to discuss. We'd already reached the most delightful pact without the slightest need to negotiate the terms. Only once, she asked me with a heavy, broken breath, "Are you all right, Kian?" I panted with difficulty, at last uttering an "Uh," and nothing else. Was she worried that I might die of delight, or only making sure I was enjoying myself enough?

Luckily, I'd relieved myself that morning already, or else a fertile flood might've dripped all over the poor donkey's bloated belly and Mehri's skirt, which would've been hard to explain. But Mehri showed no concern about being discovered, either. Maybe she thought I hadn't reached puberty yet. Maybe she

didn't mind having some fun and then blaming it all on me at the
end. Or maybe she was seeking an excuse to shout at her foolish
husband for allowing this to happen; for his careless decision to
put this horny child behind his innocent wife. What a child! What
a ruthless rascal! Ruining a wife's innocence single-handedly!
What an innocent wife! Really! Was this woman teasing me too?
Not that it mattered. At that moment, she could mock me or kill
me a million times as long as she just let me stay in that divine
position some more. Only my stupid fear of other riders detecting
our hanky-panky on the donkey stopped me from opening the
buttons of my shorts, drawing my entirrrrre manhood, and sliding
it smoothly under her skirt to find the gate to paradise.

Mehri kept the donkey at a slow pace to better coordinate our
moves. Maybe she was trying to lose everybody altogether, so
that we could go hide in a private spot. We trailed all other riders
with more distance every minute. So they kept yelling at her to
catch up. They were keeping an eye on us so kindly, assuming
that Mehri was afraid to push the donkey too much. Poor bastards
just had no idea how courageous she was, more than all of them
put together! She shouted back at them to stop fussing about us.
Yet, all these yelling back and forth were getting on my nerves.
Mehri called them idiots in a whisper and I giggled—not merely
for her sense of humour, but more so for her opening up to me
against those gawky adults. I was really mad at them, too. Their
kindness was just interfering with her concentration on my penis.
Imbeciles!

I kept gauging the situation ahead of us. Although we had the
opportunity to go further with our adventure, that final move felt
too bold for me. Not for the fear of falling off the donkey or Mr.
Mahjar kicking my ass, I just didn't dare doing anything that
needed the use of my hands or could startle Mehri. Maybe this
was a lame excuse for my gutlessness! But apparently, I couldn't
stop being a caring person despite my desire to become a true,
powerful man as soon as possible. The feeling of guilt, even for
minor sins, was already spreading its roots in my brain, even

competing with my powerful sexual drive. Maybe she would've received my full manhood with kindness, I couldn't bet one way or another; though I believed she would have. As if I hadn't been a mystified child all my life, now lust was making me even more confused and helpless.

5

My reluctance to let go of Mehri when we reached the almond orchard after forty minutes was probably noticed by others the same way Mehri felt it. All the exhausted, depressed donkeys had come to a complete stop and everybody had dismounted except Mehri and me. I embraced her with passion. I'd never hugged anybody ever in my life, let alone the way I'd held her in the last fifteen minutes of our donkey ride. At last, Mr. Mahjar came over and peeled me off Mehri's back with difficulty. He probably thought I was still scared of falling down. I quickly put my hand in my pocket and grabbed my inflated manhood, to stop it from showing off and demanding what it believed to be its absolute right in that moment. It seemed it'd never deflate again or at least not within the next few days. Mr. Mahjar asked Mehri, "Why is your face so red?" And she replied, "Too much sun. And this donkey jumped over a lot of rocks and ditches." Didn't I tell you these adults lied all the time? *What sun? What ditches?*

I recalled the traditional donkey race in Iran, where racers ride someone else's donkey and the one arriving last is the winner. Each rider pushes toward the finish line so that his own donkey is left behind at the end of the pack. That day, our donkey won the *trophy*, but Mehri and I lost. We lost the chance of fleeing and hiding somewhere, just because men didn't stop fussing about us falling behind. Only losing them would've brought us a magical victory. Still, that special donkey ride in that wonderful afternoon must be considered the greatest ride of my life. It was my first blissful experience satiated with an amazing mix of love and lust with lasting effects on my future affairs and fate.

Everybody strolled through the orchard for three hours, ate almonds, chattered, and filled their sacks. But me, I just followed the adults—mostly Mehri of course—in a haze. All along, I dreamt about our return trip. On the way back to our cottage, at the end of the day, I would get a chance to finish the job that my beautiful Mehri and I had started on the donkey. I thought the late afternoon shadows would conceal the details of bodies riding the donkeys. So many lustful adventures I'd created fast in my active mind would remain invisible to other riders. All afternoon, I only built beautiful fantasies. I imagined all the details of my plan and tried to build enough courage to be ready this time. Meanwhile, I chased Mehri with tension to guard my prey and property.

I had no appetite to eat my sandwich or almonds, as my mind could only focus on Mehri and our return trip. I kept checking my watch impatiently for the end of day, like a restless ghost waiting for darkness to show his presence! But, after all that daydreaming and anticipation, I was forced to return with the other kids in a car. When other women noticed how few almonds I'd put in the sack for Narges they laughed at me, while everyone poured a portion of theirs in my sack, to keep Narges happy, I imagined. I felt bad and sad, especially for Mehri who had to ride the donkey back alone and miss my sentimental vulgarity. She peeped at my sad face twice with a witty pity.

We were scheduled to return to Tehran the next day. So I never got a chance to understand the meaning or significance of the episode on the donkey, for me and for Mehri, maybe for the two of us together. What kind of a reaction must I show or expect if I happened to be alone with her in a corner? The only clues consisted of a few accidental and timid exchanges of glances in the crowd when we had dinner or breakfast with everybody else. She avoided my eyes with tension as if suddenly remembering only now to be shy, after all. She appeared too serious sometimes. It was hard to believe she was the same woman who'd been so generous to me on the back of the donkey. Her behaviour mostly confused me more than it hurt. I wondered whether I'd violated the allowed boundaries, or stopped too soon. I couldn't imagine approaching her, not even for some normal conversations. I felt embarrassed saying even a simple "*Salam*" to her. Yet I thought about her a lot. Now suddenly a new blank chapter seemed to have opened up in my life, while I just remained sad and clueless about how I should go about writing the pages as delicately as possible. I wondered whether she was indeed the *mysterious* woman that the gypsy had forewarned me about the previous summer. She was behaving so mysteriously already!

6

Despite my romantic mood after that spectacular donkey ride with a mysterious goddess, a much smaller, but funnier, mystery also amused my brain when I analysed the Iranian donkey racing. The way riders rather fight one another so fiercely just to make their lazy donkeys win, instead of themselves, felt odd. Although humour is probably the main purpose, the manner men pride themselves in having a winning donkey than being the best racer themselves reveals a lot about human brain and a nation's culture. For one thing, people valuing their possessions, including their donkeys, above their own success and self-image is educational. To humiliate and exhaust themselves to death so willingly merely for a chance to brag about their possessions, even a measly lazy donkey—the laziest one, in fact—is mind-boggling!

Near the end of the summer, Father returned with a brand new black Mercedes 220 and lots of presents for everybody. Narges behaved like she'd forgiven him already. Maybe she considered the amount of money she'd wasted throughout the summer, out of Father's bank account, enough retaliation. Father had given her access to one of his bank accounts with a large balance, out of guilt perhaps or to ensure we'd survive for a few years without him. Maybe he'd considered the chance of living in Europe with a mistress, awhile at least. Why rush back to the bosom of his nagging wife and too many business hassles crushing his spirit? The affairs of the new subdivision were getting quite nasty. The whole neighbourhood blamed him for the lack of proper services and security. He'd invested too much money to give up now and scrap the project, even if possible. On the other hand, not enough buyers were attracted to move the project ahead as planned.

Narges had spitefully spent the money in his bank account on jewellery, clothing, furniture, antiques, and travelling. She gave away a good portion of it to the teachers and then in Mashad to Imam Reza's various charities and funds. I bet if Father hadn't returned in time, she would've had trouble paying even for the basic food or servants' salaries. I haven't seen anybody with a lesser sense of responsibility for money or budgeting. Father was upset with her retaliation, but kept his calm. I saw his shock and anger, despite his knowledge of Narges's financial inaptitude and lack of common sense. But he surely knew he couldn't do a darn thing about her clear retaliation. The only thing that perhaps had occurred to him for getting even with her was to leave all those pictures from his European tour around the house casually. If she dared use those pictures to ask for a divorce, he'd be happy to oblige her.

Even more bizarre was Narges's real or fake indifference to his revenge. She kept silent about all the incriminating pictures left intentionally in his study so leisurely, yet nobody could miss all that fury and spite covering her face for weeks. I checked his pictures with numerous women, during the trip, in parks, on the beaches, or around historical sites. For a long while, after Father's return in his sparkling Mercedes with some air of triumph, the atmosphere around our household was so freaky, more than ever.

Apparently, Narges realized the game Father was playing. She swallowed her pride and decided to stick it out a bit longer still. She seemed fully resolved to wait for another chance to retaliate even harsher herself. Leaving him would be a foolish reaction on her part and an easy way out for Father, I reckoned, like handing him his freedom on a golden platter. The way she looked at him, so spitefully, showed how determined she was to make him pay horribly for everything he'd done in Europe. I knew she'd surely succeed. She'd definitely cook up another brutal retaliation of her own soon. It was merely a matter of when and in what form. Pondering their looming games and vengeance against each other frightened the hell out of me. I wondered why Father didn't act to divorce her rather than waiting for her to ask for it. Especially in Iran, those times, it was much more normal, easier, and with little financial consequences, for a man to divorce his wife without her consent. Was he keeping her out of pity, for the sake of his social standing, or was he afraid of her wrath?

In my opinion, at least one of those punching matches, when Father beat the hell out of Narges, was way overdue, although we all knew it wouldn't help their relationship and my frustration with her at the end, anyway. She'd go right back at it, lying and bitching the next day, first thing in the morning, while bruises on her face and body would show for a week or more. The only benefit of those cuffing and kicking displays was that they made me feel avenged for two minutes at the end. On the other hand, it was amazing how their rows and even hard punches apparently only stirred her sex hormones going by their noisy love the same evening, which meant twenty minutes of torture for me. I guessed Father was simply apologizing! This was merely another one of their weird sicknesses, I tell you. It made it hard to fathom their relationship and personalities, on top of spoiling my two-minute joy earlier in the day watching Father's punching regimen to tame Narges. Still, I believed my two-minute pleasure was worth hundred times the twenty minutes of my torture later in the same evening during their futile, temporary ceasefire in bed. I reckoned all my anguish was only a tiny sacrifice I should embrace gladly as long as she got a good beating first.

The million-dollar question was why and how Father had been controlling his rage for such a long time?! How many more months or years did I have to wait for another show? I wish he could hear me and show a bit more of his depleting manhood.

New questions were added daily to the long list of mysteries piling up for years. At the top of the list, now, of course, stood Mehri Mahjar, the woman who had showed me the heaven on the back of a donkey, but then left me out in the cold. My love for her after failing to find the gypsy woman raised all sorts of fresh imaginations in my big head and chewed the rotting cells of my brain, but I didn't know what to do about it. Worst of all, I wasn't sure whom I loved more these days, either: the gypsy woman or Mehri? And they both were out of my reach, anyhow. The fierce competition in my head between these two goddesses both teased and appeased my soul—all for nothing. Was it time to choose and love one of them more at least—most likely with neither of them ever coming into my life, anyway? Where was my fate leading me?

PART II

The Woman

CHAPTER EIGHT
The Pretty Cockroaches

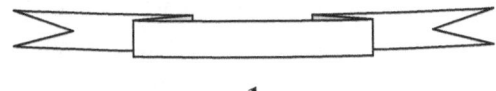

1

A bizarre atmosphere was brewing around me at Royal club and the parties I attended with my loving parents. It appeared that the dozen or so pretty women in our close circle of friends were now gauging me with some enigmatic fascination, if you don't mind my bragging! However, I couldn't understand its meaning or the cause of this weird revelation. *Just another mystery, as if I didn't have enough of them confusing me already!* I wondered what those women were thinking or whether I was imagining the whole thing. But I felt that their stares were no longer passive like the old times. They didn't appear suspicious of my judgment of their flirting and lifestyle anymore, as though I'd at last grasped the meaning of their precious values. And they no longer hated my presence in their gatherings. On the contrary, their vibes now felt delicate and warm.

They'd also stopped their habit of arguing about my looks, as if they'd settled their differences about my genetic sources at last. This was a delightful change all by itself. I'd really hated their guts when, in the past, they'd insisted that even a small feature of my body resembled Narges's. A woman had once said that wives and husbands look alike eventually, anyway. Her dire stupidity to arrive at such an absurd conclusion was unbelievable; unless she was sucking up to Narges or mocking her. Imagining that Father or I would eventually resemble Narges was funny and insulting.

On the other hand, I felt proud now that most of these pretty women insisted that I looked a lot like Father—at last. Not even my rather big nose apparently ruined this resemblance, anymore! Their compliments helped me boost my ego, yet their sneaky attention didn't seem to be related to my looks, either. Unless it related to their amazement about the horrible odds for Narges's son looking rather handsome. The Eight Wonder of the World! But I had two gorgeous grandmas, I wanted to shout at them. I should've asked Mustafa for his mother's photo.

Sometimes, they seemed to be gossiping about me, too, while peering slyly at me and giggling. Not knowing the cause of their odd behaviour was irritating. Yet I enjoyed their furtive glances and teasing smiles. After all, I was a naive, horny boy looking for love, attention, and adventure, if you haven't gathered already! I had no idea how to deal with the situation, though. Instead, I only smirked to show off my growing courage around pretty women. That was the best I could do for now while trying to read their naughty minds. Sometimes, I took their mischievous interest—or whatever the heck it was—as their respect for my entering high school or the way I often wore a suit like grownups nowadays. Perhaps my height and arrogance had convinced them I'd come around and become another impressionable phony adult like them, after all. Or maybe they were teasing me for getting the highest overall score in Tehran in my last year of the elementary school. Father kept bragging about it to everybody. So, perhaps these women were merely mocking me, like my classmates, for being a geek. Sometimes, I thought people, perhaps even Father, imagined that getting all those high marks had something to do with Narges's influence at school and the Education Board. What nonsense! But how could I explain that Narges and my teachers loathed my guts enough to do just the opposite if they could find an excuse to give me lower marks?

Long story short, I was just dying to know the cause of my sudden popularity and what those sneaky women were saying behind my back. For two months, this absurd mystery drove me nuts, I tell you, although I enjoyed every moment of that sneaky attention. Then one evening, when I was dozing off in my bed, a shocking thought startled me. I jumped and turned on the light. I was in shock, but my newest theory made total sense when I imagined and reviewed the women's furtive teasing and giggling around me. Yes, I'd finally discovered the reason: Mehri had shared our hanky-panky on the donkey tale with her gossipy pals. Now the answer was so obvious I felt stupid for taking so long to figure it out. I ran to the kitchen and poured myself a glass of cold water. I gulped it with tension, filled the glass again, and returned to my room. Still in shock, I dreaded the consequences of the information spreading around. I cursed my slow brain.

I could hardly breathe. It was hard to believe that Mehri had done such an outrageous thing, especially considering her cold, serious look around me all along. Did this mean that her husband and other men also knew about it? Oh, my God! My mind got busy sorting out so many questions. I had more reasons to run away from home now; or at least hide in my room forever. But how could I convince my parents to stop dragging me with them everywhere? How could they find a new midnight gate-opener at such a short notice? Unable to sleep almost all night, I tried to solve my new dilemma.

In the morning, however, I was convinced that I had all the necessary answers and nothing to worry about. I wasn't really in big trouble, after all. This conclusion made sense, however, only after making a phenomenal discovery about the power of women. I decided that neither Mehri nor the other women had divulged my vulgarity to their husbands. It was only a secret amongst them, which they could use forever to tease me. I wasn't sure whether Narges was included in this conspiracy or not. I could possibly figure that out later if I really wanted to, but it wasn't a big deal if she or even Father had learned about it. They wouldn't kill me for my cute sexual curiosity. Instead, I wished to know the extent of the details that Mehri might've revealed to others. In the end, again, I concluded that she'd in fact told them a lot, instead of being stingy with her account of the details or my manhood. Their sly giggling hinted that she had in fact told them quite a bit, maybe even more than I deserved or shown her.

My initial panic and embarrassment turned into a crude sense of gallantry and arrogance, in fact, after figuring out all the angles of Mehri's scandal. I also felt proud of myself for tackling such complex psychological analyses so fast. Most importantly, I was glad to be out of the closet at last. Ready for action, you might say. Ready for any kind of hanky-panky that any of those cuties would like to share with me. Those secretive pretty creatures! 'Pretty cockroaches' would probably be a more fitting description of them. Weren't they snooping around people's lives, spreading gossips, crawling all over the dance floor, and teasing me all the time? But then what was Narges doing in the midst of them!? *The pretty cockroaches and the homely lonely one!* They were driving me nuts, all of them, in their own ways.

Mehri's telling of such a hot secret showed that they all shared similar secrets among them. They appeared so cool and careless about the risks of their secrets getting out, too. Their nerve to talk about their scandalous adventures with one another so casually felt amazing and bizarre for my naïve mind. Their bonding power had blown my brain. Surely, women were the stronger gender, not men, considering their nerve to trust one another so casually, despite their horrendous sense of jealousy and rivalry. I made a mental note to be more careful in the future. Yet I was now also quite ready to rip the rewards of my *dirty* reputation! I had finally arrived in the scandalous world of petite aristocrats!

The only question was why Mehri had been so cold toward me all along then. Three months had passed since our incomplete adventure in Damavand. Her attitude was odd considering her eagerness to share that obscene secret with a bunch of depraved friends. If her experience with me had been exciting enough to risk sharing it with others in such a hurry, why not act on it, too. All the clues showed that she'd come out with a good memory. So what kind of a game was she playing?

Still my deductions didn't give me enough nerve to act, either. They only frustrated me more for not knowing her motive and how to raise her interest to follow up on our 'hanky-panky on the donkey.' Was she still messing with my nerves, trying to tame or intimidate me? Had she merely taken the upper hand in case the secret came out? Had she been afraid that I might open my big mouth to some kids in the club or parties? Now just imagine the kids at the club starting a wild rumour of their own! Such a vile gossip would've actually outshined even the grownups' regular rumours. Soon the adults would whisper among themselves with surprise and praise, too: "He did what?" one might ask the other. "You mean on a donkey!?"

2

Not going to school with Narges had improved my life in so many ways. In particular, I didn't have to bear the excruciating, suspicious silence that lingered when Narges drove me to and from school. And no more facing my classmates' idiotic chanting —*bachenaneh, bachenaneh*. Father dropped me near the high school every morning. Early in the evening, I met him around his office or somewhere else to go home together. This gave me some freedom after school. It also gave me an opportunity to know Father better. We discussed many topics on the long road to and from home. I learned that he was indeed a smart and cool guy. For one thing, he suggested that I sleep in my grandparents' house anytime I wanted. This simple solution gave me the chance of staying late in the city without worrying about taking the bus home and fighting the hungry wolves. I wondered why this idea hadn't occurred to us sooner. The answer became obvious right away: Narges disapproved the plan. It turned into another topic for Narges to nag at Father. I appreciated his sacrifice to endure her abuse just to give me a bit more freedom. I couldn't figure out why she opposed this solution. She ignored me when I was at home, anyway. The only possible reason, I thought, was that she was about to lose a good chunk of her control over a slave who had reduced the workload of our servants for years.

When driving home one day, I asked Father, "Do you know what Narges means when she keeps telling me, 'Curiosity kills the cat'?"

"She says that to you?" Father asked with a chuckle.

"Yes, too often in fact, when she doesn't want to answer my questions or thinks I'm nosy."

He burst into laughter. "I heard it in England three years ago and told her a few times myself."

"What does it mean?"

"Exactly what you've thought. But she should say, 'Curiosity *killed*, instead of *kills*, the cat.'"

My grandparents' house was in the middle of the city, on Kakh Avenue. Grandma gave me a key to the house with deep reluctance. She was unhappy about taking part in a scheme that Narges opposed. She was a bit scared of Narges like everybody else, I believed. She'd tasted her malice a few times in person whenever she'd made a suggestion. She'd witnessed Narges's sudden rage toward others on different occasions, too. Anyway, Father's words were always respected, mostly because he paid for their living expenses. He'd also repurchased their house for them when Grandpa was forced to put it out for sale to pay off his debts. Grandpa was another rich to ruin story in our family. Still another mystery I had to crack.

My new high school friends were much smarter than all the morons I'd befriended before. Actually, they proved quite useful to me to learn about life in the city. We went to the cinema and parties together. We strolled around the city and blabbered about dating girls and how to fool them to sleep with us. Sometimes we went to a café to pick up girls, but all those efforts proved mostly depressing instead of pleasant. Those young girls were either too snobbish or too romantic. We could never reason with them about their snooty attitude or boys' urgent needs. They were also too much controlled by their parents. I didn't really mind having a girlfriend my age, but my experiences with girls had only pushed me more toward finding a woman. For whatever reason Narges assumed, and spread a rumour, about me having at least one girlfriend. I believed she had a hidden motive like usual, which I'd discover later. I only grinned when someone tried to grill me about my mystery girlfriends. I reckoned my silence would raise Mehri's jealousy, while showing everybody that their secrets would always be safe with me.

Overall, my dreams were coming true, at last, with lots of freedom and exciting possibilities. Often, even nowadays, I've wondered what would've become of me if Father hadn't come up with the idea of using my grandparents' house and learning about the city life. How fast would've I perished in the haunted subdivision if I had to endure the entire high school in that setting as well? How many people would've I ended up killing, maybe even Narges, with Father's handgun? On the other hand, under this wild scenario—murdering Narges and all—the outcome of many peoples' lives would've changed for the better, especially Father's and perhaps even Narges's, too.

Alas, our dreams often prove shallow once they come true. You think I could now forget about Royal Club and parties to heal my old wounds for being in those places all my childhood. No. No way... Now that I was no longer forced to go to the Club and parties, I craved them more than ever. The reason? I was now addicted to those pretty women who appreciated me from a safe distance. Their subtle flirting gave me a special thrill. What I'd hoped to get from the gypsy woman felt possible in the arms of those sexy women. I could learn to become another one of those gigolos roaming around the dance hall. All I had to do was to stick around and learn the tricks of romancing women. Their soft flirting was satisfying enough already, but there was much more to learn and do. I imagined all kinds of passionate hanky-panky coming my way soon. It was just a matter of time before they threw themselves at me one after another. That kind of passion seemed impossible with the snobbish girls of my age whom I met in some juvenile parties. So, I often tagged along my parents to the same places I'd been going, and foolishly resenting, all those years.

The only hassle was that now a lot of eavesdropping and probing was necessary to learn about my parents' evening plans and act accordingly. Most nights, I invented various excuses to ditch my pesky friends and rush home with Father, so that they dragged me with them to the Club or parties. I also had to make up stories for Father who wanted me to spend more time with my friends, as though he abhorred his scheme for me becoming more independent going to waste. Or maybe he now suddenly realized, after all those torturous years, the damages of raising me in such sinful environments that he and Narges attended most evenings. In return, I usually claimed my friends were busy or crazy, to get Father off my back.

Meanwhile, only Mehri's indifference hurt, especially when I mused over her enthusiasm on the donkey, sharing the story with her friends so eagerly, and my subtle efforts to show my devotion to her, dying for another chance. On the other hand, the more mysteriously she behaved, the more likely she seemed to be the woman the gypsy had warned me about. So, by all logic, it was only a matter of time before she became *the mysterious woman who would come into my life*. In a way, she was already in my life! All these clues made me believe in the gypsy's prediction, thus worked harder furtively to learn about my parents' evening plans and act accordingly, just to be at as many parties where Mehri was.

3

I was no longer too shy like before at the Club or parties, either. My friends had taught me dancing and I'd become an expert in rock-n-roll, twist, cha-cha, and mambo with fancy moves way beyond the patience or aptitude of the old men in the club. That helped my popularity, since most women wanted to try modern stuff instead of always dancing to the old tunes with their aging husbands or secret lovers. In Iran, men were about ten years older than their wives. The women in the circle of our friends were in their early thirties, if that. But their husbands were in their forties, if not even older. The only exceptions were my parents. Father was the youngest husband and Narges was the oldest wife in the group—both forty-four years old.

Many women asked me to teach them modern dances. And then we practised together for months even after they became proficient enough. My life kept getting more exciting every week and I felt lucky for not running away with the gypsy. I was in no hurry to go to the new world, either. The thrilling fictional world engulfing me was probably painted also by all the Russian novels I'd been reading all those years. But I had to thank Mehri mostly for telling on me and thus setting the foundation of this fantasy world. I also praised the donkey that had allowed us share forty heavenly minutes on its back. That kind of soothing and erotic experience gives any young boy a lasting taste of manhood and an obsession for passion.

Maybe it was a weird coincidence or an unconscious urge that I'd started reading about Grigori Rasputin those days. The timing proved perfect, because now I imagined the pretty women at the Club or parties coddling me the same way Alexandra and other women had admired Rasputin. I roamed around the Club the way I imagined Grigori had paraded himself arrogantly in the Russian court of the Tsar Nicholas II. The only difference was that my needs were much simpler, *for now*.

So, attending Royal Club and parties also gave me a chance to boost my self-image regularly. All I had to do was to walk and think like Grigori, take in the affection that women threw at me, dance with them all night, and then use my imagination to fill in the gaps. Their soft grins and my powerful fantasies nourished my needy heart for the time being, while the future looked quite promising, too. I needed this fantastic atmosphere. I'd become addicted to all these appreciations and passions now.

Surprisingly, despite all the credit I'd given to those women for their bonding power and courage, they seemed to lack enough guts, too, to seduce a young boy and trust him to keep his mouth shut about such a novel, exciting experience. In fact, my age and inexperience proved a big barrier for the women who sometimes tried to test my readiness.

The saddest situation happened when Mehri asked me, one night so unexpectedly, whether I liked to go swimming together with her kids. I got too excited as if she were offering me sex right there on the spot. My long fantasy of seducing her and her unexpected softening led to terror and paralysis. So I just gazed into her eyes blankly—mute like a fool. Just a brief moment of surprise in my eyes was enough evidence for her to fail me again. She hadn't imagined I could be such a moron. My freakish flinch could've worried any woman. I got embarrassed and angry about my reaction even more than Mehri did—so much so I couldn't peep for many additional seconds. So what happened to all that confidence I'd tried to show off around the Club playing Grigori? I saw rage in her face for my false arrogance and silly pretences all this time. Anytime she'd decided to relax a little and believe in my readiness for becoming a man, I'd dashed her hopes fast. I'd just failed to keep up with her. In fact, I was only confusing her more every day!

She became stiff quickly herself again, while maybe worrying also about the possibility of giving me a heart attack one of these days. I felt her frustration, rolling her eyes and walking to Mr. Mahjar right away. "Honey, let's take Kian to the pool the next time we take the kids," she said, making sure I heard her.

"Sure. But I'll be going out of town awhile, you know that."

"So maybe I'll take him myself next week with the kids."

"Yeah, sure," Mr. Mahjar replied. He was in a rush to return to his business conversations with his partner. I hated the way they talked about me as another kid.

Amazed at Mehri's skill to prevent a mix-up, I got confused even more. Had her invitation been innocent then—exactly as

she'd explained it to her husband? Maybe only a peace offering
to make me realize her desire to forget what happened on the
donkey and move on? Or was it a basic test of my guts and a step
toward a more divine purpose, in which case I'd screwed up my
chance again? Was her suspicion raised, yet again, regarding my
immaturity to play the grownups' elaborate games of adultery?
Most of all, the damage to my image, once all the other women
heard about my blunder soon, felt catastrophic. I was afraid and
ashamed to be Grigori for a week. *So his infuriated soul rested in
peace for a whole week!* We went swimming, anyway, with her
tiny daughters, but Mehri and I hardly spoke beyond the essential
conversation. We didn't know how to make things better between
us without screwing up everything even more. She told Narges
she was taking me swimming as a gesture of her appreciation for
my efforts to teach her twist and rock-n-roll. The way she said it
in front of me gave me the impression that her invitation had
most likely been innocent and socially justified, but then Narges's
sharp gaze at us, especially at her, with suspicion, encouraged me
all over again, thinking that maybe Mehri still loved me and
meant business, after all. The way grown-ups, especially women
versus men, judged my degree of manhood was totally mixed up
and it differed from my own view of myself altogether as well. *It
is so hard for an adolescent to recognize and respect his or her
identity during those confusing years,* I reckoned with pain!

Not only my inability to read women's minds, but also the
war going on between my mind and mouth frustrated me. My
mouth just wouldn't open to say all those magnificent desires and
passionate words that my mind was dying to share with those
pretty women. Why couldn't they work together for once? Still,
hoping to get another chance soon, I practised sexy gestures and
words in front of the mirror in my room sometimes, to be ready
next time. I often held a cigarette in the corner of my lips, too, to
perfect my pose. I strived to build courage and get ready for the
next test, which would probably be even more difficult. Deep
down, however, I remained sceptical about Mehri or anybody

ever taking me seriously or risking to include me in their games. When? How? I was getting tired of waiting and hoping, unable to read their pretty minds, while they were hesitant trusting me, or even reading my petty mind. If only they knew how sensual my thoughts about them were! And how trustworthy I was! If they knew, we could've got down to business much sooner and things might have turned for the better, too. Many catastrophes could've been possibly prevented if only Mehri had acted just a bit sooner.

4

Among many benefits of using my grandparents' house, it could also help me investigate and solve some of the family secrets. I went there late some evenings after my adventures around the city. I grabbed snacks or beer from the fridge and relaxed in my room. Often, I mused over both Mehri and the gypsy woman, still unable to let at least one of them out of my life. I slept late, as I hardly rushed in the morning to get to school on time, anyway. I missed some of my classes for various reasons. First, I was often tired, due to all the partying during the week. Second, I'd lost my trust in all teachers. Third, my new teachers took both my friendly smirk and focusing grimace as signs of my snobbery as well, very much like my old teachers at the elementary school, as though my transcripts had also passed on this vital information to high school. During the first years of high school, I read the books on my own and got the best grades, after all.

Sometimes Grandma asked me why I wasn't rushing to go to school in the morning. I said the class was cancelled or we had gym, which everybody knew I hated. "You have gym every morning?" Grandma insisted. "Yes," I lied shamelessly. Thank God, Father never pushed me about physical education or looked down on my lack of athletic potential. Grandma and I sometimes talked about grownup stuff and the history of our family. At the beginning, she was rather fond of me. Especially, she liked my interest to learn about our heritage—that's what she assumed to be the purpose of all my questions. She was proud to brag about her past life and recount the exciting history she'd lived through. She was quite a looker and full of energy for her age.

Grandpa, on the other hand, looked too old and fragile even for a man of 69. He left the house around nine in the morning every day after a small breakfast and a long shaving routine. He had difficulty shaving the lean skin that sunk too deep inside his boney face structure. Still he struggled to do the best job possible before leaving the house. I felt especially sad for him when he had to blow his sunken cheeks out, one at a time, and hold his breath to shave those wide valleys. Sometimes he pushed the air into his cheek so hard it burst out of his mouth with a farting sound under the pressure of the razor. I chuckled watching him shave and splash cologne over his red skin, which always led to a grimace and a subtle moan. The redness of his face was from so many tiny veins in his thin skin bursting from shaving and then burning from the cologne. Still, Grandpa made sure he got as clean a shave as possible, as if going to a ball or his lover's nest every day. He always dressed up and wore a tie, but still looked like a smart walking skeleton. I respected his calm and manly pride, the leftover from the times he'd been somebody and also rich. He arrived back home at exactly ten every evening and had a small supper, always alone. He then walked a long time around the garden, or in his room during winters, to digest the tiny food he'd consumed.

Grandpa's rigid routine to leave the house at nine a.m. sharp and return at ten p.m. on the dot, seven days a week, all year round, was too peculiar. What the heck did he do with himself all day long, day after day, every single day of the year, regardless of holidays and weather, wandering around the city with no job or money? My guess for his odd behaviour was that he'd promised Grandma to observe this tough schedule if he was allowed to at least sleep in this house and maybe eat a little food, too. Unless he was merely avoiding Grandma as much as possible, while also being a punctual person by nature.

Altogether, the poor man looked lost in some special world of his own with melancholic thoughts when he was at home. He and Grandma never talked. But he asked me a few silly questions once in a while just to show his civility and a *very* general interest in his grandchildren, although I was the only one he usually saw due to his seemingly unchangeable schedule. He was drunk most evenings, anyway. According to Grandma, he went to bazaar every day and stayed in his friends' shops or in a teahouse, and maybe smoked some opium, too. I'd noticed Father handing him a few large bills whenever they met. I felt Father didn't want to leave the money with Grandma to pass it on to him. So he tried to catch Grandpa before he left the house, which caused me added agony! *Every time* Father asked me with surprise, "Why aren't you at school yet?" and I replied coolly, "We have gym." He gazed at me for only two seconds with despair before leaving. He never had time to argue or worry about me too much. This was the only hassle poor Grandpa caused me without intention. Even when I hid in my room, Father still asked for me and I had to produce and repeat myself about the fact that we had gym again. Meanwhile, I also wondered why he wasn't getting my message and leaving the matter alone. Even worse, why wouldn't he give a damn that I disliked, or could avoid, gym so casually?!

"What happened to your wealth?" I once asked Grandma.

"*Your grandpa* lost the whole thing in a matter of two years. We were the richest people in this affluent neighbourhood, except for Reza Shah and the courtiers who lived around here, of course," she replied with a mixture of pride and shame.

"How did he lose everything?"

"First he was forced to shut down his cigarette factory when the government decided to monopolize the industry. They didn't even buy him out. He was told to stop production and scrap the factory after three decades of being the only producer in Iran. Then some fools told him to invest in plastic, which was new in Iran at the time. So he tried to import plastics from Germany."

"Okay...? So what happened?" I asked.

"War happened. They claimed that the Allies had confiscated it or sunk the ship."

"That's it?"

"Yeah... He finally gave up on the shipment and life as well altogether. He never got over those shocking setbacks. At least he's still somewhat alert and can spend his days in teahouses."

5

One night, my parents had another big party, with most of the regulars attending. I had sneaked out to smoke a cigarette in a dark corner of the garden. As I returned to the drawing room, Dr. Afzali held my arm and whispered, "Let's go out for a second."

I followed him with apprehension, wondering what the heck he wanted from me. We hardly spoke despite our spooky eye communication in the past and my fading sympathy for him as a humiliated husband. Especially in recent months, I'd been in fact too busy with my own flirting routines in the Club and parties to notice him much. We walked in the garden toward a dark spot and hid behind a large rose bush. He took out an object from his pocket and extended it toward me.

"Can you keep this for me without telling anybody?"

It was a narrow, thin, rectangular, bronze object about seven inches long with no familiar shape, like a useless artefact.

"What is it?" I asked.

He peered at my confused eyes, pondered awhile, then pulled the two sides of the object apart and folded them together on the opposite side until a long shining blade appeared from inside the bronze covers. It was about six-inch-long, one-inch-wide that stood at the end of a heavy yellow handle. It was huge and scary, but I was mostly confused about his intention. Why did he have this murderers' dagger and why should I hide it for him?

"Why do you want me to keep it?"

"Just hide it for me for a while," he said.

"But why?"

"I don't want it around the house. It's only for a short time."

The matter felt fishy and bizarre. Yet, the idea of playing with that dagger, and possibly using it for a good cause, was exciting, not to mention my surprise and pride about his trust in me as a reliable confidant. In fact, I'd already decided that I really liked to keep it for myself, *if possible somehow*, but mostly I didn't know how to reject an adult's request. *Maybe I'll claim, later on, that I've lost it,* was the quick thought crossing my mind. On the other hand, having a dagger in my possession without my parents' knowledge was somewhat risky for me. I wished he'd at least tell me something about it, but he was too nervous to discuss or even hold it in his hand any longer. Gutless to ask for explanation, I reached to take it. He folded the dagger back into its original shape and handed it to me.

"Here... Go hide it right away," he said. "But don't mention it to anybody, okay?"

"All right."

"You promise?"

"Yes."

I put the dagger in my pocket, went back inside, and hid it in my bedroom behind a pile of papers. As I returned to the drawing room, Dr. Afzali stared at me suspiciously, as if gauging the safety of his secret with me. I nodded and went to the dance area to check on my pretty students.

In recent months, the Afzalis had taken over the spot that the Mahjars had occupied for many years as my parents' best friends. The Mahjars were suddenly less favoured, while the Afzalis got more attached to my family. Mina had become Narges's best friend, which was a bizarre revelation in itself. I didn't understand the reason for this sudden switch, but wondered if Mina had told Narges about Mehri's hanky-panky with me in Damavand. I didn't care anyway if she had. But I didn't like this idea of my parents switching their best friends a bit. It just didn't make sense! I was attracted to *mysterious* Mehri more every day, while our relationship felt more ambiguous and neither of us dared to do anything about it. We only flirted from a safe distance without expressing our emotions or even speaking a few casual words to each other. Yet I believed we'd get there soon. Soon things would work out for the best and I'd get another chance with Mehri. Maybe in bed this time. Perhaps once I grew a little bit older and smarter, she'd find me ripe for her needs. So, I simply hated my parents making my and Mehri's job harder!

6

I took the dagger out of its hiding place almost every night when I was alone in my room. We played in many heroic roles together and pondered many wild, soothing plans. Unlike the fatsoes, my new friend, Mr. Big Dagger, seemed adventurous, too, always suggesting great ideas, especially for teaching people some good lessons. Meanwhile, I kept wondering why Dr. Afzali couldn't hide it at his house. Was it really his or had he stolen it from someone else? Why didn't he want anybody else to know about it? Why wasn't he, for example, asking Father to safe-keep it for him instead of dealing with a confused juvenile like me? Did he think I was more reliable and mature than Father?

Anyway, I loved the dagger more every day. It was beautiful and heavy, so full of itself, one of the best-crafted objects I'd ever seen. These rich people could somehow find even their weapons in such gorgeous form. The blade was extremely sharp and shiny. The alloy looked so sturdy but delicate like a mixture of steel and platinum. I knew that one thrust with that dagger in Ahmad Javid's belly would rip his intestines and liver into a hundred pieces. I didn't understand why I was still so mad at him even though my life had improved so much and I hardly met those fatsoes anymore. I still wanted to cut his balls at least, though.

All along, the kids kept bugging me whenever they heard the shots Father blasted in the air regularly. They insisted that I'd lied about my access to the handgun, while I loathed my gutlessness, too, to wave it around their faces. So, I decided to show them the dagger for now at least. I told them it was mine and warned them to be careful about arguing with me too much. I was no longer trying to impress them as much as I was trying to scare them, especially Ahmad. They sure looked timid enough very quickly, which made me feel like a man. I didn't have time to be their leader, anyway, even if they begged me. Why did I want to be a leader ever? Who has time for it in this day and age with all these pretty women dying to fool around? Chasing women was the only purpose of life, if you asked me then. Doing anything else in life besides satiating our lust would be silly as soon as we aren't slaves to our egos or careers for survival. Being a leader to help people felt absolutely futile now, especially, since I'd already found humans irreparable.

Ironically, my new view of sex as life's highest priority kept triggering my old thoughts about the inherent tyranny of lust, as if I'd now found a great topic to prove God's dire guilt in causing humans' endless misery. I was getting too obsessed now with the mystery of God's intention for making lust quite potent in His creatures—especially for these lousy, wicked humans, as if He'd built this particular species only for enriching His universe or at the very least playing a major role in keeping Him amused with their lustful feelings, thoughts, and actions.

Surely, digging into God's or Nature's mysterious means and genius was just for amusing myself with some wild imaginations. On the other hand, it was hard to ignore some plausible notions about God's efforts to tackle many aspects of *creation* through *procreation*—by (ab)using other creatures, especially humans. Most likely, lust was one of His main gimmicks, out of millions, for running His universe at our cost, with slavery and suffering merely for occasional, often humiliating, sex. For all humans, but especially me these days, this wasn't fair, since sorting out my life priorities now felt quite excruciating all by itself.

Accordingly, humans' huge power to destroy God's creations, mostly by stopping their procreation duty—by defying His zeal to force lust so deeply into our being and ruining our spirits—was a serious remedy to consider. We had to do it, I thought, for our sanity or maybe even out of spite for the Main Creator. My only dilemma about God's level of guilt was whether this intense lust voltage had been intentional or just a design error now crippling us. *Gosh, my thoughts are getting more ridiculous every night!*

After writing all this drivel in my diary, I thought maybe I was nuts, after all. These absurd ideas were screwing my mind fast, compared with pre-puberty era when women and sex had not infected me so badly. Then, life had felt rather balanced in line with many urgent concerns for a normal human, even in a child's mind. That kind of crude existence was easier to justify, although it had still felt frustrating and tough for a curious boy in a broken family. Now, finding myself in this rowdy crowd in Royal Club, and even amongst people in general, felt too surreal so often.

Sometimes, I wondered whether those playful women were only using me, maybe for provoking their husbands' jealousy or merely dancing their long nights away. Contrary to my past wild imaginations, dancing wasn't merely a sexual tool. It had other purposes too. But I tried to disallow these depressing thoughts discourage me. I believed sex would come my way soon, too. Yet even more important than sex was passion to fill the gap from my childhood. Therefore, it was a win-win situation for me and those women. For now, we only pampered our desires in private and hoped for nice things happening soon to make up for all this wait and anticipation. Their husbands also looked comfortable with my innocent games and flirting, since they still saw me as a shy fourteen-year-old boy. At least I was more reliable than those nutty gigolos roaming the Club's dance hall with their hungry stares at women. In fact, the more I danced with their wives, the less time and chance the real gigolos got with any particular woman and the safer those husbands felt. So, I was really doing everybody a favour—except for the older gigolos, who glared at me and my dance manoeuvres with spite!

Still, I worried and agonized sometimes when I imagined that the husbands might be right; I knew nothing about seducing older women, let alone the married ones. The fear of being ridiculed or killed by their husbands just paralyzed me. Being a gigolo was probably not a straightforward, easy profession, after all. Yet, I couldn't give up my obsession and sexy dreams now. *Too late for my retreat or redemption!*

After three months of enjoying the company of *Dr. Dagger* and killing many people in my dreams, the Afzalis were visiting us again on a Tuesday night. Once the formal guests left, only the Afzalis were still around, chatting with my parent on the big patio next to the pool. I walked to the garden to grab another piece of cake from the dish on the table. My fifth that evening, I believe.

Dr. Afzali kept gazing at me and then asked, "Have you told anybody about the *thing* you're keeping for me?"

I was startled. That was the dumbest question anybody could ask me in front of my parents and Mina. Why would he reveal our secret so casually? Was he really that stupid?

"No...," I mumbled.

"Can you go bring it?"

This was really too much! I was amazed at this idiot's way of handling a secret that he'd begged me to keep confidential. Now he was asking me to fetch this frightening dagger for him under the curious eyes of my parents and Mina. How could a person be so selfish and inconsiderate? I knew Narges hated guns, but she loathed daggers and motorcycles even more. To her, these two objects were the most outrageous inventions in the world. Guns weren't found in Iran, anyway, as only military personnel had access to them. She might faint if she saw the dagger in my hand.

I lingered, as though hoping a miracle would stop the need for me to go to my room and bring the dagger. Maybe the asshole realized his stupidity and stopped asking for the dagger until later. I wondered why he would disgrace himself in front of everybody for using and trusting a child with such a huge secret. And then embarrassing me in front of everybody, too. How dare he?

But the idiot sounded serious. He wanted his dagger back right away. Narges, Mina, and Father looked perplexed by my hesitation. Why was I frozen like a statue instead of fetching whatever the heck I'd been safekeeping for this idiot? The idiot! I wished Dostoevsky hadn't written his account of the particular *idiot* he knew. I could probably write about a much stupider idiot myself—after getting a chance to read his novel first, of course. I could write a much bigger book about this dreadful idiot in front of me. No wonder everybody wanted to get a taste of his wife! I felt good for explaining his pathetic life in my diary, including his pitiful conversations with his brother, General Afzali, in the Club. *I'll put them all in my book someday,* I promised my angry ego.

At last, I realized my hesitation was futile. All the stalling gimmicks I'd perfected over the years to bug Narges wouldn't work tonight. I didn't even find the guts to say I'd lost the dagger. So, I went to my room and waited about ten minutes, hoping that people out there would pick up a different topic for conversation. I felt so miserable parting with my faithful friend of the last three months so unexpectedly. I kept caressing it and saying goodbye to it. Having this friend had been a good source of distraction with some kind of a healing power. I tried to gather the guts to go back and claim I couldn't find it. But I feared the consequence of making such outrageous claim in front of everybody. At least Narges would not believe me and would probably go search all the corners in my room. I resented my gutlessness to lie even for keeping such a good friend. So I returned in despair with the aim of passing on the dagger to Dr. Afzali without others noticing it. But everybody stopped talking and stared at me again. Dr. Afzali was actually the one drawing the audience's attention to me by stopping their hot conversation and gazing at me again.

I stood bewildered again myself, wondering about his bizarre behaviour tonight. Was he drunk or mad? Meanwhile, the curious spectators wondered about my ridiculous behaviour. Their eyes kept wandering from me to Dr. Afzali and to the shining yellow object in my hand. All I was hoping was that at least the idiot wouldn't tell them what it was. I hoped he'd just slip it in his pocket and end this mockery. I gave the dagger to the idiot. He made a gesture to put it in his pocket. But you could just see his pressing itch to show it off to everybody.

"What is it?" the nosy Narges asked.

The idiot looked around with a phony hesitation. I could see the glee in his eyes for the opportunity of showing off his toy. I bet he'd counted on Narges's nosiness already. So, he opened it before everybody's eyes eagerly with an idiotic grin. Narges shrieked in surprise. Father remained silent in shock. Mina grew a big smirk on her face as if mocking her silly husband. Her eyes revealed the depth of her thoughts: *How much more evidence you people need about my husband's idiocy.*

"You gave this thing to Kian?" Narges yelled at Dr. Afzali. "Are you out of your freaking mind?"

Dr. Afzali giggled. "He was only hiding it for me."

"This is a terrible thing to keep in the house," Narges yelled.

"Don't get too excited… It's not good for your heart."

"Thank God you're not my doctor," she yelled.

"Amen!"

"I can't believe we're keeping daggers and handguns in this house and letting this boy play with them. It's all Noori's fault," she growled and left, Mina following her fast toward the kitchen.

"Are you going to take care of Nosrat and his father at the Club?" Dr. Afzali asked Father after the women left.

"Consider it done. I've already told Bashiri to get rid of them," Father replied. "Bashiri has realized that Royal Club is not a place for people like Nosrat."

"I almost went there to kill that son-of-a-bitch. Only your promise to get rid of him stopped me from slitting his throat," Dr. Afzali shrieked nervously.

"Yes, yes. I understand. That's the right thing to do. He's gone. He's history," Father promised.

"That's good…"

"It's a pity, though, that his father had to be fired, too. He was such a great cook," Father murmured in despair.

CHAPTER NINE
My Generous Uncle Jamal

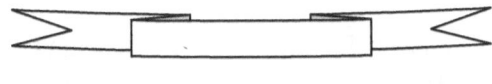

1

My youngest uncle, Jamal Noori, had only thirteen years over me. We could've been childhood playmates, actually, if I were conceived right after my parents' matrimony. This was the only good outcome of Father's marriage at the age of twenty-two, I imagine—unless somebody took my birth and being a blessing, too! We had a nice relationship, though we hardly met. During elementary school, I was cooped up in our house and seldom visited our relatives. Jamal was rarely in Tehran, anyway. He travelled around the country and built bridges and roads for the government. He was a civil engineer or something like that. He came to Tehran for only a few days every month, so our paths seldom crossed. But, now, I tried to stay at my grandparents' house whenever Jamal was in town. His charm and charisma resembled Father's, although his obsession for sex and women surpassed even Father's, and actually seemed endless. So, I was hoping to learn some of his outgoing personality and maybe even his knack for chasing women. That was the kind of relationship I couldn't have with Father despite his cool personality.

In those times, some sensible boundaries prevented kids from feeling too relaxed with their fathers. Such a liberal person poor Father was, he meant to remove this barrier between us and make me open up to him. We talked a lot about everything, including girls. Sometimes, I gathered my courage and asked him touchy questions, too; like the time I asked him why he went to Europe without Narges. His answer was brief: "Because husbands and wives need breaks from each other to stay sane." Yet, Father and I could never get too personal, because of the family secrets he wished to keep from me, and also because I wanted to hide my crude opinions from him, especially my growing cynicism about people and God.

So I shared with Jamal lots of silly stuff I couldn't raise with Father, the way two good brothers or pals do. I could relax and be vulgar even without worrying about his view of my sanity. My other three uncles and one aunt hadn't inherited as much of his charisma. They were nice people, too, but their striking contrast with Jamal and Father was quite odd. They were too conservative and timid, whereas Jamal and Father were adventurous, witty, and horny. I liked their spirited, fun-loving personalities.

Grandma usually had to leave the house whenever Jamal was in town. Sometimes Jamal asked her directly, "*Maman,* when are you going to *Dadash's* house?" She expected Jamal's notice to vacate the house if she hadn't shown signs of doing so already. Her tense anguish all day, anticipating Jamal's order any minute, seemed funny to me. Yet, she wanted to resist only for stressing that the big house still belonged to her, not Jamal. Sometimes she simply wanted to stick around and take care of her spoiled baby —to cook his favourite meals and make up for his unhealthy diet while travelling. She also craved the chance of filling his ears with her gossips about other family members and the headaches they caused her. She usually had plenty to complain to him about me. She could whine for hours about the way I was ruining her privacy and all the extra work my presence caused. Most of all, however, she hated loose women monopolizing him and limiting her chance of spending time with him. Yet Jamal always won. He had no problem with my presence or Grandpa's arrivals late in the evenings. However, he didn't want Grandma witness the stream of women, mostly prostitutes, coming and going. He kept them all night and maybe for days as he wished.

Jamal was expected back in Tehran the day after Dr. Afzali asked for his dagger in front of my parents. This was in the spring of 1971. That night, I put a few shirts, pants, and socks in a small bag along with a few books that I needed for the rest of the week. On the way to school the next day, I told Father I'd be staying at my Kakh residence a few days. He always laughed whenever I mentioned 'my Kakh residence.' By the way, Kakh in Persian means palace—thus, the street name due to the Shah's Palace in the neighbourhood. Besides the humour, Father was thrilled to see me benefit from the scheme he'd cooked up. He was still fighting with Narges over it. *Oh boy, I feel nostalgic even now when I think of my cosy city residence.* Having a place away from my morbid parents, the horny servants, and the rotten fatsoes, whenever I wanted, was just so precious. I cherished that luxury then and miss it now, after decades, when I need some mental rest so badly. Father had been spot on about everybody needing frequent breaks away from people around him, to clear his head. A refuge to hide from the rest of the world for a few days. For Father, that place had to be Europe for almost three months!

2

I went to my *Kakh* residence—the Palace—right after school, hoping to make a plan with Jamal for that evening. I'd called him during lunch break and Grandma told me he'd gone to rest in his room. But when I arrived, nobody was home. Of course, Jamal might've gotten my message and ignored it. Nobody could stop him from running with the most appealing plan at any moment, which often led to ignoring his previous commitments. I never held grudges against him for his sloppy attitude or forgetting his promise of maybe just ten minutes earlier. His good humour and charm easily made up for his lax personality. On the other hand, I wondered whether Grandma had passed on my message to wait for me. She probably hadn't. Despite her religious fanaticism, she often lied like the rest of us. My friendship with Jamal bugged her plenty, too. She was the one suffering the consequences of his influence on me.

As much as Grandma hated leaving the house when Jamal was in town, she enjoyed the excuse she'd found to ditch me too often even when Jamal wasn't around or hadn't ask her to leave. She visited our relatives, especially her daughter's and sons' families, more frequently just to avoid all the extra hassle my presence apparently caused. She stayed away for days and weeks, mostly out of spite for me, while hoping so naively that her vengeful, long absences would discourage me from going over too much, so that she could get her normal life back.

Her sneaky plan worked somewhat initially, as being alone in that huge house depressed me. All that quiet crushed my chest, although I liked my cosy Palace. So, I brought some girls to my room when Grandma wasn't around, the same way Jamal did. But soon she learned about my new sins and loathed my guts for pushing her nerves. She abhorred her scheme backfiring, while I enjoyed the way I'd confused her. Abusing her absence annoyed her even more than my regular barging in. In return, she stopped sharing her plans about visiting relatives with me at least. If I called around to find out, she rushed back home to spoil my life. So, now my efforts to learn about her plans or whereabouts only backfired. Still her struggle to limit my invasion of her household decency failed most often. I'd already learned a lot from Jamal about putting my needs above other people's rules. Following Jamal's footsteps, in particular ignoring Grandma's needs and orders, was boosting my arrogance faster than everything Grigori had done for me so far. So, the more Grandma hated Jamal's wicked influence on me, the closer I felt to him.

The big dilemma I'd caused Grandma was funny enough, but I also enjoyed her despair and frustration when I fooled her with the same games I'd been perfecting with Narges all my life. Sometimes, she pretended to be having a heart attack because of me. I knew she was faking the whole thing, though. I'd heard that we can have only three heart attacks, but Grandma had already pretended to have at least a dozen of them on my account alone. Anytime she had one of them, she just went to her room with her hand over her chest and fainted on the bed. In ten minutes, she was snoring and I knew she wouldn't be cooking any dinner that evening. The whole show was to deprive me from a hot meal. But I didn't mind. I liked the sandwiches that the deli in our neighbourhood made. I bought myself a big, delicious sandwich and ate it in my room. Sometimes I bought sandwiches for Grandma and Grandpa, too, and put them in the fridge for them.

So, not giving my message to Jamal that day was surely Grandma's another form of retaliation, I reckoned. In return, I started calling some girls I knew. I tried to convince them to come over and they refused with all kinds of lame excuses. They were usually afraid of their parents or had run out of excuses to get out of the house. That was a major problem with girls, even though our society was imitating the Western lifestyle so fast in all respects. "Say you're going to study with a friend," I kept pushing them to no avail. Overall, most girls were either too lazy or simply crazy, going by their mood swings alone. They were too practical and anxious to find a husband—even if they were only five years old—to leave home for good, instead of only fooling around. Only seldom they wanted to spend time with a good-for-nothing high schooler like me, if they happened to be in the mood for horsing around that exact moment.

So, in the end, that night I decided to check out some of my freaking schoolbooks. I had to prepare for the upcoming final exams, but I hadn't been in the mood for a long time now. Even looking at the lines in the textbooks nauseated me. Reading each topic a couple of times and doing a few of those damn practices were enough to get passing grades. Yet, I couldn't concentrate like before in the elementary school. What was the point of studying so many useless subjects like algebra, chemistry, or the Koran, anyway? It felt like a complete waste of my precious life, especially since I was right in the middle of my philosophical gibberish about life. The entire concept of existence felt pointless, anyway, never mind praying five times a day! For sure, I wasn't planning to become a mullah or a rocket scientist, either. So studying the Koran or physics' formulas felt foolish for sure. There must be at least one thing more useful to do in this empty world besides sex, yet I wondered what the heck it might be! *Has anybody figured this out yet?!* I liked to know.

Around eight p.m., the sound of key turning the lock on the front door startled me. It was too early for Grandpa's arrival for sure. So I ran out to welcome Jamal. But the loud laughter of a woman echoed in the hall before she entered ahead of Jamal. I turned back and watched them from my room. They went to the table in the hall to empty their bags of food. When Jamal noticed me at last, I waved at him. He came over and we kissed on the cheeks, while the pretty woman watched us from the hall. She was also pretty tall and big again, like most other women Jamal usually liked to date, especially in terms of the size. He didn't introduce me to her, because we walked inside my room quickly.

"Do you want to have dinner with us?" Jamal asked.

"No, thanks. I already ate something," I replied.

"Are you sure?"

"Yeah… You go ahead and have fun with your friend."

"What're you doing?"

"I'm studying for my exams."

"Okay, then. Go back to your books. We'll talk later."

"Sure."

I just sat on my bed and stared at the wall in a haze. *Now what? I have nothing to do now,* I pondered, feeling lonely and depressed, while my mind was suddenly in a different plane only imagining what Jamal was doing with that gorgeous big whore. The notion of 'nothing to do' felt ridiculous, though, as my poor conscience nagged again about the piles of readings I refused to attack. I had to think hard soon. I could be careless about my life and all, but adding to my dad's list of worries was unfair. I had to find a way to get a bit more serious about school, just a tad would do, my conscience stressed. Narges had been right, after all, about losing my concentration and consciousness if I was allowed to live a reckless life in two different residences.

Guilt-ridden, I opened the math book and glanced over some pages with disbelief and disgust. Everything, every single line or formula, looked cryptic. I had no idea what the hell they meant. I used to be the best pupil in math. What had happened to me? Luckily, I found a good excuse for my inability to focus: Jamal and the whore were laughing so loud too much, making a racket around the kitchen preparing their dinner. They were probably drunk already. He came to my room with a bottle of beer. And that was it for that night's plan to study, I decided as I grabbed the beer. I just lay on my bed, sipped the beer, and began fantasizing about Mehri. If she'd been there we could've had a party. Then I imagined Jamal trying to steal her from me. I always imagined that he, like Father, could look at any woman, talk to her for a minute, and she'd fall into his arms before realizing what had hit her. Still, his appetite for prostitutes didn't diminish, either. My sole consolation was that Mehri was nowhere close to Jamal's taste in terms of her size. For a handsome guy like Jamal picking only larger women with huge asses and breasts seemed bizarre, as if making up for his own rather petite physique.

3

Near ten p.m., their noise and laughter stopped. From the crack of the door, I watched them go to Jamal's room and close the door behind them; just in time before Grandpa's routine arrival. I went to the kitchen and found it tidy. The drunkards had somehow managed to clean up their mess before going to bed. I left my empty beer bottle and grabbed a fresh one from the fridge. In my room, I continued my own private party with Mehri in my dizzy head. These days, I thought much less about the gypsy woman— at last. Yet I never forgot how she'd turned my mind and life around and I still craved seeing her, too. After I emptied the big bottle of beer, I fell asleep with my clothes and the light on.

Jamal's shaking my shoulder woke me up. I rubbed my eyes and he smiled. He had only his shorts on.

"Hey, let's go to my room and meet Shahla?" he said.

"No, I want to sleep," I said in a drowsy voice.

"Oh, come on. Don't be silly. She wants to see you."

"What time is it?"

"It's only midnight. Come on, let's go."

"Has grandpa gone to bed?"

"Yeah…," he said and pulled my arm to get me up my ass.

I followed him to his room with my brain still half-sleep. He closed the door and stood behind me. In front of me, Shahla was sitting naked at the edge of the bed with a cute smile on her face. Her legs were crossed, but still I could see the man-killing hair between them. Her plump upright boobs stood with pride on her white full body. I waited in confusion for ten seconds and gazed at the gorgeous whore.

"This is Kian, my naughty nephew," Jamal said to her at last, chuckling. He was quite drunk and his eyes were red.

I nodded and stood quiet while enjoying her body, despite the layers of fat bulging out here and there and her big ass occupying half of the bed. With curiosity behind a soft, playful grin, she kept gauging me as well. We were all drunk, going by the lingering silence, blank stares, and hesitations.

"This is Shahla, my friend," Jamal said at last, giggling again.

"*Salam*, Kian," she said.

"*Salam*, Shahla," I replied before the daunting silence befell upon us again and we gazed at each other like zombies.

My calm, for a schoolboy studying a young naked woman's body from close-up for the first time, was admirable. Of course, I'd already seen a million ugly nude women during my preschool years, when Narges took me to women hammam—the public Turkish bath. In fact, I still had nightmares sometimes whenever the sight of so many vulgar old women haunted me. Witnessing them walk around so shamelessly with their wrinkled pussies, boobs, and asses had been disgusting. Those horrific scenes could traumatize any child, especially a boy, perhaps for life, I claim categorically. They have most likely been a major source of my oddity and view of women. More humiliating, when I'd grown, even in grades one and two, a few times Narges had sent me to the hammam in advance to ask the operator if they'd still let me in after gauging my age and size firsthand! The greedy operator always said fine after staring at me with scepticism and weighing Narges's request. Then, later, some supposedly embarrassed or shy customers usually whined about my presence at such age. Seeing Narges's flabby body in itself might've been too shocking and damaging to the depth of my psyche for eternity. Therefore, my enigmatic apathy toward Narges might've also been partly due to having seen her wrinkly naked body too much. I wish Freud could shed some light on my fresh intricate theory.

By the way, a few girls I'd convinced in recent years to get naked for me had been creepy silly. They'd insisted on turning off the lights first and getting undressed only under the sheets. They pretended to be shy, but I believed they were embarrassed of their messed-up growing bodies. Obviously, none of those chubby or puny figures, which I'd only touched like a blind man under the sheets, could compare with the delicious full body of a woman, especially those huge breasts in front of me and picturing puny Jamal on top of her. Yet I was relaxed and amazed at my fading shyness in recent months. Or was it only the effect of the beers making me enjoy one of Jamal's whores instead of throwing up? *So another God's purpose for high dosage of lust was to ensure we horny males jumped even on top of ugly broads or whores, often even if we weren't drunk enough!*

"Go ahead, kiss her," Jamal said.

I was nervous about the game I didn't understand, but kept my composure with great effort. I wished somebody would tell me what was going on. Surely, I wasn't about to ask a dumb question, either. So, I moved forward, leaned, and kissed Shahla on her cheek. She stroked my face with her soft fingers.

"No, I mean kiss her lips," Jamal ordered like a sadistic army general. He was enjoying his authority not only over me, but even more so over Shahla. They were drunker than I'd thought. I obeyed his order and planted a quick kiss on her lips.

"You can kiss her anywhere. What do you want to kiss next?" Jamal continued and Shahla giggled, while opening her arms and gazing at me with a grin.

Her breasts spread with utter glamour above her fat belly. The devil in my head was quick to offer a plan: *Start from her belly button, move up a foot, lick those breasts, and then go back all the way down.* Then it crossed my mind that Jamal had probably contaminated all those areas already. I felt disgusted touching that stained flesh, let alone kissing or licking it. That slut! Who was she anyway? A prostitute? I'd admitted to myself, of course, that she was somewhat sexy like Mehri. They both had the same soft bright skin. Shahla was probably not even thirty. Then I imagined Mehri glaring at me, as if warning me about cheating on her. She was a slut in her own way, I thought in anger for a moment.

I felt tense, imagining those jerks, Jamal and Shahla, were teasing me now that they'd probably run out of other kinds of entertainment for the evening. I got mad. I was drunk and sleepy too. Jamal, my regular friend and protector, appeared like a total jackass. Sometimes I got agitated for no goddamn good reason, I tell you. And this was the worst time to let my rage spoil all the fun I could have—the golden opportunity that Jamal was offering me on a silver platter. The grinning goddess sat right there before me with her arms still open, but her legs crossed with a slight sign of shyness. I wanted to hide myself in the hair between her legs. I really did. Instead, I was crippled by God knew what—maybe my false pride or fear overpowering even that high-voltage lust. *Is human psych so weird or what? Are we made so enigmatically or what, with so many conflicting urges challenging lust?*

"What're you waiting for? A formal invitation?" Shahla said with a teasing tone and they both burst into laughter. Besides their annoying laughter, her comment sounded too sarcastic to me, like the way Narges always mocked me. This was the last straw. Like a back-broken camel, I moaned and blasted out of the room. I could never, for the life of mine, understand the madness that came over me and made me behave so weird that evening. I bet if Shahla hadn't talked like Narges, the outcome would've been different—for the better or worse, I wouldn't know, though!

I dashed to the kitchen and drank a large glass of cold water. Then I went to my room. I thought Jamal would come after me and force me to go back and finish the game, but he never showed up. I felt sad for no goddamn good reason. Still, I cried myself to sleep, all along dying to know why I felt so miserable. In fact, my abrupt, random weeping for no damn reasons has been puzzling for me, like some kind of an odd mystery in itself!

4

The next day, I heard Grandpa staggering around the kitchen, making his breakfast. Then he shaved in the washroom with the normal torture, going by all the farting noises and moaning. As soon as he left the house, I got out of the bed, ate a piece of Taftoon bread and feta cheese, and left for school with a guilty conscience. I imagined that soon Father would be informed of my regular tardiness. The freedom I was giving myself was just ridiculous. I hated to see him angry, especially with me. But what could I do? Especially today, I was still too depressed by the last night's event to worry about school. Besides, Grandpa's morning routine always delayed my day if I wanted to avoid having a silly chat with him so early in the morning! I grilled my brain about my last night's attitude. Everything I did these days felt bizarre and moronic the next day. The meanings of things changed from one minute to the next, especially if I had time to think about them. I felt sorry for not playing along with whatever goddamn game Jamal and Shahla were trying to play with me. I should've remembered that Jamal would never do anything to harm me. So why did I behave like a jerk instead of pouncing on the grand opportunity he'd offered me?

My overreaction and then weeping in my bed must've surely been a sign of a big turmoil inside me crippling even my potent lust genes. I had to sort things out somehow for myself soon. But first, I knew I had to go back to Jamal with my pathetic pride in a big mess. I must apologize and promise to behave properly the next time Shahla would be around.

At home, I found a note from Jamal, saying he'd return soon and wanted to talk to me. I made myself a sandwich with cold Kookoo, a tasty mixture of minced beef, eggs, vegetables, and potatoes, all fried together. Jamal arrived in a great mood, singing one of his favourite songs those days—*Strangers in the Night* by Frank Sinatra. He was always whistling or singing an old tune. His imitation of Mario Lanza was perfect, too, especially when he sang *Come Prima*. He had a deep voice. Recently, I'd been trying to imitate him and sing foreign songs, too, especially the Italians and Americans. My voice also sounded deep and smooth, as if this talent ran in our genes. Singing was another gift from Jamal, though I forgot all about it soon—no priority. I wondered if Father had a similarly great voice, but he never sang around the home at least. He only whistled when in a good mood or dressing up, probably planning about seducing another woman soon.

Jamal suggested to go for a walk. Kakh was a delightful neighbourhood in the older part of Tehran, with a narrow, shady, cool main street. Through a side street, we walked to Pahlavi Avenue and strolled on the sidewalk next to a rapid stream that rushes between two rows of tall plane trees. Actually, the same pattern of a stream between two rows of ancient plane trees runs on both sides of the wide avenue. The long tree shadows kept the sidewalks cool and cosy for such a hot summer afternoon. Jamal mentioned the pleasure of having this natural setting right in the middle of a heavily developed city like Tehran. I nodded. We were just making odd conversations to recover from last night's catastrophe.

"What's the problem with you?" Jamal asked with tension at last. I couldn't say whether he was still irritated about my reaction the night before or worried about his own behaviour and possible drunkenness.

"Sometimes I go crazy, I suppose. Sorry," I said.

"I guess… What'd you think I was trying to do?"

"You wanted me to do it with that whore…"

"She's not a whore. She's a very respectable woman in fact."

I burst into laughter. "Respectable, my ass!"

"No, I'm serious. She's in fact married to an important man."

"And still she comes out and stays with you all night?"

"She's smart, too, ha? She knows how to spice her boring life sometimes, especially when her husband is travelling."

"Is she in love with you?"

"She likes me, I guess, and she likes fun even more."

"And she wanted me to kiss her anywhere I wanted, too?"

"Yeah…! What's wrong with that?" he asked.

Jamal looked more puzzled about my naivety every second, more than I was by his perception of the world and women, which sounded awkward but simple. He behaved like someone privy to a special type of wisdom—to live free like the animals in the jungle. Yet I couldn't, for Muhammad's sake, understand how these women's minds worked. Was there some knowledge about manhood and women that Father had neglected to teach me? Was Jamal wondering about the same thing?

Still my brain couldn't fathom the sinful worldview of Jamal and Father as normal, and the chance I was totally off the mark with my dumb questions. "What kind of a respectable woman would do this?" I asked. "I thought she was a prostitute."

"Well, even if she was, why did you run away?"

"I told you that my mind sometimes takes a vacation without me. But I don't like prostitutes anyway."

"Why? What's wrong with you?"

"I don't think anything is wrong with me usually."

"No, something is wrong with you all right."

"You think so?"

"Yes. Someone running away from such a pretty woman must be sent to the madhouse right away. I'm amazed. Really!"

"Why would a respectable woman let me kiss her and all?"

"Well, she was a bit drunk and I'd asked her to do it for fun."

"For fun!?"

"I thought it'd be a good experience for you to become a man. Besides, she'd been on my case for a while for kissing her cousin in a party. She wanted to get even with me. She was trying to make me jealous, too, while retaliating. So I let her."

"Only a kiss? What'd you do with her cousin?"

"Well… Maybe a little bit more than a kiss."

"I knew it. Is Shahla coming back to see you soon?" I asked, daydreaming about another crack at kissing her all over. If she really had to take her revenge, I had no right to stop her and I mustn't be too fussy about everything. Besides, I really wanted to become a man as soon as possible even if I must take big steps and make great sacrifices!

Jamal burst into laughter. "Now you want her, silly boy. It's too late."

I was embarrassed but laughed along with him, anyway.

"Why?" I asked with sorrow.

"Because the bird flew out of the cage. She's gone."

"Gone where?"

"Nowhere special. She's just mad at me."

"I don't understand…"

"She couldn't believe I'd go through with this game. One minute she insists on taking her revenge and the next minute she fights with me for letting her take her revenge."

"Is she crazy or something?" I asked.

"Women are always hard to figure out," Jamal replied with a sigh. "Besides, when she was sober in the morning, she felt cheap and guilty for playing this game, the same way you felt about it the night before. She said if I'd really loved her I would've not been so casual about letting her kiss you."

"She has a point, although she's probably crazy, anyway."

"She just wanted to blame me for pushing her into a difficult position and for testing her courage to take her revenge. Before asking you to join us, I had to either let her take her revenge or beg her to forgive me. She wanted me to promise not to betray her again, but I couldn't bring myself to beg. She was testing me, too, to see how far I was letting her go in front of my own eyes. Some women really enjoy playing nasty games," he said. "You never know what they really want, anyway."

"You guys also laughed so idiotically, like teasing me. Maybe that made me nervous, too, for not realizing what was going on."

"All of it was to keep our faces straight for the 'daring' game we were playing. We were trying to look cool, I guess."

"So now she's realized that you don't love her for sure," I said. "First you make out with her cousin and then offer me to her, too, so casually."

"But it's also your fault," Jamal said.

"How do you figure?"

"Because I tried to do something for you. Instead of thanking me, you just ran away from her like an idiot. She got angry for being turned down instead of having some fun with you. You humiliated her. You saw her as a slut and you made her think more than necessary. She felt that perhaps she was really a slut."

"That's good for her and her husband then. I made her think a little. I did everybody a big favour, I suppose."

"She'll get over it soon and find another man. Don't worry."

"I'm sorry for causing you a major loss then," I said.

"Don't worry about it, boy. We were bound to split, anyway."

Yet I wasn't sure if Jamal was telling me the whole truth. In fact, I thought he was only putting me on. He was a master at it. He never changed his story, but I kept doubting his account of who Shahla was. For some reason I preferred to think she was a pricey prostitute, rather than a respectful married woman. Maybe I was too naïve. But I really hated seeing so many pretty women cheating on their husbands so casually. I was sick of it all already.

"Do you ever think about having a special woman in your life, instead of fooling around with different women? Maybe marrying her?" I asked Uncle Jamal.

"Not yet. How about you? Do you have a special girl?"

"No. But I think I love a special woman."

"Good. Good. Who's she?"

"A married woman. Her name is Mehri, but don't mention it to anybody. Narges and Father know her."

"So you've been busy, ha? I thought you were still a virgin."

"I haven't slept with her if that's what you mean…"

"Have you kissed her at least?"

"No, I haven't kissed her yet, either."

"Have you told her that you like her?"

"No, not yet," I replied, annoyed with his pesky interrogation. I couldn't tell him that I'd instead knocked on the door of her heaven even though I hadn't still kissed her or expressed my love to her.

"So basically you don't have any relationship with her. It's all in your imagination, ha?" Jamal asked.

"No… It's not only my imagination."

"So what? What's she for you then?"

"I just love her."

"You love her? Are you a poet or something?" Jamal said in his usual mocking tone mixed with a chuckle.

"Yeah… I love her. What's wrong with that?"

"Oh, boy… You're more naïve than I'd thought."

"What's wrong with loving someone, tell me?"

"You say she's married. What do you expect to get out of your love fantasy?"

"I'm working on it, don't worry."

"Listen, Kian, forget about this love business. Just fool around with girls your age, for now at least. Okay…? I thought you were smart."

"I'm as smart as my dad was, I suppose!"

"What do you mean?"

"Well, I have some questions about Father's decision to marry at such a young age, as if being in love or something."

Jamal giggled. He tried to hide his frustration about the topic I'd brought up out of nowhere.

"What kind of questions?" he asked.

"Well … Was he in love with my cranky mother?"

"Don't speak like that… She's a nice woman," he said sternly, trying to hide both his shock and subtle amusement.

"You think she's nice?"

"Of course… Don't you?"

"Maybe sometimes. But she's usually nagging and sometimes nasty, too. And she's kind of ugly for Father, don't you think?"

This time Jamal laughed loudly a long time. When he finally stopped, he took a handkerchief from his pocket and dabbed the tears running from the corners of his eyes.

"Oh boy, you're really funny sometimes."

"I didn't mean it to be funny," I said.

"Then you have some issues, don't you?"

"I'm just curious about so many secrets around me. Maybe all these questions in my head have made me mad, who knows?"

"It's good to know! At least you realize and admit it yourself!" Jamal said with a giggle.

I was glad that I'd given someone in my family a heads-up about my messed-up mind nowadays. "So tell me, do you know if Father was in love when he got married?"

"I don't know," Jamal said with hesitation.

"Could you be serious once, instead of mocking me?"

"I'm not… But why are you so interested in this stuff?"

"Because I like to know about my parents. Is this a crime?"

"Well, okay. But I already told you that love is for poets."

"So?"

"Is your father a poet?"

"No!" I replied.

"Here we go… That's your answer."

"So why get married if it's not for love?"

"If you like a person and get along nicely, you may want to share your lives together. That's all."

"Was Father at least attracted to Narges?"

"You're really serious about this?"

"Very serious indeed."

"Will our discussions stay only between us?"

"Yes. Everything we discuss or do will always be kept secret."

"Okay, then. Let me think…"

"Think about what? Just tell me the truth."

"No, I don't think Dadash Jalal was very attracted to Narges."

"Why did he do it then, especially at twenty-two while having a good time with women as well—like you?"

"It's a long story. But I was only two years old myself."

"But still you know the story, don't you?"

"More or less. Dadash Jalal told me some of the story and your grandma told me the other parts of it."

"Great… You're then the best person I've been looking for to solve this mystery."

"Mystery!" Jamal burst into laughter again.

"Yeah. A big one, I'd say. Don't you agree?"

"Well, I can see how this matter could turn into a mystery for an uptight person like you."

"You think I'm uptight?" I asked. It was a new picture of me!

"Sometimes you are… Yes."

By this time, we'd reached Shah Reza intersection. We went inside the famous confectionery at the northwest corner of the intersection. Jamal led the way to the counter and bought us two *Napelonies*. We both loved this delicious Persian pastry, so we stopped talking to concentrate on our *Napelonies*. Then we started walking back home.

"So, are you going to answer my question?" I asked after we walked a long time in silence. Jamal kept thinking hard, tensely.

"I have to think about what I can tell you."

"Don't you want to tell me everything?"

"Listen, your father and I have shared a lot of secrets. He's been my best friend all my life."

"Do you have trouble sharing everything you know?"

"You be the judge... I've been trying to be your confidant the same way Dadash Jalal has been to me. How would you feel if I shared our secrets with somebody else, especially someone so close to you?"

"I understand. Obviously I don't want you to share anything with Father about what I tell you."

"So you can see my problem about sharing his secrets with you. Some issues in families must remain secret, especially from the kids. I don't like to say things that may offend your parents or make you feel less of them."

"Your hints sound more disturbing than whatever the truth might be."

"Maybe. So let me think about your question. I'm going to Hamadan tomorrow. I'll be back in three weeks. Then I'll tell you whatever that is useful for you."

"I guess I can wait three weeks for you to make up a story. But from the sound of it, the real story must be bizarre?"

"Maybe. It's mostly sensitive. I'm only trying to be careful... Such a romantic jackass you've turned out to be."

"Did Father introduce you to girls when you were a boy?"

"Yes, a few time..."

"Is that why you tried to pay back Father's generosity last night through Shahla?"

"Maybe. I like you anyway. I had many siblings and relatives to help me if I needed someone to talk with."

"I wish I had an older brother like you."

"I'm him. You can always depend on me. But don't try to solve all the mysteries in this family. Forget about the past."

"I wish it were that easy," I said with a sigh.

Quieting my nosy brain wasn't easy at all while a new question bugged me all of a sudden: I wondered why my parents didn't have any other children. All the other families around us had at least two kids. My parents being the only exception—with a good excuse obviously—still appeared weird. For me, having no siblings was a source of both relief and grief. I might've enjoyed having a brother or even a sister or both or more, to share some of our misfortunes together. I bet we could've ganged up against our parents and driven them nuts. Just imagine a few of us rascals bugging Narges all day and night. She would've been the one begging the gypsy woman to take her with her to some place away from her nutty husband and children. Maybe my siblings would've brought peculiar personalities, too, thus changed this family's lifestyle altogether. But under the present circumstances, if they were supposed to suffer like me, they were better off being unborn. Lucky souls! On the other hand, since I was a selfish boy, anyway, I wished I had three brothers and two sisters, rather than another mystery to solve—about their absence.

Had Narges and Father really known the grimness of their marriage and parenthood capacity from the beginning? Had they decided not to add more headaches to their long list of problems? In that case, they deserved a Nobel Prize for peace—the peace of their unborn kids! Sometimes they appeared wise despite their odd ways of living, for example, for not leaving me alone at home in the evenings. This decision, in particular, was bearing fruits finally. Suddenly, my past tortures and all my recent hard work in the Club and parties many evenings made perfect sense. A delightful chapter had started in my life at last while I fooled around with many gorgeous women. Those exhilarating contacts were worth even the huge torture of being my parents' midnight gate-opener, even in the height of freezing winters. I really needed to see, smell, and dance with those sneaky, pretty women —those cockroaches.

CHAPTER TEN
Rendezvous at Radio City

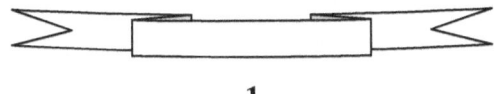

1

Since the Afzalis had become so lovey-dovey with my parents, we rode back and forth to Royal Club and most parties together. Father picked them up on our way to wherever we were going. We usually went inside the Afzalis' house and waited, no matter when we arrived. Often Mina was still dressing or fussing over her meticulous make-up. Her colourful face was rather dollish compared to the gypsy woman's clear reflection. I wondered what the gypsy woman would think about Mina's makeup and personality. Dr. Afzali said jokingly a few times that if someone washed Mina's face, he'd find a new woman. "I have two wives for the price of one," he said. I thought Mina was pretty enough without dolling herself up, but she perhaps thought makeup was necessary to glorify her presence and dazzle men more than all those other pretty cockroaches.

The rivalry amongst the women to look the prettiest in those parties was bizarre. Except, of course, for poor Narges, who had given up a century ago. She put on some makeup, anyway, but she never exaggerated because she knew it was useless—only a waste of time and makeup. My poor mom! The way she pouted and focused to put lipstick on her narrow lips was so funny. She just killed me with her fuss to stay inside the lines that she drew with a special red pencil first around her lips. In those moments, I felt for her in a soothing way and didn't mind kissing her cheek.

Everybody knew that she cheated by drawing the lines very much outside her lips' natural boundary.

By the way, I didn't remember having ever hugged Narges or feeling to do so. Only once a year, on Norooz—Iranian New Year —we kissed each other on one cheek as a cultural obligation we had to observe. And then we were immune from kissing and hugging for another year.

I was surprised about Narges and Mina becoming such close friends. Mina was no longer snooty with Narges. On the contrary, she suddenly seemed taken by Narges's wisdom and wittiness. She always laughed at her jokes—her sarcastic remarks, I must say. Narges hardly knew or bothered telling jokes, but she was very good at making witty comments that offended some people and made others laugh. Anyway, Mina was very fond of Narges these days and I wished to know why. Yet, I didn't have time to add this bizarre development to my list of mysteries requiring investigation. I didn't care, anyway, except for the fact that my darling Mehri was less around my family and me nowadays.

As a rule, Dr. Afzali sat in the passenger seat next to Father and I sat timidly between Narges and Mina in the large backseat of the Mercedes. Still, I felt claustrophobic sitting so stiff between these two creepy ladies. Being too close to Narges felt icky due to the ancient cold war between us since my birth. The faint scent of henna on her hair also bothered my nostrils a bit, in spite of the perfume she wore everywhere but on her hair. The damn henna always competed with her perfume. So I preferred to stay clear from her as much as possible.

It also felt awkward sitting next to Mina—a woman with a lousy reputation at the centre of wild gossips. Especially after witnessing Dr. Afzali's pain all those years, Mina's behaviour at the Club disgusted me. Some rumours and clues had helped me put two and two together and conclude that Mina and Nosrat Yaghobi, the chef's son at the Club, had been having an affair or contemplating one. Even more rumours circulated at the Club after Father forced the firing of the chef and banned Nosrat from the Club. People complained about letting such a great cook go and we all missed his exquisite chicken kebob in particular. I had my own theory based on two clues. First, Dr. Afzali had asked me to hide his dagger for him just to minimize the risk of killing Mina with it in a moment of madness. Of course, he could've used any kitchen knife if it'd really become necessary. But killing her with that expensive, hunting dagger would've surely looked more professional, premeditated, and prestigious. Second, his words to Father the night he asked me to return his dagger still rang in my head, "I was just about to go slit that son-of-a-bitch's throat." He'd asked Father to arrange the firing of the chef and banning Nosrat.

So I felt horrible sitting near Mina in Father's car or at the Club. I wondered why my family took the risk of befriending these people—a possible whore and a potential murderer—and actually parading them now as their best friends. Many families always craved being close to Father at least. Thus, the Afzalis' sudden popularity was a new mystery. Some other reasons also made me uncomfortable sitting too close to Mina: I was still rather shy around women despite my regular imitation of Grigori. It seemed that the hornier I got, the shier I felt for sexual contacts. I bet Freud had an answer for this, too! Also, I didn't want to give Mina a wrong impression if my body touched hers by accident. She shouldn't think that I was another softy for her showy charm, like so many other guys always sucking up to her. I was too proud and pure to sit next to an ill-reputed woman, let alone the possibility of a mix-up when my elbow rubbed against hers when the car swerved round the corners. So, I always cringed in the backseat of the Mercedes to avoid Narges and Mina. Poor me! How much torture my destiny entailed!

Of course, you might rightfully ask again, 'Why the heck was I still willing to accept all this humiliation of going places with my parents so often in the first place? Why tolerate the sense of suffocation in the car, too? Why stick around old married women now that I knew a few girls my own age?'

Well, if you really want me to repeat myself, I couldn't ignore Mehri while she enticed me sneakily. Although she often seemed cold toward me, she sent me enough vibes to stick around her. She knew and applied the exact measure of charm to keep me hopeful. She seemed to expect me to be at all those places for the right moment. I had intentionally hidden myself from her a few times and heard her asking Narges where I was. I did it to enjoy her desperate enquiry just before presenting myself abruptly and making her grin with a sigh of relief! Therefore, I simply couldn't disappoint her in me any more. Grasping what she was doing to me or expecting from me was tough, yet a delightful torture I embraced for a chance to love her in a more intimate manner soon. We had a special kind of love affair that only she and I could grasp and enjoy. So I had to be wherever she was, just in case she decided it was time and that I was ready at last. I had to prove my loyalty to her by my regular presence and our furtive flirtation. I was willing to bear all the embarrassment of tagging along my parents at my age, even now that I had a city residence and Father insisted that I use it. My behaviour appeared bizarre to others, too, especially the Afzalis. But I didn't care because I was under Mehri's spell. I longed for making love to her desperately —an inescapable God-given torture, anyway.

Two other major reasons also existed for my rising addiction to all the hoopla in Royal Club and other parties. First, being a dance teacher for all those pretty women boosted my pride and persona. Second, the extreme, vile symptoms of the bourgeoisie at the Club, including the gamblers' lifestyles and the vulgarities of the crowd on the dance floor, were turning into an invaluable educational setting for me. I felt I was learning a lot simply by observing the people around me. It was a peculiar environment that hardly anybody could imagine, let alone get the privilege of studying from close-up. They provided lots of material for my diaries. Like a mad scientist, I filled many pages and notebooks with my new discoveries and feelings. Those writings helped me keep my anxiety in check, while filling my slack time when I was lonely and depressed in one of my residences with no desire to do any homework. Overall, the adults' attempts to win me over with their offerings were bearing fruits and I enjoyed their attention. I was rather adapting myself to their lifestyle, even though I still resisted adopting their showy values.

The awkwardness of sitting close to Mina vanished soon, anyway. Nature worked its magic as I leaned more toward Mina to avoid Narges when the car swerved around the corners. That sneaky 'relativity theory' again! It mixed with the force of gravity around the corners and I fell all over Mina. She also knew how to engage a young boy with her alluring smiles and affectionate words. She made me relax soon. My coldness and snobbery never discouraged her. So, in return, I rationalized soon that her guilt was not proven! Besides, who was I to judge her? So when our bodies touched, I found lesser and lesser reasons to cringe or be careful. I let myself go, the way I assumed Grigori would. I was still basking in the good vibes that the women in the Club and parties sent my way. And my growing confidence wasn't going unnoticed by Mina, either.

Mina had a friendly personality. I reasoned that this might've led to her image as an easy catch. I bet Dr. Afzali was the one having the toughest time figuring her out. I imagined the absence of concrete evidence to establish her guilt caused him a great deal of frustration. His inability to believe the rumours or establish Mina's treason hurt him the most. Several months after asking me to return his stupid dagger, I developed another new theory. That is, I discovered his motive for asking me in front of Mina and my parents: The poor bastard was only trying to send a subtle message to Mina, but also the whole world through my parents. He was announcing that he wouldn't hesitate to slay Mina or any man who might betray him. That was indeed a clever way of sending a dire message, while implying that he'd been patient long enough with Mina and her lovers. Then I realized he hadn't been an idiot, after all. I was sorry for him and angry with myself for thinking of him as an idiot when he'd indeed been so cunning.

I admired his diligent plan, including the whole episode of asking for his dagger in front of my parents and Mina—at the cost of my extreme humiliation in front of everybody, of course. Idiot! He'd been hiding the dagger and taking all the reasonable precautions to control his temper. "But my patience has limits. I own this big dagger, which I will use to cut your throat if you get close to my Mina." This was how I read Dr. Afzali's mind and his way of warning people around him, especially Mina.

But you know what? I also remembered Mina's smirk when she saw the dagger. She showed, with great arrogance, that she didn't give a damn about his subtle threats. She appeared quite fearless. After I'd put all these facts together in my head, I'd found a new perspective of Mina. Her courage and determination to live her life as fully as she desired without hesitation had now created a positive image of her in my mind. I admired her soft arrogance when she only smiled to sporadic gossips regarding infidelities and revenge.

Mina demonstrated her talent in drawing people's trust as we shared the backseat of the Mercedes to go many places with my parents. Perhaps she noticed my change of attitude and my new positive vibes toward her, too. She spoke to me like addressing another adult with no effort. She was the first person giving me a true sense of becoming an adult and being somebody. I started to believe, for the first time, that I was in fact at the threshold of manhood and I was welcomed by a gorgeous representative of adults. Perhaps it was time to stop doubting myself. She asked me about school and my imaginary girlfriends. One time, when she had a party, she came to me and whispered whether I wanted some whisky. I was flattered by her offer and said yes quickly. My parents noticed me drinking whisky and getting a bit drunk, but didn't object or react. I bet they also noticed who had offered it to me, but made no fuss about any of those things, as if they were all in this sinful skim together. That was my first attempt at drinking alcohol, thanks to Mina again. I enjoyed the taste and feeling of whisky. And I appreciated her initiative and courage to introduce me to this exhilarating experience. So I, too, became kinder and more relaxed around her. Her love of life, free spirit, and fearlessness, mesmerized me—especially since I found not enough of these qualities in myself, despite my efforts to imitate Grigori and Uncle Jamal.

Mina had an open mind and she was free like a gypsy. Her strong personality complemented her natural warmth and charm. If somebody told me that Mina had been a gypsy, I would've definitely believed him. Then I thought, again, how the gypsy woman would judge Mina's character, regardless of her makeup, if she learned everything I'd discovered about Mina now!

2

One night, at Royal Club, I noticed Mina near the dance floor watching my new rock-n-roll moves. As her beloved husband approached her anxiously, maybe hoping to ask her for a tango, she pointed me to him and said, "Aren't his moves incredible?" Actually, I felt she'd said it rather loudly for my benefit in such a noisy place.

"Yeah…," Poor Dr. Afzali replied with despair, probably even sensing the game Mina was starting. He just glared at me briefly before reeling back to his table.

"Hey, Kian, would you teach me your new moves?" she said.

"Of course…," I replied.

We practised a few new steps I'd learned from my friends, then a slow Italian song started and the dancing crowd changed gears. Mina turned to leave the dance floor but then stopped.

"Would you like to dance this tango with me, too?"

I looked around and noticed Dr. Afzali staggering toward the bar in despair.

"Sure, if you like…," I replied.

As we held hands, she embraced me tightly. The warmth of her body and breath startled me, but I didn't make too much of it. I only took a glimpse of Mehri who was checking us tensely.

Mina's subtle attempts to wrap herself around my puny body became noticeable, though. It was simply quite different from my previous dancing experiences with other women. A few times my cheek rubbed over her hair and temple. Her pretty fingers were slim but firm. Her hand was warm and its bright white skin was soft. Then it began pressing my hand in waves. She squeezed my hand off and on until my dumb mind realized it was a signal. So I squeezed hers in return, in harmony with the rhythms she kept transmitting.

After so many years of daydreaming and hoping, it was still hard to imagine my fortune was about to change. However, the firework and celebration had already started in my head. At last a woman was talking my language, but I didn't know how to speak myself or what to do next other than repeating this ludicrous hand-squeezing thing. So, all we did, we just raised the volume and frequency of the squeezing to acknowledge the message— over and over (instead of 'over and out,' which is customary for transmitting messages). The more we did this, however, the more nervous I got, since it seemed she was expecting me to do or say something. I feared failing this test, too. We embraced each other tighter, very close to the borderline where nosy eyes around us could detect the insanity Mina and I were exhibiting on the dance floor. To me, our embrace could seem quite suspicious to others, especially Dr. Afzali, but Mina was careless and didn't find it too much. *You take away one of my toys and I find another one soon,* she was probably announcing to the whole world. For me, I just had to trust her judgment. It was easier and more fun to trust her, I reckoned. Still, I was ashamed and horrified for not knowing what I was expected to do or say urgently, if anything at all.

We kept dancing off and on all evening, squeezed each other's hands firmer, and embraced tighter rather casually. We'd already sent and received, in the first tango, a clear message about our desire to start an affair. So, at that point, we were only expressing our fast rising infatuation, through firmer and faster squeezing of each other's hands. Our shameless hugging only indicated how hard we wished to squash each other's body if everybody went home and left us alone. All the cells in our bodies would merge in a few seconds, let alone our sexual organs. I trembled and felt embarrassed whenever Dr. Afzali peered at us with confusion. *How many of her toys should I smash,* he was probably thinking. I tried to avoid his eyes and look natural, but a criminal's eyes always betray him, while avoiding the victim's eyes becomes tough, too. My eyes kept turning to him as much I tried to elude him. I was nervous, but Mina's courage and cool helped me keep my composure. She was already running the show, while helping me boost my confidence, courage, and arrogance. Suddenly, I figured that all my gallantry was actually a fair retaliation for the way Dr. Afzali had humiliated me so carelessly in front of Mina and my parents the night he'd ordered me to return his stupid dagger. Idiot! The idea of revenge gave me enough nerve swiftly to embrace Mina's body and become reckless like her myself. Forget that idiot. I believed Mina sensed my sudden bravery and felt pleased with my tight squeeze, which I imagined was more potent than a thousand words.

Mina and I hardly spoke to each other all evening even though we danced quite a bit together. We just squeezed each other's hands like two dumb lovers. She was probably waiting for me to say something, I felt with agony again, but had no idea what to say. Even worse, I couldn't gather enough nerve to say anything even if somebody whispered all the right words into my ears. The fear of failing the test again had already paralyzed me. I imagined Mina also had difficulty saying something to a juvenile whose capacity for this kind of vulgarity was questionable, in spite of his eagerness to imitate Grigori. Especially, seducing the underage son of her closest friend required a lot more vulgarity. It would surely be a scandalous adventure that could damage her reputation beyond repair—maybe far past all the big milestones she'd already reached. On the other hand, all these risks would make this affair more exciting and boastful for her if only she could trust me to keep such a horrific secret—such a taboo.

We both had our reasons to keep our mouths shut, instead of clarifying the purpose of all that hand-squeezing. My left hand had turned into a holy shrine for me, though. The smell of her Nina Ricci and the subtle pain in my left hand from all that squeezing kept me in a trance. *Boy, she had a strong grip for such delicate hands.* She could probably kill me in her embrace when we started having sex together soon. For such a graceful lady, I wondered where she got all that strength. I found the answer right away, though! It was all the power of love, my love, of course... My love had already turned her into a superwoman, no doubt. I didn't wash my left hand for two days until the smell of Nina Ricci faded away.

3

Swimming in soft clouds with Mina, a crucial issue worried me: Obviously, the promise of a magnificent relationship with her felt delicious. But she'd surely share the information with Mehri and her gang at the club. So courting Mina would mean losing Mehri. Was I willing to make this big sacrifice after loving Mehri for so long? Mina was pretty, but Mehri was a goddess I had cherished religiously. She'd become even more precious to me than the gypsy woman had been, maybe because she'd kept me hopeful all along, while I'd missed the mysterious gypsy. We had played many erotic games and exchanged many romantic gestures all along, not to mention our heartfelt hanky-panky on the donkey! I also felt that Mina was most likely rushing to lure me to overdo Mehri before she got the courage to claim me for herself. So if my hunch held water, Mehri was planning to seduce me soon. Mina had sensed it too. Maybe even Mehri had told her directly. She was probably waiting for me to grow up just a few more months. Or maybe she was waiting for me to find the nerve to express my love to her in plain words, romantically, rather than trying to stick my penis up her ass on a donkey as a show of my affection!

My hesitation to choose between Mina and Mehri was now spoiling my life and sleep. It also showed my gutlessness to act. I was merely wasting precious time. Mina had proven to be more willing, competitive, courageous, and pushy, of course. I already knew how competitive those women were. But Mina's boldness had given her the edge. This meant it was now my turn to show my gratitude and guts and prove my trustworthiness in a manly manner. It was high time to stop beating around the bushes and expecting those ladies do all the hard work. But what if Mina had been teasing me, bluffing at a moment of drunkenness, or only trying to raise someone's jealousy—most likely Mehri's? It'd be embarrassing if I finally dared say something and she put me down nicely. She would then rush to report my exact words of passion to Mehri, too. They would probably laugh their hearts out and also tell all the other women! Mehri had done it once already and now it was Mina's turn to prove to everybody that she could tease me even better.

Weirdly enough, Dr. Afzali's wrath was now the least of my worries. The thrill of loving Mina washed over, a hundred times, the fear that he had uselessly tried to spread around. The poor bastard had done his best to forewarn those jerks who intended to seduce his beloved wife. He threatened one seducer today and the next one surfaced from another corner the next day, especially this idiot who'd already seen and touched my dagger! Yet, not his big dagger, not even the guns of Navarone, could now keep me away from Mina's pussy the way my wild imagination guided me. My past empathy for Dr. Afzali and my sense of conscience had all nicely evaporated. The only thing I felt was love for Mina.

At last, I decided to wait for Mina to give me another hint the next time we met, if she were still interested and sober this time.

4

Mina didn't disappoint me in our next meeting at Royal Club. It was full of staring, dancing, and hand-squeezing again, so much so I suspected *again* she was *really* in a hurry to outdo Mehri before she started her own plan to seduce me soon! I watched and suffered Mehri's stealthy monitoring of my behaviour, but then couldn't disappoint Mina, either, and ignore her urgent advances. I was already in a big jam before even starting any relationship. Finally, in the car on the way back to the Afzalis' house, I decided to do the last test before getting into real action. I grabbed Mina's hand softly when the car glided in a dark street, after making sure Narges couldn't see my gallantry. We pressed and caressed each other's hands with passion—without music and dancing for the first time. Right away, I knew I must express my love soon. I had to speak out before we broke each other's fingers.

By the time I went to bed, I'd made up my mind to call Mina in the morning to declare my unconditional love. Then, I burst into laughter about my thoughts in the car about the chance of breaking one of our fingers out of sheer passion and screaming abruptly from the terrible pain. Besides shattering the peaceful silence in the car, while everybody usually snoozed on the way home, maybe even Father's startle made him lose the control of the car and smashed it. Then everybody would've looked at my or Mina's broken finger in shock and asked how it happened! I was glad these silly imaginations had not rolled in my head in the car, making me laugh abruptly like an idiot, as loud as I was now in my bed, and startling Father and everybody else, after all—only by my silly thoughts and laughter.

So, I called Mina's house the next morning when I knew Dr. Afzali and the kids weren't around. I was relieved when Mina answered the phone herself and not her maid. I felt she'd been waiting for my call for many days, or at least since last night.

"*Salam…* this is Kian," I said with a shaky voice. I didn't dare calling her by her first name. It would've sounded weird to call her Mrs. Afzali, too, considering the purpose of my call. So I skipped using any name in my greeting

"*Salam*, Kian. I was just thinking about you," she said. These women really knew how to put you at ease. Her comment was perfect to get me going. I was now full of nerve and arrogance.

"Yes, me too. We should meet."

"We could have coffee someday perhaps."

I didn't like the way she said *someday… perhaps*. It sounded rather sloppy and unromantic. After all that hand-squeezing and the pain in my fingers, I thought it was urgent to love each other and all! How could she be so casual now that I'd proved my bravery and passion, after everything we'd been through?!

"Soon I hope," I murmured with gloom.

"Sure, someday soon," she replied.

"Where can we meet?"

"Do you know the coffee shop next to Radio City?"

"Yes… I go there all the time."

"I'll be in that area the day after tomorrow around four."

"Okay… Should we meet in front of the café?"

"Yes...," She replied. "We'll pretend to meet by accident and I'll ask you whether you'd like to have a cup of coffee—just in case somebody sees us."

5

I tried to run out of the classroom, but my friends blocked my way and asked about my rush instead of going around with them. I had no time to explain anything even if I cared to share my hot secret with them. They just kept horsing around while I cursed them and tried to escape. At last, I agreed to go with them and then fled under their bewildered eyes. I had only ten minutes to get to Radio City, so I ran the whole distance in the crowded streets like a lunatic.

Panting like a hound, I arrived at the rendezvous on time, but no sign of Mina. I bought a whole pack of Winston from a street vendor and lit a cigarette. Thank God, I'd realized just in time to be prepared to offer cigarettes to Mina from a packet rather than pulling one from my breast pocket and giving it to her. Recently I smoked only Winston, which was rather expensive, but I usually bought only a few cigarettes at a time mostly as an old adolescent habit perhaps. I was a rather rich kid, although Father didn't give me any allowance. Anytime I asked him for money, he merely opened his wallet, which was always full of bills. He let me take as much as I wanted. It was nice of him to let me decide how much I needed at a time. But the task of asking him for money every week was a drag. Even more torturous was to decide how much to take from that big pile of large bills. On the other hand, now it felt quite silly to ask him for a fixed allowance.

I took a drag on the cigarette and pondered how I should go about expressing my love to Mina. I'd been thinking non-stop about this matter and worrying since we'd set this date. Was it necessary to say I loved her, liked her very much, or something in that range? It also felt necessary to me, as a man, to offer the right reason for our affair, in the right way, and right away. Although she'd started the hand squeezing, I was the one who'd asked her for a date and thus should be ready. As if I had to convince her or something! Yet, in fact, she'd seemed to be waiting for me to say or do something from the first time she'd squeezed my hand. But what? How? I didn't even know how I should be addressing her: Mrs. Afzali or Mina or darling! How could I become so personal and call her Mina after calling her Mrs. Afzali for the last eight years? Since I'd been seven years old! So many issues made the task of getting personal with her too awkward. On this ground alone, I almost changed my mind about having an affair with her, after all. It felt too complicated already. Breaking all those rules and barriers, only because we'd squeezed each other's hands like maniacs, seemed impossible. It all felt too absurd and surreal.

She was already eight minutes late. This was a good excuse to run away from this madness. As I turned to escape, I saw her coming toward me in a tight skirt lined just above her knees, a beige blouse, and a designer leather jacket. She strolled on high heels with elegance and her long blonde hair spread over her shoulders. Yes, some Iranians are natural blondes, too. She was one, I reckoned. I believed she didn't tint her hair because the colour had been consistent all those years. More evidently, I'd never heard gossips about the matter. It would've been simply impossible to avoid gossips regarding any blonde hair, had it not been its natural colour! Narges alone would've not allowed that!

When she got closer, I noticed she was carrying a big brown paper bag, too, with the tips of a few celery stalks sticking out of it and staring at me. Heavens, I almost burst into laughter the way she embraced the brown bag with her gloved right hand. The big bag of celery messed up her exquisite pose in a comical manner, except that the colours of the celery and her gloves matched. I tried to control myself, but I couldn't move my eyes off that bag of celery that seemed to be taunting me. For a moment, it crossed my mind that she was a madwoman. Maybe she was teasing me, coming to our date with a bag of celery. The damn thing was just spoiling the scene of her elegant approach toward me—the scene of two lovers' first rendezvous. The next moment, I thought she was coming here only to tell me she'd changed her mind and must go home to cook that celery for dinner. In the final moment, I thought I loved her, anyway.

"Do you smoke a lot, Kian?" she said as she got close to me and found me speechless with a cigarette dangling at the corner of my lips.

"No... *Salam...*"

"*Salam...* Do you like to have a cup of coffee with me?" she asked, as if using a secret code that must be pronounced out loud for legitimizing a contact. And as though she wanted to ensure she wouldn't be lying to anybody in case forced to swear how we'd ended up having coffee together!

"Sure... I'd like to have a cup of coffee with you today if you have time!" I replied with a subtle giggle and sarcasm, trying to play along with all her funny theatrics and follow the protocols as properly as a gigolo should. I looked at the half-smoked cigarette in my hand and decided to keep it.

I knew the place, so I led her toward the upper floor where lovers went to hide in a cosy corner. She climbed the narrow stairs with her full, curvy ass moving from left to right at my eye level. I wondered how soon I'd be touching the soft skin of those gorgeous globes. We found a table in a corner. As we sat, I hid my schoolbooks on the empty chair next to me, took another puff at my cigarette, and put it out in the ashtray. She put the bag of celery on the empty seat next to her, and took off her jacket and the long green gloves that almost reached her elbows, a few inches below her half-sleeve blouse. A waiter took our order for regular coffee. The tips of the celery stalks still peered at me from down there, trying very hard to demolish the legitimacy of our rendezvous. It was ridiculing me. I glared at it in return like sneering my enemy.

"It's a present for you," she said with a grin.

"What?"

"The celery…"

I laughed. "I was only curious why you're carrying it?"

"I just bought it. It's a good cover in case someone sees us."

"It is?"

"Yes. Whenever I go out, I always buy something to explain my wandering in the streets or going places," she said.

"But it clashes with your outfit," I said like an insulted fashion critic. *Is she going to bring a bag of celeries or other vegetables or maybe a rack of lamb to all our rendezvous?* I wondered with despair.

"I must be careful," she said.

Her logic didn't make sense, but I decided to let it go. She looked beautiful and I kept staring at her.

"How many girlfriends do you have?" she asked.

"None. I told you before too."

"Why not?"

"I don't know."

She gazed at me with a teasing grin, the same way she and other women did it at the Club. The long silence and her stare reminded me of my duty to clarify the purpose of our meeting right away. But the idea of her waiting for me to say something romantic made me tense like hell, as if I had to make a big speech at the United Nation. I'd been really sweating over this matter too much, but I believed it must be done. Enough hand squeezing! *Gosh, I've always been such a bore.* Anyway, I gathered my nerve and said, "I like you very much." I felt the tension in my voice and she noticed it, too. She only smiled. Here, I'd said it… I'd done my duty… It wasn't such a difficult thing to do, after all, the way I'd tortured myself over it the last few days. But now suddenly a big load had come off my shoulders at last.

"We must be careful around people," she said as if my tension had worried her.

"Okay," I said like a good boy promising his mom to behave when the guests arrive.

Promptly I realized I wasn't painting a very pretty picture of my manhood. So I swiftly took out the pack of cigarettes out of my pocket, pulled a couple out of it and offered them to her. We each took one, but I didn't light the cigarettes. Instead, I dropped the pack of cigarettes on the table casually in a serious gesture, grabbed my cup of coffee, and sipped it a couple of times. She held the cigarette casually with a smirk, too, as if undecided about smoking, after all. Still, she looked amused watching me play the role of a cool gigolo trying to make a point. *Finally*, I put down the cup and lit her cigarette first.

We smoked our cigarettes pensively, stared at each other with admiration, and listened to the soft music pouring from the speakers hidden in the ceiling. I couldn't think of anything else to say and it made me nervous. I felt we'd already run out of topics to discuss. She just kept gazing at me with a grin. Ironically, many questions rolled in my head that I wished to ask her. But posing those types of queries wasn't a smart strategy for now, perhaps ever. I wanted to know how much of the rumours about Nosrat and she were true. I wanted to know why she was so cruel and careless toward poor Dr. Afzali. *It was maddening how my*

slow brain could ponder only touchy topics this minute! Thank
God, I still had enough sense to stop my innocent curiosity from
jeopardizing my chance of winning her love. Narges's corny
warning, *Curiosity killed the cat...,* sounded most relevant and
wise at that moment. I had to get over my sense of ethics and my
scepticism about the kind of person I was choosing for an affair. I
had to forget my cynicism about modern social values spreading
fast in the Iranian society. Instead, I began basking in the pleasure
of having a mature girlfriend who was twice my age and married
to a jealous and threatening man.

Mina broke the dreadful silence at last, thank goodness. "You
always remind me of Anthony Perkins."

"I do?" I asked with surprise. We were both tall and slim and
my hairstyle looked a little like his as well. But I never thought I
resembled him at all.

"Yeah. I think you look like him, especially your hair."

"His hair is black, I think. Isn't it?"

"I guess. But you look like him, anyway. Take my word for it.
Don't you like to look like him?"

"I do. But I really don't think I look like him."

"Oh, my God, you're as stubborn as your mother," Mina said
with a cute chuckle.

"You really think I look like Anthony Perkins?"

"Yes. You appear mysterious and quiet, too, like him."

"Maybe you think I'm a psycho, too, like him in the movie?"

"No. I'm sure you're a good boy."

"How do you know?"

"At least I hope you're not a psycho... Are you?"

"Maybe I am... Don't I look like one sometimes?"

"Not a psycho!" she said.

I hated the subtle hint in her tone. "But what? Only crazy?"

She laughed. "No. All young boys go through this phase."

"What phase?"

"They like to draw women's attention. But it's okay."

"That's what you think I'm doing?"

"You're cute. The women in the Club like you. Most of them don't mind fooling around with you."

"Are you kidding me?"

"No, I'm serious. You come across as a boy who appreciates women the right way. That's what they think about you."

"Does Narges know this too?"

"Oh, no. Don't worry. They don't let your mom in on these secrets."

"But Narges is very smart. She probably knows what they think. Even I've felt some of what you're telling me."

"You have?"

"Yes."

"Like what?" Mina asked.

"The way they tease me in recent months."

"It's because you're growing up and getting handsome. Most women have a fantasy about a young lover like you."

"Wow. You're telling all their secrets already."

"Because I trust you... I'm sure you'd never mention our conversations to anybody. Right?"

I was tempted to challenge her: *How come it's okay for you women to always share your secrets?* I wanted to ask her what Mehri had told her and others about our hanky-panky on the donkey. I was dying to know this one at least. But I realized that she wouldn't tell me the truth, at least not today in our first date. Besides, I wasn't sure whether those women took my gallantry on the donkey flattering, cute, or vulgar.

"You can trust me. I don't talk much, anyway," I said at last.

"I've noticed that. Why don't you talk with people?"

"Because their pretensions kill me. I hate their guts."

"But not mine, ha? You don't hate my guts as much, ha...?"

"No, I like you. I told you." This time I expressed my passion without tension. I sounded so cool. I was surely on my way to become a great gigolo very soon—a good sign for both of us.

"Why do you like me? I'm old!" Mina said with a deep tone of self-pity. It sounded as if she were fed up with aging already.

"I think you still look young and pretty."

"You think so?"

"Yes."

"Thanks. I hate getting old. I already have some wrinkles around my eyes."

Oh my God! I started to worry about the reason she was choosing me for a lover. Of course, she'd use me wildly for sex to enjoy life fully before aging beyond repair. But she probably wanted me more to confirm her charm and boost her confidence. Her self-pity saddened me. First that damn celery and now this. I'd assumed she was a confident woman. I'd imagined she wanted me because I was such a handsome man! Not because she needed a guinea pig to test her youth and beauty every day. Selfish woman! Yet none of these setbacks could stop me even an iota from preparing myself for her needs. *Who cares!* I told my finicky brain to shut up and let's move on. In fact, knowing about her frailty could now give me an edge to test my manhood better. I liked to know her age, but believed asking her would be rude and make her even sadder. I had to keep too many questions— the only ones my sneaky brain offered today—to myself for now. But I reckoned she was at least twice my age. Maybe I could trick Narges to tell me her age difference with Mina!

"I think you look gorgeous even with those tiny wrinkles."

"You're so sweet."

"Besides, you can always put on more makeup to cover them, I guess," I said as a presumed joke with a silly grin, just before realizing the vile air of sarcasm hidden my suggestion. My loose mouth and crazy brain had finally decided to work together to make a complete fool of me, after all. I was still child for sure!

She stared at me with a smirk, probably equally confused, like myself, about my stupidity or wittiness with completely opposite meanings and effects for our looming affair.

"Do you think I wear too much makeup?" she asked tensely.

"No, but I'll take care of you to stay young forever, anyway," I said with tact and confidence seriously, hoping to make up for my blunder. I sounded like we'd been lovers for ages and I was born a gigolo, getting more artful and passionate every minute.

"I'm such a lucky woman, Kian. I know…"

It was getting dark outside. We'd been chitchatting, gauging each other, and drinking coffee for two hours. I asked the waiter for the bill and left him a big tip, making sure Mina noticed it.

We got out of the coffee shop cautiously and strolled toward her house. It would take us about forty minutes to walk all the way, but she didn't seem to mind. She was determined to saunter on her medium heels with the big bag of celery and she wasn't showing any sign of leaving me soon, which I took as good clues about our flourishing love affair. Still I was worried about her tiny feet walking in those shoes two kilometres. I wanted to call a taxi for her but loathed letting her go. I wondered again how women could do it so naturally, as if they had a special gene merely in charge of walking on high heels. We held hands in side streets with less traffic. When a car approached, we separated. I was amazed at our courage. We discussed the possibility of someone driving by and seeing us so cosy hand in hand. But we touched each other again, as if mocking destiny. I imagined we looked ridiculous together holding hands, while I carried a big load of schoolbooks in my left hand and she kept the bag of celery close to her chest with her right hand. Yet, we were enjoying every moment of this exotic experience. At last, I was receiving the kind of attention I'd craved all my life. Getting it from such a pretty woman was incredible, beyond belief.

We stopped inside an alley near the main intersection leading to her house. It was time to say goodbye at the end of such a memorable day.

"When can we meet again?" I asked.

"We can meet when the kids are at school and Hassan is at work. Call me one or two days ahead when you can skip school and we make a plan to go somewhere."

"Somewhere? Like where?"

"Like coffee shops or cinema or some place else, we'll see."

"Okay," I said with a wide grin and squeezed both her hands firmly, as a tactful competition to show our growing passion. She squeezed our sore, mingled fingers even firmer, which made me cringe and almost moan. Like any thriving love affair, ours was already out of hand and hurtful, especially for our fingers. I wished we could stop this reckless proof of passion and our senseless competition to show it better, but I liked holding hands with her a lot. So I had to find a way to address this touchy issue without breaking her heart or letting her think that my hands were weaker than hers. Then I got sad thinking that her fingers were stronger only on account of so much practice in many other love affairs before me. I wondered if she'd, or could've, squeezed Nosrat's large hands as firmly as she did mine. Perhaps she was now only making up for all the humility she'd felt due to Nosrat's his hands alone!

With a mix of jubilance and confusion, I started toward my city residence. It was about the same distance we'd walked from the coffee shop. This could give me enough time to wind down after such an exhilarating day. I couldn't still believe I had a lover now —at last. Having a city residence—the Palace—not too far away from my beloved's place was another blessing. I seemed to have everything that a man needed. I smelled Mina's perfume that was stuck mostly to my right hand this time. It kept me in a trance, while I contemplated the purpose and the likely consequences of loving a gorgeous woman like Mina. I wondered how long I could keep her interested in me and how I should go about loving her. I wanted to make it eternal, but did she actually love me enough? I mocked her fear of aging, but my self-esteem was even lower than hers.

CHAPTER ELEVEN
A Dangerous Affair

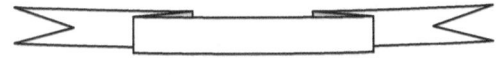

1

The woman!

Mina seemed to be the one. She was mysterious enough all right! At last, the gypsy's prediction of meeting a *mysterious* woman before travelling to the new world seemed to have come true. *Hooray...!* I pondered this amazing fortune on the long road to my grandparents' house. This had several serious implications, though. First, it rather proved the gypsy's psychic power, which meant I should be careful about the affair. But how I could be careful if I really wanted to fall in love with Mina right away. Should I reject her? Did I have a reason or willpower to deprive myself of this opportunity after three years of search for a woman to love? In fact, Mina could've been merely the result of my keen search for a lover and not a proof of the gypsy's psychic power. Maybe Mina wasn't yet the woman the gypsy had meant. She must've been clearer about 'the woman' if she'd really wanted to help me. Maybe Mehri had been the one the gypsy had meant, which I didn't have to worry about now, all thanks to Mina! In fact, Mehri seemed more mysterious than Mina, after all. I'd dodged the bullet then... possibly!

Before reaching my grandparents' house, I'd decided to love Mina without hesitation. I wouldn't allow any mumbo-jumbo spoil my feelings for her. To follow the gypsy's advice somewhat, I'd just be *careful* not to raise Dr. Afzali's suspicions too much about my affair with his wife. That was a sensible step to keep my promise to the gypsy and make her happy. But I couldn't think of anything else to be careful about.

Grandma asked edgily whether I was hungry and I said yes. She brought me a big plate with rice and eggplant and beef. I sat behind the table in the hall to eat, but she stopped me. "Aren't you going to wash your hands?"

I was surprised because she usually wasn't as picky about cleanliness as Narges. I stared at her to show my dislike of her sudden nitpicking. She stared back at me without blinking. So I went to the washroom and gazed at my face in the mirror. It didn't look so gorgeous after all the love tension and lack of sleep in recent nights. Thinking about Mina was already taking a heavy toll of my life. I smelled my hands and decided that I couldn't wash off the Nina Ricci. It was the proof of having a woman in my life. Not any woman either. I had a woman who looked like a fashion model and was full of energy, beauty, and pride. I liked to sleep with Mina's perfume in my nostrils until morning. So, what I did, I just turned on the faucet and let the hot water run for one minute. Then I waited another thirty seconds pretending to be drying my hands with a towel. Then I came back and sat behind the table.

"You still smell like a whore," Grandma said. "Where've you been?"

I got mad since she sounded like Narges. I'd never expected her to be vulgar or confrontational. Though, I guessed that this arrangement, my comings and goings at my pleasure and asking for food, had now finally driven her nuts, going by her tone of voice and choice of words. Also, maybe she thought I was full of sins going to a whorehouse or something. I was too unholy to harbour for a religious person and all. She had enough trouble with Jamal already, and now I was following in his footsteps so fast, too. More trouble and sins around her.

"What you mean, Grandma? I haven't gone to a whorehouse if that's what you're afraid of," I cried. I felt I must put her in her place, instead of showing any sign of weakness or getting timid. I wasn't going to quit coming here and she should get used to it.

"I'm going to talk to your mother about all this."

"About what? About what?" I cried, threw the spoon and fork on the table, and rushed away.

I went to my room without supper. She didn't come after me, either. I knew she'd tell on me to Narges, but I didn't care. I'd passed that stage of my life to be afraid of Narges or anyone else. Not even Dr. Afzali with his stupid dagger scared me too much. I was in love. Still, I decided to talk to my dad about his mother's behaviour. He was good at putting her in her place. So was Jamal. A few times, I'd been startled by Jamal's method of taming Grandma. I remembered two incidents very much like tonight right at suppertime. Grandma had made a silly comment that upset Jamal. What he did, he just grabbed the four corners of the tablecloth with all the food and dishes on it, took the whole thing with one big thrust to the window, and threw it outside. The sight of all that food and broken dishes scattered all over the ground was funny and terrifying at the same time. Grandma ran off to her room and stayed there for the rest of the night. But Jamal kept talking with me in a calm manner. Sometimes he apologized as if he'd only sneezed. He then said, 'Let's go eat *chelokabab*,' and we left. I was sure my dad would straighten out the situation with Grandma. He wouldn't let Narges interfere with my social life, either. Yet, I decided that the next time Grandma said something silly or insulting, I'd do exactly what Jamal did. I had the strength to grab the tablecloth and throw everything on it out the window.

All along, I knew that not even my Kakh residence was a place to find my lasting peace. Grandma wouldn't allow that. She took Narges's side, the same way I'd noticed all women took one another's sides at whatever price. The way they supported one another gave them their enormous power over men. Why would they ever change their tactic then? So I had to find a home for myself soon. This reminded me of the other advice the gypsy women had given me: "Plan for your travel to the new world." If her prediction about a mysterious woman, probably Mina, had come true, then her prediction of my travel to the new world held water, too. But the idea sounded ridiculous now—maybe a bit funny altogether.

I lay on my bed and weighed my options. The wisdom of the gypsy woman was obvious now. By 'planning' for my travel to the new world, she'd tried to make me realize the need to work on my grades in order to obtain the exit permit. But pursuing any kind of plan to get good grades was a tall order, especially now that all my thoughts were focused on Mina. I simply couldn't imagine how it could happen. After graduating from high school, all young boys were forced to serve in the military for two years unless they entered university. For going abroad for education, boys should have high grades and pass the national university entrance exams as well. Only ten percent of students could get into top Iranian universities. Being one of them sounded like a joke. With the kind of grades I was getting at high school so far, and my limited motivation, my chance to pass those exams was nil. I was surprised about my educational standing collapsing so fast in only a few years—with no or only a little fault of my own, too, I reckoned, *of course*! I was always at the top of the class in elementary school and now I was sinking to the bottom of the barrel in high school. I could hardly get the grades to pass even the simplest courses nowadays. *How did it happen?*

So, the idea of travelling to the new world was too far fetched, mainly due to the growing grudge between my textbooks and me with no foreseeable peace in sight. My parents didn't like to send me abroad, either. Most importantly, I loved Mina too much to consider putting even a short distance between us. Travelling to the new world was now only a good laughing matter, unless Mina wanted to go with me. Falling in love with her so fast and deeply was amazing! I was surprised myself! Anyway, Mina was my real new world now. For once, I had to learn to live for today in a real world. I had to relax and let destiny take its own course. I fell asleep as soon as I settled on this brilliant strategy.

2

I sort of pushed myself to at least attend school more regularly before Father got smart about my lousy lifestyle. I called Mina every day and we chatted about fifteen minutes on the phone. She went out with her friends every day while her image danced in front of my eyes and distracted me in the classroom. I skipped school one afternoon and we went to the movies. She suggested it so casually, like a suicidal maniac. I couldn't say no, despite my concern. My pride wouldn't let me appear less brave. Showing any hesitation about the plans she suggested would only reflect my immaturity to deal with the adventures we'd agreed to pursue together. I was in a pact with a fearless general running the war of nerves. She was my leader. I felt I'd never be a leader of anything in my life. In the cinema, we just held hands while sitting straight like kindergartners—a scene even more pitiful than the idea of two desperate sinners merely seeking a secluded place to hide. I wanted to at least lay my arm over her shoulder and let her put her head on my bony chest. However, only holding hands under our jackets or something was allowed in theatres—the limit she imposed so ridiculously seriously! I thought she had some kind of answer ready for any kind of situation we might get caught in; I mean, in case somebody found us together. Yet, she seemed to be really enjoying the movies, so much so I often felt she liked them more than me. Sometime, I felt I was only an excuse to go see her favourite films, rather than a beloved to cherish in that bizarre refuge. She was confusing me a lot already! Her love of movies was quite irritating and humiliating, I tell you.

Once she chose the zoo for our afternoon excursion. It was far from the city centre where we lived. So I skipped school again with an exhausted conscience bitching about my lost senses. Then, seeing all those animals in such a poor state depressed me more every minute, while we passed by their cages a hundred times that day. They all looked puny, sad, or dying of something. Especially, seeing the tiger in such misery infuriated me. I wanted to open its cage and let it go eat the zookeeper if the poor thing could gather enough strength to get there. I also wondered if any of those lost creatures had any love life or sex at least! They didn't seem to have energy to fart, let alone get horny.

I wished to get out of there, but Mina had planned to spend the whole afternoon at the zoo. She had the sources and wisdom to know what places and types of movies her friends and family would least likely go to in those odd hours, I imagined. Still, all afternoon, I wished I had the guts to ask her about the particular excuse she'd invented to offer in case somebody saw us in the remote zoo during school hours! It just had to be a masterpiece, I reckoned with great admiration for her ingenuity, assuring myself she knew what she was doing. All along, keeping all these touchy —possibly childish—questions to myself was torturous.

Anyhow, we strolled on the same short path a thousand times. We tried to talk about movies and the stuff happening at Royal Club and parties, including the gossips and possible affairs often shaping around us. We talked about high school and teachers' arrogance a little bit, too. But I merely felt depressed, guilt-ridden for being in that pathetic place for so long instead of attending the real zoo at the school alongside my monkey classmates. We passed by the tiger's cage a hundred times, and I got angrier every time, until she decided it was time to go back home, at last. We were among the last few people in the wretched zoo, so I suggested breaking the tiny lock of the tiger's cage just before leaving, but Mina refused with a cute smirk.

We went to the Club as usual at least once a week. Mina and I danced almost at the same rate she did before with Nosrat, while I imagined the message in her subtle smirk to the audience, *What do you think about my new toy? Didn't I tell you that I'd soon find another one even younger and handsomer?* Sometimes, I ran to the garden, hid in a dark corner, and smoked two cigarettes when I thought I was only Nosrat's replacement. Sometimes, she let me sip her wine or whisky in front of others. But as far as smoking was concerned, I still hid it from everybody but Mina.

Dr. Afzali monitored the situation from a distance. Probably he assumed I was still the same shy boy who always sat on the couch with a critical mind. Maybe he was thinking, *He's only safekeeping Mina for me the same way he did it with my dagger, although he's dancing with her too much.* I liked that he didn't take me too seriously. Still, I tried to keep my guards and said 'No' to many of Mina's orders to dance with her, sip her whisky, or other stuff. I was rather certain she didn't mean to provoke her husband as long as she could pursue her playful adventures, too. However, I was getting a feeling that she was eager to show off her influence over me to other women in the Club and parties, especially Mehri, who stared at me with spite and angst all along.

I didn't think Mina had revealed our affair to the women yet, but she was giving them enough clues to guess for now. She was playing a game with them as well. Meanwhile, Narges and Father watched my gallantry in passing. Yet, Father seemed pleased with my popularity as a dance instructor for all those pretty women and learning some of the social skills he valued so much.

3

Jamal returned on a weekend as he'd promised. I went to my Kakh residence after two weeks since Grandma and I had our little skirmish. As expected, she'd vacated the house for Jamal's benefit, but also in anticipation of my likely visit. I felt a bit sorry for her with an even tinier shame for annoying her sometimes, often deliberately. Jamal said he had plans for the evening, but promised to meet the next day.

I walked toward my friend's house, about thirty minutes away. Feri was becoming a good friend of mine—my ideal kind. He had social skills, intelligence, and a great sense of humour. He was a good dancer and played classical music on his piano. We chased girls together and always competed for the prettiest one. Girls often walked in pairs on the streets and usually one of them was much prettier. I wondered if any psychological reasons drove these phenomena. Whenever we succeeded in luring some girls, we fought over the same girl. We teased each other like idiots in front of them to impress the one we both wanted. Sometimes, I intentionally focused on the girl he wanted. The other girl got fed up and the rest was predictable. They just gave up on both of us as two immature, spoiled boys.

Yet, we never gave up fighting, sometimes even over an ugly, snobbish girl. We enjoyed our senseless urge to compete, despite appearing childish and crazy. The funniest part, of course, was that he believed to be as handsome as I was. Yet, I mostly blamed his coddling mommy for his silly overconfidence. Her regular nonsense about his good looks, especially when I was around, had evidently confused the poor guy. She wore thick eyeglasses, which were obviously due for a major upgrade.

I laughed behind the scene, though, while learning a few good lessons in psychology as well. To me, Feri was crazier than I was since defeating me felt more important to him than getting a girl —not the prettiest perhaps, but a girl at least. For me, losing those girls was a blessing, as I was stuck in my fantasy world among all those lovely women at the Club. So, I enjoyed our competition and then seeing Feri lose a girl was the icing on the cake. But Feri suspected nothing about my juvenile game behind our seeming serious competition. I pretended to be angry, too, but chuckled secretly about our bizarre behaviour and his admirable tenacity. His senseless obsession to defeat me showed his false pride and need to feel superior at any cost. Aren't we humans so weird or something? I suppose I wasn't a good friend, after all, depriving him of the girls I didn't want, anyway. Then again, these episodes were in fact educational and excellent experiments in psychology to prove my own idiosyncrasies and idiocy the most. Anyhow, in the end, Feri was getting what made him happier: my defeat. And he got what he deserved, too—no girls. He was weirdly jealous and so full of himself, but it didn't bother me and our friendship a bit. We were nice to each other at so many other levels. At least we weren't spiteful. We were only silly and sick in different ways.

We shared lots of secrets, too, Feri and I. But I was hesitant to tell him about Mina. Knowing his loose tongue, he might say something stupid in front of my parents about an older woman around me just for teasing me or accidentally. He might do it also to avenge our ongoing quarrels over girls. Still, I was dying to tell him, Jamal, and the whole world about Mina that day, as if a wild force pushed me toward his house to explain why I ditched him sometimes after school or skipped school so often. Maybe I'd even confess to my grand gimmick of fooling with him around girls. But then the whole evening, I didn't find the right mood or nerve to make any of those confessions. I decided to wait a while longer and assess the risks before opening my mouth. Suffocating from all that burden, still I convinced my eager, impatient tongue to bear with me a few more weeks, please.

I had the same urge and doubts (plus the same quarrel with my tongue) the next day when Jamal and I went to Melat Park.

"Did you put your story together?" I asked Jamal after we bought ice cream and sat on a bench near the big fountain.

He burst into his usual lighthearted, contagious, loud laughter. It always sounded exactly like Father's.

"About your parents' marriage?"

"Yes, the story of Romeo and Juliet!"

This time he laughed for twenty second. "You're really a piece of work, you know?"

"Yes, everybody says so." I laughed too, as though approving the humour of my sarcasms today.

"I'll tell you everything Dadash Jalal has told me only if you promise to never mention them to anybody."

"But how do you know Father has told you everything?"

"He's told me the story the same way several times. I'd also heard parts of it from your grandma. Some of them are a little private and funny, too, but I'll tell them exactly as he told me," he paused before continuing, "You aren't a child anymore."

"I hope not. Is the story shocking or something?"

"Not really… I just don't want you get a wrong impression about your parents."

"Don't you worry. Everybody seems to know about Father's escape on the wedding night and the low chance of a romantic start like most normal marriages."

"Although his escape doesn't say anything about love."

"Well, okay. Can you please tell me the damn story?"

Jamal stared at me awhile until I looked down timidly. My impatience was probably making him rethink his options.

"First promise to keep it confidential forever and don't get too hyper, either."

"Okay, I promise."

"It all started with your grandpa's bankruptcy."

"Grandma told me that story briefly."

"Okay. After government made him close down his cigarette factory, somebody in the bazaar convinced him to invest the rest of his capital in plastics that was new in the Iranian market. He signed two major contracts with a German company to import plastic products and build a plastic factory in Tehran. Nobody knows the details and why he paid for a large portion of these projects in advance. His friends might've swindled him. Or maybe a good deal just went sour. In those times, the banking systems and insurance companies weren't sophisticated to protect importers and investors, especially since the Second World War was escalating.

"Within a few months, the shipment is on its way to Iran with the documents in your grandpa's hand to release them from the customs in Khoramshahr. Then, they tell him that the shipment is sunk or confiscated by the Allies since Iran is allied to Germany.

"In shock, your grandpa struggles to locate the merchandize and get help to release the confiscated shipment. But he failed as the situation kept worsening. Germany and its industries are now in trouble, and the Allies are too engaged with higher priorities to care about confiscated shipments. A friend proposes that the only person who could possibly help Grandpa would be Reza Shah himself, because releasing this cargo has some economic benefits for Iran as well. The King could get the government officials to at least look into this matter closer. Perhaps they could also contact the German officials for assistance with the German exporter, the shipping company, and collecting any useful information."

"I couldn't imagine my parents' love story involved the World Wars and Kings!" I blurted sarcastically.

"Are you bored already?" Jamal exclaimed with tension.

"No, sorry, please continue…"

"Anyway, for contacting the King, the friend suggests finding someone related to the court. Then maybe your grandpa could bribe or convince him to take his message to the King and ask for his help. When your grandpa fails to find such a person, the same friend offers to help him find the right contact by spending some money. Your grandpa agrees and the friend finds Mr. Taibi, whom I believe you know very well?"

"Ozra Banu's husband, right?"

"Yes. Do you know what his job was?"

"Reza Shah's shoemaker, right?"

"Yes. He had a shoe factory too."

"Okay… then what happened?"

"Your grandpa's friend invites them to his house to discuss the project.

'I hear your shipment has been confiscated?' Mr. Taibi asks.

'It looks that way, although some people say that the Allies might have sunk the ship already.'

'So you don't know exactly?'

'No. Nobody can say where the hell the shipment is.'

'Yeah, it's a tough situation with the damn war.'

'Can you help me, please?'

'Well, I'm here to hear your story.'

'Naturally, I'd like to pay for your trouble somehow.'

'I still have to know what you expect from me.'

'Well, just tell the King my story in some detail. Ask him to order an investigation into this matter.'

'I guess I can do that. But I can't guarantee what he'll do or what the outcome will be.'

'Of course. I'm not expecting you to perform miracles. Just try to convince the Shah that this project has significant economic benefits for the country. That's all I ask.'

'Okay.'

'Can you tell him that we're close friends?'

'Are we?' Mr. Taibi asks with humour.

'We could be. You look like a good man.'

'Then I'll tell the King we're good friends.'

'It'll help a lot, I imagine.'

'Maybe! It would've been ideal if we were related.'

'Of course. I wish we were.'

'I hear you have a few young sons?'

'Yes. That's true. I hear you…'

'Great! I have only one daughter. How old are your sons?'

'The eldest is twenty-one and the next one is eighteen—'

'Your first son is the same age as my daughter.'

'Well, isn't this a great coincidence?' your grandpa says.

'Would you like to come to our house on Friday night to meet my family, with your wife and son, of course?'

'Sure.'

"Your father had always been a troublemaker around the house, although he's finishing his studies at Tehran University," Jamal continued. "He'd been wild for a religious family, mainly for drinking, chasing women, and not coming home for days and weeks. So your grandma has been in favour of finding him a wife to possibly bring some order into his life away from his vulgar friends. Your father and grandma also realized that their lifestyle would change quickly if some financial solutions weren't found right away. So they listen to your grandpa's pleas and agree to go to the Taibis' house."

"I can imagine what happens next," I said hastily. "The damn World War II forced a silly marriage. Reza Shah's alliance with Germany is responsible for my existence."

"Yes, you are just another war casualty!" Jamal replied.

"But why would Father go along with this shenanigan?"

"Don't you want to hear the whole story?" Jamal asked testily.

"Sorry," I said. "But isn't the rest straightforward?"

"Not quite. Nothing in this story is straightforward or logical."

"Okay, sorry. Please continue…"

"They meet the Taibis… Your grandma is on side and pushes your grandpa to convince Jalal to marry Narges. Besides losing their house, Jalal's sinful life is killing her, the same way you're doing it to her nowadays. Like father, like son!"

"I can never compete with Father on anything," I said.

"Don't be so modest. From what I hear, you've caused your grandma lots of grief already, way beyond Jalal all those years!"

I giggled and Jamal continued. "Anyhow, your grandpa has a private chat with Jalal about the matter.

'So what do you think, son?'

'I'm too young to marry, especially to that ugly girl.'

'She's not ugly. Why do you talk so rudely…? *Besides*, she's educated and I hear that she's very kind.'

'Besides, besides…!' Jalal snaps. 'What can I do with her education and kindness in the bedroom? Besides, I'm not ready to get married. Besides!'

'You'll like her if you spend some time with her, I promise. Give that poor girl a chance.'

'I already did by agreeing to come with you to their house last week. I'm still having nightmares.'

'Stop being a clown. This is exactly why your mother insists to find you a wife.'

'She thinks I'm a clown, too?' Jalal asks with a giggle.

'Think about your family at least. If I can't get the shipment soon, we should all go sleep in the street. Are you ready for that?'

'I'm going to find a job soon anyway.'

'How about us? Don't you care about your old mother?'

'But how can you ask me sacrifice my life for money?'

'Your mother and I don't see it as a sacrifice. You'll be settling down and getting a grip on your life.'

'You two need new eyeglasses. But my eyes work perfectly. So I won't do it.'

'I'll make a suggestion and hope you accept it as a present to your parents.'

'What suggestion?'

'Spend a few hours with Narges to know her better. If you still don't want to marry her, I won't ask you again.'

'Only if you promise not to ask me marry her again.'

'Okay, I promise. I just want Mr. Taibi think that I did my best and only you two couldn't relate after meeting alone.'

'Okay... Maybe you could actually keep him in limbo for a while, too,' Jalal suggests slyly.

'You mean, let him think it may happen later?"

'Yeah... Maybe he gets the job done, anyway...' Jalal replies.

'Gosh, you're so clever and kind... Thanks, Jalal...'

"So your grandpa arranges for Jalal to meet Narges in private. Dadash Jalal told me his conversations with Narges many years ago for teaching me something about life and finding a proper wife. He said he agreed to see her only for formality and making his sad parents happy. All he meant to do was to kill a couple of hours with Narges and maybe tease her a bit, too.

'Did they tell you that I was adopted?' Narges asks Jalal.

'No. Nobody mentioned that,' Jalal replies with surprise. But he's impressed with Narges's frankness.

'This is typical of this hypocritical family,' Narges replies. 'I'm sick of it all. I'm going to run away soon anyway.'

'Run away where?'

'Anywhere. Just out of this house, away from this family.'

'Do they treat you badly?'

'My parents are often busy working or partying. So my father is trying to find me a husband to rescue me from this madhouse.'

'I hear that he's connected to the court?'

'Yes, he is…'

'So maybe he can get one of those princes to marry you! You might even end up becoming a queen!'

'Don't be silly.'

'No, I'm serious… Those princes would be lucky to have you as their bride—such an educated, pretty princess,' Jalal says.

'We'll see… but I must get away from here soon…'

'But you'll probably put yourself and others into trouble, not to mention losing your chance of meeting those princes.'

'I don't care.'

'Make sure to lose your shoe on the road at least, so the prince can find you…"

'Stop fooling around…' she says. 'I must escape or kill myself. Which one would you choose if you were in my place?'

'Oh, it's really hard for me to choose for you. You can always flip a coin or something if you can't decide.'

'Are you always this funny?' Narges asks.

'I heard you're a school teacher.'

'Yes.'

'That must keep your mind busy. You look like a smart girl and can *probably* find a good husband *eventually*.'

'But I'm now a prisoner in this house. I need a good man who appreciates my kindness and devotion. I'll be a great wife.'

'I'm sure you'll be. I bet a lucky bastard, most likely one of those princes, will snatch you soon. Just wait and see…'

'But you don't want to marry me! I can't wait any longer.'

'It's early for me to marry and I'm not a good man, anyway.'

'The sooner you marry, the sooner you'll concentrate on your business. You'll become a better person, too.'

'Maybe. But I have other stuff on my mind besides business.'

'Finding a good wife is hard… But don't worry about me.'

'Okay…'

'Nobody cares about anybody. Why should you care?'

"Anyway, Jalal leaves Narges with pity and guilt for teasing her so much," Jamal stopped and stared at me.

"So, she'd been nagging and arguing even then," I said.

"It sounds that way, doesn't it?"

"And you remember those old conversations in such detail?"

"Only most of their funny chitchat that Dadash Jalal told me twice. It was actually much more than I remembered today…"

"Yeah, they've been funny from the start…," I said.

Surely, Narges had been suffering in that house, I reckoned, living with Ozra Banu and all. Her tenacity, especially about the idea of running away from home or killing herself, had also been interesting. It rang a loud bell! These urges were probably genetic and I'd inherited them from her, too, plus her knack for sarcasm and lying and on and on. I'm her son for sure!

Uncle Jamal broke my thoughts. "Your father has always been a kind and naïve guy despite his rowdy character."

"I think so too… Then what happened?" I asked.

"He feels pity for both Narges and your grandpa. He said he felt obliged to make many people, especially your grandma, happy. She'd actually been weeping and begging him to agree. He said that giving his consent to his father had been the dumbest decision of his life. He feels anger and embarrassment even now, after all these years, whenever he thinks about his stupid decision. He was advising me to never get sentimental when I'm choosing a wife and stick to my own needs and welfare, instead of making emotional decisions out of pity for anyone the way he did—not even if you are in love with someone."

"So that's why he married Narges? Out of pity?"

"Yes. Maybe you should know about another twist, too."

"What twist?" I asked.

"Your grandpa and Mr. Taibi arrange for the engagement, with a subtle hint that the marriage might depend on the couple's final verdict and the outcome of Mr. Taibi's efforts to locate and release your grandpa's shipment with the King's help. So, your father and Narges meet during the following five months. Narges keeps feeding Dadash Jalal with more gloomy stories about her life and plays the role of a neglected girl. Every day he feels more obliged to rescue a poor, pure girl from the hell she'd portrayed to him. Meanwhile, Mr. Taibi's pleas with the King aren't bearing any fruit and your grandpa realizes that the situation is turning more hopeless every day. While the pressure for wedding grows gradually, your grandpa feels only more depressed and finally acknowledges the end of his career. So he calls Jalal to a corner.

'My dear son, Jalaleddin Khan. I'm sorry for putting you through all this hassle for nothing.'

'Why? What's happened?'

'I don't think anybody can help me with the shipment. The King himself is abdicating and the Allies have occupied Iran.'

'So, now what? The shipment and all your money are gone?'

'Looks that way. I'm tired. I'm sick of all this begging and putting you through so much pressure.'

'I'm sorry, Dad. I wish I could do something.'

'You're a good son. I thank God for giving you to me.'

'Is there anything I can do?'

'No. You're free. I'm going to talk to Mr. Taibi myself and tell him that the engagement is off. You don't need to marry Narges.'

'Let me think about it, Father. Maybe I should still marry her.'

'Why? Do you like her now?'

'No, I feel sorry for her along with other factors.'

'What factors?' your grandpa asks Jalal.

'First of all, Narges has always been a victim. Now if we change our minds about this marriage because a deal has gone sour, the news will kill her. She'd probably commit suicide or run away and die somewhere."

"Do you think she's crazy enough to do that?"

"Yes, I think so," Jalal replies with a sigh and mixed feelings.

"And still you're ready to marry a crazy girl like her?"

"I guess so. Besides, maybe still some hope exists for finding the shipment. A good contact or opportunity may come up any day as a result of all the work Mr. Taibi and the King have done so far. If we break the engagement, and Narges's heart with it, Mr. Taibi might sabotage or at least stop whatever chance is still there to recover your shipment.'

'But all these speculations have been going on for such a long time. I do not want to make you suffer any more if you don't think Narges is the right person to marry.'

'There's also something else that I'd meant to speak with you about,' Jalal says.

'What is that?'

'I've heard some rumours that Mr. Taibi has found a solution, but is keeping it a secret until he's sure Narges and I are married.'

'Who told you that?'

'Narges, of course…'

'And you believe her?'

'I don't know. But she says she's heard it herself from her adopted mother,' Jalal replies.

'Well, that's horrible if Mr. Taibi is really doing this—kind of blackmailing us.'

'It is, but maybe he's really desperate to find a good husband for her daughter and doesn't want to lose his chance this time.'

'Well, I don't blame him in a way… You're a good catch.'

'I think she's also told him and others that she loves me a lot.'

'Well, it's surely getting too nasty and complicated. But we cannot go accuse him now or after your marriage about having a solution or keeping it secret.'

'I know… I cannot even discuss it with Narges or accuse her of lying now or later, either,' Jalal says.

'Oh, my son. You're such a bright and caring man. You're the light of my eyes. But my job, more important than releasing the shipment, is to release you from your obligation if you're not fully comfortable with it. I've felt so guilty all this time.'

'Don't worry, dad. I can always divorce her later, can't I?'

'I guess… Still I can't do this to you. You don't need to worry about me or anybody else as of this moment. I just don't think anybody can rescue the shipment from the Allies now, anyway. I doubt Mr. Taibi having a solution, either. But I also hate to think or say that Narges is lying to you, too. I really hope she is not!'

'But we can never be hundred percent sure about any of these things, especially about Mr. Taibi having a solution or not,' Jalal replies. 'I can't say if Narges is lying or not, either...'

'You're right. But what I've told you today is the best advice I can give you. From this moment, you're the one who must make all the decisions for this family, especially for your own welfare. So go take your time to decide what you wish to do.'

"So your father spends a few more days to think everything through. Unfortunately, he still ends up making a decision that only later he realizes to have been wrong. He decides to proceed with the marriage for all the reasons he'd mentioned to his father, out of pity for your weeping grandma, and maybe other reasons we don't know. At the end, nobody could help your grandpa with the shipment. Soon he turned into such a quiet, confused person you've seen all your life. It's a miracle he's still alive and keeps going around and seeing people."

"Father's sacrifice for everybody was absurd. But maybe he deserves all the pains Narges has been giving him," I said.

"Why do you think he deserves it?" Jamal asked in shock.

"For his nasty deeds before marriage, like going to see Narges with the intention of teasing her so much, especially about all the princes lining up to marry her," I said with a giggle.

Jamal burst into laughter. "Maybe he does then. But he knew he was making a big mistake. That's what's been bugging him all his life more than anything else, because he knows he did it to himself. He knows he cannot or shouldn't even blame others for his stupidity. He thinks Narges had manipulated him, especially by lying about Mr. Taibi's schemes and imminent solution."

"What's the story of Father's escape on their wedding night?"

"Yes. That's another funny story."

"Funny?"

"As I said, Dadash Jalal realized the absurdity of his decision. On the wedding night, he drinks and smokes a lot to calm his rage. He told me it felt like his life was coming to an end and that he couldn't do anything about it. He keeps dancing and joking all night with the guests to hide his tension. Maybe he makes a total fool of himself during the ceremony. Somewhere near the end of the big party, your mother tells him: 'You're a lucky man.'

'I'm lucky!? Why?' Jalal asks.

'Because I agreed to marry you! I'd rejected so many suitors before you showed up.'

'So you think you did me a favour by marrying me?'

'Of course. Even you said I might get a marriage proposal from one of the Shah's sons...'

'Oh, God, what have I done?'

'Besides, you're all rude. You're all a bunch of drunks.'

"Dadash Jalal asks his friends to arrange for a trip right away before he loses his mind and kills Narges already."

"Wow... So why did he go back home?"

"Well. That's still another point he wanted to teach me," Jamal said. "One can't sort out these events and communications easily in one's mind or deal with them. He couldn't leave her, especially when your grandpa's fate was still in Mr. Taibi's hand. Jalal also realized later that Narges had most likely said all that nonsense because deep down her pride had been bruised by the way Jalal had behaved on the wedding night and gotten drunk."

I knew about Narges's clever mind, sensitivity, and her need for revenge. So, the reasons Father had told Jamal made sense. I was sad, so I turned down Jamal's offer to go to a party with him.

The quiet in my room later in the evening helped me relax and take in the glorious epic of my parents' marriage gradually. I felt somewhat happy for having solved at least one of the old mysteries. To celebrate, I began fantasizing about all the gorgeous women I adored; all three of them together: the gypsy woman, Mehri, and Mina. I needed their help to forget about my parents' pathetic life quicker.

CHAPTER TWELVE
The First Kiss

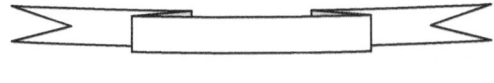

1

F eri and Jafar were waiting for me outside the classroom as I got out. I was depressed since I hadn't spoken with Mina today. When I'd called her at the regular time, nobody answered the phone. Jamal's story of my parents' freaky beginning was still pricking my mind a little, too. I wondered about my essence as a by-product of an antagonistic long affair between two genetically and emotionally disturbed parents on top of a loveless growing environment all my life.

Feri insisted that I go with them—to walk around the popular streets near the shopping areas to pick up girls. Then we usually went for dinner some place, unless some other plans came up. They liked me to go with them because, in recent months, I'd become an expert in starting a conversation with girls in the streets. At least they kept saying that just to stir my ego to do the dirty work for them: to soften snotty girls. Boys and girls go to separate schools in Iran. So our only method of contacting girls was to chase them in the streets. We needed courage and skill to say the right stuff to them and overcome their snobbery. Even the idea of going near girls paralyzed most boys. My odd skill came merely from my indifference toward girls, while my mind craved only women. Especially now with Mina in my life, I was simply too arrogant. Chatting with girls felt like kidding kindergarteners. Sometimes, I was actually quite rude, talking down to them the same way I spoke to our servants. Ironically, as another mystery of the universe, my conceit usually worked well and we ended up having coffee with them. Feri and Jafar benefited most from my bizarre approach without knowing the force behind my rising haughtiness. They told everybody at school about my vulgar method of luring girls. My huge transformation from a rather shy boy to such a jerk was amazing, but certainly reflected the evils of my adolescent experiences in vulgar parties and clubs! What surprised people even more was that, once we picked up the girls, I left after spending no more than half an hour to have a cup of coffee with them. Witnessing my cool departure without even asking for anybody's phone number in fact increased those girls' interest in me. Feri was sad, however, to see me not in a mood at all for competition anymore.

My friends gauged the girls passing by, while I just wondered about my next step with Mina. We weren't progressing as fast as I'd imagined in my dreams. Going by my fantasies, we should've by now tried many thousand methods of sexual acrobatics. But Mina and I hadn't even kissed after three weeks of dating. I needed some courage to kiss her. I wondered where she went every day while I was stuck in the classroom and daydreamed about her without grasping a word that teachers blabbered.

"Why aren't you interested in girls anymore?" Feri asked.

"Who said that?" I replied.

"I said that! You don't stick around after all the hassles of picking them up."

"I have other stuff on my mind."

"Like what? Are you hiding a girl from us?" Jafar asked.

"No."

"Oh, yes... I bet he has a girlfriend and hiding her from us," Feri said. "Are you afraid I might steal her from you?"

"I bet she's ugly," Jafar continued.

I didn't reply as my mind focused on a distant sight. Oh boy, my eyesight was amazing those days. Like having binoculars inside my irises. The tiny object I'd spotted from this distance looked like Mina. Her walk in high-heels, the blonde hair, the figure and clothing were all familiar. My sixth sense.

"He asked you a question," Feri said. "Is she ugly?"

I started running like a gazelle escaping a horrendous forest fire. Except that I was sprinting around people and cars on the busy Takhte-jamshid Avenue. After a hundred feet, I just turned and waved at my friends without stopping. My sudden madness had surprised them, but I had no time to explain anything, which had to be some kind of a lie, anyway. Actually, I had to lose them to save my secret. With my incredible start, I was out of their sight the way only a lover could. As I approached the dot that had triggered all that energy in me, the figure went inside a pharmacy. I slowed down and hid in an alley to make sure my friends hadn't chased me. Then I sneaked into the pharmacy and proved my eyesight's power, as I just bragged about it already. Mina smiled at me when she finally saw my frantic eyes admiring her.

"What're you doing here?" she asked.

"I was with my friends and I saw you. So I ran to catch you."

"Good. I'm getting some pills."

"I called you at noon."

"I went out with friends earlier today," she replied casually, as if our routine telephone conversation wasn't important anymore.

The pharmacist gave her a receipt and said the pills will be ready for pickup later in the day. She took the receipt and we got out of the pharmacy. I made sure Feri and Jafar weren't around. Then I walked with Mina toward her house.

"We haven't spent much time together recently," I said.

"Because you shouldn't miss school too much."

"But seeing you is more important to me now."

"Oh, dear Kian. Thanks."

"I really mean it."

"Do you have school tomorrow afternoon?" she asked like she'd just arrived from France and didn't know that all Iranian schools were open all day, except for Fridays.

"I'll skip it."

"You want to come to my house?"

"Is it okay, with the maid and everything?"

"If you come around, let's say, one o'clock, I will let you in myself. Don't ring the bell and don't talk when I open the door. Just go upstairs and wait in the drawing room."

"Okay." I was too excited suddenly, imagining all the good things that this kind of sneaking around could mean.

"Can you get my pills from the pharmacy on your way?"

"Yes. What is it?"

"Oh, just my birth-control pills."

"Birth-control pills?" I asked with panic.

"Yes...," Mina replied. "Is that a problem?"

"No... I can do that...," I replied with hesitation.

Asking for the pills under her name, especially those private sexy kinds, sounded risky. The pharmacist knew Mina very well by the way they chatted and chuckled. He surely knew Dr. Afzali as well, at least from his reputation as a heart surgeon. 'Are you related to Mrs. Afzali?' he'd probably ask me, I thought timidly. 'Or only having sex with her, you bastard?'

We strolled toward her house for thirty minutes and held hands now and then. Her sweet voice, grin, and smell rejuvenated me. I felt alive again after three days of separation, which had felt like eternity. I was now addicted to her perfume. It shut down all my nerves. I forgot school, my parents, and the rest of the world. All my worries evaporated smelling Nina Ricci. And I got edgy again when Nina Ricci faded. I sniffed my unwashed hands for many days between our dates while thinking about Mina all my waking hours! Especially in bed before falling asleep, but also in the classroom, my hands usually covered my nose.

How would I survive without Mina and Nina now? The germs on my hands were just having a ball, too, I imagined. Maybe they liked the smell too! Mina would probably understand if I asked her not to change her perfume, because it kept me alive when I wasn't with her. I felt that this was another kind of quirk growing in me. I was hoping, however, that my obsession for her and her perfume would lessen once I got a chance to have sex with Mina —*Tomorrow!* I would probably regain my sanity a bit tomorrow. Sex with Mina would kill my addiction to Nina, too! Or maybe my madness worsens, like the way Dr. Afzali was trapped in her spell! In my case, it might get even crazier, because of the way I usually got too obsessed about something or someone. My dire obsessions to unravel family secrets and my search for the gypsy woman were good examples. The gypsy was responsible for my biggest obsession—herself—but also the way I perceived and pursued my life in recent years.

2

The next day, I walked into the pharmacy lost in a load of wild imaginations with the receipt in my trembling hand: Maybe the guy knew what I was up to from the way Mina and I had met and whispered the day before. Maybe he knew I was going to her house right now to give her those pills, so that we could have sex. Maybe he would call Dr. Afzali and ask whether he knew a guy with my descriptions and whether he should give me the pills. Thank God, he was sunk in his own thoughts and didn't even look up at me. Maybe he'd had a fight with his wife just before I'd arrived, unless his indifference was only a trick.

I hid the private package in my pocket and rushed away, as if smuggling a classified document for espionage. If Mina had any good explanation for my carrying those pills, in case I got caught, she had forgotten to tell me! She surely exposed me to so much risk, *on purpose perhaps,* as if getting a special thrill playing these games. With the name 'Mrs. Afzali' written on the box in large prints, having those pills felt riskier than carrying Father's handgun in the streets. It'd clearly prove my crime if the police or Dr. Afzali found them on me. I'd be accused of a crime that I was only going to commit later, in half an hour. Though, at least, now I knew that she took those modern pills, which made sex easier, safer, and nicer. Oh, God, how would it really feel? I got quite anxious about my upcoming crime and my sexy dreams coming true shortly. *But I must be calm and brave today,* I decided fast. I must prove my manhood at last. So I marched with pride and purpose toward my lover's house, my penis leading the way.

I'd checked and adjusted my Sarcar a hundred times with other watches and clocks all day. I didn't want to arrive early, wait behind a closed door like an idiot, and raise the neighbours' suspicions, too. But I didn't want to keep Mina waiting at the door like a doorman and getting upset with me, either. I had to start this splendid stage of our affair on a good note.

I was really proud of that gorgeous watch, but the damn thing also humiliated me whenever I checked the time. It embarrassed me for having begged Father to buy it for me. Anytime I looked at it, my cynicism about materialism felt too shallow. I hated my hypocrisy, for the way I'd craved that Sarcar the minute I'd seen it in the window of the fancy shop in Shahreza Avenue. It was a very reliable watch besides its beauty, but somehow I didn't trust it that particular day. I imagined it'd retaliate for my hesitation about materialism on the day I needed its help the most to arrive at Mina's house at exactly one p.m. for a very important business.

The door was a crack open as I got there. I pushed it a little and Mina opened it. She pointed at the stairs going up and stood in front of the steps going down, trying to block the view from the hall in the lower floor. I climbed the stairs and waited near the drawing room. Mina closed the door with caution, looked into the hall on the lower level one last time, then came up and led me into the drawing room. She pointed to the end of the large room where it connected to the dining room. We sat on the sofa. I guessed she'd ask me to hide behind the table in the dining room if we heard the maid's footsteps coming upstairs.

"Isn't your maid coming up here?" I asked anxiously.

"She has nothing to do here. She can hardly walk anyway. She'll be busy cooking dinner for the next couple of hours."

"You're really brave, Mmm... Mina!"

"No, you're braver than me today… Finally calling my name after all this time… You brave man…"

"About time, ha?" I said with relief, but also grief for being so gutless too long. "But you're the bravest every day."

"Why?"

"For everything we do around the city. The way you look so careless about it all, the maid coming up here, or maybe even eavesdropping."

"I often have guests and she's used to it. Besides, she's almost deaf."

I burst into laughter. "That's another point. You know how to pick a practical maid for your needs. A deaf and lame one."

Mina laughed and grabbed my hand. I thought it was the right moment to stamp my first kiss on her voluptuous lips. I leaned forward with great confidence, rather sloppily, mind you. I squinted like a hunter and aimed for her lips a little too fast. She turned her face and stood up as if I'd been out of order. I stared at her in silence with embarrassment. She walked the length of the drawing room to its far end, stopped, and watched me like a judge pondering a verdict. I gazed at her in confusion.

At last, she approached me cautiously with a grin, stood above my head, and played with my long hair. Then she bent and kissed my lips from that awkward angle. Oh, it was so sweet. I couldn't move an inch and my neck started to hurt from holding it pressed backward. It was a delicious kiss, so I let her stand above me and kiss me in such a dominating posture as much as she wanted. Finally, she stopped kissing and sat next to me on the sofa. I could breathe again, thank God.

I wondered why she'd stopped me from kissing her and then returned after a minute to kiss me upright while leaning over my squashed head and neck. My first thought was that she wanted to be the one setting the timing for our first kiss. Too romantic, ha? But my quick second thought was that she wanted to be the one running the show, not me. Maybe I'd been too bold for one day, first calling her by her first name and then trying to kiss her, too!

Where was I—this petite adolescent—going with all that sudden boldness? Anyway, to me, her attitude felt weird and it sucked. So much unnecessary drama, if you asked me. I could've gotten a whiplash from that awkward kiss! But it was really tasty too.

"What kind of feelings you have for me?" she asked with hesitation.

"I love you," I replied without hesitation.

"You do? Are you sure?"

"Yes. I'm sure."

"Since when?"

Gosh! I had no clue how long I'd loved her. She was starting to sound like an interrogator, probing me the way Narges used to do in yesteryears to set the time for finishing my homework and getting back to housework—her chores.

"Since we danced together at the Club, four, five weeks ago," I replied after some thinking and hoping my response was proper.

It wasn't. It probably sounded not satisfactory to her at all, since she frowned and kept gazing at me for a long while. Maybe she was expecting to hear that I'd loved her secretly for the last two or three years at least. Maybe even since the first time I had laid eyes on her as a toddler. Thank god, she finally decided to give only partial credit to my answer just to let me pass the test, barely. She grabbed my hands and kissed my lips again. I wished I understood her logic, grading system, and the clues my answers had provided! But I was glad I'd gotten at least a passing mark and maybe we could now go to bed please.

We kissed for fifteen minutes without speaking—exactly like silent movies. Dead silence while I was almost out of breath again. Her kissing was firmer than her hand-squeezing, I tell you. Should I start undressing her? I decided to use my basic instincts in the politest manner without rushing this time. On the other hand, if I was supposed to speak sexy or moan, I didn't know what, when, or how. I should've paid more attention to Narges when she'd tried to give free lessons to the whole neighbourhood all those years.

My lips were going numb from kissing the same spot, but it felt rude to stop. I began cheating a bit, though, by caressing and kissing other parts of her face with frequent, fast returns to her lips. I felt an urge to lick her neck when my left eye caught that soft, white skin with a pretty vein beating smoothly, the exact spot vampires would enjoy sucking for blood. I fancied drinking a few drops of her blood myself, which would probably taste like a dry red wine. I pushed my fingers into her dense blond hair and kissed her earlobes and cheeks. She played with my hair very passionately, too, as though taking some kind of revenge. My long hair was a mess, I was sure. Her balding husband was probably also responsible for the way she clutched and curled my hair, as though finding such a full silky hair now gave her all the rights to mess it up as much as she wished—just to make up for her regular deprivation!

The long silence made me edgy, but I didn't want to say 'I love you' to her again. She had conned me once already today to admit my deep love without bothering to say that she loved me, too—like it were my official duty to love her. I considered doing the same thing myself: Asking about her feelings for me before following immediately with, 'Since when.' But then I decided not to drag a confession out of her, mostly because I didn't have a grading system, anyway. Instead, I felt like biting her neck so that she'd scream, moan, or complain—anything to interrupt our long, monotonous foreplay. *When are we going to bed then?*

Touching her bare legs felt just marvellous, as I let my hand navigate toward the plumper areas near her buttocks. The higher it moved up her legs, the more blood rushed into my veins, as if the centre of the gravity was right there between her legs. It was drawn toward the black hole where no object cares to escape from. But she slapped my poor hand every time it approached that dark formidable gravity. How could any other force compete with the sucking energy of a black hole, I was amazed! But the force of her slapping my exploring hand kept throwing it off its course. The explorer finally changed course and moved toward her chest that throbbed under her blouse with its buttons undone. My sore fingers caressed her soft skin a little and then inched toward her breasts. Those two gorgeous globes had grabbed my attention. I landed both my hands on them over her bra. But when I tried to remove the bra or slip my hands inside it, again she slapped them. They were getting red and burning from all the slapping—only for following my sneaky brain's orders. When not slapping me, she just kept pulling my hair playfully to keep me in line, while abusing the opportunity of messing up a fluffy long hair further as well. I wondered whether Dr. Afzali had ever had enough hair for Mina to play with. Her zeal to make up for many years of hair deprivation was clear and comprehensible, but getting a bit out of control.

"Why do you keep slapping my poor hands?" I asked her at last. "They're only doing some exploration."

"No exploration!"

"Why not?" I asked with grief, almost telling her, *Then you can't play with my hair either…!*

"Because if you love me you won't do these things. Besides, I don't know what you do with other girls."

"I told you before, I don't have any girlfriend."

"But you go out with girls, don't you?"

"Sometimes."

"I don't like that. You must prove you love me as you say..."

"Prove? How?"

"You'll have to figure it out yourself," she said.

"And meanwhile, what're we going to do?"

"Everything we did today. Don't you like kissing me?"

"Yes, but…" *How much you want me to kiss the same thing?*

"I like kissing you, too, and going to the movies and other places."

I was confused. Totally dumbfounded! What she was offering me was a million galaxies away from what I'd imagined about loving a woman. All the nice novels I'd read, including *Madam Bovary*, agreed with my imagination. Jamal's stories with women agreed with my dreams, too. Even the young girls I'd dated had been more liberal than Mina, except for insisting on keeping their virginity and doing everything under a blanket, and as long as I didn't try to look at their bodies. With so little Mina offered, she expected me to give up the joy and humour of dating other girls, too. And then prove my love and loyalty to her as well, while letting her mess up my hair as much as she liked, as if she'd just bought herself an obedient, shaggy puppy to play with. It just felt like too much sacrifice and commitment for me with no tangible rewards! I really had to make a decision here. Maybe Mehri would still prove to be a more cooperating lover if I approached her in a direct, gentler manner. Now that I'd gained confidence about dating women, maybe I could express my love for her right away. I could beg her to forgive my short, totally meaningless romance with Mina. Even judging by our 'hanky-panky on the donkey,' I'd probably get better results with my beloved Mehri sooner. And she was even prettier than Mina. *Oh gosh, on top of all the lust related pains I've whined about already, now even more of its side effects were becoming the added sources of my suffering. How can our brains work under all these pressures and confusions that lust alone causes for humans?*

"Who's your tailor?" Mina asked as though the negotiation about sex was over.

"Karami," I replied with surprise. "Why?"

"I know a good tailor," Mina said.

"I know a good tailor, too," I said sarcastically, still struggling with my disappointed, angry penis trying to rip off my trousers and my brain still working on new lust related theories.

"But I really like the suits this guy makes."

"Is he expensive?"

"A little, but he's worth it."

"I'm not planning to buy a suit, anyway."

"I'd like him to make a suit for you as my present."

"A present? What for?"

"Just because I love you," she said.

Her timing to express love couldn't have been more perfect. 'Love' felt magical, like a sacred gift delivered from Heaven by a handpicked crowd of angels floating over the clouds and playing a serene harmony of harps and horns. Love felt maybe even worth my celibacy, because I'd waited too long and needed badly for ages to hear someone expressing her love for me—especially after the long suspense Mina had kept me in. I'd heard some lousy love phrases from girls, but I'd never thought or felt for a second they knew what the heck they were talking about. But the way Mina said it, I knew she meant it. She certainly knew what she was saying and what love truly meant. I forgot all the torture she'd given me all afternoon. I forgave her for causing my hands' redness and pain. Now, love felt hundred times more precious and fulfilling than sex—my imagination of sex, I mean. So, I was forced to postpone my encounter with this supposedly delicious experience again. Then again, I heard the devil laughing with an ear-piercing roar.

"How can I explain the suit to my parents?"

"Just say that you'd saved some money."

In the end, I decided to ask Father for money for a new suit. I could use the money on my growing extravagance around Mina. When I asked him for money a week later, he just opened his wallet as usual and I took fifteen-thousand rials. He was surprised for the first time by the amount of money I took. It was certainly a substantial sum of money, even for the kind of suit that Father's famous tailor made for him. But it ended up being less than the twenty-thousand rials that Mina spent on the suit.

Mina and I kissed and hugged some more that day. Then I combed my hair with great difficulty before following her down the stairs. She ensured the maid wasn't in the hall on the lower level. We planned to meet in Café Naderi the next day after school and go to the tailor. She opened the door and I sneaked out. After walking five city blocks, I realized I'd forgotten to give her the birth-control pills. I stopped and thought about going back, but didn't feel comfortable knocking on her door in case the deaf maid answered it by fluke. So I kept walking toward my city residence with fear, as if carrying a ticking bomb that might explode any minute.

3

Waiting anxiously for the last bell the next day, I planned to ditch Feri and Jafar, but again succeeded only after a major squabble. I couldn't understand their clowning sometimes, especially when I told them I was busy. The outcome, I arrived at Café Naderi late and found Mina already sitting at a table, looking bored but still busy gauging the patrons keenly. We ordered coffee and smoked cigarettes before going to the tailor, which was two blocks away, on the second floor of an old building. We looked at many fabrics and finally she chose a dark blue with fine maroon stripes. I liked it too. The style she chose was a three button tight jacket with padded shoulders, which looks totally ridiculous these days. I feel embarrassed now even looking at my pictures in that suit ages ago, but then boys believed they were so lucky to live in an era with such a fantastic fashion sense. I bet every generation feels this way, while we spoiled humans keep making all kinds of weird clothing, which we also throw away quickly so idiotically. What a weird species!

We left after Mina fussed over everything long enough. The stairs going down was empty and rather dark. So I grabbed and kissed her with great passion. I really loved her the way she was showing her love. We exited the building cheerfully at last and strolled down the street. She turned and gave me a tender smile, pleased with my sentimentality in the stairs, then stopped.

"Do you have a handkerchief, Kian?" she asked.

I checked my pockets. "No."

She opened her purse and pulled a pinkish silk handkerchief. She began cleaning all over my mouth, like wiping up ice cream off the face of a three-year-old kid.

"What is it?"

"Lipstick. Lipstick is all over your face, darling."

I just stood still like a good boy to let her finish. Suddenly, my eyes caught Feri and Jafar in a short distance ambling toward us. It seemed they'd already seen me as well, while Mina still kept cleaning my mouth with her pink handkerchief very seriously. I wondered if they'd followed me from school and were going to confront us now. Anyhow, there was no time to warn Mina and hide. The best I could do was to stop her from cleaning my face and whisper, "Let's go. My friends are coming toward us."

Mina shoved the handkerchief in her purse as Jafar and Feri stood in front of us.

"Hey, Mr. Kian Noori," Jafar said playfully. "Where're you going?"

"Nowhere special...," I replied with tension as Jafar and Feri checked Mina out with utmost curiosity.

"Is she your mother?" the asshole Jafar asked.

All the passion and joy on Mina's face a second earlier turned into a grimace and then gloom. Still she managed to deliver a sad smirk.

"No. We must go. I'll see you guys tomorrow," I said while grabbing Mina's elbow and thrusting her forward, away from those two morons.

I looked back after ten steps. They were still standing there and watching us, probably thinking I was crazy going out with a woman twice my age.

Mina was pensive. She remained quiet for a long time. I couldn't find the right words to relieve her tension, either. At last, she broke her dreadful silence.

"You better forget about me."

"Why? What're you talking about?" I asked with panic.

"I'm too old for you," She said. Her fear of aging was all over her eyes again and she looked pathetic. The wrinkles around her eyes suddenly looked as deep as she'd whined about them in the past, as if the sun and her swift shock had widened them.

"You're not. Besides, I love you. Believe me?"

"I believe you. What're you going to tell your friends?"

"I don't know. I guess I should tell Feri the truth. That's the problem."

"Why do you have to tell him?"

"Because he comes to our house regularly and he knows my parents. I have to tell him to keep his mouth shut."

"We must be really careful, Kian."

"I know," I said. But, in fact, I didn't understand her sudden sense of caution. The way she behaved! The risks she took, they all looked like she was dying to get caught. I didn't understand the games she played. Who was she playing those games for and why? Was she doing all these tricks to make Dr. Afzali more jealous and mad? Or was she merely giving him enough reasons, including the new affair with me, to divorce her? To regain her freedom somehow away from the poor doctor.

"By the way, did you pick up my pills from the pharmacy yesterday?"

"Oh, yes. I'm glad you asked." I took the small package from my jacket's pocket, looked around us, and then handed it to her quickly before a CIA agent could photograph the transfer of the evidence. As she took it, I breathed a sigh of relief.

"It felt like carrying a bomb anytime I remembered it," I told her. "Thank God, I kept forgetting it."

Mina burst into laughter. She looked so beautiful to me and I loved her, I thought with glee. I felt lucky she was mine. Maybe Dr. Afzali felt she belonged to him. But he was mistaken... He was totally mistaken. She was all mine. And I hated the fact that she was taking those pills only for Dr. Afzali's benefit.

4

During the following four weeks, Mina came with me to all the four fittings and a final try on the day I picked up my suit. She was too fussy. She made the tailor work hard for the money she paid him. At the end, it looked great, however. And it made me look handsomer, despite the silly fashion those days. She was pleased to create an aristocratic-looking Kian. I thanked her and kissed her again in the stairwell when we left the tailor shop. I told her I liked the change pocket inside the side pocket. Except that I'd keep my cigarette lighter in there. The next time we met, she'd bought me a brand new gold Dunhill lighter, in the box and everything.

Every time we'd gone for a fitting, we'd first met at Café Naderi as though by accident. We had coffee and pastries and whispered like lovers for one hour. Then we strolled to the tailor. On our third rendezvous at Café Naderi, I met her close friend, Parvaneh. When I arrived, the two of them were having coffee and chatting. Mina introduced me while Parvaneh appraised me with some lustful appreciation. I sat and ordered coffee too. The way the two friends continued talking and included me in their conversations was bizarre. It sounded as though Mina had told her about her affair with me two centuries ago. They treated me very much like an old story. Naturally, I felt offended a bit by the way they seemed to view the affair too ordinary, like some kind of window-shopping they did every day just for the heck of it. A normal state of affairs for sensual pleasures. After being around Mina for three months now, however, I was finally learning not to be surprised by these kinds of eerie social behaviours anymore. I'd myself told Feri about my affair with Mina. In spite of his initial shock, he admitted to finding the affair cool. He promised to be careful around my parents and in case he met Mina at our house by accident.

"So why did you laugh so loud when Jafar asked whether Mina was my mother, you asshole?" I asked Feri with anger.

"Just the way he asked it and the reaction in your face, but mostly because I'd seen your mother already," he replied with a chuckle.

"Jackass…!"

Even after my suit was delivered, Mina insisted Café Naderi was a good place for meeting supposedly by accident. So we kept meeting there once a week. She thought people would believe our story in case some enemy found us. But the few people who saw us having coffee together were her friends. A great place for desperate housewives, I guessed, especially during office hours when their trusting husbands were hard at work and grieving over their depressing lives. Therefore, we were safe in Café Naderi, or simply Mina wanted me to believe so. I'd gotten used to her risky routines and I wasn't worried about meeting her friends. None of them belonged to the group in Royal Club, thank God.

Mina and I went to other places too, where she believed the chance of getting caught was minimal. In particular, we went to the cinemas showing old movies in the afternoon. We still didn't kiss in public places or at the movies. We only held hands under a jacket or something like naïve teenagers, while the vulgar ones made out all around us so energetically. We saw all the Anthony Perkins' movies, but we went back to see *Goodbye Again*, again and again. I loved the music and Anthony played his role really perfect. I was proud of myself, if I were supposed to be Anthony. The more Mina pushed me to go see that movie again and again, the more I felt her love for me, since she kept saying I resembled Anthony. So I loved her more, too, the more we saw that movie.

She was living in a fantasy world and I was dragged into it as well. It felt as if we were imitating the scenes and feelings of the romantic movies we saw. The amorous tune from Brahms' Third Symphony, the one used in *Goodbye Again*, was always ringing in my head. I bought the record and listened to it as often as I could. And my clothes and hands always smelled Nina Ricci. I sort of worried that Narges would ask me something about my smell any moment. She could certainly detect the smell of Nina Ricci and knew the person who normally wore it. But I didn't care anyway, though I hated my inability to think of a reasonable answer to give her in case she asked. The romantic life in Mina's fantasy world had consumed us and we enjoyed it so casually like a legitimate couple.

I talked to Mina every day on the phone. Now, she always waited for my call, she said, before leaving home, to go wherever she went to spend her afternoons with friends. The best time I could call her was around noon during the school lunch break. If I could skip afternoon classes, she let me go to her place. But we only cuddled, kissed, and expressed our eternal love for each other. Our love was growing fast and I felt attached to her with all the fibres of my being. I couldn't imagine life without her. One time, when we were strolling toward her house in a shady street, I felt my life's emptiness without her. So I told her, "Please marry me."

She was shocked. Then she giggled. "You're only sixteen years old, my darling."

"Does it matter?" I asked.

"It matters a lot. Besides, I'm still married."

"Divorce him. I really love you, Mina."

"I love you too. But you shouldn't think about marriage."

"Why not? I have only one more year of high school. I'll start working and we'll live together *happily ever after*," I said wittily.

"Hassan wouldn't allow it. I have two young kids too."

"But you seldom see them. They're always with the maid or at their grandparents' house. You're never around anyway."

"Are you saying I'm a bad mother?"

"No. I mean, they don't need you."

"Your father will go berserk if he finds out you even speak about marriage."

"But he married at a young age himself."

"Well, that's another good reason he'll certainly give you...; that any marriage at a young age is doomed."

"How do you know that?"

"About what?" Mina asked with tension.

"Has he told you his marriage is doomed or you're saying that from your feelings?"

"Most people can see something is not quite right between your parents," Mina replied with panic. "Your mom complains to me sometimes, too. But please don't mention these words to anybody. I hope I'm wrong, anyway."

"Okay, I won't. But I don't care what my Dad thinks about my marriage."

"Don't you love your father? He really adores you."

"I like him a lot too."

She stayed quiet. I realized how utterly romantic I'd talked and dropped the subject, too.

"Besides, you'd have to do a lot of education and travelling before even thinking about marriage...," she said in a motherly tone.

Her tone of voice and ideas depressed me. Suddenly my old promise to the gypsy woman to focus on my plan to travel to the new world crossed my mind. Such a crazy hallucination! The stupid idea had been buried in a deep grave in recent months. It sounded like a madman's words now. I'd surely been under the gypsy's spell when I'd promised her to plan for going to the new world. Mina was my new world. I'd already arrived. I'd taken the gypsy's words too seriously. Such a wild imagination!

I even imagined, rather humorously, that maybe Mina knew about the gypsy's prophesies somehow. Or perhaps she had a similar psychic power and a crystal ball, too. I'd thought many times that Mina could've been a mysterious gypsy herself, just going by her easygoing, strong, wild personality.

I laughed even harder anytime I recalled my bigger promise to the gypsy: to be careful about the mysterious woman I'd meet before going to the new world. They were the same thing, and Mina was both, anyway: the mysterious woman and my new world. I found no reason to be careful with Mina. There was no reason to believe I was under her spell. How could the new world she'd built for us be harmful? In fact, it felt just the opposite. In that new world, I was no longer feeling lonely and anxious the way I'd felt one year earlier, maybe all my life. My madness had disappeared. I'd felt someone's love for me for the first time in my life; all that wonderful touching, kissing, and real affection; all that messing up each other's hairs; and the opportunity of heartfelt passion, love expressions, and tender communication with someone who really understood me. Now, *only* the idea of travelling to the New World, presumably the U.S., sounded like a silly fantasy altogether. Instead, I had to push Mina and myself into the evolving blissful reality satiating our deprived longings for love. Now, Mina was the true reality. Mina was my eternal reality in this new world.

I believed Father loved me, too, but he'd never showed it in any tangible manner other than by opening his wallet for me or defending me against Narges and Grandma sometimes. Anyhow, I couldn't imagine any parental love, or any other kind of love possibly out there, could match the love of an angel like Mina. Now I had finally reached the highest order of blessing God may ever bestow upon a human. Now I had a goddess to worship every day.

I was in heaven. But still Godless!

CHAPTER THIRTEEN
Grigori of Royal Club

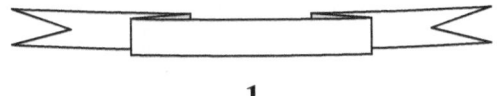

1

I wore my new suit to the New Year, Norooz, party at the Club, with the heavy gold lighter safe in the side pocket. Even Father was impressed, but also surprised that another tailor than his own could do such a marvellous job. He asked me who the tailor was and I said Naraghi. I just couldn't lie to him despite my concern about the chance of him going to Naraghi and learning about my suit's history—especially about the blonde, mysterious woman fussing so much over everything and paying for it. Then I figured he'd never give up his own pricey tailor serving the ministers and aristocracy in Tehran, including his dear friend, Prime Minister Hoveyda. He wouldn't abandon him even if the good tailor kept ruining his suits or proved to be another sly spy.

Mina wore the pendant I'd bought for her with half of the money I took from Father for the suit. I believed I'd done a great job finding that special treasure at Mozafarian after one hour of haggling and hinting about being Narges's son. He remembered Narges and her nonsensical purchases of jewellery very well. He might've even assumed I was buying the pendent for Narges, although I asked him, before leaving, not to mention anything to her about seeing me recently or selling me the pendent.

The puny pendant blinked subtly like a distant star on Mina's expansive chest, with her breasts about to burst out of her tight décolleté dress. It looked quite small and cheap compared with the jewelleries other women showed off that special night. The contrast with Mina's regular glittering jewellery was even more startling and raised a lot of curiosity. I hadn't meant to make her look less flashy, but felt proud, anyway! I was impressed by her sacrifice to wear my present, instead of keeping it only for casual occasions. It just revealed our immense love once and for all. Another positive outcome was that now a lot more attention was paid to her gorgeous chest with no glowing jewellery blinding men's lustful eyes—an extra source of agony for poor Dr. Afzali caused by me.

Ironically, with such drastic change, Mina radiated a special aura and class, too—for wearing only that tiny pendent! Many women, especially Mehri, checked out the pendant with envy. They were surprised but also jealous. Her courage and novelty had blown their minds away. Mina touched it and showed it off while talking to them about it. Her bragging looked funny, though, as if it were a trophy she'd won in a major tournament. Now, she was showy in a different manner! I was dying to know what the heck she was telling them about the pendent and peering in my direction stealthily. My eyes followed her everywhere she walked, although I tried not to make my peeps too obvious. Dr. Afzali was doing the same thing from another corner, so we often ended up staring at each other instead of Mina.

Mina and I danced only seven times to minimize the chance of giving the wrong impression to people. Too late probably! My gorgeous suit and her tiny pendent had raised enough suspicions already. Yet, various clues hinted that many of those nosy women already knew about Mina's new secret. This didn't surprise me, as she'd shared it with her other friends whom we'd met at Café Naderi. How these women trusted one another with such fatal information blew my mind still after all this time. It really did.

My popularity had also multiplied ten times with the start of the New Year while I basked in my new world. Grigori would've been so envious of me that night, or at least proud of me as his protégé. Maybe I was only imagining everything. It was hard to

figure out what went on in those pretty cockroaches' heads. I
strived to absorb the alarming information before deciding about
the situation around us and the level of danger. After all, I had to
protect my affair with Mina—as well as my head—before some
provoking rumours blew Dr. Afzali's top at last.

I felt Mina had also told other women about my suit being her
present, going by the witty compliments many women made
about it all night. They invited me for a dance as well, which I
accepted while trying not to make Mina jealous. I was always
careful not to spoil our nice love affair, although she seemed to
enjoy my popularity with women more than I did. She goaded
me and looked generous with her friends, letting them get a taste
of her property. They could touch and test the purity of the puppet
she'd created, as long as we all remembered her kindness and
ultimate ownership. On the other hand, maybe other women
were merely testing the strength of Mina's claim over me. Or
they were only eager to spoil her fun somehow just for the heck
of it, if they could. These were, after all, the nicest scenarios I
could imagine about those women's intentions and their sneaky
fuss around me that night.

With all the courage Mina and other women had given me
throughout the evening, I approached Mehri. She'd religiously
refrained from making any comment about my suit or showing
an interest to dance with me. Her anxious stares had, however,
caught my eyes often enough throughout the evening. If anyone
in that group was certain about Mina's new secret, it was she. I
remembered her shapely body from the day we went swimming
with her daughters. She was the one who had given me the best
taste of sex, even after my long affair with Mina. My sexless life
with Mina had now found a heavenly meaning, though. I liked it
that way myself. She was becoming the goddess of love, a sacred
image that sex might destroy. Obviously, this was an absurd and
confusing image infecting the brain of a love-thirsty juvenile like
me. My mind was apparently screwed up about the connection
between love and sex, thanks to Mina. Therefore, while Mina

was the symbol of love, Mehri still remained the focus of my sexual dreams—the goddess of sex. That appeared to be the only solution: to have both—a goddess of love and a goddess of sex. So, was it time to focus on the sex goddess now that the love goddess seemed happy? Would the two goddesses allow it? Would I dare betray the love goddess? As an evolving gigolo, I reckoned there was no rule for having more than one mistress at a time. Surely, Grigori had had no problem with that!

"*Salam,*" I said to Mehri.

"How're you, Kian."

"I'm fine. Thanks. I wish you a happy Norooz."

"You too. Next year will be your last year of high school?"

"I hope so!" I said with a smirk.

"Are you still getting good grades? At the top of your class?"

"No. Not really. I'm just hoping to graduate next year."

"What happened? Why aren't you studying enough?" she asked with a sudden air of compassion, as though hoping to get a confession from me about the cause of my distraction right there and then. Maybe I'd admit my stupidity and tell her about my sexless affair with Mina. Maybe she was hoping that I'd do such a noble thing as a sacrifice to buy her love and a ton of sex.

"I don't know."

"You do… I know too! You can tell me," she said firmly with inquisitive eyes, like begging me to confess and get it over with. Please open up and give us a chance for infinite intimacy. She'd forgive me and we'd start our own affair after kicking Mina out.

"Would you like to dance this tango with me?" I asked her.

"Okay… I always admired you for being such a smart boy," Mehri replied after looking across the hall and exchanging sharp, meaningful glances with Mina, as if still mad at her for betraying her and jumping the line to seduce me.

"Not anymore, ha?" I dared ask her while grabbing her hand and she only grinned, pushing me into a mysterious suspense.

Mina was checking us out with a smirk and maybe a bit of stress for the first time all night. I'd been watching her all along from the corner of my eye. She tried to hide any sign of jealousy, pretending to be only amused. I knew she was dying to hear our chitchat and the cause of Mehri's last grin after I'd murmured something to her. The fight of two angry goddesses over me felt exciting. Which one would win—love or sex? Love is probably stronger but sex is definitely wilder. I noticed poor Dr. Afzali watching all of us with confusion and tension.

Mehri and I danced cosily while peeping at Mina from afar. I embraced her firmer and she didn't resist. Yet, she seemed sad and disappointed with my unwillingness to confess to her. Mina noticed how close we were dancing, but didn't flinch other than widening her eyes with a sly smirk. That famous smirk of hers always fascinated me, as though teasing the whole world. For a second, I pondered playing the hand-squeezing game with Mehri, the same way Mina had started it with me a year earlier. But I lost my nerve. I believed Mina would notice it; not the squeeze itself, of course, but the fear in my eyes. I did it only once anyway, but Mehri didn't respond. Maybe my squeeze was too light. Or maybe she wasn't in the mood for my silly games again. Was she scared of Mina for all the secrets they might've exchanged over the years? We kept silent for a long time, while I enjoyed the touch of her warm hand and her enticing smell. Her perfume smelled nice, too, whatever it was. The aroma seemed perfect for enticing any man's craving for sex right there and then. I thought I'd probably fall in love with her perfume, too, if she took me on as her sex slave. Asking the name of her perfume felt a bit risky, though. She'd probably report my curiosity to Mina. Shamefully, I realized my growing fear of losing Mina already; perhaps the way Dr. Afzali had been for ages! Unless I merely cherished our affair as a sacred sanctuary! The former was probably truer, I feared even more! I wondered if I'd drop Mina for good if Mehri just asked me to right then. When the music stopped, she pulled her hand abruptly, as if just recalling she hated me for something.

"Thanks, Kian. By the way, nice suit!" Mehri said slyly, most likely hinting she knew everything about it. What a smart slut!

"Thanks," I murmured with nostalgia, wishing I dared saying her name out loud as well... *Mehri... Will a day finally come that I call her Mehri in her face so casually the way I did with Mina?*

I watched her sadly as she went back to her corner. God, I loved her a lot. I really did. Then I peeped at Mina, who seemed to be biting her lips. I flinched and went toward the bar to get a glass of orange juice or maybe vodka if I could fool the bartender.

I believed Mina noticed the gloom in my face and Dr. Afzali felt Mina's tension and reaction. Oh, what a confusing mess! For a minute, I imagined the whole world, including my parents, were picking the variety of vile vibes circling in the air—all caused by me. Luckily, I realized right away that I didn't care.

2

I returned home with mixed feelings that night—not only for still adoring Mehri, but also about Mina's reckless leak of our affair to some women in the club. Maybe she hadn't told them everything. But, at the very least, her subtle gloating about owning me was hard to miss. Despite my joy of being loved and owned by her, what stopped everybody from spreading rumours about Mina and me? What would Dr. Afzali think? What was he waiting for? When was he going to kill us and end this charade? How much of my peculiar affairs had raised my parents' curiosity at least?

Still, the events that night, especially my flirting with Mehri, had an instant impact on Mina with a thrilling outcome for me. When we spoke next on the phone, she asked me when I could skip school to go see her. I said I was *available* the next day and she agreed. I was always available! What a model student! After our telephone conversation that day, I felt she was rather anxious to ensure her ownership over me was still intact. If so, perhaps I deserved a prize. It couldn't be another suit for sure, and I had a lighter too, so what would be her offering this time?

Following the regular routine, I arrived on time, she opened the door, and I sneaked in and up the stairs to the drawing room.

This time, however, instead of sitting on the sofa, she showed me the sheet she'd spread on the floor behind the large dining table. A large pillow was at the top of the sheet. I took off my shoes and sat in the middle of the sheet with my legs crossed like the statue of Buddha. She had a robe on with buttons from top to bottom. She lay on the sheet with her head on the pillow, grabbed my hands, and pulled me over her. She wasn't wearing a bra, so I opened the top three buttons of her robe and her glamorous breasts leaped before my eyes for the first time. The pink nipples smiled at me and I welcomed them with repeated kisses. She took off my shirt and we embraced with our naked chests at last. Then she slid my hand toward her pussy—that forbidden temple to date. I grabbed it with enthusiasm. I massaged it and played with the hair around the moist tunnel my fingers had detected. I opened the rest of the buttons of her garment and took off my trousers. I was excited more than I'd ever been. My heart banged against my chest and I felt out of breath.

I rested my head between her breasts to relax a little, but the sheer excitement had paralyzed me. After loving her so long in a sexless fantasy, this unexpected generosity of hers was giving me a heart attack. She seemed to be waiting for me to take off my shorts, too, and make love to her. Yet my erection was gone. More than a year now, in all our cuddling and kissing in previous meetings, I'd tolerated a painful erection the whole time. But, now that I needed it, it was playing a trick on me. Getting bored with my hesitation, she slid her hand inside my shorts and grabbed my penis. I saw total panic on her face. What kind of a man was I? Still she tried to keep her cool and be patient with me.

"What happened?" she asked.

"I don't know. Where can I go to pee?"

"Pee? The only place you can go pee is on the roof."

I knew what she meant. The design of their house was weird. Only the huge drawing and dining rooms were on the top floor. The washrooms and all the other rooms were in the main and lower floors, which were still forbidden areas guarded by the maid, although the temple itself was now finally open for my visit in vain.

"That's okay. I'll try to hold it."

"If you must go, just go to the roof and pee near a gutter."

Regular interior stairs go up to the flat roof of Iranian houses. So I went upstairs to the roof, naked. I leaped behind the stairs' wall in a shaded area, all along hoping the neighbours couldn't see me. In a corner near a gutter hole, I did a good job and ran back downstairs. Mina looked anxious with a smirk ready for me. I lied next to her and kissed her, worrying about my erection. The damn thing was mocking me. After months of torturing it myself, it was its turn to revenge without mercy, as if it had waited for months patiently for this exact moment. It was playing a game when I needed it more than ever in my life. I cursed it. I begged. I entertained romantic thoughts like before when we only focused on love. Nothing could convince this useless mound of flesh. I tried many ideas I invented hysterically one after another. I tried to make it realize the pleasure of visiting an exotic temple for the first time. But I couldn't fool that stubborn thing with any of my tricks or tactics. It just refused to cooperate. Suddenly, it didn't want to go anywhere and pretended to be shy. It looked ashamed too, though, if I cared to believe the way it hung its head down. But surely, it was simply another way of mocking me. I peeped at Mina's frenetic eyes. She looked desperate for sex at that instant, as if she'd promised her pussy a fantastic experience with a very potent seducer according to Mehri. My own eyes would've looked probably ten times more horrific if Mina held a mirror in front of me. What a mess! Like we didn't have enough other messes to sort out already in this formidable love affair!

"That's okay," she said with pity and a trace of anxiety she couldn't hide. "Leave it alone awhile. Just lie down next to me."

I obeyed her and she pulled her garment over our legs, as if warming me up could possibly help the situation and resurrect that wilful devil. We caressed each other like wounded soldiers. I mulled over some romantic experiences Mina and I had shared together and our hot passion all along, at least until that afternoon, before this embarrassment had made me feel so pitiful and guilty. Then I started kissing her with passion. I was back in the movie roles Anthony Perkins played. The erection came back with great poise. Thrilled from a sense of triumph, I rolled over her, found the target, and aimed with my pistol. But it lost its interest swiftly as it approached the pussy again. It was playing with my nerves and having fun while I was boiling with fury.

I was mad like hell. Then I got sad. Here was this gorgeous body before me and I couldn't do a damn thing with it, out of fear or sheer excitement. I lay back next to her again, not even daring to touch her in fear of raising her tension or hope. But Mina was gracious and speechless. She just caressed my face and played with my hair—now like a nurse tending a fast dying soldier. Yet, I couldn't feel her conviction. I wanted to ask her to let me die with some leftover pride, but I'd lost my tongue as well. She was too quiet, which made me doubt the sincerity of her sympathy.

She slid her hand down and played with my penis, but the more she tried, the smaller it got, like avenging our unforgivable past crimes. Mina and I had tortured it for too long, it would probably yell if it could speak. Nobody had humiliated me in my life as much as this…, this…, *what should I call it*, did that awful afternoon. A great deal of the confidence I'd gained in recent years evaporated in one afternoon. I agonized and worried about Mina's impression of my manhood. But I also worried about my reputation. I was no longer the Grigori of Royal Club. Too far from it, judging by the stories told about his manhood! Instead, from now on, I'd be the laughing stock at the Club. Some of my manhood arrogance surely deflated that afternoon, too, although I imagined arrogance is too deep to get crushed in a day, month, or even a decade. Mina looked pensive, probably cursing Mehri for lying to her about my manhood on the donkey in Damavand. She was definitely going to confront her for her big lie—for causing more than one year of Mina's precious life going to waste on me. Then again, Mehri would be thrilled if she heard the story!

"I'd better go," I said tensely. "Something's wrong with me today."

Mina's silence felt like her swift consent and deep relief—to kick out her source of frustration away from her face as soon as possible. She suddenly looked happy again. So I got up and got dressed rapidly, kissed her, and followed her down the stairs.

At the last minute, I said timidly, "Maybe I come tomorrow?"

"Call me tomorrow. We'll see," Mina replied.

I gazed into her eyes for ten seconds to possibly read her mind behind her playful smirk. I couldn't, so I got out, discouraged and agitated. As I staggered forward, I imagined Mina begging Dr. Afzali later in the evening to make love to her to relieve all the stress my impotency had caused her. He would probably wonder where all that lust and passion had suddenly come from; and maybe even guess what could've been behind it all! He was a smart surgeon, after all. *That bastard Kian has probably stopped seeing or making love to her to intimidate her or something,* he would imagine with a mix of fury and satisfaction.

My mind tried to offer a few more reasons for my impotency, too. Maybe my confusion about the conflicting meanings of love and sex had caused the chaos in my head and stopped sex with Mina who was only my love goddess. After having brainwashed myself all this time, my twisted brain now feared the possibility of shattering love if sex interfered with our flourishing love affair. *What nonsense..., or maybe not!* This stubborn *thing* wouldn't listen to me now, either, even if I swore that we'd all been terribly wrong about this matter. Well, the bottomline was clear: I was humiliated and it didn't really matter if it was because of love, brain, penis, or whatever. My fragile manhood had messed up my flourishing love affair.

I checked my Sarcar and decided to go back to school, but just to wait outside for Feri and Jafar. Hitting the pavement with them might relieve my anger and gloom. The exhilarating anticipation of tasting the long-overdue sex with Mina had turned into such a tragedy. I'd disappointed her in me and blown my chances for the eternal love and the big marriage I'd envisioned for us. "Call me tomorrow. We'll see," she'd said with impatience and pity. It was absurd how a simple misunderstanding between my body organs had changed my life and mood. It was ridiculous to pay for this physical confusion with my reputation and pride personally. *It wasn't my fault,* I wished to shout to Mina and the whole world!

Halfway to school, another wave of anxiety halted me in my tracks abruptly. I felt facing Feri's compulsive clowning would really kill me in my present condition; or I might end up killing him. He'd just keep mocking my melancholy to cheer me up. But I was surely in no mood for his baseless fooling around today. Therefore, I changed my direction and started walking toward my Kakh residence. *Why do people call God 'He'? God must definitely female,* I pondered as my anger with all the gods and goddesses was soaring again. *Or, at the very least, women are the privileged creatures of His kingdom!* Why? Because they don't need to worry about any damn erection. Never in their whole lives must they face the pain and frustration men feel when our manhood comes into question, not to mention the embarrassment of lying so uselessly next to our depressed beloved—sometimes next to a whining bitch. Then, trying helplessly to also justify our impotence would be even more pathetic. Those days I was too young to realize that women have at least two other advantages in this area as well: they can fake an orgasm and they don't need to worry about its timing the way men must do for women's sake. What else can women ask God for? Maybe God had felt obliged to give women all these bonuses merely for bearing men on top of bearing babies. My new discovery about God's favouritism toward women kept me amused as I strolled toward home. Maybe my impotency today was merely a divine punishment for my recent whining and blaming God for making lust so potent. *So, now, be impotent, you ungrateful creature!* But, actually, this impotency was merely another side, or continuation of, the same topic: Our obsession for sex and helplessness to conquer it easily or at all. Impotency was just further proof of God's guilt. Period.

At last, as I approached my Kakh residence, I pondered the gloomy thought of doing some studying, for God's sake. For Her sake! I was losing track of everything happening at school. Every day in recent weeks, I'd just walked in and out of the school like going to a social club only to visit my comrades. I'd lost my senses about the real purpose of people going to school.

3

At home, I found a note from Grandma saying she wouldn't be back for a few days. This was really bizarre! It was definitely a trap. She'd probably planned to arrive home to catch me with some girls. Good! If she'd played such a stunt, she needed a good lesson. She deserved a major shock and a big lesson about me. Now suddenly I had too many motives to cheer myself up and hopefully irritate Grandma in the process as well. This once—this unprecedented once—that I'd really decided to act smart a bit, Grandma had to spoil everything by daring me. Thanks to her, now I had to drop my plan to study all night. Instead, I called Goli, the girl I'd dated a few times. A man answered the phone and I hung up. I called again after five minutes and she answered herself. I asked her to join me for ice cream near her house. She agreed to meet me in thirty minutes.

I ate an apple and got out of the house again. I walked to the ice-cream parlour and Goli showed up on time. We sat there and talked about a lot of stuff and our career plans. What goddamn career plans, as far as I was concerned? I played along with her anyway, lying and hoping she believed me. She was an excellent student even though she was really pretty. I asked her how she could do it. She was surprised I couldn't concentrate on two things together—that is, social life and school. I tried to explain it to her but she didn't get it. Girls are different about these kinds of stuff, too. They can focus on a million things at one time. But boys are always distracted, especially when sexual fantasies walk all over their horny brains, which is about eighty-nine percent of the time. Anyhow, Goli was a nice gal and I really liked her. If I hadn't been busy with older women, I would've only focused on her. She had it all: very mature, smart, and liberal; pretty and sexy too. Who could ask for anything more? Never mind stupid Kian.

After ice cream and some ridiculous arguments about our imaginary careers, we walked toward my Kakh residence, which was in the same direction of her house partly. She'd come to my room a couple of times before, so maybe she was as horny as I'd become just by looking at her. Near my city residence, I asked her to come in for a glass of water and she nodded. We shared a bottle of Jamal's beers instead, which were quite big in Iran. Then we went to my room to fool around. She asked me why I didn't call her more and whether I dated other girls. I swore she was the only girl I dated. Since she hadn't asked me about any other woman, I hadn't lied, I reckoned. She asked what was stopping me from studying then, since I wasn't spending much time with her, either. I told her I didn't like living at home with my parents, but living almost alone in this place wasn't fun, either. She bought my lame excuses and felt sorry for me. So she let me take off her clothes under the sheets and we had sex for two hours without intercourse. My erection was perfect without any sign of the rebellion that had ruined my afternoon with Mina. My moody manhood! Another silly mystery.

Maybe my pussyless sex with girls over the years had become another psychological cause of my 'pussy apprehension'?! The next day I called Mina at noon, but I was nervous again like the first time I was calling her to ask for a date. The first thing I was really dying to tell her was the good news about the health of my manhood, as could be testified by Goli. I really wished to present a perfect proof to her. I wished I'd gotten a certificate from Goli to show Mina. But mentioning Goli would've been stupid—my damn sense of *practicality!* Anyway, I just swallowed my pride and kept my mouth shut. She gave me the green light for my visit at her house after some hesitation and my persistence. Her fishy reluctance to meet felt humiliating, as if she'd lost her faith in my viability as a lover or had a lot of sex last night already. Or maybe she was a psychic, after all, predicting what was in store for us!

I'm ashamed to explain the details of my meeting with Mina that afternoon while that clown tried its best to be funny again. It made Mina laugh a lot though. Our romance turned into a circus. Yet our moods got even worse than the day before, despite all the hysterical laughter. I wanted to go downstairs to find a big knife and cut the darn thing. I had to prove who the master was! But, of course, the maid would've found me, naked. So I asked Mina to go get their meat cleaver. She giggled more and caressed my face. That caressing hurt me more than a hundred insults and two hundred lashes. At last, she broke her torturous silence.

"Maybe you're shy with all this *daylight*?" she said giddily.

"Maybe… Maybe I'm a vampire," I replied with gratitude.

I appreciated her efforts to offer a decent excuse for my funny impotence, although her sympathy felt quite humiliating and comical. 'Daylight' as an excuse was laughable. It was actually insulting, and I felt so disgraced, I had to try so hard to keep my mouth shut about my previous night's amazing time with Goli. Again, I managed to stay practical and contain my angry ego. Yet, my ability to control my ego proved my growing maturity. That was the only positive point I salvaged from that frustrating situation! I didn't mention my other great theories, either, while thinking that her theory might hold water, after all. *My previous night's fantastic success had been at night, after all, hadn't it?!*

"Listen… Hassan is going to Europe for one week for a medical conference," she said. "Come back one of those nights. I'll send the kids to my parents and we can have the whole house to ourselves. We can try in the darkness of the bedroom and *see what happens*."

'See what happens,' sounded sarcastic to me again, despite her attempt to be kind. Maybe I was oversensitive those days, more than my usual crabbiness. Was she teasing my manhood?

"Okay. Let's see what happens in the dark," I said with a smirk and reservation about darkness fooling that stubborn *devil*.

I thought I should make up for all the hardship I'd given Mina recently, especially if she'd been counting on a major climax in my able hands and youthful energy. Had she expected me to give her a series of orgasms ten folds more sensational than what Dr. Afzali had ever managed to give her? Probably yes! So, instead, I told her that I loved her and kissed her all over a million times. I wondered whether my vision of Mina begging Dr. Afzali for sex last night had come true. The way she seemed so relaxed and playful, compared to her tension the day before, felt like the right clues about my psychic power and predictions. She laughed a lot and mocked my manhood rather civilly with plenty of passion.

However, the more relaxed she appeared, the more my sense of guilt and pain grew. In return, I blamed God for everything. *Would I become only a means of enriching Dr. Afzali's sex life with his beloved wife?* I pondered pitifully. Still, I tried to keep my composure, while hating my recent afternoon transformations into such a pathetic wuss, especially after my last night's proud parade around Goli. All along, I just kept telling Mina I really loved her! Yet, she didn't look convinced. When I left, I felt more miserable than the day before, since our love affair now felt shaky as well, the way she appeared agitated and out of love so suddenly, despite her relaxed humour. I felt she now doubted my love or the value of love without sex. During our entire sexless courting, she'd tried hard to convince me love was more precious without sex. And now she'd swiftly changed her position: That without sex, love meant shit. I'd arrived at the same conclusion myself since yesterday; after having been brainwashed by Mina to believe otherwise all along. Anyway, I couldn't blame her new wisdom and philosophy about love and sex. The only problem was that I'd suspected this crucial fact long time ago, while she'd only convinced me that I'd been wrong. I was dying to throw it in her face: "I told you so." But I didn't have the guts to annoy her any more than what I'd already managed in recent days.

Again, all these sexual humiliations only boosted my growing knack for blaming God for many new things, especially this latest topic about lust. I bet He knew love meant shit without sex!—just as a basic original design of His.

4

For five days, Mina and I talked only on the phone rather timidly. We both needed time to recuperate. Maybe I was a vampire, after all! At last, she invited me to her house one night after Dr. Afzali left for a medical conference. She asked me to arrive around seven and ring the bell because nobody else would be home. When she opened the door, she had a shy grin on her face.

"Your mother has just dropped by, too," Mina whispered.

I was startled. She descended the four stairs leading to the main hall, while I followed her in shock and relative terror. My mind got busy sorting out a lot of questions and tactics. What the heck was Narges doing there and how could I look into her eyes? How should I explain myself? On the other hand, I couldn't just leave since it would've appeared even more bizarre. It would've surely proved some kind of hanky-panky between Mina and me. Besides, I felt Mina had already told her about expecting me—to prepare Narges for my arrival. For Mina's sake at least, I had to play along with her plan. Maybe she'd also given Narges a valid reason for my visit. I entered and said *"Salam."* Narges gauged me calmly and answered: *"Salam!"* The look on her face was too complex to explain. It showed subtle horror and confusion among many other feelings she was striving to hide.

This episode should be considered the most awkward scene, and maybe experience, in my life. I put my couple of books and a notebook on the table in the hall and sat across from Narges. We stared at each other for five seconds before I flinched. Mina talked with great energy like nothing was out of the ordinary. Narges responded to her best friend equally loud, in their normal manner, too. Their behaviour felt bizarre all along. Both of them were crazy, I thought. Yet, I was adjusting to the situation as well. I made up my mind not to give in. Maybe Narges was waiting for me to explain my reason for being there. At the very least, maybe she expected me to leave now that the conspiracy was uncovered. She looked a little surprised, but not totally traumatized by my presence, as if she'd had some suspicions all along. I wished I knew if she'd dropped by with a plan to catch me in action.

Anyway, I proved to be more stubborn and shameless than Narges had imagined. I just sat there like waiting for my turn to get Mina's attention. If Mina was her best friend, she was my best beloved! Which one was dearer to Mina? Besides, I'd planned for that evening with Mina for five days and I wasn't about to leave without testing my luck again, once Narges left us alone and the daylight died completely. It was supposed to be a special night for us, on the mattress in total darkness. I was determined to break the spell and have sex with my darling Mina after years of anticipation and then facing so much humiliation in recent days. What stronger incentive is there in the world?

I got up, strolled across the room, and looked out the window into the street. Narges's car was parked on the other side of the road. But I'd been too preoccupied to notice it when I'd walked toward Mina's house. Of course, I had no reason to look around the streets for her car, although I made a mental note to do just that in the future. I turned away from the window and paced the room like an impatient father waiting for the birth of his first child. I almost lit a cigarette too, but resisted the temptation.

I had no idea why I was pacing the room, nor was I conscious of it absolutely. It was only a narcissistic reaction, perhaps trying to show off my rights, calm, and determination! It certainly had nothing to do with impatience, anyway. In fact, the whole time, after the first shock of seeing Narges, I was ridiculously cool. I was amazed of my arrogance compared with five years earlier when I would've been mortified facing Narges. The other reason for my pacing the room was probably my boredom. I was tired of sitting still for so long like being back in one of Narges's classes in grades one and two. Why in the hell wouldn't the bell ring and Narges buzz off?

Mina ordered me to sit down with a nervous tone. She'd probably found my pacing annoying; I did so myself right away when I thought about it. I went back to my seat behind the table on the opposite side of Narges. Narges peeped at Mina intently, rather surprised by her tone of voice and my swift obedience. I bet she missed all the control she used to have over me before I'd found my Kakh residence. *And now Mina has all the power over my deranged son.*

I opened my chemistry book and gazed at formulas blankly. I wondered if Mina's order had an ulterior motive. Maybe she'd thought I was about to leave and thus ruin her plans for a magical evening with me. I bet she'd also considered my pacing the room rude and a sign of my impatience for Narges's presence. I wished I could clarify for both of them that I was cool and I wasn't going anywhere. Let us all wait and see what happens and who wins in the end! I peeped at Narges when she asked Mina, in a sarcastic tone, when Dr. Afzali would return and where the kids were. But suddenly, for whatever bizarre reason, Genghis' image jumped in front of me. I'd stared at that picture so intensely in elementary school that all its details were engraved in my brain. The image moved around the room awhile and glared at us, as if about to decapitate us all. His resemblance to Narges was just stunning.

For another long, excruciating hour, the three of us played the waiting contest like three stubborn poker players with empty hands. Everybody was waiting for the next person to fold his or her hand and end this torturous game. At last, Narges gave up and left. She didn't even ask me if I wished to go home with her or needed a ride to some place. She merely said goodbye to us, in a sarcastic tone again, and left. All this time, I'd not spoken more than ten words. I'd only said yes or no to their silly questions and thanked Mina for bringing me tea. I'd just sat there with a serious look, as if waiting for an important business that required Mina's undivided attention in private; maybe more like waiting in a busy whorehouse for one's turn. I imagined Narges was mostly jealous for not having a young lover as well, the way Mina did. Mina's attitude was also odd in the way she seemed to take my presence and silence as a normal state of affairs with no need to ask me any question or explain anything to Narges. Actually, her attitude was quite familiar, similar to the way she'd always introduced me to her friends in Café Naderi so casually.

"Why did she come here?" I asked Mina after Narges left.

"I don't know… Sometimes she simply drops by."

"Does she know about us?"

"I don't know!"

"What do you mean? Have you told her anything? Has she hinted about anything?"

"No. Of course not! Are you crazy?" Mina shrieked.

"But this whole damn incident was weird, wasn't it?"

"More than weird, I'll say. I thought you'll give her a reason for coming here to make it look like something natural. But you just sat there or paced the room like you were waiting for her to leave. That's probably why she left earlier than usual."

"I thought you'd told her something already. I didn't want to tell a different story and raise her suspicions."

"Well. I don't know what she thinks," Mina said with a sigh.

"Do you care?" I asked.

"Well… Maybe I should…?"

"You shouldn't. I don't care either. I'm a grownup man. Maybe we should start telling people we're going to marry."

"You're such a joker. But I liked how you behaved so cool."

"You're so cool yourself. Risks you take just blow my mind."

Mina laughed and went upstairs to bring the bottle of whisky.

"You can stay here tonight if you like."

"So the kids are spending the night with their grandparents?"

"Yes, I told them I'll be out until late."

5

Mina brought two glasses with ice from the kitchen. She poured whisky into the glasses and then went to the kitchen to bring the bottle of soda. She poured soda on top of the whisky, put the cap back on, and returned it to the fridge. On her way back, she grabbed a bowl of pistachios from the kitchen counter and put it on the table between us. Then she reeled back to bring a plate for pistachio shells. She was making me dizzy walking so much back and forth, like a nervous teacher. I didn't understand why she had to return the bottle of soda to the fridge and then go fetch it again ten minutes later. But I let it go.

"Cheers, my darling," she said, sitting next to me at last.

"Cheers, my brave beloved," I said and we sipped our drinks before I leaned and kissed her lips with great passion. I felt she was happy despite our weird encounter with Narges.

"Do you have cigarettes?" she asked.

"Yes." I took the pack of Winston out of my pocket and we each took a cigarette.

She went to the kitchen again and brought an ashtray this time. I lit our cigarettes with my golden Dunhill lighter, put it on top of the Winston pack, and admired it from the corner of my eye. I could never quit smoking as long as I had this beautiful lighter. I couldn't give it away or drop it in a drawer in my room, either, since it was her present and it was gold, too. I was stuck. Of course, I was dying to know whether it was totally gold or only gold-plated. It just felt imperative to know for some odd reason! Mina had mentioned it was gold, yet I couldn't stop wondering. I didn't dare go check it out, either, just in case it wasn't pure gold. The dilemma of confronting Mina about it, or not, would kill me. Meanwhile, not knowing was nerve-racking. A lighter is a daft present to give to your lover, especially a gold one, I tell you. Maybe I felt that way in that moment because I was mad at Mina those days for my own impotence!

I grabbed her hand and caressed it tenderly. Then I kissed her white beautiful fingers one by one. They were so enticing, as were her feet, toes, eyes, lips and hair. Her red lipstick matched the colour of her nail polish on her fingers and toes. I was just having a ball, enjoying all that red hue on many fast moving parts of her body, which made her look so sexy, but also reminded me of the gypsy women and her knack for red. We just sat there, drank whisky, smoked cigarettes, ate chips and nuts, and chatted for an hour about many scenes from the movies we'd been seeing together. Then, we nibbled on tasty sandwiches she'd prepared for us along with more whisky.

As we got drunk, we even tried to explain the meaning of love by analyzing many romantic tales in books and movies. Love was a new experience for both of us. And yet we felt like two experts on the matter. She, in particular, sounded like a love guru. She was thrilled for being in love at last like she'd discovered it in me after a long painful search. Her romantic expressions sounded odd, though, as if she'd forgotten our disastrous sexual episodes a few days earlier and her frustration. Was she changing her mind again about the importance of sex? Oh God, I hoped not! *Why are women so mysterious and erratic to figure out?* Anyway, I decided to avoid negative conclusions and stressing out myself again. We agreed on many life issues, too, aside from romance. Especially, it was precious to learn she wasn't materialistic at all —again like a gypsy—despite her determination to compete in aristocratic settings.

That night in particular, Mina looked vulnerable, judging by the way she talked with such a soft, sincere voice. Like she was going to commit suicide the next day. Her casual hints revealed her marriage to Dr. Afzali had been mostly based on customs and family decisions and not her love for the rich doctor, who was seventeen years older than her. She believed she was my first love and I never corrected her. The idea of bringing me such a powerful experience gave her some kind of thrill. Her words and facial expressions showed she was really enjoying the romance she'd created for both of us. Our first taste of true love.

I wanted to believe her. I wished to believe our love was the real thing. But my doubts in some moments prevailed when I remembered the rumours about Mina and Nosrat, the chef's son. I was dying to ask her to explain her feelings for him and whether the rumours had any basis. I really did. Was I really her first and only love? I also felt mad when I imagined Dr. Afzali making love to her, to my beloved, the person I declared love to so often from the bottom of my heart. How much longer could I bear this? How much longer should I allow this? How could she allow it? How could she make love to somebody else if she really loved me? But I knew better. I was wise enough for my age despite my random madness. So I kept all my questions to myself. Nor did I care to explain my infatuation for the gypsy and Mehri and Goli. She didn't need to know about my furtive passions, if they could be considered love.

Around eleven p.m. she suggested we go to bed. I said okay with terror. She asked me if I liked to take a bath with her. I said yes with tons of conflicting imaginations. She ran the water into the tub as we undressed with fantastic hopes. Our moods had built up smoothly all evening. The whisky had made us relax. I had a great erection before the tub was ready for us. So I took one of the big towels from the rack and spread it in the middle of the bathroom. There was no time for thinking. We lied on the towel, and, to my astonishment, I could make love to her without any trouble. Oh, God. The black hole finally sucked and killed me with its amazing heat. She moaned and howled, and so did I, from both ecstasy and relief after two weeks of guilt. Now, I really, really loved her. I said it out loud a hundred times and she repeated my words eagerly. I begged her to marry me. Please... please. She said okay, okay. What a wonderful world.

We washed each other in the tub. Then we got out, stood in the middle of the bathroom holding our towels, yet all the kissing and licking made us only wetter. At last, we managed to go to bed. I asked her to let me sleep on the side she slept every night. She understood my paranoia and said she'd changed the sheets that very morning. As she turned off the lights, the moonlight poured in from the centre of the half-closed curtains. I pushed the blanket away to explore her body and I was aroused again. I kissed her flesh from forehead to toes. Soon I was making love to her again like there was no chance of getting another erection after tonight. We growled again even louder this time in the quiet of the house. At last, we kissed goodnight like husband and wife. I imagined how magical it would be doing this every night. Like husband and wife. I was so happy. I was a real man, at last.

"Remember, you promised to marry me," I whispered.

"Just imagine we're married now. What's the difference?" Mina murmured.

"The difference is not having to sneak around to see you."

"This is more fun and more natural than being married, I can tell you that. Take my word for it," Mina said.

"It's more natural this way? How can you say this?"

"Of course it's more natural. What is marriage?"

"I love you, Mina. I really do. I want to make love to you every night."

"We will…"

"How? How can I make love to you every night from my grandparents' house? It's still not that long!"

Mina burst into laughter. "It will be soon. Let's sleep now. You have to go to school in the morning, darling."

"Okay. Goodbye again," I said, trying to be romantic.

"Goodbye again, my darling," she whispered. "Do you have your books for tomorrow? Have you done your homework?"

"Yes, mommy. Goodbye again." *What homework!?*

6

My love for Mina grew five times faster every single minute after that night. I saw Goli too, since I liked her, but my heart belonged to Mina. Mina and I met in Café Naderi and went to the movies and other places as usual. We made love in her house once a week at least, usually during day light, while I mocked her old theory about the cause of my initial impotency. We touched each other at the Club and parties, too, and in the car when Father drove us to those places. We kissed anytime we found each other in a secluded corner. People were used to my frequent escapes to dark places to hide my smoking habit. Everybody, including my parents, knew about my smoking, but I still couldn't bring myself to smoke in front of them. Yet I sipped Mina's whisky and took a puff from her cigarette in the crowd sometimes. We only smirked when people noticed our sneaky deeds. I believed I was paving my way for the day I'd come out of the closet, drink and smoke openly, *and maybe even announce our marriage!* And Mina, she probably pretended to be only helping a naive enthusiast like me get a taste of the grownups' mannerism. Yet, she seemed to be having fun with me in the public as well, in her own way. I tried to hide my rising arrogance and pretended to be as shy as I'd been in the older times, mainly for Dr. Afzali's benefit. Thank God, it seemed to be working. He probably still saw me as a helpless child abused by women, including Mina, just for fun. But I often also thought he was an idiot, after all, for not taking me seriously still. All along, those women's sly, probing stares continued to baffle me. Now, I believed even Narges realized the gravity of my affair with Mina. She looked cool about it, while our attitudes felt bizarre more than ever, now with our rivalry for Mina's affection, on top of our old competition to bug each other. Actually, her friendship with Mina was growing as fast as my love for Mina was. Those weird grownups!

I wasn't motivated about school at all. All along Goli had tried to put some sense into my head. She even offered to tutor me, but I refused. When Mina realized the mess I was in, however, she gave me an ultimatum. She was so angry and serious. She told me if I failed even one subject, she'd drop me like an old sock. I believed her and somehow learned to focus a little more. Goli came over and helped me, too. So, I passed all the subjects with good grades. I knew I could do a good job if only I got my mind into it. Mina's ultimatum did it and I finished grade eleven. I was really looking forward to my last year at high school and starting my real life. And hopefully marrying Mina right after graduation or at most within a week.

7

Grandpa had a stroke in the summer of 1973 and passed away. For over five weeks, we engaged in various memorial services for him. We didn't go to the Club or other festivities, where our friends continued dancing their nights away without us. They attended the memorial services, too. The women, however, looked like a bunch of strangers without their regular makeup. I saw their real faces for the first time. Most of those pretty women looked quite ordinary without makeup. Some looked utterly ugly and mean, indeed—like real cockroaches, in fact! I hadn't seen so many lifeless eyes in one place in one day. It was another major eye-opener for me to witness how so many women had been painting themselves into pretty dolls with some decent characters. But not Mina and Mehri. They looked even more gorgeous in my eyes without makeup. Grandma cried her heart out and talked lots of nonsense quite consciously. She was trying hard to play the traditional role of a mourning widow. She kept chanting, "What am I gonna do without him? Why should I live without him?" Her attitude really sucked, I tell you. I hated her guts for talking like an idiot. And for being so foolishly phony. As though nobody recalled her disregard for Grandpa all those years. The sound of her monotonous moaning was driving me nuts. What a hypocrite Muslim! A few times, I was really tempted to shout, "What the heck are you talking about, old woman? When was the last time you talked with the poor man. When was the last time you showed him a little affection and respect?"

She just chanted the same words with plenty of moaning like a taped message every fifteen minutes or so when another person came around to offer his or her condolences. Especially, I went berserk imagining Narges playing the same charade and saying the same words if Father died. I realized I'd just have to kill her on the spot with my bare hands if I ever had to witness such a travesty. I wouldn't probably have the patience to go find Father's handgun. In my opinion, the only two individuals who were truly sorry for Grandpa's death were Father and Uncle Jamal. They cried a lot.

Uncle Jamal stayed two weeks, so we talked a lot about many things. I even confessed to my love for a different older woman, now, without mentioning her name and he didn't care to know, anyway. He wasn't thrilled with my 'childish sentimentality,' as he put it, but he looked happier when I told him about Goli. She came by one evening during Grandpa's main memorial service. Some of my friends came over as well. Mina and other women gauged Goli curiously and maybe jealously, but I introduced her only to Uncle Jamal. He liked Goli quickly and ordered me to be nice to her. I promised to do my goddamn best, while stressing I loved the older woman much more. He finally seemed okay with that as long as I kept Goli. But overall, he looked cynical about my passion for old women, although he did it a lot himself.

"Is she here today?" Jamal asked me, as if planning to go kick that old bitch's ass out of my life.

"No...," I lied.

Once Jamal suggested we go for a walk after getting fed up with the mourners, especially Grandma, pretending to be sad at the great loss of Grandpa. I was bored myself being in that crowd for so long, too, but I had to stick around every day at least out of respect for Father. Anyway, we sneaked out to get some fresh air.

"Have you now cooled down about your parents' wedding circumstances?" Jamal asked.

"In what way?" I asked with surprise.

"Well, I noticed your frustration when hearing the story."

"You mean, getting angry with Narges?"

"Yes... But as I said last time, she's a good woman in some respects."

"In some respects..."

"You won't tell the story to anybody, right?"

"Right. When I promise you something, I keep it."

"But you may break your promises to others?"

"Of course... That's what you always do yourself."

Jamal burst into his contagious laughter. "Anyway, I'm only worried about my words causing unnecessary trouble around your family. Narges seems mad at me these days."

"I haven't said anything to her. I won't mention our discussion to anybody. But I have a couple of other questions."

"Still more questions...," Jamal blasted. "Like what?"

"First of all, I want to know why Narges hasn't been nice to me. What does she have against me?"

"You're asking more personal questions every time."

"Because I've lived with these sad dilemmas every day."

"I'll tell you, but you must promise again not to repeat my words to anybody, not even your lovers."

"I promise."

"In the first place neither of your parents wanted children. They took all the precautions, but then you were conceived by accident, I guess. That was the first blow to her."

"No wonder I feel like a wreck so often then…"

"Yeah, you've been a sneaky, persistent thing from the start," Jamal said with a chuckle.

"Did Father tell you these things too?"

"Some of it, but I also saw some stuff myself."

"Father looks all right about my being around."

"Of course, he was happy when you were born. But Narges… Well… She didn't want children, especially a boy."

"Oh…?"

"Yes. She was terribly disappointed when you appeared. She cried for months and refused to breastfeed you. When she started to accept you somewhat, one year later, she dressed you like a girl and let your hair grow long until you were three years old."

"Oh, boy… She's always been a psycho!" I blurted.

"That's why your father hid most of your childhood pictures. He couldn't fight with her all the time, so he compromised in many ways. When Dadash Jalal took you to the barber and made you look like a boy, she went ballistic. She was mad with both of you for a long time."

"I see… She's surely been crazy. Why hasn't Father divorced her all these years? That's my next question."

"First, he felt indebted to Mr. Taibi. And then, after you were born, he was trying to protect you and give you a stable home."

"Why indebted to Mr. Taibi?"

"The situation with your grandpa's shipment went nowhere. So when your father graduated from university, Mr. Taibi insisted on lending him a substantial amount of money to invest in real estate. He also introduced your father to many influential people who helped him all those years to get where he is now. He's rich and a major government official all thanks to Mr. Taibi's initial assistance and influence."

"When did Mr. Taibi die?"

"Six years after your parents married. Your dad had repaid his loans, but could never forget owing his success to him."

"So how did Ozra Banu lose all of Mr. Taibi's wealth?"

"She's always been an irresponsible person. She took some lovers who swindled her. They forced her to throw exotic parties every night and they gambled with her until they sucked the last dinar out of her. Then all those lovers and friends vanished. They left her alone to rot in misery."

"Who were these people?"

"Some were old family friends and some were among the group that Mr. Hariri invited to his parties. She competed with Hariri for many years in the kind of fancy parties they threw for their sleazy friends."

I was happy that many of the old mysteries were solved, and that most of them had been answered by Uncle Jamal alone. Still, instead of cooling down, I was eager to know about the details of some of these stories, especially about Ozra Banu and her love stories. They must've been funny and depressing at the same time. Narges and Father had probably suffered witnessing the daily demise of Ozra Banu, but remained helpless to do anything about it. How horrible it must have been for Narges in particular.

CHAPTER FOURTEEN
An Alley Named Agony

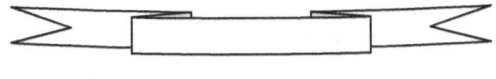

1

In the latter part of 1973, Mina wasn't cheery like usual. She was quieter and met her friends less often, too. She looked pale and tired. However, I liked her this way even more, because she appeared more serious and pensive, like me. Best of all, she now looked too mysterious pleasantly! She had more time for me, too. Our relationship felt more stable and progressing fast in the right direction. I met her four times a week on average and we had sex on two of those occasions. When I questioned her mood, she only blamed Hassan, who was too grouchy according to Mina. He also accused her of infidelity. How could I blame either of them? The way this Hassan—Dr. Afzali—peeped at me felt hostile, too. I wondered why! He had no reason to suspect me! Had he found some evidences? Were my regular cheek-to-cheek dancing with Mina, sipping her drinks, and taking a puff from her cigarettes enough clues? How should I know where to draw the lines? So I'd left it to Mina to do it for us, while I wrestled with many other endless thoughts of my own. Had Hassan possibly found out that I visited Mina in his own house—his sacred sanctuary—some afternoons? Maybe he was wondering how to confront a child for screwing his wife! How would people and legal system react to his hitting a tiny boy, no matter how naughty the child might've been?! What a sneaky, nasty child, in fact! Anyway, I still liked to think that my affair with Mina was a fair retaliation for his act of humiliating me in front of Mina and my parents the night he'd asked me to return his dagger. The only question was how many times I should sleep with Mina to call it even. I'd come up with a round fair estimate of one thousand. After that, I had to marry her. My rough estimates also indicated it'd be right about the day I'd graduate high school. Just another great coincidence—or maybe even a sacred sign!

Overall, I didn't like a bit the way Hassan glared at me with a hint of suspicion. Sometimes the thought of being killed with the same dagger I'd hidden for him for three months made me shiver. I'd played a lot with that dagger. I missed it a lot and wished to see it again, but not in my heart. It had helped me threaten the neighbourhood kids. Now it could become the device of my own death. What if Hassan killed Mina? How could I live without her? I'd have to avenge Mina and kill him, I supposed. I'd kill him with Father's handgun, no doubt. But, my revenge wouldn't solve my problem. What would become of me without Mina? I should kill myself, too, to join her in heaven immediately. Mina and I weren't any less devoted to each other than Romeo and Juliet had been. So I must die for Mina, too, one way or another.

Mina's state of mind affected my plans, of course. Actually, the situation imposed a kind of emergency on my naïve mind to rescue her from the mess she was trapped in. As a man, as her lover, I felt responsible for her welfare. I felt guilty about the way Hassan treated her. I was the one causing her the ongoing agony of infidelity, which I presumed would depress even a person as cool as Mina.

But my own life was also in shambles. I had severe doubts about my life and future. I couldn't focus on school at all and my situation had gotten worse than ever before. The school's new policy to accept the tuition in two instalments had given me the chance of keeping half of the money Father gave me to pay my tuition. I used the money on my extravagant lifestyle and all the activities I shared with Mina and my friends, including gambling. We drank alcohol and played poker or billiards when I wasn't with Mina or sleeping. After asking me a few times to bring the balance of the tuition, the administration expelled me. They said to come back only with the money, but I had no guts to tell Father what I'd done. I couldn't tell him I hadn't been attending school for the last three months. Besides, I didn't like going to school, anyway! I didn't even know what topics students were studying in grade twelve. I didn't dare discuss the matter with Mina, either, let alone ask her for a loan. So, all I could do was to blame the school's sudden flexibility, with childish humour, in my confused head. Their idiotic new scheme had fooled me to keep the money and now I had to pay a big price for my—any curious child's— natural enthusiasm to test the new policy.

I was so close to graduating from high school and starting an independent life if only I could control my demented temptations. Some days, I even admitted to my insanity myself, for ruining my life and future for no goddamn reason other than a messed-up mind wasted on love. But I couldn't help it. I gauged my options: Dropping out for good and looking for a job, or repeating grade twelve. I kept all these secrets to myself, of course. Mina was clueless about my expulsion or social life, let alone my gambling and playing billiards every morning. Many afternoons, I found refuge in her arms, though. Every time we met, especially on those occasions when we embraced each other's naked body and made love, my nerves calmed down. Her embrace was my only source of relief, which I needed on a regular basis to keep my madness in check. She couldn't even imagine I could be such a reckless idiot about my education, although she never asked me how I could skip school so many afternoons to be with her. She had no idea about my agonizing thoughts and feelings behind my romantic words, either. She was sunk in her own mysterious world, anyway. But she was my angel—a sexy angel unaware of her beloved's devilish acts and I had to keep it that way. She had enough headaches to sort out already.

On top of all these pressures, I had to keep a straight face and hide my problems from Father, too, especially the expulsion. So I kept him engaged in my life instead of avoiding him. I tried to respond to his encouragements to share my thoughts with him. He always tried to be an open-minded and liberal father, and I loved him for that. In fact, as I'd matured and developed some moderate opinions, he and I had found more topics to discuss. But at that critical point in my life, in particular, I had to engage him in any kind of conversation to minimize his touchy questions regarding school and my career plans. I had to show lots more interest in social issues, the economy, politics, his business and job, or other topics, as long as I could occupy his mind whenever we were together. I was running out of topics when I recalled my old curiosity. Other than being a good subject to discuss, maybe Father could actually help me find the answer, too. So, one day on our way home in his car, I asked him:

"Where do you think those colourful pictures of ancient kings and conquerors in history books have come from?"

"I don't know. Why?" Father asked.

"I'm just curious. None of them has the painter's name or a date on them. So how can we be certain they're even real?"

Father turned around with a smirk and then looked ahead on the road again. "Why is it so important to know how those people looked?"

"It's just good to know whether those pictures are real or only someone's imagination, especially this Genghis Khan's. I like to know where they found his picture," I replied.

"They probably got it from some archives or a museum."

"Did they have archives and museums those times to keep all these collections for centuries, especially with all the wars and destructions our ancestors were enjoying?"

"I honestly don't know," Father replied with a bit of distress, maybe even pondering his ignorance about such critical points related to our history, not to mention the chance for an ongoing fraud.

"How can we find out?" I asked, mainly trying to keep our conversation going, which had now led to this silly question. I felt he, too, like my teachers, was getting tired of my silly questions and might send me to the principal's office any minute. *Just get out of the car,* he'd say, stopping at the curb. However, I was so desperate to keep Father's mind off main issues somehow.

"Probably the book publishers know. If you get their names, I'd get someone to check it out... if it's really important!"

"I can find my old textbooks and get the publishers' names if you think it is possible to sort this out," I replied eagerly, although I wondered about my endless naughtiness, too. Was it admirable or merely deplorable?

"We can always try. You're really serious, ha?"

"Yeah... At least I want to know who painted this Genghis Khan's picture."

"Why are you picking on this rotten Genghis Khan?"

"Because his picture in some books looks a lot like Narges," I replied.

Father burst into laughter, almost losing the control of the car.

"Show me the picture when you find it," he said.

2

I found the old history textbook the same evening and showed Genghis' picture to Father in his study. He nodded a few times while staring at the picture and laughing his heart out rather silly. Narges heard him and came over with tension to see what was amusing us. Father closed the book and only stared at her, as though appraising her with a new perspective all of a sudden. She scrammed with disgust after glaring at us awhile. Father agreed with me about the resemblance, thus appeared even a bit more curious and determined himself to help me. He promised to get someone to talk to the publisher and find out where the picture had come from. I was thrilled that this mystery might be solved soon, too. One less worry in my life!

Father and I agreed on so many issues despite our different political opinions. As I mentioned before, he'd turned into a pure capitalist and a full-fledged advocate of the United States. I leaned more toward Marxism personally at least as far as human values were concerned—not quite related to my high compassion towards people, but more so the result of feeling the need to keep a leash on all kinds of humans' natural defects, including greed and arrogance. I never brought up our political differences with Father, especially his lifestyle that appeared a catastrophic, sad example of the Western culture to me. In the past, he'd been the one forcing conversations in order to get me out of my shell. But now I was the one asking him for advice on a regular basis, just to keep his mouth shut about touchy topics such as education, career plans, or personal matters, even though he often tried to raise those very same subjects. Still, he seemed pleased with my sudden enthusiasm to share my feelings and thoughts with him. I also worried about my candid attitude and sudden sociability soon raising his curiosity about something fishy happening around me or simply getting tired of my nonsensical queries. For now, however, he looked happy with his suddenly talkative son and I felt safe.

If you like to know, with Narges the situation was too easy. We still hardly spoke or discussed any personal issues. Yet, she probably knew a lot about my secrets. For one thing, her contacts with the women in the Club gave her some access to my love life. She knew I smoked and drank. I suspected she'd already called my school and learned about my expulsion. Yet, out of spite for Father, who had let me live in two residences, she kept silent. The reason, you might ask. She didn't want to correct the situation. She wanted to wait long enough until my demise was complete. Irreversible! Until I flunked. Until I ruined my life for a woman. Until Father's stupidity for trusting me was proven. That would give her an opportunity to double her pleasure: To scold the father and son together and then enjoy the fall of their friendship, too. Anyway, Narges and I had long quit interfering in each other's affairs. And I didn't care much about her plans to destroy me, either.

Only once did I find it necessary to raise a touchy topic with Father, even though I knew it could push me into some slippery grounds. It could lead to the kind of discussions I'd been trying to avoid all along. But I had to address this topic, as it felt necessary that Mina and I did something about our future life together. The present situation was too inconvenient for both of us. I was losing control of my life altogether. And she was probably fed up with Hassan's silly accusations. So, I decided to test Father's leniency for my getting married soon. I was hoping to see him dancing in my wedding instead of facing his anger and rejection. After a long debate about life and marriage, I offered my final position.

"I'm a kind of person who must get married young, *too*," I said in a serious tone and then whispered, "like yourself."

"Why? What kind of a person is that?" he asked.

"I can focus better on my life and career if I'm not engaged in silly affairs that go nowhere." I almost said *like yourself* again, bur fortunately stopped my tongue in time.

"But do you know how difficult it is to have a family?"

"I'll get used to it."

"Why do you want to get used to silly things. Get used to good stuff instead. What's the rush anyway? You haven't even gone to university."

"University? What's the point? Most people go to university, study something, and then choose a different profession." Again, I almost said, 'like yourself,' but luckily kept my mouth shut. "That's crazy, don't you think?"

"No, I don't think… Education always gives you a higher platform to start your career. Otherwise, you start very low. Unless you're lucky, you'll always remain a far distance behind the ones who go to university."

"Like yourself, ha?" I couldn't stop myself this time. "You were merely lucky then?"

"Yes… in a way. Besides, I have big plans for you in politics."

"I hate politics," I said and then added with glee after a pause. "Unlike yourself."

"But we need smart people to run this country. Why do you want to get entangled in marriage and its troubles when you must be concentrating on education and career? You could be a cabinet minister someday, I promise."

"A minister? I don't care about being a minister in a cabinet, commode, or church..." I tried to be funny to hide my rising frustration with his resistance and silly suggestions.

"Stop being a clown...You and I should spend some time soon to review your plans for your future."

"Review my plans for future? What about my future?"

"For example, we must decide what you'd like to study at university. Do you want to become an engineer, a doctor, an economist, or what?"

"Even if I go to university, which is very unlikely, I'd like to study psychology."

"Psychology? Why psychology? We don't have a minister of psychology in this country. As far as I know, no psychologist has ever gotten a high government position in any country."

"But that's not the point. Not everybody should aim to be a minister or a member of parliament."

"What's the point then? Who's gonna help this country then?" he asked me, frustrated.

"The point is that I'd prefer to study in a field I like, and that is only if I ever decide to go to university."

"We'll discuss this later. But as for marriage, put it out of your head. You're too young to know how much trouble you'll face the minute you marry."

For a split second, I thought I should remind him again that he had married at a young age himself. But I realized it wasn't the time to confront him regarding this sensitive matter, especially since I already knew he'd been forced into that situation. He'd done it only out of the goodness of his heart, despite the stupidity of his mind. I should stop being a jerk and abusing his patience. I decided to stop arguing with him altogether. It didn't feel like a good time to continue this conversation, but then a great idea struck me.

"What if I love somebody?" I asked with excitement, proud of my fast thinking for once.

"Love? At your age? It's the worst thing."

"Why? I can't risk losing someone I love because of my age. I'm a grownup now," I said. I was about to say that I was also going to be a high school graduate soon, but quickly stopped my mouth from uttering such an unlikely promise. I mustn't give him any hope that I was on track to finish high school that year.

"You're still too young. There're many other opportunities for a young, handsome guy like you to fall in love in the future. Don't worry."

"But I love this person now. I really do."

"Who's she anyway? Who's her father?" he asked with stress. Yet, signs of flexibility showed in his eyes, especially if her father was an aristocrat or a prominent officer in the government.

I knew mentioning Mina, my real love, could cause a big chaos. *Besides, I didn't know anything about Mina's father!* So I made a compromise.

"Her name is Goli. Her father has a big tire factory and he's very rich." I was too clever, I thought. By using Goli as a guinea pig, I could at least establish the possibility of getting married at a young age. Once he got used to the idea, I could serve him the bigger shock later. *Although I realized how tricky it'd be later to tell him that now I suddenly loved Mina more than I loved Goli!*

"Well, maybe we could visit and get to know Goli's parents. Then we can wait for you two to finish your education and see how things go."

"So you're willing to meet her parents?"

"Yes. Of course. If it makes you happy, I'll do it. I really like you to be happy and successful."

Tricking him felt cheap. I was lying to him left and right. I'd never want him, or even myself, to meet Goli's family. I'd never thought capable of so many things I was doing to him. For one thing, I was betraying his trust in me all the time I was skipping school. But I was trapped and I had to solve my problems one at a time. Anyway, I loved his liberal attitude and open-mindedness —very precious qualities for the near future in fact, when I could find the right moment and courage to tell him about my true love, Mina. The one, and the only one, I really wanted to marry.

3

A few days after my tortuous conversations with Father, I met Mina at her house. In recent months, I'd always imagined Dr. Afzali barging in on us during one of those vulgar shows that Mina and I exhibited without care or shame. We'd become more and more relaxed about the affair, as if loving each other was our most natural right and legitimized all that travesty. Who the hell was Hassan to consider even as a relevant piece of this puzzle? Nobody else mattered, either, not even his or her basic opinions about decency. When Hassan didn't show up to murder us, I wondered if he'd had difficulty leaving the hospital during his shifts or was only trying to avoid a situation that would require divorcing Mina or murdering a child. Despite my fear of being slaughtered at such young age so innocently, I was ready for the consequences, whatever form it took. I was tired of going on like this. If he did the honourable thing and divorced Mina, then we lovebirds would get a chance to build our own nest. And if he killed us, we'd reunite in heaven and have a serene life away from all the present hassles and worries—if we assumed religious claims about afterlife held water, of course! This was one of those rare occasions when I hoped Grandma's divine nonsense could actually be considered a sane option for planning my life.

I'd hidden my hallucinations from Mina regarding Hassan catching us together. I thought she might feel guilty for my fear of decapitation by her mad husband. Or she might get anxious about my fancy to get caught to end this masquerade. Our love was too precious to let these petty concerns blemish it or worry Mina. So

I bore alone all the turmoil and terror inside me to prevent Mina's further stress. Another big sacrifice by me! She never revealed her views, either, about the chance of Hassan catching us. Either she knew something I didn't, or she was also trying not to taint the beauty of our love by the unchangeable reality surrounding it. Maybe she didn't want to worry me, the same way I was careful not to burden her.

Anyway, after we enjoyed our great sex that afternoon, we lied on the floor of the dining room and smoked our cigarettes. By the way, in spite of all the pleasure, doing it on the floor was destroying my boney knees. That was another complaint I was keeping to myself for now, while thinking seriously about a way to express my pain and concern to Mina. Instead, I told her about my recent discussions with Father. I said he eventually seemed flexible about my marriage at a young age. I hoped the news would thrill Mina. But if it did, she didn't show it. She just kept silent. *Maybe she was jealous that I'd already handled my part of the deal—giving a partial heads-up to Father at least—whereas she still had the challenge of putting Hassan on notice sooner or later!* She didn't even ask how I'd convinced Father and what had been discussed. I thought she looked pensive merely because of her concern about many hurdles ahead once we decided to get married and the way we were going to announce it to the whole world. I tried to imagine the riot at the Club when people found out. *The Marriage of Grigori!*

After a long silence, she asked, "But you haven't told him or anybody else about us, right?"

"Only Feri knows. I had to tell him after seeing us."

"Yes. You told me that. But nobody else, right?"

"Right."

"Oh, by the way there's something I should tell you," she said with a smirk.

"What?"

"Mehri doesn't mind having an affair with you," Mina said casually.

I was stunned. I just didn't know what to make out of this shockingly absurd proposal. Especially after pouring my heart out to her about our upcoming marriage, Mina's casual comment sounded too insensitive and vulgar. I wondered whether she was teasing me or testing me. Was she possibly stating a fact? Or, the worst possible scenario: Trying to dump me! At the same time, I was flattered that Mehri had at last come to her senses. I was truly thrilled, despite my doubts regarding the truthfulness of Mina's bizarre message. Yet, I thought, some kind of truth must exist behind Mina's confession, maybe a demented type of truth, maybe a conspiracy, but something nonetheless. The bottomline was that her message had given me a delightful shock. It had filled me with both happiness and sadness at the same time.

"How do you know this?" I asked with mixed emotions.

"I know many things, Kian," Mina replied. She sounded too mysterious and sneaky, that pretty cockroach.

"But, how did you exactly learn about this?"

"She told me herself," Mina replied in an even more casual tone.

"She told you to tell me?"

"No. Not like that."

I kept silent while dealing with my sudden confusion.

"Do you want me to arrange it?" she asked at last to break the silence. A big smirk made her look absolutely mysterious.

"No," I replied with anger. I couldn't believe my ears. My pride was shattered by the way she appeared so casual about her indecent proposal. Was she willing to share me with others? Was some kind of trade happening behind my back? Was she gauging my loyalty as a final test before agreeing to marry me? If she was testing me, then my reaction was perfect, but I should make a major confession right now: I am still very sorry for saying 'No' so fast before thinking. In fact, I should've said, 'Yes, yes, and yes' on that fateful afternoon and then waited for the new course of my destiny to unfold. I should've said 'yes' even if I was sure she was only testing me. One way or another, my life would've taken a different course right there and then. I should've said yes at least for finding the truth, instead of still suffering, after all these years, for not knowing Mina's intention and scheme that afternoon. *Oh, what a pity! How inexperienced and stupid we are during adolescence, especially when we want to be in love!*

Even right now, at my prime age, I still wonder if I'd had a chance to understand and love Mehri. Did she really love me too? I believe she did. Had Mina told me the truth? I believe she had. These questions have been torturous all these years, even today. I still get frustrated every time I read my diaries about that dire day. Pity, we make such major mistakes so easily and lose the greatest opportunities of our lives. A sadder part of this episode was that I couldn't gather from Mina's expression whether she was happy with my answer or disappointed. Neither one of us brought up the subject again even once, though, not even a hint of it. However, the mystery of Mina's proposal and Mehri's possible love would remain both delightful and depressing for me forever.

On the other hand, my quick answer, the resounding 'No,' to Mina's question shows my absolute idiocy and devotion to her at the time. Only in hindsight, saying 'Yes' to her question makes perfect sense. But all these after-the-fact thoughts say nothing about the 'messed-up Kian' then. At that time, I was under Mina's spell. I didn't want anybody else, not even Mehri. I didn't need time to weigh my options before uttering my firm "No" to Mina's mysterious question. *That's a pity.*

4

Two months later, sometime in April 1974, *monsieur Hassan* went to Europe again for another conference for a week. It'd been a long time since he'd gone away and since I'd had a chance to stay overnight with Mina and have sex on a soft bed. I was looking forward to spend a few entire nights with her and practise my role as her future husband. By the way, I had started calling him Hassan in front of Mina, while she only smirked at me with a mix of respect and spite for my growing arrogance. I figured I might as well do so after having screwed his wife for so long—slowly reaching midway to get even with him after his dagger business. Hassan and I were stuck in a kind of a binding partnership those days, whether we liked it or not. We both loved our business deeply, but loathed our partnership.

Mina and I followed the routine we'd invented the first time Hassan went to a conference. Gosh, these conferences are real marriage killers, I tell you. Mina always did something extra every time I stayed with her overnight. She tried hard to make our evenings more romantic. She made tasty dinners for us after sending the kids to her parents. She lit the candles on the dining table, in the bedroom, and in the bathroom. I brought a dozen glowing red roses for her. She often had a vase with water ready in the middle of the dining table. She was a great cook. I knew she'd be a perfect wife for me, because I loved food almost as much as I loved Mina. She possessed the greatest combination I could dream of in a wife. What else could I ask for?

That night, we had a great fiesta—a special experience I'd never forget. The dinner was delicious, I suppose, as we were quite drunk by the time we started eating, anyway. But I recall how fast I was wolfing while Mina teased me about my endless appetite. We had tea and dessert afterward. Around eleven p.m. we relaxed in the bathtub together and then made love on her soft mattress again and again. I was truly happy as we smoked our cigarettes—so were my knees.

"Oh, Mina. You're my eternal love. What am I gonna do if you're not in my life even for a second?" I said from the bottom of my heart with absolute devotion.

"I'll always be in your life. As long as you want me to."

"For ever. I want you in my life forever. Whatever it takes," I said with deep emotions.

"You can't imagine the joy you've brought into my life."

"Tell me. Tell me how much you love me," I begged her.

"A lot. I love you a lot. I love you more than my children."

"More than your children...? Really...?" I asked with a mix of surprise, panic, guilt, and delight. I'd always felt guilty for stealing so much of her love that belonged to her kids, not to mention her time away from them. I put myself in their shoes and felt so lousy.

"Yes, I do. Can you imagine that?" she said with a sigh.

"No, but there's a good way to find out."

"What's that?"

"Let's have our own kid just to test our love."

Mina burst into laughter. "That'd be interesting!"

"You really think we'd love each other more than our kids?"

"I will. I'm sure about it," Mina said.

"Me too. So let's make a baby together to prove our love. Hassan wouldn't find out."

"Oh, my darling. You're really crazy!"

"Stop taking your birth-control pills right away."

Mina only laughed.

"I'm coming here every night until Hassan returns."

"Oh, not every night. It's not possible."

"Why not?"

"Oh, so many reasons. Kids for one thing."

"How about tomorrow night?"

"No. Not two nights in a row..."

"How about the night after?"

"Call me in the morning as usual to confirm it."

"Sure. I must hear your voice in the mornings, anyway."

"By the way, how can you manage to call me around ten o'clock every morning? Aren't you in the class?" Mina asked and I wondered whether it was the right time to share my secret with her. But I realized the story of my expulsion from school could cause havoc. This wasn't a good time for honesty. I just couldn't screw up my chance of enjoying her bed while Hassan was away and my knees agreed, too.

"I simply get out of the class to make the call. It's easier to use the public phones when all other students are in the classrooms."

"Ah! Okay."

The way she always bought my regular lies and nonsense was amazing, but it also made me wonder if she really believed me or just didn't have the urge to find out about the horrible things she was imagining I was doing. She was a psychic, after all, right?

5

When I called Mina in the morning to confirm our evening plan, she said she wasn't feeling good and cancelled it. Her response sounded lousy when I asked what exactly was wrong with her, but I let it go *for now*. She said she'd be staying in bed or at least wouldn't be leaving the house.

Around five o'clock, I called her to see how she felt. Maybe we could meet later if she felt better and the kids weren't around. I was going to tell her she didn't have to worry about feeding me that night. A big sacrifice on my part, I tell you! All I wanted was to lie beside her and embrace her. We didn't even have to have sex if she weren't feeling up to it. So many sacrifices I'd prepared myself to make just to be near her. But the phone kept ringing and nobody answered.

Feri, Jafar, and I explored the streets like usual when I had nothing better to do. Feri kept advising me about coming back to school. I was tired of him pushing me to talk to my dad about the money I owed to the school. Especially today, I couldn't worry about anything but Mina. I called her from every public phone in our path as we strolled in the streets of Tehran. A few times we came across some pretty girls eager to meet flirty boys. Feri and Jafar pushed me to go talk with them, but I wasn't feeling up to it. I felt sick and I told them to forget about girls tonight. Instead, we went to a restaurant for dinner.

At eight p.m., I got too worried. I was dying to see Mina and finding out what was happening. So I took a taxi to get to her house fast. I rang the bell fearless of the consequences, even if her kids answered the door. But nobody answered. Maybe she'd gone to a clinic or something. I kept chain-smoking cigarettes while hanging around her house like an agitated ghost. What could've happened to her? I was worried sick. I felt like throwing up that big *chelokabab* I'd eaten earlier for supper, but nothing came out of my throat.

It was dark around nine and I still paced the street. My worry about her health turned into some form of paranoia, followed by a nauseating thought: Maybe she hadn't been ill, after all. And if that were true, only two possibilities existed: She either had used sickness as an excuse to be with her friends or kids, or was seeing another man. This last possibility made me puke. Luckily, I was then in a side alley away from the main street and my vomit splashed all over the wall out of immediate sight. I wiped my mouth with a tissue, covered the mess on the ground with several tissues, and staggered toward the main street. I got out of the alley and walked toward her house to ring the doorbell again. But, halfway there, the headlights of a car approaching the house in a slow speed alarmed me. I tried to escape back into the alley. Yet, I imagined the car occupants had already noticed me. They'd probably seen me fleeing amidst the car's intense headlights. It illuminated the whole street all the way to the alley. I ran and jumped behind the wall in the alley at last.

I hid until the car's headlights were turned off and the street was dark again. I peeped cautiously into the street and saw a black Mercedes parked right in front of Mina's house. I couldn't see the car's occupants, but two ghosts seemed to be sitting there and chatting. After two minutes, the passenger door opened and Mina got out. She was elegantly dressed as if returning from a cabaret or something. She looked healthy and gorgeous too, even in that dark street. She walked to the door, opened it with her key, and went inside. I prayed the car drives away. Hopefully, the driver had only given her a ride home from somewhere. I prayed hard. I wanted to go inside and ask Mina for an explanation. But after four minutes, the driver's door opened and a man got out. He locked the car's door and kept peering around with caution.

He gazed in my direction for a long while, but couldn't see me in that dark spot. Then he started toward Mina's house, still peeping at the alley. When he came closer to the curb, under the lamppost, I recognized Father. He looked handsome as usual despite the worry on his face. He went inside Mina's house at last.

I was mad, I was sad, beyond all my previous experiences of madness and sadness. I was devastated and humiliated, all my guts shaking inside me. I punched the brick wall and wailed from pain. Then I walked back to the edge of the alley and stared at Mina's house. I wished the door would open any second and he'd get out. Leaning against the wall, I was frozen in my spot, gazing into the spooky distance with a blank mind. I wished to evaporate in the massive darkness engulfing inside and outside me. I wished the ground would open up and swallow me whole. I was dying for a chance to see Mina right away. I needed to ask her for an explanation. I counted the minutes, but nobody came out of her house. Still I waited and prayed that he'd leave any second. But he didn't. I mourned in that corner for what felt like eternity, until eleven p.m. Almost two hours had passed since the devils had arrived. I was stunned by the cruelty of destiny. The reward of loving her for three years. I wept my heart out in that alley of agony. I banged my head against the wall. I touched my head and felt the sticky blood on my fingers, but I didn't feel any physical pain. My frozen brain had already numbed my body, too. Not even a hundred slashes of Dr. Afzali's dagger would've given me any pain in that dark alley. I was too numb to even moan if someone crushed my bones one by one. The two people I loved the most in this world were probably making love at my expense at that instant. They'd betrayed me at the worst possible period of my life. They'd broken my heart when I needed their loves the most. They'd abandoned me when I was so vulnerable. A big bang echoed in my head, then another bang and another. Then everything around me went dead. I'd become deaf or the whole world had collapsed suddenly. Cars passed by me without any noise.

Sometime later, I found myself lying on the pavement of the dark alley. I gathered all my energy to peel myself off the ground. I stood on my shaking legs and peered one last time toward Mina's house. The black Mercedes was still parked there with utter arrogance, shinning nicely over the darkness surrounding it. Like a drunkard, I staggered toward my grandparents' house. It took me about an hour to get my numb body there. I fell down many times in the streets and I just sat still on the cold asphalt. A few drunks and perverts passed by me and peeped at me with pity, but they didn't dare come close to me, probably thinking I was a madman. They just ran away quickly. I was surprised when I got home. I had no idea how I'd gotten there, but I recognized the house and the entrance at least. I stood there and gazed at the door for five minutes. I didn't know what I was supposed to do and why I was standing out there like a zombie, staring at a door. I took out another cigarette from the pack in my pocket and lit it. My only good luck that excruciatingly long evening was that I'd brought two packs of Winston with me, as though I'd anticipated a catastrophe and a need for that many cigarettes. I was already halfway through the second pack. Luckily, I had a few more packs of cigarettes at home. I lit another cigarette with the one that was almost done.

Two minutes later, I threw away the cigarette butt and started searching my pockets for the key to the house. It wasn't there. I checked all my pockets a hundred times, but the key was lost. Maybe it'd fallen out of my pocket when I'd taken something out of it in the dark alley or when I was lying on the pavements somewhere along the way. I had to ring the bell or sleep in the street. I wasn't in the mood for staying in the street any longer tonight and I was dying of thirst, too. So I rang the bell, feeling a little guilty for waking Grandma up at that time. If she saw me in my condition, she'd freak out, I was sure. She'd already had enough trouble with me. She'd complained to Narges a hundred times. This time she'd have a real heart attack. But again, under my present condition, I didn't care about anybody or anything. I rang the bell again and again. Every time, I let it ring longer. At last, I let it ring for a minute, holding the button with rage. Then I started to bang on the door with all my strength. No answer. I was surprised of my decency, brains, and patience to think and shout, "Grandma, it's me, Kian," just in case she was afraid to open the door this late for a possible intruder. Still no response…

I got really angry. I kicked the door near the lock with rage. The latch securing the lock was knocked out of the wooden frame and the door opened before me. I got in and shut the door behind me. The lock was intact but the latch lay on the floor. The doorjamb, where the latch had been, was broken into a million pieces. I went inside, took a chair from the hall, and put it behind the door to keep it closed. Then I went to the fridge and took a cold beer. I opened it with anger and took a sip, as though it must make me forget the world or kill me right away. I wondered whether I could seriously expect such a miracle from that poor bottle of beer. At least it tasted good, and even those few seconds of distraction helped my madness a bit. I lit a cigarette too. I smoked and drank beer until two a.m., only staring at the walls. My mind was dull.

PART III

The New World

CHAPTER FIFTEEN
The Witch of Royal Club

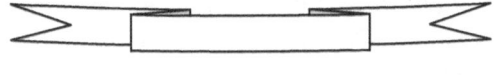

1

My chest was about to explode, as if stuck inside a crushing vacuum. No sound echoed even from outside the house. My Kakh residence resembled a big tomb and I was trapped inside it, doomed to die soon. At two in the morning, I reeled numbly from one room to another looking for a soul to embrace, or a hole to escape. I peeped inside Jamal's room. He wasn't there. I peeked inside Grandma's room. She wasn't there. I needed any sign of life, even a crawling cockroach, to tell me I was still alive. I went to my late grandpa's room. It was the gloomiest place in the big tomb. Yet I stood near his photo in a haze for five minutes before sensing his sad spirit swashing from one corner to the other, maybe worried about my spirit; or agitated by the devil surging inside his favourite grandson's body at that moment. I went back to the hall and turned on my heels sluggishly half a dozen times, staring at each wall a few seconds at a time. I hoped Azrael would break through any of those walls and take me away. No such luck! I lurched to the living and dining rooms when I heard some loud laughter. No one was there either. Only twelve chairs around the big table stared at my miserable face. Then I reeled to my own room. It was the darkest and dampest place in the tomb —too haunted and chilly. Was it supposed to become my grave? I was quite ready, so I lied on my bed and waited to die. I waited and waited. But nothing happened and I didn't die. I was still too restless. So I went to the kitchen. Then I stood in the middle of the hall again. I had no idea why I walked everywhere, but couldn't stand still. The sense of suffocation got unbearable as soon as I stopped walking. Life was being sucked out of my flesh torturously slowly. I was looking for a refuge, but it was nowhere to be found. I begged for a big miracle, but it wasn't inside the house, nor was it out there, I knew. I'd luckily escaped that hell only two hours before. Outside, only misery meandered instead of miracle. Agony was in every alley. I had no sense or idea who I was and why everything around me looked so horrific. My chest was too tight to breathe, so I just leaped left and right like a slaughtered rooster. I swung aimlessly like a lonely feather toyed by the wind. Then a wild storm began to blow inside me and thrust my body forward fiercely. I started running. I ran and ran until I ran out of breath. Still I couldn't stop. Then, the fierce fear of suffocation made me scream, as though a big giant held my body tight in his grip and squeezed the last air out of my lungs. The storm inside me was tearing my guts into pieces, too. I just raced around the tomb and screamed at two in the morning. Then I began taking my clothes off with rage. I tore up my shirt. I chucked my watch as the last item on my body. I was now only a horrific howling tornado in the tomb. Only God knew how long I ran and screamed in nude. At last, I collapsed.

I found myself next to the oven in the kitchen. I was sitting naked on the cold tiles and sobbing silently, no more sound or air left to escape my throat. I was glad nobody was home. The next second, I was sad nobody was home. I crawled to the living room and sprawled on the carpet. The house was quiet again. The madman was face down on the floor, exhausted. At last! But still not dead, unfortunately.

I missed Narges! Such a crazy delusion! As If I were an infant again, urgently needing to return to the womb, away from this tomb. As if looking for a real refuge and soothing compassion. But why Narges? How was this mad illusion even possible, even in my current state of hallucination?

I wanted to think, but I had no mind. What the hell was now happening around me? Why was everything turning round and round in midair? Mina's face floated around my depleted body a few times, too. Sometimes she peered at me with pity. Sometimes with a sad smirk. Sometimes with sheer indifference. The same familiar gestures, exactly like the ones she'd given Dr. Afzali a million times during the years I'd been watching them. Still I loved her, I thought. Loving the lost love—as if I could go back to the past and undo everything. Then I hated her, I felt. Hating my desire for her love—as if only hatred could push me into the future. Yet the future felt too gloomy without her. What future! I'd lost control of my future. The only future I'd pictured during the last three years was the one in her arms, and it was all but gone now, burned in an earthly hell, buried in an alley named agony, all in a matter of five hours. Moving forward, however, felt inevitable. I couldn't turn the clock back.

There it was—the ugly reality that had knocked me out flat so unexpectedly, with utmost cruelty. All the affairs I'd witnessed in the Club and vulgar parties hadn't prepared me for this moment. I'd never assumed I could be on the wrong side of this reality. I'd never imagined I had to learn so soon in my life that I was as doomed and vulnerable as any of them in those masquerades— even worse than Dr. Afzali. Poor humans. Poor us! Such helpless creatures we've ended up being!

2

The daylight woke me up. But before even opening my eyes, another blast of suffocating panic-attack crippled me. I was still lying naked on the carpet in the middle of the living room. I was breathless and numb for a long time, until my nerves calmed down a bit at last. I thought I must've slept for a couple of hours or so, which felt like happy news. I could possibly survive this crisis then. Soon I might even end up stronger than I had ever been; I badly wanted to believe. I might even come out of this experience a real man. At last! This was perhaps a good test of manhood. My mind was beginning to work. The arrogance I'd built throughout the last three years was emerging, trying to help. It was proving useful now that I really needed it. I thought about Grigori. Maybe a bit like him! I sat up. Then I went to the kitchen to find some food. Fast improvement—I started to feel somewhat alive as if coming to from a long coma.

Now what?

I looked for my clothes all over the house. Each one was in a different room, some of them in torn pieces. I found my Sarcar, too, at last. It was on the top of the kitchen cupboard, where by accident its brown wristband hung over the white cupboard door. Otherwise, I would've never imagined looking for it on the top of the cupboard. It was still working fine without even a scratch on it.

I felt hungry. *What should I eat?* I had feelings again and I could make decisions, too. I looked inside the fridge and took three eggs. The bottles of beer grabbed my attention and I took one of them, too. I drank it while frying the eggs. It was so darn refreshing. Beer had never tasted so amazing—it just revived me. The big beer bottle empty, the eggs fried, I found some Taftoon bread and sat down for breakfast.

Next, I checked the front door. It was a crack open. The wind had pushed the door ajar, along with the chair I'd put behind it for security. I picked up the broken pieces of the doorjamb, which were scattered all over the floor, and examined them carefully. I was surprised my mind could focus. I put the pieces together like a jigsaw puzzle after two minutes, which made me smile. But I couldn't fix the broken doorjamb and repair the latch, nor could I fix the shattered love. What could I fix then? The idea of finding a carpenter and waiting around for him felt beyond my patience at that moment. I had to escape that tomb before another anxiety attack knocked me out again.

I looked in the kitchen drawers and found a large bottle of glue, which was probably good only for paper and cardboard.

But that was all I could find. With a ton of that glue, I put the broken pieces of the doorjamb and the latch together, back in their original order. The finished masterpiece looked so funny and clumsy, like a kindergartener's artwork, but that must do the trick. I put the chair back in the hall and waited for the glue to harden. Then I closed the door and locked it from inside very gently, especially when turning the doorknob and engaging the lock. It worked but the glued patches looked fragile. If somebody knocked on the door, the whole thing would fall apart on the floor again, but I didn't care. That was the best I could do considering my mood and patience; although I imagined I could write a quick note as a warning and stick it to the front of the door, "Please don't knock, the bell works perfectly."

I found the spare key I'd made for emergency and got ready to leave. I locked the door from outside with great care and waited one minute to see if the smooth wind blowing outside the house could break the lock. It didn't, so I assumed the lock was secure enough for now. I considered blaming robbery for the broken lock or just denying everything. However, I realized no robber would have my limited conscience to repair the latch and leave empty-handed, too. I should've left the doorjamb unfixed with the door wide open, for some robbers to come in and steal a few things. I felt sad for my slow thinking and fixing the door. I didn't feel like going back to break it again and leave it open this time. I decided not to even bother about lying. YES, I'd broken the door and I wasn't sorry for anything, because I couldn't sleep in the street. So, let's get going, I told my annoying conscience and lurched forward.

I went to the billiard club, where I'd felt secure during the last five months in the mornings and sometimes afternoons, too. I had to distract my mind for a while by chatting around or playing pool. At noon, I called Narges at school. I knew she'd be in the staff lounge. They called her to the phone.

"I won't be going home for a long while."

"Why?" Narges asked with surprise. The tone of my shaking voice, despite my intention to stay cool, had apparently revealed the severity of the situation to her.

"Can't explain. I just have to stay in the city for now."

"For how long?"

"I don't know."

She remained silent, perhaps curious about my decision and whether it had anything to do with her. Yet, her pride stopped her from asking me more direct questions. I bet she imagined it was because of her. Then I suspected she knew about the catastrophe the night before already. Maybe she'd been expecting it all along.

"You need anything I can bring for you?" she asked at last.

"Yes. Please bring my shorts and shirts and shoes and a few trousers. Imagine I'm going on a trip for a few months."

"Okay. Anything else."

"Yes. Bring all the textbooks and notebooks on my desk."

A major problem with living in two residences had been that my textbooks and notebooks had also lived in two places. While they all travelled with me back and forth at different times, we often lost track of one another. We often ended up being in the opposite locations as we commuted between the two residences, as if they were tricking me. During all those years in high school, as much as I tried to plan, I usually didn't have the right books and notes for my classes and doing the assignments. Obviously, without access to the right books and notes, studying had been eight times more difficult. So, my poor performance at high school wasn't entirely my fault, as you surely agree! Blaming my sneaky textbooks isn't merely a joke. Something fishy was really going on behind the scene as well!

I played pool some more, but I was too agitated to focus for a second. I thought I should clarify the situation with Mina finally to settle my nerves a bit. It wouldn't be wise to abandon Father, Mina, and maybe the whole family without a proper justification. I had to confirm the reality of the horrific event I'd witnessed the night before to avoid any dire mix-up. Maybe I'd tortured myself for nothing out of sheer stupidity! I got out of the billiard club and stood near the curb with indecision driving me nuts. I lit another cigarette and tried to find the best course of action. Talking to Mina on the phone seemed useless. So I took a cab and arrived in front of Mina's house in ten minutes.

3

I rang the bell, quite reckless about the possibility of the maid or even Dr. Afzali opening the door. Luckily for Mina, she opened the door herself. She was shocked, but I didn't give her a chance to talk or think. I pushed her out of my way and climbed the stairs to the drawing room. It looked so gloomy, too, like the tomb I'd lived in the night before. It was no longer the love shrine I'd prayed in with all my *nazr* and *niaz* during the last three years. The scene of our romance in her bed two nights before and our promises rang in my head and felt so surreal. All my silly hopes, to be with Mina forever and marry her, all that love making on my aching knees, all those laughter and kisses, all that messing up each other's hairs, they all felt like the act of Satan in my body. All that romance I'd wasted on her! Mina entered the room slowly with bewildered eyes. I saw a little sign of fear on her face for the first time after all the years I'd known her. *How horrific I must look myself to stir such terror in her,* I wondered with pity and pride.

"Sit down," I ordered her.

She obeyed me after staring into my eyes and noticing my rage. I paced the length of the drawing room awhile and gauged my strategy to interrogate her. Now I was the judge. I walked back, stood near her, and glared down at her for ten seconds. I remembered our first kiss in the same spot and position, except that, in that instance, I was sitting and she was standing—just the opposite positions. She'd imposed her dominance over me to give me the first kiss three years earlier. But now, I was the one standing. *Yes, now I was the judge!* I held the dominant position this time and I wasn't even going to give her the last kiss. No more kissing. *Oh, what madness!*

I felt sad about the idea of not kissing her voluptuous lips ever again. She looked timid and her eyes looked damp. Still, those anxious eyes mostly appeared to be hiding a lot of treachery. And yet, she still emanated her famous smirk, anyway—the same sly smirk she'd often delivered to Dr. Afzali and a few times to me, too. A confusing mix of passion and apprehension covered her face as she gazed at me with no sign of shame. My own mixed emotions were even more torturous. I felt I still loved her. I still loved her courage. But I hated her as well. I hated her pride.

"What is it, Kian?" she asked sternly with of sudden resolve.

"You tell me. Is there anything you wish to tell me?"

"No… Like what?" she replied with confidence.

I bet she was dying to know whether the person running away in the dark last night had been me. I was eighty percent sure they had seen me running away in the midst of the car's headlights. Or maybe they'd noticed a man running away and turning into the alley, but weren't sure it had been me. I didn't want to give her any clues about anything. That was a part of my plan to test her.

"Are you sure?" I asked her.

"Yes."

"What'd you do last night?"

"Nothing."

"Nothing happened last night that you want to tell me?"

"Not really," she replied coolly.

I slapped her so fiercely her head span from left to right. I'd say it was fiercer than the slap the woman on the train to Mashad had blown in my face. I felt good. She put her gorgeous hand on her red face and tears gathered in her cunning eyes. Yet she still kept smirking.

"Slap me… Kill me. But I love you," she said with a shaking voice. "Kill me if you like, but I'll always, always love you…"

I was tempted to do both: to slap her a dozen times and then kill her. But I saw no point in any further violence toward her, for my own sake. To leave my final mark, I stood on her pretty toes with the heels of my shoes. I pressed them with rage. I'd always adored her delicate feet. I wanted to cry myself for squashing those gorgeous innocent toes. *Innocent, my ass,* I thought the next moment. They'd probably lured so many naïve guys like me.

"You big liar," I shouted.

"Tell me what is wrong, Kian. Please."

"You're the one who must tell me something."

"Something? Like what?"

"The truth. Just tell me the truth," I begged her, although I kept my commanding tone of voice.

"I don't know what you want me to say," she insisted.

Her arrogance and hypocrisy made me even madder. She was determined not to confess. She had a fixed strategy of her own. It sounded like a strategy she'd followed all her life. She'd surely used it all the time with all her past lovers. Poor Dr. Afzali had probably faced her denials a million times. *What a bitch!* Her tenacity to deny the truth was as severe and irritating as Narges's. This analogy and feeling made me so mad I slapped her again.

"I don't want to see you anymore," I said.

"Why not? Tell me what is wrong?"

Talking with her felt useless. I wasn't going to tell her what I'd seen either. I had a fixed strategy of my own, which I believed was the best, especially considering Mina's apparent aptitude for lying and denial. But more difficult for me was using the word 'Father' in a sentence to tell Mina that I knew she slept with him *as well.* Even thinking those words was driving me nuts, let alone speaking them aloud to her. The whole reality was beyond my imagination, let alone drawing its picture for Mina. Recalling the image already made me so sick I almost puked.

"For the last time, is there anything about last night you want to tell me?" I asked with utter frustration.

"No. I told you," she answered with absolute calm.

I marched toward the stairs and she followed me, trying to hold me. I pushed her away and walked faster toward the door.

"Kian, please. Please tell me what is wrong. Stop, Kian!"

I rushed down the stairs, opened the front door and banged it against the wall with rage before jumping out. She ran outside and kept calling me in whispers. But I was gone. Gone. Gone.

I strolled in the streets for two hours, trying to get used to the idea of life without Mina somehow. But it was difficult to set aside such deep memories. I had to scrap my plans for a life with her, but I had nothing else to connect me to the future. The idea of going back to Grandma's house to sleep alone or face her rage sickened me, too. I couldn't stay in that tomb, for a few days at least, until the memories of the previous night died a little bit. So I walked toward my school to find Feri. I got there in time. I asked him to let me stay in their house for a few days and he agreed. We found Jafar and began our normal fooling around the streets. Then we went to a restaurant for dinner. I called Narges from a public phone and told her I'd be staying with Feri for a few days. I didn't want her or anybody else to worry about me or call the police to find me. I wanted to hide from everybody and everything, but I didn't want to get lost, not yet at least.

4

I stayed with Feri for a week. His mother was a nice woman and I believed she liked me, as long as I didn't tease Feri for not being handsome enough. Her wild imagination of Feri's looks alone could taint anybody's view of her sanity! It happens, perhaps, when a woman has only one son who looks prettier than her three daughters. Apparently, she was hoping to dump one of them on me, too, while those girls showed their own tenacity to seduce me with their vile, comical charm. So staying in that house, with four homely women hoping to lure me, perfectly showed my fear of going to the tomb I'd lived in the night before. On school days, Feri and I had breakfast together every morning before leaving the house. He went to school and I went to the billiard club. We met at the end of the day and had dinner somewhere before going home. I really missed Mina. But Mina was history. I'd begun to smarten up. I decided to raise some money to pay for the balance of the tuition and go back to school. The big shock of being back at school could possibly set my mind straight, to forget Mina. The only problem was just the matter of finding the money. Feri and I joked around and laughed a lot about my desperate situation and our lousy solutions. Once he suggested, "Go home one day when your parents aren't around and steal your dad's gun and one of your mom's nylons to pull over your face. You'll be set to rob a bank." The other option was to steal and sell one of Narges's jewelleries or antics.

I decided to hit the textbooks at least, so at the end of the week I went back to Grandma's house. The lock and the doorframe were fixed. In my room, all my textbooks and notebooks were sitting together for the first time this year. I organized them for a serious attack on their useless contents.

I called Narges at home with the news of being back in Grandma's and busy for the nation-wide grade-twelve exams. She insisted to bring me some food and to talk with me and I said fine. I also called Goli, whom I hadn't called for four weeks. I asked her to help me catch up with schoolwork and prepare for the exams. She laughed her heart out as she assumed I was joking or something. It took me ten minutes, laughing along with her, to convince her finally that I wasn't kidding. She agreed to help me. Such a gem she was.

Narges arrived around seven in the evening with a few big pots of various Persian foods she knew I loved. She put them in the fridge and told me I only had to warm them up before eating.

"Why don't you want to come home?" she asked.

"This is a better place for me to concentrate on my exams. They're difficult," I said.

"Has anything happened between you and your father?" she asked as though she suspected something was out of the ordinary between the father and son.

"No."

"Ha...! So why did you break the door of this house?"

"Because I'd lost my key and had to get in somehow past midnight. Nobody answered the door, either."

"Where'd you get a new key?" she kept interrogating me.

"I had a spare in my bedroom."

"Your grandma is really furious, you know?"

"No. I haven't seen her for a while."

"She almost had a heart attack when she got home and put the key in the lock."

"Why?" I asked with a serious tone. But I was quite amused imagining what might've happened.

"She puts the key in the lock and the door breaks down in front of her eyes. The sound and sight of all the bits and pieces falling on the tiles almost killed her," Narges explained. "Your grandma was quite hysterical when she called me."

I tried to control my laughter.

"It's not funny. She might've had a heart attack. I came over and calmed her down before calling a carpenter."

"Where's she now?"

"She's staying in your aunt's house. She asked me to tell your father that she won't come back to this house as long as you're staying here."

"Oh, good."

"What do you mean?"

"I need a quiet place to study, as I said."

"I don't know what your father is planning to do about your grandma's ultimatum, but it looks like he's taking your side. He doesn't look interested to discuss the matter with you or ask you to leave this place."

I could think of a million reasons why Father didn't want to upset me anymore. Most likely he preferred that I stayed in my city residence as far away from him as possible, for now. Neither of us found the present circumstance suitable for us to be too close. How could we look into each other's face?

"Good. I'll have to stay here for now," I replied.

"I'll bring you food every three days. Leave your dirty clothes in a bag for me to take with me. I've got a key from your grandma for coming and going," she said.

"Okay. Thanks."

"Do you need anything else?"

"No."

Narges left with a sign of resignation. Nothing else she could do with this son and his father. Uncle Jamal called me two hours later. Grandma had gone through the big hassle of finding him just for telling him about my madness and breaking the lock. She'd taken her time to make Jamal angry with me. I was sure she'd even wept on the phone.

"What's the matter with you?" Jamal asked on the phone. "Are you now gone totally nuts?"

"I believe so," I replied.

"So somebody must do something for you," he said.

"Like what? What can anybody do for my madness?"

"Find out exactly what's wrong with you. To give you some medication or take you to the madhouse."

"These things won't help. Only I can possibly do something about my problems," I said.

"Are you going to do something then? You know what your problems are?"

"I'm starting to know and I'm hoping to find a way out."

"Is there anything I can do to help, too?"

I thought for a second. "Yes."

"What is that?" he asked.

"I need some money quickly."

"How much?"

"Thirty thousand rials," I said.

"What for?" Jamal asked.

"I've used the tuition money for personal stuff. I haven't been going to school the last five months."

"Now, I really think you're crazy. I could never imagine you'd become this reckless."

"Well, actually, it's probably all your fault I have become so reckless like this; you've been a bad influence on me, as Narges and Grandma have always said so," I replied with a chuckle.

"Is that a fact?"

"Yes, that's a well-known fact. Everything is your fault...," I said tensely with another silly giggle. "So you must lend me the money now at least."

I was thrilled for my chance today to tease him a little and maybe take my revenge, too, for the time he'd blamed me for Shahla's retaliation and leaving him. 'It is your fault that she's gone, since I tried to do something for you,' he'd said, and many other words that had haunted me for weeks. 'Instead of thanking me, you just ran away from her like an idiot. You humiliated her.'

"Why have you learned only my stupidities," Jamal said at last. "I have tried to teach you a lot of good stuff, too."

"Like what?"

"Well...," Jamal murmured, thinking, apparently unable to find anything good he might have ever tried to teach me.

His pensive desperate silence revealed the big commotion within him, as if pondering his own rotten character for the first time, so out of the blue! He seemed in agony, although he seldom appeared remorseful for anything, as though he'd never dealt with his conscience.

So, I tried to break his silence. "You shouldn't tell anything about my problems to anybody, either," I said. "Remember our promise to keep all the secrets?"

"I'm not going to tell anyone. But, is all this madness related to that married woman you'd told me about?"

"Yes, but it is over now..."

"I tried to warn you, but you never listen," he said with rage. "That was another good thing I was trying to do for you, but you ignored me..."

"I know you did... Thanks. But I was in love."

"Have you got your brain back now?"

"Yes, I promise..."

"What's your plan then?"

"My friend tells me to rob a bank," I said with a giggle.

"Why don't you tell Dadash Jalal the truth?"

"Never. Don't consider that an option. I rather flunk."

"What if I lend you the money? Are you sure you can go back and finish high school?"

"Yes. I'm sure. I'll pay your money back somehow, too."

"Okay. I'll give you the money in four days when I return."

"Thanks, Jamal."

The cliché that every incident is for a greater purpose was proven to me again. I could return to school, because my money problem was resolved, because angry Grandma had called Jamal, because I broke the door, because I lost my key, because Mina had cheated on me… on and on…

5

The next day, I gathered my nerve and went inside my estranged school. Witnessing or relating to such a hopeless hoopla after five months felt weird. Even odder, my long absence hadn't changed a thing and everybody was still doing the same old boring stuff! Now high school felt almost as useless a place as university!

"See who's back!" Mr. Ramzi, the administrator, said with a mocking tone before peering back over some stupid papers quickly. The fact that he recognized me immediately after so long was both flattering and discouraging, as he probably had time and energy only to recall the faces of big troublemakers.

I smiled and stood in silence while he tried very hard to look serious and pretend to be ignoring me. *For what end, I wondered!* Except, in fact, he was doing me a favour with his timely conceit merely confirming my earlier view about schools upon arrival.

"What do you want?" he asked at last.

"I want to come back to school, Mr. Ramzi," I said.

"It's too late for that. Next year maybe. But I'm not even sure about letting you back next year, either."

"I'll bring the money I owe you in four days."

"I'll believe you when I see it."

"But I'd like to know what happens if I give you the money."

"This is the money you owe us and must be paid. That's all."

"How about the national exams. Will you introduce me?"

"Of course not. You've missed most of the school year. It's against the rules to introduce you. You won't be able to pass the exams, anyway. It'd also damage the stats of our school's passing percentage. It'd ruin our good reputation. *You* know that!"

"I'll not only pass, but also get very high marks in the national exams. I promise."

"Impossible."

"Please."

"You've missed mid-term exams too. What do you expect me to do about that?"

"Just trust me."

"No way. It's against regulations."

"What is this stupid regulation? I'm promising to give you the money and pass the exams, too. What else do you want from me?" I shouted with rage.

"Get out of here, you jerk. Just bring the money soon. You understand?"

"There won't be any money if you don't introduce me," I screamed and kicked the wastebasket near his desk.

"We'll see. I'm going to find your father somehow soon and find out why nobody has replied to our notices," he yelled back. "I'm running out of patience with you and your family. Just get out of here, you asshole."

I had no idea about my next step as I turned to leave. I felt miserable. The world was collapsing around me fast, all because of Mina. As I opened the door, Mr. Imani, our algebra teacher, arrived and I said hello to him. In the previous years, he'd liked me as a good student. He asked me why I'd been missing his classes in the latter part of this school year. I told him a part of the tuition had been delayed and the administration had expelled me.

He looked at Mr. Ramzi with inquiring eyes. Mr. Ramzi nodded. He got furious with him and started to scream. This Mr. Imani really had a temper, I tell you. Everybody around the school knew about him and his temper. But he was also the fairest and smartest teacher in the whole goddamn school—maybe in the entire world. Mr. Ramzi was quiet like a mouse. He said he was only following the regulations.

"Piss the regulations," Mr. Imani screamed again.

I was getting scared of Mr. Imani's temper myself. He said it was stupid to destroy a young man's future due to his family's financial issues. I hadn't really said anything about my family's finances. And he apparently didn't know who my father was! Many people in Iran have the same last name as my family. Luckily, my words had given him a wrong, but highly useful, impression without my fault or intention. I explained the money was ready and all I wanted was a chance to prove myself.

Mr. Imani forced Mr. Ramzi to accept my proposal. We agreed I could attend the classes if I believed they could help me at that point, but I'd take the final internal exams with all other students. If I passed them, they'd give me some midterm marks, too, and introduce me for the national exams. I felt a bit proud of myself, but I owed everything to Mr. Imani and my *magical* luck *again* for bringing him to the office just in time.

I went home in a rather good mood, except that Mina's image and memories persisted in spoiling the chance of pushing some calm inside my numb skull. I tried to overcome those images and crushing thoughts by focusing more on the details of my plan to catch up with all that schoolwork. I had to embrace this immense opportunity to finish high school, but, more importantly, to get over my agony. There was no other way and I had to change my life quickly. The damage was done. I was still in love, and I had to pay a hefty price for everything. A badly broken spirit. And hatred toward the father I'd adored all my life.

I felt very proud of my sound decisions and rational behaviour during such a tough period. With all my confusion those days, how quickly I'd ditched the idea of stealing Father's gun to kill at least Mina was amazing. Her crime was unforgivable for sure, especially since I blamed her also for ruining my plan to chase Mehri. How uselessly loyal I'd been to Mina, even rejecting her offer to arrange my love affair with Mehri. Losing Mehri merely for Mina was now more hurtful than losing Mina herself. Mehri had tried to warn me, but I'd ignored her with my utter idiocy. Still I was glad that I'd overcome all that anger, instead of killing Mina.

For the first time, I also felt the depth of agony Dr. Afzali must've endured for so many years because of jerks like me, but mostly for making one mistake of loving and marrying Mina. On the other hand, he was an idiot to still love her so desperately when a juvenile like me had managed to drop her easily, despite the fact that I believed I still loved Mina even now more than anybody has ever loved that slut.

A few times when I was drunk alone in my city residence, I wondered whether it was too late to go find Mehri and tell her that I was ready. I could tell her that I'd loved her all along for the last six years and not Mina. That was surely the fastest way to forget Mina, too. Fortunately, as soon as I sobered up, I realized the silliness of pondering those kinds of thoughts again. It felt like another stupid plan by a madman! Romance, especially with an older woman, is always bound to burn you, I told my broken heart. There was nothing that could be done about the lost love and that evil woman—the witch of Royal Club. In fact, all love affairs fail somehow sooner or later. That was my new belief and my way of calming myself. *So what's the point of chasing Mehri now? Let's forget Mehri too. I must forget about all those pretty cockroaches, once and for all, for good.* It was time for Grigori to retire. *Oh, my dear beloved, Mehri, I still love you. Alas, I won't be seeing you again because I won't be going to the Club and parties with my parents anymore. I hope you miss me too. I hope Mina burns and dies in hell a million times for separating us.*

CHAPTER SIXTEEN
Preparing for My Big Escape

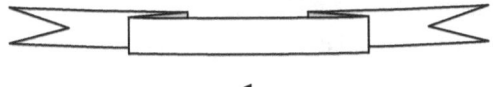

1

I stood at a difficult crossroad, where I had to make many tough decisions all on my own. All youngsters arrive at this point, I suppose. It's just the matter of proving one's resilience. At least I was living in a perfect setting for serious thinking. The privileges of living alone in a quiet house in the middle of the city became most obvious now, especially for getting Goli's help. Except that I sometimes felt guilty that this opportunity had come at the cost of forcing my grandma out of her home. The drama around this situation made me sad but also chuckle. She had to seek refuge in her daughter's house. She came over on a few occasions only when Jamal was in town. She only talked with him. She took a few more personal items every time and left as fast as she could. She ignored me if I happened to be in her vicinity, so I never bothered to say hello to her anymore. I was a bad grandson amongst my many other bad qualities, not to mention my sins. Especially, I feel embarrassed now—but not then—about leaving the stained sheets—the proofs of my repeated sins with girls—for her to wash by hand herself or to set aside, with disgust and screaming, for the maid who came by every other week. I knew she'd complained to Narges about it.

I remembered the older times when Grandma and I still got along nicely. Even then, what I'd done to her hadn't been decent, even though she'd been the one mostly to blame for my sins.

She'd herself only encouraged me by showing great enthusiasm to participate in my schemes that proved to be crooked only later. It had all started when Father gave me his old Zeiss Ikon camera after he returned from Europe. He'd bought a new fancy one for himself, a top-of-the-line Canon SLR with all kinds of detachable lenses. He introduced me to the art of photography, too, while bragging and displaying his techniques. Soon, however, we were competing. We tried to take the most artistic photos and show them off to each other as well as friends and family.

When I moved to grandma's house, I realized her potential as a marvellous model for my new artistic expressions. She was very attractive, even for a 66-year-old woman. Her subtle smile and penetrating black eyes gave her such an appealing character. She had a soft and bright skin with only a few wrinkles here and there. She was a complete contrast to Ozra Banu in terms of looks and wrinkles—perhaps a proof of alcohol hazard, since Grandma had never drank liquor. Anyway, I took a few pictures of her with her Islamic hijab. Taking picture in an informal pose for any unofficial purpose is by itself against the Islamic rules. Yet, she was quite thrilled to model for me with a subtle alluring grin. She looked into the camera with a charm you might expect only from professional models.

I kept abusing my discovery of Grandma more every day. I felt the same kind of pride and ownership over my model that any professional fashion photographer does nowadays. I asked her to remove her hijab and let me take pictures showing her hair. She obliged with great enthusiasm. Her hair was bundled into a bun behind her head with a hairpin. I asked her to remove the hairpin. She did. I was surprised by the lustrous, long hair she'd been hiding all those years under the hijab. She ran and fetched her comb to straighten the thick, grey hair. She let it slither over her shoulders. I took some thirty or so pictures in that session alone with all kinds of poses and moods. I asked her whether she ever used lipsticks and she said sometimes. So I took a few more pictures with the lipsticks on.

Feeling beautiful and charming are inherent needs of all women at some degree, I reckoned. Even age doesn't change this powerful urge in women. This is true even if you restrict them under the harshest Islamic hijab and rules all their lives. Past their initial shyness, they most likely won't refuse showing off their charm if the opportunity arrives. Grandma proved she wasn't an exception. At 66, she surely imagined it was her last chance to leave behind a trace of her allure and incredible beauty. I was her last hope to immortalize herself. (So she was abusing me, too, in fact!) Of course, finding such hidden talents in Grandma was somewhat shocking for me at the beginning. Yet, I didn't stop to ponder the morality of my deed. And now I feel guilty for all that callousness, too.

She was really enjoying herself though, while I was thrilled for my discovery of such an untapped source exposing my artistic genius. I was so excited with the outcome I even had many of those pictures enlarged. I showed them to some guests in a party at our house. Father noticed the pictures and gathered them quickly with incredible anger and disgust. I'd never seen him so frustrated and disappointed in me. He shouted at me in front of the crowd, including Mina, "You should be ashamed of yourself for doing such a sinful thing. How could you force your grandma to do this? How could you make such a religious person agree to show off her hair like this? Or wear lipstick? You bastard!"

I fled to my room scared stiff. I was shocked also because he'd never spoken to me that way. At the same time, I was amazed, because Father had never seemed religious and he was always running after women himself. This was the first time he was showing any kind of religious sensitivity or whatever the heck it was. When I thought about his attitude deeper later, his religious beliefs felt extremely vague and funny. For one thing, he seemed religious enough only for his own mother's benefit, whom I had now sullied with my bad influence! On the other hand, if he had even the slightest faith in Islam, he did not give a damn about his lovers going straight to hell for their lack of hijab and basic Islamic morals, not to mention his role in seducing and sullying all those poor souls and spreading so much sin around him wherever he went.

By the way, I had taken a few dozen pictures of Ozra Banu, too. But they all turned up quite soulless despite my great artistry to produce special effects and her enthusiasm to portray some charm of her own, perhaps as a last resort to immortalize herself, too, like Grandma; or perhaps to compete with her after she saw a few of the earlier photos I had taken from Grandma. But, at last, it became obvious that Ozra Banu would be absolutely useless for any kind of artistic expressions. Her inerasable smirk and deep-rooted malice ruined all her pictures.

I hid from Father in my bedroom for a few days. Maybe I shouldn't have abused Grandma despite her own enthusiasm and role. But I wished I could tell everybody she was guiltier about this matter than I was. I wanted to explain how she'd encouraged me subtly beyond my belief. I could tell on her but I didn't. I guess this showed a little bit of my decency, after all. I just kept my mouth shut and accepted all the blames. Father was mad at me for one week before trying to make up for his outburst by asking me to go to the movies together—the two of us only. He never again mentioned the photos, which he'd confiscated. Sometimes, I thought maybe his harsh reaction was only a sign of jealousy after he saw the artistry I'd shown in those colourful pictures. Maybe he wished he'd thought about this subject and taken the pictures himself. Grandma was his mother, after all, not mine! Maybe he wished he'd immortalized his mom himself, especially now that he'd realized his mom's hidden wishes and proclivity. Maybe he could've even rescued his mom from the religious grip that had ruined her life! I don't know! In the end, I couldn't figure out which interpretation matched Father's mind and personality best: Artistic jealousy, a crude Islamic prejudice, or any other complex motive, including his guilt for his own sins.

I felt sorry for Grandma for exposing her feminine tendencies to the whole world, which at the same time revealed her shaky religious beliefs, too. I also felt sorry for all other stuff that Jamal and I had done to her. I recalled those occasions when Jamal had thrown all the dishes and food out the window. A few times, he did it only because food was too hot. He shouted, "Why is this too hot?" and there went the whole thing out the window. He didn't even wait for an answer. I wondered why he couldn't wait a minute for the food to cool down. Besides, how was this matter in any way poor Grandma's fault? Jamal's lack of conscience and logic made me think he was only looking for an excuse to stick it to her for whatever reason. Maybe he had problems with his mother, too, like me. Although I truly liked Jamal, sometimes I believed he was a complete ass and cuckoo. At the same time, deep down, I wished I had guts like him to do similar stuff to Narges and get away with them the way Jamal did. I could sort of understand Father holding grudges against grandma for begging him to marry Narges in hopes of solving their financial issues, but what was Uncle Jamal mad about? Both Father and I owed our good looks to Grandma, so did Uncle Jamal. Yet the three of us hurt her the most, instead of kissing her feet for the great gift she'd given us. Of course, Father and Uncle Jamal had inherited Grandma's *too* delicate physique as well. Especially Uncle Jamal was rather short and semi-feminine, which he hoped to make up for with his charm and good looks. It worked sometimes but not always, it seemed. Luckily, I was the tallest in the family, like grandpa, although Narges and Uncle Mustafa were tall, too.

By the way, Jamal somehow found out about the pictures I'd taken from Grandma, too. Maybe Narges told him. She was quite ecstatic the night Father saw the pictures and attacked me in the party. She had such a good time during those moments and the following week while Father was mad at me. She got sad again, of course, at the end of the week, when she found out Father and I had made up and he was taking me to the movies. Jamal got angry with me even more than Father had. I couldn't understand these two atheists, reacting so passionately to such a small matter. Why were these two womanizers so prejudiced and sensitive only about Grandma's hair or wearing lipsticks? What did they have against the art of photography? What had I done wrong? Deep down, however, I felt their sentiments without being quite able to explain it. I knew I'd been wrong.

Another point crossing my mind, when Grandma glared at me those days (when preparing for my grade-twelve exams), was that she abhorred me, amongst many other valid reasons, for the fact that my artistry had brought her an everlasting disrepute. She might've felt deeply ashamed after hearing about his sons' overt reactions to the photos. She'd probably been even more surprised about this matter than I had been. Her sister and other children had surely scorned her directly, too. Anyway, the bottomline was that I was a bad grandson for so many reasons, especially tainting her image as a devout Muslim. For six years, I'd kept giving her more reasons every day to resent me. And now I feel guilty for not recognizing Grandma's hurt feelings at the time and for not getting a chance to ask for her forgiveness. This is another big curse I believe is cast over me forever. Sorry Grandma.

2

Narges brought me food every few days. I felt sorry for her, for going through all that extra hassle to deal with her son's endless conundrums. For the first time, I felt she looked worried for me. I felt we were both learning a bit about compassion toward each other and in general at last. Take that as another blissful outcome of breaking up with Mina, I told myself. Maybe a little too late, but a good start nevertheless. I told her I could manage somehow to eat outside. However, she insisted on bringing me food and checking on me in case I needed something. I believed she was happy about the situation, as she'd guessed something had gone wrong between Father and me. Maybe by supporting me in my time of need she could increase my animosity toward Father. She might've even felt a bit guilty for somehow causing the roots of my lingering unrest, crooked personality, and present agony grown over the years. She knew I was facing turmoil. I gathered this mainly from the anecdote she once told me to raise my spirit.

She said, "I was in the kitchen a few days ago chatting with the servants. I told Rahim you're going through a rough time and that's why you're avoiding all of us. Do you know what he said?"

"No," I replied.

"He said any time boys in his village behave weird like this, it just means they want a wife. That's how a boy sends a message to his mother to find him a bride."

I smiled and stared into Narges's eyes with some affection. I appreciated her attempts to cheer me up.

She continued, "So, what do you say? Is this true? Do you want me to find you a bride?"

I burst into laughter and she laughed aloud with me. This was the first time we were laughing together from what we'd said to each other.

"Is that a yes? Should I start looking?" she said giddily. She was enjoying her own sense of humour. Perhaps she'd realized at last that she could be funny without being sarcastic.

"No, thank you," I said.

"But let me know if you changed your mind," she said with more loud laughter.

"Okay. You'll be the first one to know."

I believed her contacts with Mina had given her a chance to realize that both Mina and I were going through rough times, with a possible *and imaginable* connection. I imagined Mina wasn't probably too happy about losing me, either. It had always been difficult to understand what went on in her pretty head. The risks she always took, her ingenuous love of life, and all those affairs made her appear mysterious. She was really *mysterious*, exactly as the gypsy woman had predicted. Yet, I believed Mina sort of loved me, too—amongst God knew how many other men and boys! The point I wasn't quite certain about was Narges's knowledge of Father being the cause of my turmoil, too. But, if I had to bet, I'd say she knew about that as well. She'd most likely seen enough reactions by me, Mina, and Father in recent weeks, plus the shattered door of Grandma's house, to suspect that all these events and reactions were somehow related.

Father hadn't contacted me for three weeks since the incident. That by itself proved many things, including his guilt. He knew what was bothering me. He knew that I knew about his affair with Mina. He'd probably seen me running in the headlight of his car. At least he knew it by now, after Mina telling him about my unexpected visit, slapping her twice, and then pounding her toes. I tried to imagine Father's face, either getting angry with me for torturing his mistress, or chuckling, enjoying my assertiveness. I realized he was in an odd position, too. I also wondered which one of us he loved more: Mina or me. Was it possible he himself had encouraged Mina to seduce me in order to make a man out of me? Had he just attempted to do something similar to what Uncle Jamal had tried to do the night he asked me to have sex with his girlfriend, Shahla? Had Mina told him how much I loved her? In all, he knew by now, if not for a long time before this incident, that I'd been seeing Mina. He possibly knew about my love for Mina, my marriage proposal to her, and my anger towards him because of all these affairs and the incident. He would've called me if he hadn't been feeling *some kind of* guilt. He would've surely tried to know why I hadn't gone home or made any effort to see him at least for getting some money.

But you know who called me so casually? Mina. The nerve of this woman. The first night I'd returned to my city residence from Feri's house, she called. She said she was in Parvaneh's house and that she said hello. You can't imagine how cool she was on the phone, as if nothing had happened between us. As if I weren't hurt at all. As if she didn't remember how hard I'd slapped her. During the week I'd stayed in Feri's house, I'd thought about her all the time, but only for erasing my memories of her. So her warm conversation on the phone sounded absurd. Were she and I living on different planets? Was this just one of her proven tactics she'd often used on other men, especially poor Dr. Afzali?

"When are you coming to see me?" she asked like she'd just returned from a trip and wanted me to buy a bouquet of roses like old times and go welcome her. Her serious tone and arrogance made me chuckle, while I wrestled the devil inside me insisting to forgive her.

"Never. I never want to see you again in my life. Don't call me here, either," I replied.

"Why? At least tell me why you're acting so strange."

"You think I'm acting strange? You're actually crazy, beyond strange."

"I agree. I'm crazy about you," she said. Again, I must stress my amazement. Listening to her was like hearing a four-year-old kid talking. I recalled the beginning of our relationship when I had a hard time calling her by her first name like she was such a godly figure, and not the child on the other side of the phone this minute. How stupidly polite I'd been around women in the Club and parties before learning about their deep frailties and deceit.

"I don't care and I don't believe you, anyway," I said. "I must go. Don't call me again."

"Please, Kian. Let's meet and discuss everything."

"No. Never."

"Why?"

"I've told you the reason a few times already. You just keep saying you don't have anything to tell me."

"Because there's nothing to tell."

"Forget it. I can't deal with you. You win."

"I win what? Promise to call me soon when you cool down."

"I won't. Besides, I really have to focus on my exams from now on..." I paused as a great idea crossed my mind. "Besides, I have a girlfriend now and don't want you in my life."

A long pause followed her sigh of surprise.

"You love her?"

"Yes."

"Is she the same girl I saw in your grandpa's memorial? What was her name?"

"Yes. The same girl. I really love her."

"More than what you always said you loved me?"

"Absolutely. I don't love you anymore, anyway."

"Okay, Kian. I wish you a happy life," she said.

"Okay, Mina," I replied with a cool voice. But my throat was clogged and tears ran down my cheek.

3

I smoked freely around the house with several ashtrays filled with cigarette butts. Not a rational behaviour, of course, but I couldn't help it, especially with the gold Dunhill still in my possession. I didn't know what to do with it. Narges made sarcastic remarks about my smoking, but I simply ignored her. I believed I was thinking straight and behaving quite rational for a broken boy. I was starting to act firm like a man at last. Destiny or the course of the events in the last seventeen years, especially the last three, had brought me to this critical moment of remorse and awakening. So now, I had to try to play a major role regarding various issues, take charge of my life, and plan seriously for my future.

Jamal lend me thirty thousand rials and emphasized it was only a loan, which I must repay soon. Otherwise, he'd have to collect it from Dadash Jalal, he stressed. He tried to sound very serious, making sure I paid the school this time and really got down to prepare for the upcoming exams. He wanted to make me feel responsible for my actions and decisions. I only chuckled while he kept making his threats. We both knew how hollow they were. Although, a minute later, I felt he'd most likely do it if he happened to merely dislike me one day for a simple matter. He'd proven to be an extremely spiteful, conceited, and angry man.

Mr. Ramzi grabbed the money, but emphasized with anger that they'd introduce me for the national exams only if my marks in internal final exams were above eighty percentile. I agreed. Feri and Goli believed I was dreaming about doing nine months of school work in such a short period all on my own and getting such high marks, too. Still Goli promised to help me. Now I had a big priority and goal in my life, totally different from everything I'd been doing during the last three years. I had to prove my true self, to recreate a smart Kian, in less than two months.

It is always helpful to support your short-term goals with longer-term plans and that was exactly what I tried to do. Of course, graduating from high school would by itself bring me some freedom and a sense of accomplishment. I realized that. However, deep down, I felt a stronger incentive could help an impossible task according to Mr. Ramzi, Goli, and Feri. Luckily, I'd found my long-term plan as well. Especially after my last telephone conversation with Mina, it'd become clear that I had to run as far away from her, my parents, the life of aristocracy and clubs, and all the phony people around me. I also had to give Grandma her home back and plan to make my own living. Thank God, all these goals could be combined and achieved if only I acted on the gypsy's advice to plan for my travel to the new world and work. But how? I had no financial or moral support to pursue such a grand scheme. Yet I decided these obstacles should be handled somehow. My long-term objectives were too sacred to dismiss because of the logistics.

Imagining a bright future in the new world had boosted my spirit another notch and clicked a switch in my head. I drowned myself deep into my textbooks and Goli's notes. I woke up at six in the morning and went to bed at midnight. I did nothing but studying and I met nobody but Goli. She came by only for short visits to clarify difficult concepts. Neither of us felt like spending even two minutes on romance. We didn't even kiss. For me, my hurt feeling after Mina stopped my urge for romance with any woman. Narges saw Goli once when she came to drop off food for me. Both Goli and she were surprised when I introduced Goli as my girlfriend. I did it to hurt Mina. I knew Narges would tell her how beautiful Goli was and how happy I looked with her in my life. She'd tell Mina that Goli and I appeared like an ideal couple.

More timely and helpful, my sentiments pleased Goli, too.

Nobody knew about my plan to travel to the new world. In particular, I couldn't upset Goli at the time I needed her so much. I felt guilty sometimes for my treachery. I wished I could take her with me, but it felt like an impossible dream. I couldn't take her regardless of the price I had to pay for not having her in my life. I wasn't even sure if or when I'd dare to love someone truly again. She was surprised by my incredible determination to catch up. But she could never imagine that preparing for my big escape was behind all that energy. In all, I couldn't drag Goli into my risky future, despite my dire desire to share all my dreams with her. I had to prepare myself for hardships and couldn't ask her to share them with me. There would be enough difficulties ahead already without carrying the burden of the big responsibility for her, too. I couldn't speak out and apologize for not including her in my absurd dreams, either. I was stuck and had to just control my conscience, emotions, and big mouth. *Stay practical, you lover boy. No more love for a while—maybe a long long while…*

4

Sometimes I got out of the house for fresh air or strolled with Goli in the quiet neighbourhood. Around this time of year, many students sit under the tree shades of Kakh Avenue and study their asses off. Witnessing their labour and determination to pass the excruciating national exams and get into universities pushed me to work harder myself. The limited space at top universities in Iran brings the best out of these young geniuses and raises the bar for all. Most of them are poor and live in crowded, warm, and noisy houses. So they come to these cool streets, which, despite the traffic, are much quieter than their own tiny homes. They studied all day and night, ate very little, and slept sporadically in a corner of the street or next to a tree. Poor, desperate, motivated, and extremely intelligent, every one of them was an enemy in my tough situation at that point. And there were just too many of them, pushing up the standards and the passing percentile beyond humans' normal capacity. Still I enjoyed watching them. Maybe I hated being the only one torturing myself for some imaginary future—which would probably prove as lousy, anyway. They made me feel good about myself as well, compared with the bum I'd been the last three years. I felt proud to fight hard for similar objectives, although those jerks were really making it impossible for me. I really liked those guys, or at least enjoyed the scene of so many of them suffering like me.

The fresh air and the calm hoopla in the streets revived me. Every time I returned to my city residence, I found myself blessed to have access to such a quiet, cool place—and beer, too, if necessary. Goli was also blessed, living in a luxurious house with lots of privacy and all. I told her I wished I could bring some of those poor guys into my Kakh residence—to the Palace—and let them study in our large, quiet garden or even indoors perhaps. She said she'd do the same if her parents let her. We were not trying to be cute or nice guys. Believe me. I knew she was telling the truth. What a gem. On my part, however, I doubted my own sincerity and depth of compassion sometimes when my chronic cynicism regarding human nature questioned the rationality of helping people. Of course, I hid these demented sentiments of mine from Goli as well.

Goli suggested to shake hands and agree to never forget how lucky we both were. Those kinds of her emotions made me adore her even more. I really loved her in my stupid way. I was so lucky she happened to be around me at the time I needed some emotional support after leaving Mina. Naturally, I never told her about Mina. Sometimes, pondering my plan to abandon Goli soon made me cry.

Many sporadic thoughts and feelings also overwhelmed me occasionally and I couldn't concentrate for one or two hours. For one thing, my feelings for Father were harsh but also confusing, at times, when I tried to figure out his guilt. Despite my edgy emotions, I wanted to be rational. The question was whether he'd known anything about my affair with Mina before the incident in front of her house? How could've he reacted if Mina had been his mistress even before she'd started loving me, too? Yet my rage always overrode any rational thoughts that crossed my mind. I wondered how to react in case we happened to meet. Should I just run away from him? Should I confront him? I couldn't keep Mina out of my mind, either. I'd told her that I despised her, but I still loved her whenever my rage was subdued for some reason, maybe by a beer. I'd told her I didn't want to see her, but I was dying to see her and have sex. This was weird because I knew I didn't want to even kiss her ever again. It felt awkward to even speak with my father's mistress. Yet, I took out her picture from the hiding place, stared at it, and reminisced many exhilarating moments of our long affair. I imagined Mina and Father talking about me, too. What would they be saying to each other about the situation? I also spent hours pondering the logistics of travelling to the new world. It was no longer the matter of if, but only the issue of how. I had some basic ideas, but they all still needed a lot of polishing and rethinking. Until one night, by a fluke, I recalled Uncle Mustafa, Narges's half-brother.

All those years, Uncle Mustafa had visited us only a dozen times. He'd met Father and they'd become good friends. This was another blow to Narges's ego—to witness the two men she disliked for different reasons were now so close. The more poor Narges had resisted the idea of socializing with Uncle Mustafa and his family, the more Father had been eager to do so, which in turn had most likely made Narges hate both of them even more. I couldn't say whether Father really liked Mustafa or humoured him only out of spite for Narges. I also imagined the high chance of Narges seeing Mustafa as a *cause,* or at least the *result*, of her mother's decision (whether she'd been pregnant or not) to give up Narges. I'd suspected this scenario myself, let alone Narges who now felt like a direct victim of this incident leading to her lifelong misery, while Mustafa had enjoyed a real family. For a spiteful person like Narges, especially, even seeing Mustafa was now hurtful, let alone considering any chance for liking him. *No wonder she couldn't like him at all!*

Uncle Mustafa and I, however, felt genuine warmth toward each other. I'd written the details of his first visit to our house in my diary along with his telephone number. I found the number, jotted it down on a piece of paper, and laid it on a corner of my desk. I looked at it for a week and pondered the manner of telling him everything. I needed guts to ask him for such a major favour. However, more awkward was the task of revealing my freaky relationship with my parents.

One night I decided to simply jump in and try my luck with Uncle Mustafa, instead of waiting for courage any longer. He was surprised to hear my voice, as I'd expected. I told him I had some issues to discuss with him in person if he was planning to come to Tehran soon. He said he'd be coming in ten days. I gave him my phone number and asked him to call me only at that number. He promised to keep our telephone conversation and subsequent meeting confidential.

5

Uncle Mustafa and I met in the lobby of Bahar Hotel where he was staying. Making such a big request, which also revealed my murky relationship with my parents, felt embarrassing. So I asked him lots of absurd questions, like how and what his kids were doing! My clownish conscience whispered in my head, *Since when you've become such a sociable and caring guy!?* Uncle Mustafa was polite and patient with my gibberish, but eager to hear the main issue. At last, I gathered my guts and looked into his eyes with determination.

"Do you remember your offer outside our house the first time you visited us?"

"I'm not young, *pesaram*. Please refresh my memory."

"You told me to call you if I needed help."

"Oh, yes, of course. Tell me what you need."

"Money... Lots of it," I said with presumed humour.

"How much?" He smiled but looked confused.

"I don't know... A lot, I guess... I'll pay you back as soon as I find a job in the United States."

"Oh! Are you going away?" he asked with a smirk. "Will you be back for dinner?"

"I'm serious," I said with annoyance.

"Sorry Kian, but your plan didn't sound serious to me."

"Why not?"

"For one thing, you can't be serious about working there while going to college. I don't recommend that."

"I'm going there only to work," I replied as if I'd received a job offer from Gerald Ford to help him in the White House.

"That's even worse. Is your family okay with your plan?"

"They don't know it."

"Why? What's going on, Kian?"

"Father and I aren't in good terms these days. I've never been close to Narges, either."

"Why don't you want to go to university here?"

"Because I like to live in the United States."

"Oh! Sorry! I didn't know," he said with another smirk.

"You're not serious today at all!" I said, my famous grimace warning him.

"But life in America isn't easy, especially for foreigners. I've been there and I have a business there, too."

"Well, this is something I must figure out for myself."

"But you must first discuss it with your parents. I can't do something that might upset your parents with me."

"I don't want them to be involved."

"Then I don't know how I can help you?"

"I understand. I only asked because I recalled your words. You rolled down your car window and—"

"Yes, yes. I remember it now. I still like to help you, but not behind your parents' back."

"Okay. Sorry for bothering you."

"It's not a matter of money, you should understand."

"Then lend me some money and I'll promise not to mention it to anybody."

"No, that's not the right way," he said with a smirk.

"Why?"

"Because now I know what you need the money for. I can't hide a project of this nature from your parents."

"What if I come back in a few months and ask for money to start a business."

Uncle Mustafa burst into laughter. "I'm sure you wouldn't lie to me, would you?"

I stared at the floor. "I'll find money some other way. Don't worry..., but please don't mention our conversation to anybody."

"Well," Uncle Mustafa said with hesitation. "I don't know. I'm now concerned about your situation at home and plans more than anything else."

"Worried about what?"

"You've shared your strange plan with me and it doesn't sound rational to me, especially if you're not going to discuss it with your parents. Promise me not to do anything rash without their knowledge."

"I can't promise anything," I said.

"You're putting me in a tight spot then, I hope you realize."

"Why?"

"How do you expect me to sit on this information now?"

"At least promise me not to talk about it until I really decide what to do."

"Only if you promise not to leave Iran before letting me know far in advance."

"Okay. I promise. I should go do some studying...," I said and stood up. I decided to worry about breaking my promise to him, or not, later. I was sorry I'd discussed my plan with him. I hadn't imagined it would put a big dent in my plan instead of helping it.

Uncle Mustafa walked with me to the street. He appeared anxious, but I said a quick goodbye to him and rushed away.

I strolled in the streets with anger but also scepticism. Some six years back, a gypsy had put a senseless idea in my silly head and now I was pursuing it like a crusade. What was I trying to run away from, other than my parents? I could easily do the same without leaving Iran. How could I trust the possibility of finding a better life in the new world? I knew nobody there and the chance of finding a good job in America, I was told, was quite slim for foreigners. I walked over an hour all the way back home instead of taking a bus. I had to evaluate my radical plan one last time before trying to find money some other way. Maybe I should stay in Iran and serve the two-year mandatory military service as an option to stay away from my family and maybe grow into a man as well. Or maybe I could go to a university in another city in Iran. Maybe I could go live in Isfahan near, or with, Uncle Mustafa? I had many options sounder than going to the U.S.

Yet, after the long walk home and thinking, going to America still felt urgent, as though the gypsy woman's spell still haunted me and President Ford was really desperate that I start my duties right away. I wished the gypsy were around to reassess my case. I wished she'd come back and tell me, "Forget what I'd told you. Don't go anywhere. I'd made a mistake." Until then, however, I had to stick to my original plan and disallow indecision cripple me. I'd find money somehow no matter what. Perhaps I could rob a bank, after all, or sell a few of Narges's fine jewelleries to Mozafarian or another jeweller.

6

I hated my promise to Uncle Mustafa. Even worse, however, I wondered whether Uncle Mustafa would keep his promise for now at least? It all depended on how much he trusted mine. I was myself pondering leaving Iran without telling him. So how could I expect Uncle Mustafa to trust me? Maybe grownups have a higher integrity, I thought for only a second. Then I realized he wouldn't trust my promise, since grownups are more experienced and know people lie and break their promises easily. So I couldn't trust him. I needed a way out of this mess, but I couldn't find a solution all day. Instead, I got more frustrated and angry with Uncle Mustafa every minute.

I couldn't concentrate on my studies and practices Goli had programmed for me. A lot of time was being wasted because my deal with Uncle Mustafa had gone sour. Instead of getting his support, I had to keep his mouth shut. Finding the money now seemed much simpler than quieting Uncle Mustafa. I settled on borrowing two or three pieces of Narges's jewelleries for good as part of my advance inheritance. One piece would probably pay for my plane ticket and one year of living expenses in the U.S. in case I couldn't find a job. But to be on the safe side, I'd borrow three of her jewelleries and sell them in Tehran or take some of them with me to the U.S. I even made a clever plan for doing it one afternoon when my parents weren't home and servants were in their room, busy with some kind of perversion or taking a nap. Narges probably wouldn't even notice the loss or only blame the servants. She'd probably forgive them quickly, maybe without even bothering to interrogate them.

But what to do with Uncle Mustafa? I had to find a way to distract him. After some thinking, I realized he wouldn't trust me if I told him I'd changed my mind. Even if he believed me, he might still mention my abandoned childish plan to Father. And if Father heard about my crazy plan, he'd stop me. He could simply tell the passport office to never issue a passport to me without his consent. He had many ways of stopping my departure. So Father shouldn't get the smallest clue and thus I had to stop Uncle Mustafa at any cost, short of killing him, I hoped.

7

Uncle Mustafa called me himself early the next morning. He sounded anxious and asked to visit him in the evening. But I was reluctant to do so before inventing a special plan of my own.

"Is something wrong?" I asked.

"I don't feel comfortable about the way we left off our chat yesterday."

"In what way, Uncle Mustafa?"

"So many questions are now bothering me, Kian. I'll tell you at dinner tonight."

"Can't we talk now? I'm behind with my studies."

"I'll go pick you up and take you back home quickly after dinner. You must take a break to eat, anyway."

I just couldn't say no to him, although I didn't like him as much these days. He picked me up around seven p.m. and we went to a nearby restaurant.

"Narges's son is like my own son. I've totally meant this whenever I called you my son," he said after we ordered.

"I appreciate it, Uncle Mustafa," I said with a smirk.

"Especially now that you're not talking to your parents, you've suddenly put a heavier load on my shoulder. I must be closer to you and more informed about the stuff on your mind; I hope you understand?"

"What stuff?" I asked. I loathed the tone of his voice and the idea of my sudden obligation to him, too.

"I like to know about your plan to leave Iran, of course. I want to know how you intend to get the money, what you're planning to do in the U.S., the issues you have with your parents, and why in the hell you don't want to tell them about your intention to go abroad."

Boy, he was getting on my nerves really fast. Still I decided to stay calm. "Because I don't want to argue about it with them. Father, especially, might try to change my mind. And he's the last person I want to meet or argue with."

"Why are you avoiding your father? Can I possibly mediate between you two?"

"I can't discuss it with anybody or Father himself. This matter can't be fixed."

"But he's your father. When I think about the possibility of Hamid doing the same thing to me, my heartbreaks. Please be reasonable. Let's find a way to reconcile between you two."

"No. That's impossible. I understand that you can't help me. That's fine. I won't bother you anymore."

"Kian, *pesaram*, please don't talk to me this way."

"But I'm really under a lot of pressure these days."

"That's exactly why I find myself more in a bind," Uncle Mustafa said. "I just can't walk away and ignore your stress and problems. We should find a way to work this out between us or I must go talk to your father about it. I want you to understand my dilemma."

"Well, I like to solve this matter between us, too, but how?"

"I don't know either. But, as I said, you must be either open with me completely or let me talk to your father and relieve my conscience from this bind a little at least."

"I've been open with you. I don't know where I'll get the money yet, but I must go live in the U.S."

"Oh, my dear God. How can we solve this mess?" Uncle Mustafa said with a deep sigh.

"If you just lend me the money, I'll repay it to the last dinar."

"I already told you that money isn't the issue here."

"But maybe you shouldn't worry about other stuff."

"How can I do that? I'd be betraying my sister if I hide your drastic plans from your parents. Narges is a tough woman to deal with already. I can't make my situation even worse with her."

"I understand, but I don't want them to know."

Uncle Mustafa just kept staring at me and pondering. The waiter started to serve our dinner and we got busy with our food without speaking a word for about twenty minutes. Surely, we both had special dilemmas to handle and we couldn't think of a compromise. I sort of understood his position, too, but I couldn't worry about him. He still looked anxious and quiet like me after we finished our supper with great appetite, as if our tension had no side effect whatsoever. Thinking that at least we seemed to be sharing the same high degree of love for food made me tickle and feel better. At last, he said he was ready to take me back home, but just before I got out of his car he had a last word for me.

"I'll call you in four days. I'd like you to tell me then about your intentions honestly. If you're still planning to go away, you must tell me about all its details, including how you're going to get the money. Then I'll decide what the right thing is for me to do under the circumstances. Hopefully, I've made myself clear to you tonight?"

"Yes, you have. Thank you very much!" I replied tensely.

"Either way, I must discuss a bit of our conversations with at least one of your parents. You can choose which one you want me to talk with."

"But you promised you won't talk to anyone for now," I said with anger.

"I can't keep this promise. It's not the right thing to do."

8

Uncle Mustafa had really pissed me off this time. I wished I dared scream at him and curse him. I couldn't concentrate to study for one whole day. What was the point of studying like a maniac, anyway, if I couldn't go to America? I could always graduate from high school later, possibly next year, if I really wanted to. Still, as a last resort, I invented a lousy solution that I hoped would satisfy Uncle Mustafa, too. If not, I had no other idea and had to just sit back and let fate keep pushing my pathetic life. Once I settled on this strategy, I got back my courage and concentration and attacked the textbooks again.

Uncle Mustafa called me on the fourth day as promised and we met in Bahar Hotel again. I started explaining my plan right away.

"I still think I should go to the U.S. and your financial support would make it easier, of course. My suggestion is that you let me make the arrangements. Once everything is in place you talk to

Narges about my plan and tell her that I don't like anybody else to know about it until I leave," I said.

Uncle Mustafa kept thinking for three minutes. I'd come up with this plan by assuming that Narges could be convinced of the rationality of my plan. Actually, she might be happy to see me run away. At least it'd give her another huge chance to blame Father for the way I'd become because of his mistakes.

"It is not a very good plan," Uncle Mustafa said at last. "But I'm willing to consider it if you agree with my conditions."

"What're your conditions?" I asked.

"First, you must keep me informed about everything from now on. But the main condition is that if Narges doesn't wish to keep your plan a secret, you shouldn't get mad with anybody and let her do whatever she thinks is necessary. And if she says no, I won't be able to help you."

Now it was my turn to think for about four minutes. At last, I realized I had to agree with his conditions. Hopefully, by the time we were going to inform Narges, I would have my passport and a better chance of running away even if Father was informed a few days before my departure. I also hoped Narges wouldn't reject Uncle Mustafa's proposal if he explained my reasons to her with diligence.

"Okay, I agree with your conditions," I said.

"All right then, let's shake hands on this." he extended his hand. I shook it and we both smiled.

"So you'll lend me money until I find a job in America?"

"Yes, I will, don't worry."

"I also owe thirty thousand rials to my uncle. I like to pay him back if I leave Iran. Otherwise, I'll work and pay him myself."

Uncle Mustafa burst into laughter. "I like your openness and sense of humour. You sound exactly like Hamid."

"I know I'm asking you too much, right?"

"Well, let's see... You're asking me to lend you money for travelling, another thirty thousand to pay Uncle Jamal, then also guarantee to keep sending you money as long as you ask for it."

"That's what you brought upon yourself six years ago!" I said with a grin.

"That's true. Don't worry about money. What'd you use the thirty thousand for?"

"To pay my high school tuition."

"Didn't your father pay it?"

"I used the money for personal expenses."

"You live too expensively even in this cheap country!"

"I'll promise to live very economically in America."

"You won't tell me what's gone wrong between you and your father, ha?"

"No. Please don't ask. It's a sensitive issue."

"Okay, I understand," he said with a grudge.

"Great. I hope we don't have to talk about Father anymore, right?" I asked. I felt I'd sounded like Narges—straightforward and rude. But, to be honest, I was losing my patience with Uncle Mustafa and his diligent interrogation for doing such a simple thing. I didn't understand all his fuss.

Uncle Mustafa only nodded. He'd noticed my frustration. He'd certainly had many situations like this with his own kids and was familiar with young people's testiness *once in a while*. Most likely *regularly*!

"Don't you get along with your mother, either?"

"No. We've never been close. You know how she is…"

"Yeah. She's stubborn like you," he said.

"And many other things…"

"You must get a student visa then."

"Sure. I'll get an admission from a college or something."

"Have you decided what you're going to study?"

"Nothing. I'll only get an admission letter for visa. But once I get there, I'll find a job."

"This plan doesn't work for me at all," he said sternly.

"What do you mean?" I asked.

"My other condition is that you must go straight to college and get at least your bachelor degree before looking for a job."

"But college is just a waste of life nowadays," I said.

"Your radical ideas can't convince me, Kian. My conditions are firm."

"You're forcing me to do something new any second," I snapped.

"I guess I am. But education is a main condition. I thought I'd made that clear already?"

We left Bahar Hotel and chatted some more as we strolled for a block together. He mentioned his kids and the difficulty of communicating with them, which was sometimes tougher than his recent dealings with me. He was trying to make me relax. He confessed he found our communication much more normal and open. I said all kids have difficulty opening up to their parents, as though I were a wiseass professor of child psychology. Even more bizarre, he now seemed to trust me to be a good source, if not a professional advisor, to sort out his problems with his own kids. I also told him I appreciated having him and Uncle Jamal around me, which partly made up for the lack of siblings, too. Not that all siblings could communicate, but some did, I could imagine. In the last minute, he told me to think seriously about his condition to go to college.

I hated distractions under my present circumstance. I had so little time and I'd organized every minute of it with only five hours of sleep every night to catch up with all the readings and exercises that poor Goli had put together for me to do. So, fussing so much over Uncle Mustafa's conditions was affecting my schedule, energy, and mood. Yet a quick decision was necessary. I couldn't even discuss my complex dilemmas—my secret and planned betrayal—with unsuspecting Goli. She was my auxiliary brain these days; mine was filled with formulas and concepts and other junk. At last, I decided to go study psychology, which could have other benefits for me as well: It would give me some time to familiarize myself with the new world and find a good job later without any financial pressure. Studying psychology might help me figure out myself, too, as I realized I was only a lost young man, if that. I needed lots of time and expertise to find a more reliable, real Kian in me, if there was one.

After making this hard decision, I could concentrate on my scheduled studies. I reduced my sleep to three hours every night, while drinking lots of tea to stay awake. Uncle Mustafa called me to arrange for another dinner and discussion. I said I'd accept his condition to go to college, but no dinner out tonight.

"What subject you'll study at college?" he asked.

"I don't know yet. I'll decide later," I said, trying to get rid of him. I still remembered my bad experience with Father on the same topic, while he sternly warned me that there has never been a Minister of Psychology in any country!

Uncle Mustafa was quiet for about ten seconds and then said, "Kian, remember I must get Narges's consent before buying your plane ticket; at least a week before your departure. If she says no, I cannot do anything for you; I want you to remember that."

"Okay," I said with the intention of closing the deal. Besides, maybe by then I could find another way of running away without his help and knowledge. "Let's wait for my graduation and see if any of these steps would be necessary."

"Is there a chance you might not graduate?"

"Yes, but I'm trying hard to avoid another setback."

"Good boy. Good luck. Keep me posted…"

"I will. Thanks, Uncle Mustafa. I appreciate your help."

"You're welcome, *pesaram*."

CHAPTER SEVENTEEN
Abandoning a Beautiful Angel

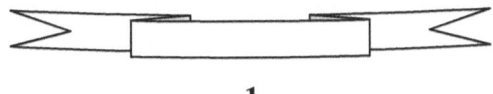

1

Sometimes, I thought the gypsy woman had been more than a psychic. She'd been an angel with a special mission to save my life from taking a horrible turn. I wanted to believe in this omen in order to stick to my ambitious plans at all cost. Her warning had pushed my pride to drop Mina without hesitation, instead of believing her claim of innocence or playing her games forever. Resisting that much charm was difficult for any mature man, let alone for a love-thirsty kid like me. Even my infatuation for the gypsy had been an omen in itself—to prepare myself for the heartbreak of all love affairs. So, her command to plan for going to the new world must have a divine purpose, too, although it'd caused only havoc so far.

I followed Goli's tight deadlines and guidelines to catch up with the grade twelve courses, took the internal exams, and passed them with flying colours. Mr. Ramzi was really pissed off for having to fudge a set of good marks for my mid-term exams and introducing me for the national exams, which I passed with still higher marks. Next, I had to study even harder for taking the nationwide university tests. I was accepted for a few fields of studies at Tehran University. I could go to any university, indeed, with the kind of marks I got. All these achievements qualified me for an exit visa, too, without doing the military service. So, I was finally ready to go build myself a fantastic future in America!

Throughout this atrocious sequence of studying and taking a thousand tests, grappling with Mina's memories was the hardest challenge. I used different gimmicks to calm my yearning for her. Praising my willpower, in particular, boosted my ego and eased the pain of not seeing and touching her. I just kept thinking that my timing to dump her couldn't have been any more perfect. If I'd continued seeing her even one extra week, I would've not graduated from high school or done all the other stuff. Instead, Mina would've simply driven me to my ultimate madness the same way she'd done it to poor Dr. Afzali and others. Father was probably another one of her victims. Overall, the separation felt like a blessing more every day despite the pain I still couldn't shake off. The old saying that there is a reason for every setback in our lives—God's wisdom—was proved to me again. So I thanked Him too. But I was too hurt and sad to forgive Him yet. Sadly, my lifelong doubts about Narges and God have always remained quite deep to overcome easily. Some of us get damaged too much to believe in God despite the divine signs we receive now and then. But I was also worried about my childish atheism. I didn't wish to remain a blasphemer because of Ozra Banu's possible contamination of my mind.

I sent my school transcripts to a dozen colleges in California because many of my classmates talked about its fantastic climate and fun atmosphere. Goli was accepted to the medical school at Tehran University, as she'd planned. She kept asking me which school I'd chosen and I told her that I hadn't decided. I was still hiding my plan to go away. Poor Goli! I knew I might be losing the greatest opportunity of my life if I let Goli slip out of my life. But if that were true, why would God send the gypsy women to tell me to go to the new world? I got a bit confused when I tried to sort out this dilemma. However, I'd become fully obsessed with my travel plans at that point. So I just couldn't jeopardize my fantasies by telling anybody anything about my big plan. In particular, if Goli knew, she would've been the only person who could convince me to stay in Iran to go to university together. I would've had real difficulty refusing her request the way she'd been so patient with me. I owed her my sanity and success with all those difficult exams.

I chose Pepperdine University out of a few colleges accepting me, because it was near Los Angeles. I got my student visa and passport, too, all along informing Uncle Mustafa of my progress. He promised to come to Tehran to organize the final stage of my departure and I had to make sure he did it right.

We met again in Bahar Hotel's lobby to agree on the details. He seemed to have a contract with this hotel near Ferdosi Square or owned it. Being near carpet stores and not too far away from Tehran's main bazaar was perhaps convenient for him due to his business. We strolled to a café and ordered *paloodeh*, a special Iranian delicacy.

"How long is it since you last saw or spoke with your dad?" he asked while passing thirty thousand rials in an envelope to me to give to Uncle Jamal—like paying for the information he was demanding. He'd forgotten or was ignoring his promise two months earlier not to raise this topic again. But I let it go.

"Four months," I whispered while grabbing the bag of money.

"Four months?" Uncle Mustafa shrieked.

"Yes."

"I wished I knew what kind of misunderstanding could bring so much agony and separation between a son and his father."

"It's not a misunderstanding," I replied. I felt depressed for no goddamn good reason and tears gathered in my eyes. Maybe I missed him but I was too stubborn to admit it.

"And now you want to leave him without saying goodbye," he said sadly. He was probably putting himself in Father's shoes.

"He's the main reason I'm leaving Iran," I said, but quickly realized my lie and felt horrible for my idiotic behaviour, blaming my parents all my life for my own insecurities and idiosyncrasies.

"What if you don't see him again? Don't you care?"

"I don't know...," I murmured.

"Are you planning to come back to Iran eventually?"

"No. I'll never return," I said. I felt homesick already thinking about everything I'd be missing: My friends, Goli, the memories of Iran, the Caspian Sea, and possibly Father, too. How could I do that? But I had to. That was what a madman must do to prove his insanity.

"I'm sad hearing all these things. I wish I knew what's behind these childish rows, but I hope you know what you're doing."

"Maybe someday I tell you, but not now."

"So Narges is the one I must discuss your plans with. Right?"

"Yes."

"I'm sure you know I really preferred to talk with your dad. I get along with him much better than I can with my own sister. Your mother is usually hard to handle. It'd be a big task for me."

"I know what you mean," I said.

"When're you planning to leave?"

"I have plane reservations for ten days from today."

"What if your mother insists to pay for everything herself?"

"No, I don't like that option. I hope you don't mind?"

"No. I'll support you as long as you need me."

"I'll ask you for as little money as possible. But it may still be a lot, because you're forcing me to stay in school."

"Absolutely... You should never forget our deal. Maybe someday you don't need my money, but you must continue your education. I'm sure you'll never put me down."

"I'll never break my promises to you and Uncle Jamal."

"You're a good boy. I just don't understand what's gone wrong to cause the mayhem you're putting us through now."

"By the way, don't tell Narges the date of my departure. Tell her in a few weeks. After I flew out of Tehran, tell her I'm gone."

"All right. Do you want to come to the meeting and explain your plan personally?"

"No. She or I will say stupid things and ruin everything fast."

We went over the details of his mission and how he should convince Narges. Then I left.

2

Uncle Mustafa and I met again after his meeting with Narges. He'd had a hard time convincing her to meet him for coffee. She still resisted accepting him as a relation. What a stubborn woman! I'd inherited this fabulous trait from her as well. Only after Uncle Mustafa had stressed on discussing an important matter about me, she'd agreed to meet him.

"What is this?" I asked Uncle Mustafa when we met and he gave me a set of papers.

"This is the transcript of my conversations with Narges."

"Transcript…? You wrote down your conversations?"

"No, I decided to tape it without her knowledge."

"You did…? Why?"

"First of all, I wanted to keep a proof of her consent or refusal for my records. Second, just in case she refused to help, I wanted to let you listen to our conversation personally and believe me. I also wanted you to know the exact words and promises I've made to her on your behalf. Always remember these points. Keep these papers to also know how you felt and acted these days."

"And then you also made a transcript?" I asked with surprise about his diligence and wisdom. In fact, I was shocked by his amazing foresight about the good chance of Narges changing or denying her words later. How he'd reached this valid conclusion and impression about Narges in such a rather short period of knowing her blew my mind.

"Yes, I got my secretary in the Tehran office to do it before I added my edits to explain the moods as well for your benefit. So take a few minutes and read these papers," Uncle Mustafa said.

I started reading the document:

"When she arrived at the coffee shop, she was anxious and curious.

'Have you seen Kian?' your mother asked immediately.

'Yes, we meet rather regularly.'

'Oh…!'

'Yes. He wants to go to college in the United States.'

'What? He told you that?' she asked with terror in her eyes.

'Yes. I don't know why he's not speaking with you or Jalal.'

'I don't know what's going on. Everybody's acting bizarre.'

'Who's acting bizarre?' I asked.

'Both Kian and his father. I'm not quite sure what has gone wrong between them.'

'He doesn't tell me either,' I said.

'He must talk with his father if he wants to go abroad.'

'He doesn't want to do that. That's why he wants me to help him.'

'You?'

'Yes. But I told him we need your blessing at least. He wants you to keep everything a secret until he leaves.'

'But his father will be angry with me for not telling him.'

'Why? Would he stop him if he knew?'

'I don't know. But I wished Kian wouldn't do such a stupid thing. I'm going to talk to him right away.'

'I believe he doesn't want to talk about it with anybody.'

'But I'm his mother.'

'He's made up his mind. We've been discussing this matter for the last three months. He's really serious about leaving.'

'Last three months? He never mentioned anything to me about going abroad," she said with hurt feeling.

'He's not been quite sure how to handle this issue.'

'So what do you want from me?'

'I've told Kian I can't help him without your permission.'

'My permission?'

'Yes.'

'He's been doing everything his way. He's been out of our control for five years. Since his stupid father let him live in his grandparents' house.'

'I'll be lending him money for his travel and education. He'll repay me once he gets a job. I'm comfortable with this plan.'

'I don't think his father or I like this arrangement.'

'Why is that?' I asked.

'We prefer he goes to university in Tehran. He's not in the best condition to live alone without his parents.'

'He seems to be doing fine to me. He sounds mature. He's only stubborn, like some people I know in his family,' I said. She ignored my sarcastic joke except for a glare.

'I don't know what to say,' she said with gloom. 'He's mad at me already. All these years! Now if I stop him he'd probably stop talking to me forever.'

'It's difficult to know what he'll do with himself and his life if we don't let him follow some kind of dream he's now built for himself. He thinks that he must answer to his calling.'

'What calling?'

'Going to the new world.'

'That stupid fortune-teller. That's the idea she put in his silly head. I remember that.'

'Well. There may be a reason for that. He must try, and learn, to become a man. Living alone in a foreign country might teach him that.'

'What do you think I should do?' she asked.

'I think you should let him go. Go see him if you want, but don't argue with him.'

'How about his father? He'll be furious.'

'Did you actually ask his father what's wrong between them?'

'Yes. He said he didn't know. He said kids go nuts at this age.'

'You believe him? Do you think he knows what's wrong with Kian?'

'I think he does, but he's not going to tell me. That's why I'm afraid. If I don't tell him about Kian's new foolishness, he'd be so angry. He may kill me.'

'But Kian thinks it's better that his father doesn't know about his plan.'

'I wonder why? When is he planning to leave, anyway?'

'In two or three weeks.'

'That soon?'

'I guess."

"Hmm…"

"So what's your decision?' I asked her.

'The situation might get worse if we try to keep him against his will.'

'I agree…'

'Can you explain everything to his father later and convince him?'

'Yes, I will, although it'll be hard for me to justify hiding this matter from him.'

'In that case, I guess I have to say yes and get ready for my husband's rage when he finds out.'

'I think this is a wise decision, if I may say so. But you're the one who's choosing the best option under the circumstance. You're the one who can stop him now and must deal with his father and other stuff later. I'm only telling you all the facts and I want to wash my hands about the possible consequences.'

'So he can't go if I ask you not to help him?" Narges asked with some satisfaction.

"Yes, that's the bottomline. He needs your permission…"

'That's fresh…! But I understand.'

'I'm glad you do…'

'We'll pay you all the money you give him.'

'That's not necessary. He doesn't want you or Jalal involved.'

'He's gone mad, his father is gone mad, and I'm now in the middle of this mess,' your mother said and started weeping.

'He's a good kid with some problems that he wants to solve on his own,' I said.

'God help him.'

'Do you need time, maybe one or two days, to think about your decision?'

'Not really. If you're sure we must let him go, then let him go. I'll deal with his father later. Who cares if he kills me, ha?'

'I've agreed to help him only after he promised me to go to college and get his degree. I trust him to keep his promise to me.'

"She left after a few more minutes of general chitchat," Uncle Mustafa told me after I finished reading the transcript.

I stared at Uncle Mustafa with guilt for causing everybody so much headache all the time.

"Thanks, Uncle Mustafa, for handling it so nicely, especially taping her. Keep it safe because it might become handy," I said.

"I know. I'll safeguard it with my life. You keep these papers and read them if necessary, too. There are tons of information and sensitive points in this transcript for all of us to remember.'

"You're right… I might actually need them someday when writing my memoirs…"

"You must know that all this hassle was also your fault."

"My fault? Why?" I asked.

"Because it would've not been necessary to do the taping and other stuff if you'd let me talk to your dad instead of Narges."

"Yes, you're right… Sorry…"

"As you noticed, I also wanted her and your father to know, and also document, your promise to me to finish college."

"Yes, I noticed it. I'll keep my promise to you…, I promise."

Uncle Mustafa chuckled and said, "Your mother asked me to tell you to take care of yourself and write a letter sometime. I don't know why she couldn't say these things to you personally! Your family is very strange."

"My family is the reason I'm leaving," I replied, but quickly wondered again whether that was really true or only an excuse for justifying my own stupidity and crazy obsessions.

"But you're also part of this family. You behave weirdly too, sometimes, I must say."

"I know. Sorry. That's why I'm trying to do something about my insanity. I must go cure myself before it's too late. Maybe my parents have made me like this or gave me lots of nasty genes."

"Well, I don't mind your sense of adventure and your special plans for improving your life, but stop blaming your parents for everything. You're a grownup man now and must decide how you like to live."

"You're right, Uncle Mustafa," I said and knew that he was right. I recalled my thoughts at Jamshid's deathbed in Mashad and my promise to myself to stop being a sad brat, only blaming my parents for all my insecurities and childish mentality. But it seemed that I'd still not grown up much even after all these years. *Maybe I'm a mean person, after all?*

"She's gonna come to see you a few times before you leave."

"She's probably happy to get rid of me," I said.

"Oh, Kian. Don't say that. I bet she's really suffering. Dealing with your father and you hasn't been easy for her."

"I suppose."

At the end of our discussions, Uncle Mustafa gave me enough money to pay for the plane ticket, school, and living expenses in America for a few months. All the planning stages had been completed with great success. I was now ready to leave. Except for one major emotional matter: Goli.

3

I dreaded looking into Goli's pretty eyes and see her absolute disappointment in me. I considered the option of leaving without telling her, too. But it was such a cheap option. I still had some class and integrity left in me, *despite the random clues and surges of doubts about some meanness in my nature.* I had to face the music and get at least a bit of the punishment I deserved. I hated myself for doing this treason to her and maybe demolishing her perception of humanity altogether.

I called and invited Goli for ice cream. We'd both taken our regular rendezvous in that café as a sign of our growing love. I could never forget her angelic role after my separation from Mina. She'd probably saved both my life and soul. She didn't know this, but surely felt my sincere appreciation on top of my deep affection for her—the best way I could express it under the circumstances—at a time I was so miserable because of Mina. She was also the only reason I could leave Iran and her. If only she'd known, she might've never helped me. But I bet she would've, anyway, even if I'd told her the truth from the start; such an angel she was. And now I was going to deprive myself of all that heavenly touch and break her heart in the process, too. What a moron I was! I've realized my stupidity more every day since the day we met for the last time.

"I have something important to tell you," I told Goli in the ice-cream parlour. She looked so sweet sitting there with the spoon of ice cream dangling on her smooth tongue. I craved sucking it. I loved her playfulness even for eating ice cream. I really loved her. She stared into my eyes with anticipation. For a moment, I thought she knew everything already while I peered at her with angst. Then again, the shine in her eyes showed she was waiting for some very romantic words. The most logical, timely phrase I could say after our soulful recent experiences together would've been, "I love you," before we rushed to my place and had sex for hours after so many weeks of sensible celibacy. Any sane, romantic girl, especially Goli, would've been expecting to hear that today. But I was mute like a corpse, watching her lick the ice-cream spoon playfully just to tease me. She deserved to look and behave so horny today after months of mere education.

"What?" Goli said at last when tired of my hesitation.

"I've decided to go to America."

She froze and just stared into my eyes dumbfounded. Tears gathered in her eyes as she put the spoon down in the ice-cream dish. The muscles in her face contracted and she drooped.

"Say something," I said.

Not a word. She remained still for a long time. Then she took the napkin and wiped her lips. With the same tissue, she dabbed the corners of her eyes without raising her head. I couldn't see her eyes or tears. I couldn't say if she was crying, angry, or what.

"Say something, please," I begged her.

She looked up and only stared at me again. Yet, I could hear all the questions rolling in her genius brain. So patient. So calm and collected. Such a unique creature. How could I be such a fool? Oh, God, what was I doing? What was this obsession for going to the new world? The damn gypsy woman!

"Are you serious or only trying to hurt me?" she asked at last.

"I'm serious. I've got my plane ticket and visa, everything," I said with plenty of shame.

"You've been hiding all these facts from me all this time?"

"I wasn't sure whether I should or could do it until yesterday," I lied with pain.

"But you've been planning it all along," she murmured.

"I'm really sorry, Goli," I whispered.

"How about us?"

"Why don't you come to America too?"

"Because I don't like to go to America. I love my family and country. I've told you that a few times already. I'm happy with Tehran University. Why don't you do the same thing?"

"I must get out of here. I must go to America."

"I heard you say that. But why?"

"You know my situation with my parents. I must give my grandma her house back."

"No, you don't have to. Besides, you don't have to travel so far to achieve all of these."

"Okay, probably I don't have to," I replied pensively. I had in fact earned that house with my sheer rudeness, tenacity for sins, arrogance, and force. *Wow! With all these precious traits, I could actually be a great politician, after all, as Father always dreamed about me!* So, in reality, the house must indeed belong to me after all my hard work to own it.

"So don't go," Goli said.

"But I must go."

Goli gazed at me for a long time. She was trying to read my mind. Then she dropped her head again.

My whole body contracted from a big surge of emotions and tears gathered in my eyes. So, I got up abruptly and went to the washroom to hide my face. I felt like an idiot lost in the middle of dark woods, lonely and scared. I wept a little bit, but regained my composure soon. I got out of the washroom and returned to our table. Goli wasn't at the table, so I sat there waiting, assuming she'd also gone to the washroom. I waited for ten minutes. The waiter came around and I asked him whether he'd seen her going to the washroom. He said she'd left.

I kept calling Goli for two days and hanging up whenever her parents answered the phone. At last, I decided to ask for her when her mother answered. This was such a brave thing to do in Iran. I told her there was an urgent matter I wished to speak to Goli about. She said Goli couldn't speak at that moment. She asked me to leave my telephone number to give to Goli. She was nice on the phone unlike parents' normal attitude about boys calling their daughters. I gave her my number politely, instead of telling her that Goli already had it. She didn't call me back. Maybe she hadn't imagined I'd leave in such a rush. Maybe she called me after I'd already left. Or maybe her mother never gave her my message. I've always imagined she'd tried to find and stop me just as my plane was taking off. Now, these days, I wish she'd called one day earlier.

4

The last few days before my departure were jammed with all types of chores. Narges visited me three times, as if she'd sensed Uncle Mustafa's dishonesty about the date of my departure. It was funny how nobody trusted anybody these days! A few times, she asked me when I was leaving and I always said it wasn't still definite. I could see some type of fear and anger on her face. She tried to be kind to me and make me talk to her, but I deliberately avoided her. I couldn't think of anything I wished to talk with her about, anyway, except for a bunch of silly questions. I asked her who has been opening the gate at midnight all the time I hadn't been around, especially in the recent months. She grimaced and shrieked as though hit by a jackhammer: "Me... Of course, me. You see how much trouble you always give me, even in your absence? Now I must open the gate, too, to let your selfish father drive the car into the house."

I then asked her whether the gypsy woman had come around again by any chance during the last seven years. She said no, looking surprised about my last minute bizarre questions out of millions of more relevant questions I could be asking her these days. She was probably cursing the gypsy for causing all this chaos. I did the same myself then, and I do it even more often now, especially when thinking about Goli.

"Why are all fortune-tellers women?" I asked Narges with a giggle. It seemed I couldn't stop asking silly questions that day.

"Because women are much smarter and can see everything perfectly, even about the future," she replied with pride. "Men are mostly stupid and selfish…!"

"Are you sure that's why all fortune-tellers are women?"

"Yes… Can you think of any other reason?" she asked.

"No," I lied, as I could only think of some crooked reasons.

Many times, I almost asked Narges about Mina, too, but then always felt glad afterward that I hadn't done such a stupid thing. Anytime she visited me, Mina's image jumped in my head, as if Mina were trying to communicate with me through Narges or I were hoping she did. I wondered if they were still close friends. Maybe Narges had abandoned Mina, too. Many things might've happened that I didn't know. I didn't want to ask her anything, especially about Mina, the Club, the parties, or Father. The entire time I'd been hiding in Grandma's house, Narges had never asked me either, even once, why I wasn't talking to Father. She didn't even ask me anything about my decision to leave without saying goodbye to him. I also wondered what the women in the Club, especially Mehri, knew about my break-up with Mina. How were they now coping with my sudden absence from the scene? What happened to the foolish Grigori of Royal Club? In a few moments of madness during the final days, I also imagined going around Mina's neighbourhood and wait until she got out of her house. I just wanted to see her one last time.

Sometimes I got even crazier ideas. I thought I should have a last rendezvous with her in Café Naderi. To have coffee together. To get a chance to look into her mysterious eyes with passion without uttering a word myself or allowing her to talk. I just wanted to see if I could penetrate her cruel eyes and read the kind of emotions she might still have for me. Love, my ass! I wanted to return the suit she'd bought for me as a token of her love for me. I wanted to return the possibly-gold Dunhill lighter, too. On the other hand, I didn't mind spending one whole night with her, perhaps the night before my departure. I'd tell her I've forgiven her. Even better, I'd tell her I'd made a big mistake. I'd beg for her mercy. I'd make her love me again. I might even force myself to make love to her a few times that night. Then she'd find out only a few days later about the final act. Somebody, maybe nosy Narges, would tell her I'd gone to some place she could never reach me. Without saying Goodbye Again! At last! I still loved her. Why couldn't I get her out of my mind?

5

Two days before my departure, I went inside Café Naderi when I was passing by it. I simply found myself inside the café; that was actually how it happened. The waiter took me to the same table Mina and I had most often occupied in our rendezvous. Maybe the good waiter could read my mind, to give me my regular table. Perhaps he still remembered my generous tips to show off in front of Mina, even though five months had passed since my last visit. I ordered coffee, looked around, and noticed Parvaneh with her friend. She noticed me, too, and I nodded only as a courtesy. After a pause, staring into my curious eyes, she stood up and walked fast toward me with a grin. I considered running away, but it would've looked ridiculous and I hadn't paid the bill, either.

"*Salam,* Kian," Parvaneh said.

"*Salam,* Parvaneh." I'd always addressed her as Parvaneh *Khanum* as a courtesy for an older lady. Not anymore.

"May I sit down?"

"Yes. Please," I said, trying to appear cool and cheery despite my sudden tension. I wore a silk shirt and stylish trousers. My new handmade leather loafers looked impeccable. One of them dangled in the air as I swung my crossed leg like a child. I bet I looked good overall, though, like a real gigolo at last. I was proud of myself. I wanted Parvaneh see my confidence and tell Mina all about it. So I didn't mind wasting a few minutes with her.

"Are you waiting for Mina?" she asked. I shook my head.

"Someone else?" she asked and I shook my head again.

"You wanna come join my friend and me?"

"No, thanks...," I said, thinking that maybe she wanted to lure me now for herself or her friend who look pretty but lonely. That could've been a good way to torture Mina! Alas, I had to leave!

"You look handsome, if I may say so," she said.

I laughed. "I suppose you can say so... I would!"

She smiled. "Mina isn't feeling good these days."

"I don't know. I haven't seen her a long time."

"Yeah, she's ill. She misses you a lot," Parvaneh said.

"I don't know that either," I said.

"Yes, she does... Am I bothering you?"

"Oh, no. Not at all."

"Don't you love her anymore?"

"No. We lost our chance."

"Maybe it's still not too late. Love is a precious thing to set aside lightly, especially because of false pride."

"But when it's tainted by lies and deceit, it dies."

"Is it really dead?" she asked.

She sounded like a wiseass, perhaps trying to get a promising confession out of me—that my love for Mina wasn't still quite dead and there was still some hope—to thrill her dear friend with the good news.

"Dead. Dead. Dead," I said like a spiteful idiot.

"Sorry to hear that."

"There's really nothing to be sorry about."

"Maybe you want to see her again. Maybe that's why you came here. Is it the reason?" she asked.

I thought she had a plausible point. If I was subconsciously driven to see her and was drawn to this café because of it, I couldn't help it. But it still didn't change anything regarding my decision to never speak with her.

"No... Not really... I just came for a cup of coffee and say goodbye to this place... certainly not for seeing Mina... This is the last time I'll be in this café, anyway."

"Oh? Are you going somewhere?"

"Maybe."

"You sound mysterious. I won't tell Mina, I promise."

"She probably knows I'm going away."

"She does?" she asked with surprise. "I don't think so."

I was sorry I'd shared my secrets with her. I motioned to the waiter to bring my check.

"Do you want to meet her here tomorrow?" She asked.

I only glared at her.

"Do you want me to arrange it?"

I kept glaring at her.

"It was good seeing you again, Kian," she said with a smirk, rose, and strolled away. As soon as settled at her table, she started telling who I was—one of Mina's old toys. These women didn't even care about being so obvious about their gossips by the way they blabbered, peered at their prey furtively, and sniggered.

I paid the bill and got out of there with gloom.

6

In my long letter to Uncle Jamal, I explained a few things about my situation in Iran and why I had to leave in such a hurry. One reason, I mentioned, was to let Grandma come back to her house. I asked him to tell her I hoped she was happy about my departure and not bothering her anymore. Tell her she made me run away in such a hurry! I apologized for not telling him about my plans sooner. I said I appreciated his friendship and would cherish our good memories forever. I thanked him for his generosity to share his woman, Shahla, with me, his advice, and for letting me drink probably a million of his beers based on my fair estimates. I left the sealed envelope for him on the table in the hall.

Uncle Mustafa was the only one who knew about my flight schedule and seeing me off. So, I gave him the key to Grandma's house on our way to the airport to pass on to Narges if she wanted it. Poor guy took the key with a grimace. He gave me many last minute advice. He gave me his friend's name and phone number in Los Angeles—to contact if I needed any kind of help, financially or otherwise. He asked me if it was fine with me if he talked to Father openly later about my plans and his promise to help me. He stressed he felt obliged to explain the details to Father and why he'd agreed with my tough conditions, especially keeping my departure a secret. He wanted to mend his friendship with Father after I left. Father would probably be especially angry with Uncle Mustafa. I told him he could talk about our plans with anybody he wished the minute my plane left Mehrabad.

I thanked Uncle Mustafa for the thousandth time, kissed him on his cheeks, and walked into the secured area of the airport for boarding. At last, I got on one of those planes that had blasted over our house and pierced my ears with their noise. My dream to be in one of them had finally come true. I sat in my window seat and imagined never coming back to Iran again. Nostalgia overwhelmed me already and a lump grew in my throat.

The plane took off and soon it was over our secluded house. For a moment, I saw the familiar trees and rose bushes. I believed I saw Rahim and Batool running in the garden, maybe laughing about the times they'd teased me and giggled. I bet they missed me too. I imagined the gypsy woman knocking on our door again. But the woman at the door was probably only a beggar.

Goodbye my old home. Goodbye my dear country. Goodbye Goli, my beautiful angel. Goodbye Father. Goodbye Mina. Goodbye again, forever!

CHAPTER EIGHTEEN
Life in Los Angeles

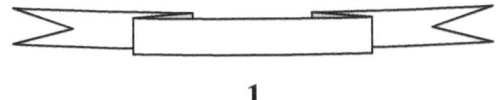

1

I arrived in the new world terribly tired and homesick. During the first couple of weeks, especially, nostalgia really hurt. My first impression of Los Angeles wasn't helping the situation, either. What the heck!? Heavy smog. Heat. Chaotic traffic on long, noisy freeways. Expensive greasy food. People who were too busy and impatient, especially around foreigners. I was deeply disappointed with the way the new world appeared compared with the heaven I'd imagined in my dreams. I missed Tehran's shady streets near my city residence, sweet Persian foods and pastries, and my funny friends and Uncles. But most of all, I really missed my beautiful Goli. I doubted my sanity seriously this time, for going through all the hassles of getting here in such a hurry. Breaking Goli's heart for what? Giving poor Uncle Mustafa so much pain for this? Abandoning Father for what kind of future? The moment of truth, you might say.

I wrote letters to Narges and Uncle Mustafa to inform them of my safe arrival and my fabulous condition. I was ashamed to say I'd changed my mind. But I also lied to stay positive and move on. I lied in hopes of restoring the fictional world I'd created for myself during all those years of fantasizing about this not-such-a-big-deal new world. I was too stubborn to accept my mistake. My silly pride and the embarrassment of facing Uncle Mustafa, Goli, and others helped a lot to stay put. Pity, I wasn't just a bit smarter and braver. I didn't realize false pride was the foulest of all human follies. Instead, I tried to learn the art of sticking it out. I tried to get used to a new difficult situation, but Father's old comment kept ringing in my head and making it too hard: "Why do you want to get used to bad things? Get used to good stuff." Simple and straightforward. Yet, I just ignored his plain wisdom. Otherwise, I should've taken the first plane back. I behaved like an arrogant lover who suffocates in his own web of lies—like Mina who had kept denying her betrayal; at the cost of sacrificing love itself. I lied to myself. Otherwise, I'd probably be living an exciting life with Goli these days somewhere amidst the chaotic environment of Iran, after the Islamic revolution.

Soon, however, a bunch of immediate worries, such as school and food and laundry, brought me in touch with the new reality. New world, harsh realities. Harsh world, new realities! These attributes best explained my situation. The stress of coping with the new demands began to compete with my feeling of nostalgia. Every day the former got stronger.

I rented a tiny room in a crummy hotel at a discount weekly rate. I was determined to manage my life as frugally as possible while living on Uncle Mustafa's financial support. I tried to be careful with his money. So, I had to sleep in a smelly hotel and eat only a small fraction of my normal appetite. Often I had only one meal a day. Everything was too expensive in this new world. After years of living in luxury and eating the best food, the new accommodation and food really sucked. I was surprised at the level of sacrifice I was willing to make, with such extraordinary determination, just to accomplish whatever the heck I was trying to achieve in the new world. My stupidity was simply amazing, especially since I didn't believe in higher education.

I was ecstatic when the first letter from Narges arrived after one month, *which showed the immensity of my melancholy when I got the letter!* She said Father got very sad when he found out I'd left the country, especially without saying goodbye to him. She said he went to the garden and sat on the bench, weeping and shaking his head. It was quite a windy day, Narges wrote. A lot of dust circled in the air, but he didn't care. He just stared at the gate and the tall walls of the garden. "Maybe he was hoping you'd come through that gate any second," Narges wrote. She felt sorry for him and went out to the garden, sat next to him, and tried to hold his hand to calm him, but he wouldn't let her touch him. So she left him alone. The servants were watching him, too, through the windows. But he just sat there and sobbed. He didn't give a damn if the whole world saw him in that sorry state. He didn't even care if spies used this pitiful incident to show his mental breakdown, Narges stressed.

She wrote she couldn't imagine Father might cry so much just because I'd left Iran. He hadn't cried half as much even when his father died. It was a new side of Father she hadn't seen before. I was initially surprised of Narges's detailed account of father's touching sentiments. But later I figured she most likely had thought that describing his anguish would cheer me up. She'd been wrong. I started feeling guilty for bringing him so much grief. Yet, my pride again stopped me from doing anything about it, although I felt really sad and bad. I felt so confused, floating between anger and guilt. How could my nerves calm down while these conflicting emotions kept fighting inside me for hours and days after I'd finished reading Narges's letter? Then I read her letter again and again. And felt angrier, guiltier, lonelier, and more homesick every time.

My reply to Narges was short. I just explained a few things about my routines out of courtesy. I tried to sound appreciative of her good deeds and delicious food in the last few months before my departure. I didn't make any comments about her meticulous account of Father's agony. I didn't know what to say. After our first correspondence, we exchanged only short letters every three or four months. I exchanged letters with Uncle Mustafa more often, though. He expected me to explain my life and education in some detail. I felt he shared the information with my parents. I guessed they were happy about Uncle Mustafa playing such an active role and keeping them informed of their idiot son's life circumstances. In her corny letters, Narges always mentioned her recent phone conversations with Uncle Mustafa and all the good news about me. She also nagged, with spite and cynicism, about Uncle Mustafa and Father becoming even closer friends. They often met when Uncle Mustafa was in Tehran. I was glad that my scheme to use Uncle Mustafa had brought him and my parents closer. Uncle Mustafa was reaping the rewards of his kindness toward me. He'd always wanted to be close to my family and now he had the honour, thanks to his moron nephew. Uncle Mustafa kept sending me money, while stressing I shouldn't worry about paying him back until I finished university and got a lucrative job. He was trying to put my mind at ease perhaps. However, it also sounded as though reminding me sneakily and regularly that I had to repay him eventually! *So study harder and get a good job soon!*

2

The hotel I was staying in was near Wilshire Boulevard close to the language school and downtown. The old neighbourhood was depressing with wrecked buildings and many homeless people. The Mac Arthur Park was near my hotel, too. So I went there sometimes to muse over my life, which always felt chaotic no matter how much I thought and planned. People warned me to stay away from the park after dusk. So I cooped up in my hotel room at nights, felt lonely, and wrestled with English lessons. In the second week, I spent one full day on the bus commuting to the Pepperdine University's brand new Malibu campus to submit more papers to the Office of International Student Services. Our university was nestled at the foothills of Santa Monica Mountains with a grand view of the Pacific Ocean. I liked the setting and my impression of life in the new world improved a great deal. The thrill of moving to my room on campus in a few months kept me going.

During my daylong bus ride that day, I wondered what kept Father from writing me a letter. He'd always been a diplomat. He could calm down his most arrogant opponents and convince them to do things his way. He could charm the prettiest women. He was probably as charismatic as Grigori. So what kept him from exercising his hypnotic power over me and getting me to like him again? Why wasn't he trying to make amends? Writing a letter erased the risk of discussing the embarrassing old incident face to face, too. My only conclusion was that he was probably as embarrassed about the incident as I was, even if we could avoid discussing it. We both knew we had to talk about the incident eventually if we ever wanted to get over it. But was he also shocked, like me, to find out about my affair with his mistress? Was he also feeling the same mixture of guilt and anger I was? Was he mad at me for ruining his feelings for Mina? Had he also realized that Mina had betrayed him, too, only after the incident? Was he still seeing her? What kind of feeling did he have for Mina these days? Was he ever in love with her, too, as much as I once was? Which one of us really loved Mina more? Was she only one of his hundred mistresses? Which one of us did Mina really love? Which one of us did she love more? I couldn't decide which one of these hundred scenarios I preferred to be true. All of them sucked. But I was glad that at least we hadn't fought over the ownership of Mina. I was glad I hadn't killed Father over someone else's wife. But I was keen to know how he'd decided to deal with Mina in the end. Had he given up Mina too?

Poor Dr. Afzali. He might've known about both Father and I courting his beloved. At the very least, he'd definitely suspected that his mysterious wife was involved with one or both of us. What a mess he'd been living in, the poor doctor. How could he be a good surgeon? How many people had died at the hospital because of his mistakes while his mind had been preoccupied about Father, me, Nosrat, and perhaps other men as well? Oh, God! What was the name of the feeling this man had for his beautiful wife? He adored her, no doubt. He needed her, no doubt. He'd foregone his pride, no doubt. But should we call it love, what Dr. Afzali felt for Mina? He was a rich, good-looking, and well-respected surgeon. He could in fact marry any woman he desired in Iran. So maybe we should say he was *madly* in love with Mina? Or he was simply mad. Love, with all its grief and humiliation. And so much selflessness and silliness. Then what had been my feelings for Mina? Had it been love too, considering how quickly I'd sort of dropped her just by my measly, juvenile willpower? Different needs, different brains, different reactions, I suppose. How about Father? Had he escaped her charm yet?

3

My roommate at the university was Robert Mauler. He was a nice guy and quite friendly compared to other Americans I'd met so far. Luck has always played a major role in my ambiguous life. I feel fortunate when I happen to be in the right mood and see life in a bright light—like when I met Robert. Over time, I've come to believe in this 'luck' thingy—despite my big share of disappointments and failures all along. I've noticed those breaks that come from nowhere and give me at least a bit of temporary timely relief, to regain some strength to go on. I've also learned that my life would've been a disaster without all the luck I was blessed with now and then. The only problem has always been my struggle with an old dilemma and two questions: Is God sending me all this luck? Should I stop being an atheist then? Yet I've never been able to convince myself one way or another, while feeling guilty about it, too. *Why can't I decide? Will I ever decide that there is a good God helping me see the truth?*

Anyway, meeting Robert Mauler was a lucky break I realized right away. In that particular point in my life, especially, it helped me rebuild my wrecked character and move forward in a city that had given me mostly a bad impression so far. I tried to get more objective about my past experiences and stay optimistic about my idiotic decision to travel to the new world. I had to keep fooling my brain every day in order to survive, alone in a foreign country. *Everything is relative and there is no point fussing about past or being in L.A.,* I thought.

Robert was taken aback initially, anyway, when he realized his roomy was *just* a foreigner with such a lousy accent. For a short while he looked distressed, so much so I felt he might go to the Student Housing Office and file a five-page complaint. But he managed to control his emotions at the end and stopped making too much fuss about my petty presence afterward, as soon as he felt like playing the role of a big brother. I let him too. But the fact that he'd *instantly* assumed to be smarter than me, since he spoke English, was both educational and maddening. He was another kind moron, anyway, judging by his ridiculous level of general knowledge, including even the English grammar itself. I thought he could help me speak English with a better accent at least. Also, he could possibly teach me a bit about life around the campus and in the city.

The weather was still warm in L.A. and people went to the beach. Robert had an old car and sometimes took me along to the beach, where I met some of his friends. A few of them were nice to me. But most of them were real jerks. I tried not to care. I just hoped to cope with the idea of being a forlorn foreigner. Among Robert's friends was this pretty girl named Daphne Cox. She was wiser than all the rest of them put together, and that was exactly why she liked me from the beginning! She was open-minded and kind; and she defended me the same way Robert did. It seemed to me that foreign students had to defend themselves somehow, or hire someone to do it for them. They had to provide a valid justification for being around, at the university and in the new world. Sometimes, they even had to prove their rights to be alive or the fact that they were human beings, too. Most people looked at foreign students with a bizarre hint of suspicion. Some jerks were even worse. They snubbed foreign students simply because of their accents. But I let it go! The so-called professors weren't much better, although some of them were very nice. The good ones tried to help foreign students, but many of them were racist and arrogant. They assumed they were superior, both the students and the professors. But when you talked to them, you realized how naive they actually were. Many of them probably couldn't find France on a map without struggling for ten minutes to find the name. Don't even bother asking me about their mathematical aptitude. I couldn't imagine how they'd come to university with such low knowledge of basic math. You stole their calculators and they were stuck. The American standard of education at high school didn't impress me too much. I bet not even one percent of those students could pass the stiff Provincial exams in Tehran. Compared to the geniuses that studied under the tree shadows of Kakh Street, how they could be even considered a high school graduate was amazing for the country leading the world. *That confusing dilemma about the essence of leadership, again, even at international level!*

I couldn't say anything about the university education yet, however. I'd just arrived. Of course, I'd had my doubts about university education even before coming to the U.S., anyway. But now my cynicism had raised many folds. So I cursed Uncle Mustafa for forcing me to live in this hellish hole—despite the gorgeous view of the ocean and mountains—instead of working in the real world. I didn't realize that racism would be even worse if I had gone to work. Anyway, I didn't fuss about the kind of education I might expect to get at university despite the much higher tuition that foreign students had to pay. It appeared to me the university accepted foreign students only for recovering a good portion of its costs, so that American students could honour the university with their presence easier!

Daphne Cox was quite different. She was smart, deep, and easy to talk with. I could express my opinions, even my Marxist tendencies, without the fear of harsh judgment or arguments. It was so weird how Americans were afraid to talk about socialism or communism and then bragged about democracy all the time. Daphne didn't always agree with some of my radical visions of life, especially my compulsive pessimism about relationships and love. She was pretty, too, though rather slim and tall for my taste. Our natural friendship soon turned into a sexual relationship after two months. She reminded me of Goli a lot. Not at all due to her looks, but her patience and intelligence. The other coincidence was that she was determined to become a psychiatrist, as if she'd made that choice at birth. I asked her a few times to explain her reason for choosing psychiatry, but she dodged my curiosity. She just said, 'No special reason.' But I didn't believe her, without knowing why. I myself hadn't decided whether to act upon my lifelong desire to study psychology. I considered getting a degree in an easier subject only to fulfil my promise to Uncle Mustafa. What would be an easier subject? Drama and theatre? With my accent? That would've been fun! But to stay in the new world I had to choose a profession. I needed a secure, lucrative job to pay back Uncle Mustafa's loans as well.

4

Starting in the third year, Daphne and I took the same courses. Having her around, especially for helping me with homework, was a great blessing. It was like Goli had sent her deputy to help me now at university. That luck thingy again! On the other hand, it was weird that I was always pushed to become the person I am today. I was forced to go to university by Uncle Mustafa. And I was forced into psychiatry because of Daphne. Of course, my childhood experiences, especially the hoopla at Royal Club, had already raised my curiosity about people's psyche, too. *How did people's tender psyches turn into such wicked psychos I had seen all my life, especially at Royal Club?* I was also still wondering whether any kind of science could help me heal Narges's hurts and anger—to make her a softer person.

Daphne presented strong arguments, too, from the opposite angle. She kept insisting psychology could help me change my negative perspective on life and relationships. She rejected my theories about the difficulty of building constructive relationships in the new era because of radical social changes and couples' growing expectations. She was an optimist facing a compulsive pessimist whom she was considering for a serious relationship. She liked me, so she tolerated me. But I suspected her natural optimism also convinced her readily that she could change me eventually. That was a lot of optimism on her part, I thought, though her goodwill was precious and cute in itself. Moreover, having an optimist around me had its advantages, I reckoned. I never liked being dogmatic, after all. I wasn't eager to adopt cynicism as a profession. All I probably needed was a beautiful, intelligent mentor and a few positive experiences to convince me there were good chances for many exceptions to my sad theories. So I liked Daphne a lot.

I also met and befriended many Iranian students in California. Many of them had to work in gas stations and restaurants to pay for their schooling and living expenses. Witnessing their torture made me appreciate my generous Uncle Mustafa even more. He was right regarding the difficulty of working and getting a good education together. Daphne was happy, too, because I had more time to spend with her instead of working. We often went to her parents' house in Pasadena, usually during the weekends, as if giving me a sense about real family and its merits. She knew I had problems with my parents and she knew about my uncles. So she always encouraged me to call them from her house. I called Uncle Mustafa often, but we wrote long letters to each other on a monthly basis as well. He was pleased with my progress, while whining about the unresolved conflict between Father and me. The closer he and Father were becoming, the more I wondered and worried about him succeeding to convince Father to share the cause of my reserved empathy toward Father. I thought Father might, in fact, tell him a distorted version of the story to get it off his chest, but also getting Uncle Mustafa's advice and assistance to resolve this bizarre, ridiculous animosity—*based on a simple misunderstanding by silly Kian, he would probably insist.*

Uncle Mustafa realized that the opportunity for sorting out the situation was limited while we lived so far apart. So, he suggested that maybe I liked to write a letter to Father. He said I could send it through him if I preferred, but I had no guts to do such a thing. I didn't know what to write in the letter after such a long silence, anyway. I didn't know whether I was ready to forgive him. How could I forgive him when he hadn't even admitted his crime? What was the crime anyway? How could I know whether he was ready to forgive me, not only because of Mina, but also for my lousy attitude all along since the incident? The more time went by, the more impossible it appeared to rebuild our relationship. I assumed that if I ever decided to write him a letter, it must start by describing my old wound. I had to justify my idiotic behaviour all this time, especially my refusal to say goodbye to him before leaving Iran. That was a tall order. I felt Father was facing similar dilemmas. So it was only a matter of who had more nerve or duty to take the first step. I couldn't do it, yet I felt guilty and suffered for not doing it.

At the same time, oddly, the reason for our break-up felt too intangible and childish every day. My love for Mina had faded away. And with it, the issue of staying mad at Father over that, or any, woman looked silly. The initial reason for the break-up was less of a barrier than my pride at this point. I just couldn't accept my stupidity. On the other hand, the crime—'his crime,' to be more precise—had caused me a lot of agony then. So the new puzzle was to decide whether to judge Father's guilt based on my feelings and reasoning at the time of the crime or according to my present feelings and rational thinking. Naturally, the matter was even more confusing when I couldn't decide what the crime had been in the first place!

5

Daphne and I were looking forward to our graduation in June 1978. She'd applied to the University of California in L.A. to get into their medical school. I was assessing my options again, while she insisted we both go to UCLA for graduate studies. I had little time to decide, too. All my life I'd believed university education wasn't my cup of tea. And yet, special circumstances always pushed me do more of it. Besides Uncle Mustafa's and Daphne's pressures, my foreign status in the U.S. was another factor that forced me to do so. Some life ironies are just comical. If I stopped going to school, I had to return to Iran or get a work permit. After some research, I realized getting a work permit wasn't easy for a bum with no work experience. I could ask Daphne to marry me to get my green card, but I didn't feel ready for any commitment. I was still cynical about loving someone truly and I was only twenty-two years old, for God's sake. She probably wouldn't marry me, anyway, if I weren't going to get higher education like her. I wasn't prepared to go to Iran, either. Especially, the political situation and unrest in Iran was beginning to worry everybody.

My only consolation these days, when I ponder my stressful professional life, is that at least my insightful reservations at the time about doing more education had been valid. It is depressing, though, that I need these pathetic excuses nowadays to feel proud and less guilty in a bizarre manner.

So, I applied to UCLA to make at least Daphne happy. I got really depressed, though, when I thought about all the work that would be needed to become a psychiatrist. I hoped they wouldn't admit me to their prestigious medical school, even though I didn't know how to stay in the U.S. otherwise. But again, Daphne was optimistic enough for both of us getting our admissions. In fact, I got the impression she already knew her father could make some recommendations. He was an important businessman and knew some influential people at the university, I presumed. Anyway, we were accepted. I discussed my options with Uncle Mustafa on the phone and he also advised me to continue with my education. He promised to pay for expenses as long as necessary. "Don't worry about repaying me until you are a rich doctor," he stressed once more, making me feel my obligation to him deeper.

He's not going to reconsider ever and let me off the hook, ha?!

After graduation from Pepperdine University, I stayed in Daphne Cox's house during the summer. Her family was very kind to me. They gave me a room and let me share their food if I happened to be around. But Daphne and I often went to the beach, anyway. I'd bought a brand new Toyota Celica with the money I'd saved over the years based on my diligent strategy to benefit from Uncle Mustafa's generosity! I'd rarely considered hoarding some of those fat loans a scam as long as I was doing it in good faith. I didn't mention my decision to buy a brand new expensive car to him, either. I didn't see any point justifying my valid preferences about using the interest-free money I borrowed from him in big chunks with no repayment plan. Daphne didn't find anything wrong with my strategy, either, since it was in good faith!

I received a registered package from Narges, which contained a gold Rolex—a gift for my graduation. Both Daphne and I were amazed at such a gorgeous, generous gift. I called Narges and thanked her. But I had a hard time replacing my faithful Sarcar that had served me for so many years and been Father's gift. Narges knew that, too, and thus giving me that specific gift. *I hated my cynical brain pushing these vile ideas into my hideous head!* At the end, I put away the Sarcar to wear the gold Rolex, while striving to suffocate my conscience nagging at many levels. What a devout, conscientious socialist! Then again, what could anybody really expect me to do? Sell the Rolex and give the money to the poor?

Now, I had everything and life in Los Angeles was so much fun at last. I raced around the city with my powerful Celica and enjoyed myself like a kid finally getting a toy. I kept checking my watch for time, even when the radio announcer or a friend said it aloud, so that others noticed my Rolex. Daphne and I went to Rodeo Drive and browsed inside the boutiques. She often shopped in expensive boutiques like Hermes, Gucci, and other trendy places. She forced me a few times to buy a pair of trousers or a shirt from them, too, or she bought them for me as a present. She insisted I get my haircut at Vidal Sassoon in the same street and I did it a few times. *I felt embarrassed and confused often, though, because I couldn't fathom, for the life of mine, what was really happening to me when all my deep socialistic ideologies and convictions melted down the drain whenever I saw pretty things or wanted to please Daphne!*

We looked around the Westwood neighbourhood for a suite to rent and share. Near the end of the summer, finally we rented a furnished suite in a luxurious building way beyond my budget, with the assumption to save on gas and parking. Walking to our new school could be a good exercise. But soon, we bought an expensive parking pass to drive one of our cars to school. Daphne and I never talked about marriage or things like that. That was a good thing about Daphne. She wasn't pushy at all except for higher education. She didn't have an agenda for all the things we did together. I wasn't even sure she'd marry me if I asked her, but I guessed she would now that I'd agreed to become a doctor like her. She suggested we travel to Iran the following summer. I told her we might do that—a big lie, I realized. I was unsure about returning to Iran for any of hundred reasons Daphne kept offering —mainly to reconcile with Father. Yet, her show of interest was cute, especially in the way she defended Father. I'd told her most of the story. She was the only one in the world who knew it as far as I knew. I had a hunch she was trying to practise her simmering knowledge of psychology on me and my parents by taking me to Iran and forcing a series of reconciliations all around.

6

The bad news about the political situation in Iran began to pour in as Daphne and I moved to our new apartment in Westwood. The news about the Black Friday was broadcasted in early September. On that day, several hundred people were massacred on Jaleh Avenue as they demonstrated against the Shah's corrupt regime.

The soldiers had opened fire on twenty thousand demonstrators. I was getting concerned about my family and my country. I was also worried about Goli. But I was happy to see the end of the Shah's tyranny as a U.S. puppet in my lifetime. I wished I could be in Tehran when it happened. For once I was optimistic about the future of Iran in the chaotic world of politics. Naively I hoped my countrymen would get a chance to taste real democracy. I hoped our precious natural resources—mostly the minds of our bright youths—be put into better use. Sometimes, I considered returning to Iran and playing a part in the revolution. I hadn't been a politically active student like many of my Iranian friends in L.A. But I was moved by the growing wave of revolutionaries trying to bring down the Shah.

Living in California had given me an opportunity to attend some regular meetings that Iranian students held for discussing socialism and democracy. I did it out of curiosity and for seeking new friends with radical ideologies. Sometimes, I even went to Berkeley and San Francisco with them for their U.S.-wide formal assemblies and conferences. They argued over some silly details when no political structure for a deemed revolution was in place to begin with. In particular, they seemed unwilling or unable to choose a capable, trustworthy leader, although many tried to push themselves or a particular person they supported for odd reasons. Some kinds of sly plots seemed to be going on for leadership by a bunch of idiots all the time, while others didn't seem to trust their characters or abilities to get the job done. A few, who appeared to be trustworthy and competent, outright refused to accept this role. This smart group had apparently realized, like myself, that being a leader was a foolish life choice with no prospects for any wise person. The rest of this radical crowd were comprised of people who participated merely out of boredom or curiosity, like myself, or were brainwashed by some political propagandas—mainly for toppling the Shah. The ultimate outcome of my new observations about leadership deficiency and the crowd's endless gullibility merely strengthened my belief about humans' inability to develop a fair, practical political system and civilization no matter how hard these devoted groups fought over their ideologies and died in their revolutions. I was glad they couldn't read my mind about them and their ideologies, although most of them observed me with some air of suspicion, as though I were a spy for Savak (Shah's Intelligence Agency). So, they never asked me if I wanted to be their leader. I was glad they hadn't! *Who has time or a priority to be a leader, ha?*

Eventually, as the revolution looked imminent, some of the more radical individuals gave up school and went to countries closer to Iran. Many went to Paris. Some joined the Mojahedin, which was the best organized and armed political group. When they began their migration—maybe a year or six months earlier —I wasn't convinced a revolution could happen. But now things were getting serious.

School started at about the same time. Our workload felt too heavy, especially since my mind was preoccupied with horrific events in Iran. But I had to go along with Daphne in selecting the number and type of courses for the first term. I felt sad for not being a part of the revolution.

CHAPTER NINETEEN
Revolution and Reconciliation

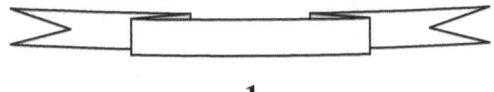

1

The Shah of Iran fled to Cairo in January 1979 after his dire attempts to defeat the crushing waves of revolutionaries failed. The desperate monarch's numerous gimmicks in the final months to show his commitment for drastic reforms in Iran proved futile.

"Isn't it funny how kings and rulers suddenly remember, and promise, they can be a better leader only when they shit their pants?" Daphne once asked and we laughed.

The Shah sacrificed even his faithful, trusted Prime Minister to save his own neck to no avail—his fate was already decided by his old masters, who imagined could now find a better puppet. By the Shah's decree, the Prime Minister, Amir Abbas Hoveyda, had been put under house arrest. This was in the early November 1978. He'd abided like a fool, instead of fleeing like the Shah and many other officials. Thus, the revolutionary forces captured him easily once they took over the country. I'd met him several times. He seemed to have been the Prime Minister of Iran as long as I recalled. He was a sharp, well-dressed bachelor, always wearing a bowtie and a carnation on the lapel of his jacket. He'd been a good friend of Father's for many years. While Father believed Hoveyda liked and trusted him, he hadn't bothered giving Father a position in his cabinet all those years. I imagined Father's lousy reputation with women stopped the conscientious Prime Minister from offering Father a promotion. The spies had apparently been successful. According to Father, Hoveyda had lived a modest life, which was proven true when the Islamic regime confiscated his assets. He'd made no effort to accumulate wealth like all other corrupt officials in the Shah's regime.

I hoped the liberals could create a democratic government and society for new Iran. But power struggles amongst few factions quickly proved my naiveté and wishful thinking again. Instead, my cynical old theories about leadership and humans prevailed. Father was removed from his high official job. I felt sorry for him and my childish old grudge toward him felt even sillier. On the other hand, I was glad he'd never been a minister in the cabinet or a general in the army. Many of those top officials were already rounded up and put in prison or executed.

I received information about Father through Uncle Mustafa and Narges. They said he was very quiet and sad in recent months. He had no job to go to and his investments were under scrutiny as well. He hadn't done anything illegal and not even received bribes, which was prevalent in Iran. But some residents of the new subdivision had found the opportunity of irritating Father and other directors of the subdivision's consortium too tempting. They'd complained to the Komiteh about their loss of savings as a result of buying a house in the subdivision and also for their suffering in this neighbourhood with limited services. Under the chaotic situation in Iran, everybody was looking for a way to hurt others for silliest reasons. Royal Club was shut down, of course, and Mr. Bashiri was sent *directly* to jail. Parties and music were banned altogether—not only on the radio or in public places, but also in people's private homes. Women were ordered to observe the strictest Islamic dress codes. The harshest Islamic rules would be applied to adultery. Therefore, both Father and Uncle Jamal had lost their lifelong opportunities for womanizing and partying, while I also wondered whether adulteresses would be stoned to death according to the Islamic laws or rituals.

No job, no women, no family, no aristocratic parties, no life, no business, no prospects, no clubs, and no son—but only one nagging wife. It wasn't hard to imagine Father's fury and agony. He often bragged about his resilience. I wished I could look into his eyes and see how much spirit and pride were still left in him.

In mid-February 1979, Uncle Mustafa called me with the news about Father's travel to Europe for some business and meeting his friends. He said this trip might do him good. Father had expressed an interest to see me in L.A. or London. He said Father was flexible in terms of timing, as he had no set timetable for returning to Tehran. Uncle Mustafa insisted I should jump at this opportunity to repair my relationship with Father. He asked me to think about the location and time. I felt bad putting Uncle Mustafa down on the phone quickly. I thought I should be a little more diplomatic once in a while, for God's sake. So I agreed to ponder his suggestion and call him back in a few days.

Daphne noticed my flustered face and asked me what was wrong and I explained Father's proposal to meet. I added I'd wait a couple of days before calling Uncle Mustafa and telling him I didn't have time to meet Father. She disagreed fast with some kind of frustration with me. She insisted that meeting Father was an excellent idea, as it might help me mend some of my deep emotional problems.

"What emotional problems?" I asked with surprise.

"Oh, Gosh, where should I start," she replied in a teasing tone.

"From the beginning. What's wrong with me, you think?"

"We'll need a few months to analyze you. We must do it sometime."

"You really mean it?"

"Absolutely," Daphne replied with a serious look.

"Just give me one example," I said.

"For one thing, you're too uptight behind your idiotic smirk. You're always hyper, although you try to hide it."

"Am I? Is that how you see me?"

"Well… How long are you going to keep a childish grudge against your father? How much do you want to stress out him, yourself, and your family over a silly matter?"

"A silly matter? Is that how you see it?" I asked.

"That's the way even you see it yourself," she shrieked.

"What do you mean?"

"Haven't you confessed a few times that even you wonder about the nature of his crime sometimes?"

I nodded with confusion and guilt. I didn't have the energy or conviction to argue with her, anyway. Deep down I felt she was right and I was stubborn. Only my false pride had been keeping me from acknowledging my stupidity all along.

"So you think we should invite him here?" I asked.

"Yes. Ask him to come whenever he likes."

"To stay with us?"

"Of course. We'll give him the bedroom and use the sofa bed ourselves. I'd like to spend a few days with my parents without you, anyway. So he can stay long enough to make up for the lost time and talk behind my back, too."

"You sound so eager to see my father…"

"Well, he sounds like an interesting man and he's your father, after all. But mostly, I really want you take care of this old matter in your head. You have enough traumas stored in your psyche. Let's deal with this one at least."

"I feel weird seeing him after all these years. You really think this is a good idea?"

"Yes. I think you two should forgive each other."

"Okay. I'll do it because you're my shrink and so persistent."

"I'll send you my bill for my services."

"Send it to Uncle Mustafa directly," I said.

"Poor Uncle Mustafa. How're you ever going to pay him back? You must work very hard for the rest of your life just to repay his loans."

"I know. That's why I'm forcing myself to stay in school to postpone his demand for payback. I'll be going to school for the rest of my life, I suppose. Or maybe he gets old and forgets all about it, if I stall him long enough!"

"It looks that way. But if you reconcile with your father, he'd probably repay your loans and you'll be relieved from your big obligation to Uncle Mustafa. This is a big incentive all by itself."

I called Uncle Mustafa the next day and gave him the best dates for Father's visit to L.A. He sounded happy, but also proud for putting some sense into my head. He probably thought I'd matured. So I didn't spoil his impression by telling him about Daphne's pressure for making the right decision. He promised to arrange everything and call me back with the details of Father's arrival in L.A. In the following days, I started to feel good about my decision, too, as well as my possible initiation to maturity.

2

One week later Narges called me with a subtle agitation in her voice. She said she was *surprised* to hear about my plan to meet Father. Yet, she sounded more disturbed than surprised. The news seemed to have shaken her, and the reason was quite clear. My hostility with Father had caused him pain and also brought the mother and son a bit closer, though I hadn't felt real affection in her attitude—going by our limited mail or telephone contacts. Her gestures of friendship had appeared mostly self-serving to me, just to keep me as an ally to hurt Father more, with obvious devious benefits for her. For one thing, she just wanted to prove Father's evilness to everybody by repeating the fact that he and I were enemies. Besides, witnessing Father's suffering from my attitude toward him had been the biggest thrill of her life. Her usual hypocrisy was obvious on the phone and I didn't give her any hope I might change my mind about seeing Father. My cold response made her more upset every second.

"There's something else you must also know," she said at last.
"What?"
"Do you remember Dr. Afzali and Mina?"
"Of course I do. I've been out of Iran only five years."
"They'd gone to Europe together for Dr. Afzali's seminar."

"So?" I asked.

"But Dr. Afzali returned to Tehran alone."

"So? What's so important about that?"

"Mina has decided to stay in London with her sister a bit longer," Narges said in a cynical tone.

"So? Why are you telling me all this? I don't care what Mina and Dr. Afzali do."

"But you know your father is in London, too?" she asked. She was probably going nuts by my stupidity or playing dumb.

A shockwave ran through my spine, mostly due to Narges's dire tenacity to stop the father-son meeting and the fact that she'd somehow learned about the cause of my hostility towards Father all these years. But I decided to stay cool and play dumb. "I still don't understand why any of this matters to me?"

"Nothing. Just a piece of information. That's all." She knew I'd grasped her message loud and clear. She was too smart to fall for my games. No matter how subtle the change in my tone of voice had been, she'd detected it.

She said goodbye quickly and we hung up. She'd fulfilled her vicious mission. Her message had raised my blood pressure and caused new turmoil in my head. Why was Father then coming over to see me while he was still involved with the woman who had given us so much agony and caused the father and son's separation? Wasn't this a horrible crime by him all in itself, which I could now offer to Daphne with pride to prove my rationality all along? Was Father hoping the news about his fooling around with my deceitful ex-lover wouldn't bother me anymore? Did Narges had any up-to-date information about their current affair and now using it to disturb me, or only bluffing merely based on her own suspicions? Only two days ago, I'd finally cooled down and agreed to see him. I'd somewhat forgiven him already. And now this. I wasn't supposed to be jealous about Mina anymore, but I was feeling betrayed again.

I realized Narges's scheme to sabotage the opportunity of any reconciliation between Father and me. Yet the idea of Father sleeping with Mina in London tortured my brain cells when I recalled her body and our nightlong lovemaking routines in Dr. Afzali's absence. I remembered my begging, and her promise, to marry me. What a wild past and haunting memories!

Was Father really so selfish to ignore that his affair in London before visiting me might drive me nuts and spoil the possibility of our reconciliation? Did he think the information wouldn't reach me? I'd travelled halfway around the world to evade these hurtful affairs. Yet, the goddamn old story was determined to follow me to my grave. Where could I escape to now? On the other hand, Father's stay in London when Mina was there could be only a bad coincidence. Was it? Should it matter to me now after all these years? If not, why was I so mad at him again? Was I still in love with Mina after half a decade, even after Goli and Daphne had shown me so much true affection and loyalty? Why was I so sad and hyper then? Why should I see him?

Luckily, Daphne wasn't around to witness my new anguish. I decided to keep everything to myself to avoid her lectures, which honestly I wasn't in the mood for. I didn't even mention Narges's call, but she noticed the fresh wrinkles of grief on my face when she arrived home. She asked me what was wrong *now again* and I told her I was only concerned about my meeting with Father. My response was honest in a way. She just nodded and left.

I wanted to call Uncle Mustafa and tell him to cancel Father's trip to L.A., but couldn't find a reason to give him? How could I explain my madness to him or Daphne again? Did it really matter if Father and Mina were still lovers? I had to accept this scenario and still forgive Father at least. It made sense if they'd arranged to meet in London now that the Islamic regime was monitoring everybody's movements and actions.

My choices were clear: To discuss the matter with Daphne so that one of us could convince the other about the best course of action. Or resolve the matter in my own agitated head alone; then stand firm about my decision if I decided to cancel Father's visit. Daphne and Uncle Mustafa would get angry about my tenacity, but I'd accept the price. I chose to decide alone, so I had to be ultra careful for relying only on my boiling brain to think and make the right choice.

A daylong painful analysis without Daphne's help was tough, but the outcome made me even prouder of myself later when I made a rational decision at last. I decided to just stop fussing over Father's affairs once and for all regardless of his choices. If he was taking the risk to see Mina under the circumstances, it sort of meant he needed her. It shouldn't matter to me if they really loved each other or whatever. I should actually be happy for both of them, for helping each other at this time of turmoil in their lives. I wasn't too mad with Mina, either. They both behaved like lost creatures of God in their own peculiar ways, but maybe they needed each other. My main interest must be to reconcile with Father only for the sake of curing my own wounds. Deep down I was eager to see Father happy. He also seemed to have suffered enough all his life, since his youth. He'd valued our relationship and his recent gesture must be enough evidence for me. He'd preferred to spend some time with me instead of staying more with Mina in London. He'd proved his true feelings for me in my absence in many ways during the last five years, too, especially weeping in the garden on a windy, dusty day for hours after my departure. All these clear clues proved his genuine love for me, compared with Narges's half-assed efforts to befriend me, mostly by badmouthing Father and buying me a Rolex. She knew her information would hurt me or maybe even kill me. Yet, she'd decided to call me just to agitate me—all in hopes of stopping the father and son's reconciliation. She knew the turmoil Father was enduring. She knew my lifelong pains since childhood. And still she continued her malice. She just seemed incapable of thinking a bit less selfishly and instead was dying to keep us in agony. I wondered where all my sudden wisdom and compassion had come from. Living with Daphne all those years and hearing her lectures had apparently washed my brain a bit for the better. Still, all this wisdom wasn't enough to stop the rage Narges had stirred up in my head. Why was she always so cruel?

3

The following Saturday night, Daphne and I went to the movies in Westwood. I wasn't really in the mood to get out of the house these days. But my gloom was driving Daphne nuts, especially since she thought I was merely making too much fuss over the simple matter of seeing my father. I wondered how she might react if she knew about my ancient love memories with Mina still haunting me and being behind my new agony. So she insisted we go to the movies to improve my mood a bit. As we got out of the theatre, somebody touched my shoulder. When I turned, Ahmad Javid smiled at me.

"What're you doing here in L.A.?" he asked.

"I go to UCLA," I replied with a genuine smile. Seeing his fat face revived some memories of our youthful mischief around the ghastly neighbourhood. How carefree we had been those days when we chased the shadows in the subdivision as the scorching sun crossed the sky. We were happy, mostly them, to waste the days away just by talking about silly stuff, including the two cute, queer dogs. Hadn't my melancholy those days been so childish in the scope of the turmoil we grownups end up facing in our boring and futile lives as we age with rising rage?

"What're you doing in L.A.?" I asked.

"I just started at USC, but been around L.A. for four years."

"Me too... I went to Pepperdine first."

The old animosity between us seemed to have passed. Maybe we'd both matured and forgotten our ancient rivalry for leading a bunch of fat morons in the neighbourhood. He'd lost some of the fat he carried then. Overall, he looked good despite his still plump face. Those striking signs of malice had evaporated from his eyes, too, and his smile felt sincere for the first time.

"So, where do you live?" Ahmad asked.

"Westwood," I replied.

"Wow… That's an expensive area for sure," he said.

I resented his sarcasm and just stared into his eyes

He continued: "You look great anyway."

"Thanks. You look handsome, too, finally… You've also lost lots of weight."

"I've been working really hard here."

"It has agreed with you," I said teasingly. "Keep working!"

"I'd rather be fat, though, instead of working like a donkey so much," he replied with angst.

"Is any other guy from the old gang here in L.A.?"

"No. No one that I know about."

"The situation is chaotic in Iran these days. Isn't it?"

"It sure is," he replied.

"What do you think is going to happen?"

"The mullahs are taking over."

"Looks like it. Who is behind all this, you think?"

"It's hard to guess which one is this time, or maybe they're in it together…"

He kept peeping at Daphne with jealousy, but still eager to be introduced. He was with two other guys, who looked Persians too, waiting for him in a distance from us. I introduced him to Daphne at last.

"Have you gone back to Tehran for a visit?" I asked.

"No. I had to work hard during summers. My father isn't rich like yours."

"Your brain hasn't changed, has it?" I asked irately.

"How's he *these days*, by the way?" he asked with a smirk.

I felt like punching him. My hasty positive judgment of him at the beginning bugged me even more than his attitude. *Anytime I try to be a bit more optimistic about humans, they just have to spoil it for me all over so quickly!*

"He's all right. He's coming over to see me next week," I said and quickly felt sorry. I didn't know why I gave him that extra piece of information when I already resented his tone of voice.

"Lucky you. He can afford to come all the way to L.A. just for a visit. My father can't even afford to go to Ghazvin these days, all thanks to your father's project."

"Your family's decision to buy a property in the subdivision had nothing to do with my father, had it? Everybody must make their own decisions based on all the information available to them. My father never gave anybody bad information."

"I don't know about that!" he replied with arrogance.

"You're still an asshole, you know that at least?" I whispered in Persian with a fake smile. I didn't want Daphne witness my argument and frustration with an old friend only two minutes after meeting him.

Ahmad delivered a smirk of his own. "Maybe I see you around. Let me give you my number," he said.

"Okay," I said. Again, I don't know why I agreed to exchange phone numbers with that moron. Maybe his *empty* attempt to stay civilized curbed my *impressionable* temper a little. If he could be civilized, I must try to be civilized once in a while, too. No... I was just too timid to reject his offer to exchange phone numbers.

We said goodbye tensely and he nodded to Daphne.

"Maybe I'll call you sometime," he said with another smirk as he started walking away. But I decided that staying in contact with him had no purpose at all. I already had a bad feeling about this encounter. I didn't want to be reminded of my past life again. So I crumpled the piece of paper with his telephone number on it and threw it away right in front of Daphne's bewildered eyes. She only rolled her eyes without saying a word. I couldn't understand why Ahmad was still so hostile about an ancient incident that had nothing to do with me at least. I really couldn't blame Father for it, either. People should be careful and wise about their decisions. That was my theory. On the other hand, it crossed my mind that maybe I'd overreacted again, as Daphne sometimes complained.

"It's our job to watch out for crooks out there," I murmured.

"What?" Daphne asked.

"Nothing... I was just thinking about that guy...," I replied. Ahmad was a university student and supposedly smarter now. So why couldn't he let go of his old childish grudges? Then I realized I'd been worse than him with bigger hang-ups of my own. How long had it taken me to forgive my own father? Five freaking years! For what? I wasn't even quite there yet, either! It'd been a long time to keep grudges against a person whom I've always loved and believed to be so liberal and bright. And all that for nothing? It's hard abandoning our past hurts, I reasoned. We can't change only because our logic says we should.

4

The following week, Daphne and I went to the airport to pick up Father. I was glad she was standing next to me when he and I were meeting after so long. The first glance we exchanged was awkward and timid as expected, but I introduced Daphne right away. He shook hands with her hastily and then turned to me and we hugged and kissed on the cheeks. He mostly chatted with Daphne, but kept peeping at me with a grin, too, while I carried his suitcase. He looked handsome and his charming smile never vanished from his face. That was the first time I heard him speak in English and it sounded funny. His accent was worse than mine, but he spoke rather fluently. I was thrilled that the initial tense moments had passed so fast.

Daphne drove while I hid in the backseat away from Father's eyes. She kept talking to make him feel welcome and to prevent any awkward silence that seemed imminent without her incessant active intrusion. She tried to include me in the conversations, too, sometimes, very much the same way the adults at Royal Club used to humour me in the old times. I was feeling like a child again, anyway. Daphne was already impressed by him and quite happy to do most of the talking, which was a relief for me. She has a knack for gaining people's trust quickly. Everybody loves her after only a short chat, the same charisma Father had. This is her greatest asset as a psychiatrist, I think. I wished I were even slightly like her in indulging people. Alas, I've been uptight all my life, I suppose, especially considering Daphne's persistence that I was. Uncle Jamal had said the same thing about me, too. I wondered for a split second whether I should get jealous already. If Father believed I'd stolen his mistress eight years ago, he had a right to steal my girlfriend now perhaps. Just to get even first! *Then we talk about where we can go from here!*

We got home at midnight. I suggested a glass of wine or beer and Father chose beer. Daphne had made some pasta salad, too. So we had a short conversation before hitting the sack. We gave our bedroom to Father and Daphne prepared the sofa bed for us. He insisted to take the sofa bed, but Daphne refused the most. He looked impressed with our good manners and generosity.

So far so good. The first encounter had gone smoothly and I was less anxious at the end of the evening, all thanks to Daphne. My positive image of Father, the one I had of him prior to the incident, was coming back to me quite fast. To my big surprise, I realized my deep love and respect for him was still intact. That was an encouraging sign, though I'd seen Mina's eyes in his in a few instants, while watching him drink his beer. Another stupid thing I did too. I smelled his jacket for any trace of the Nina Ricci when he took it off to go to the washroom. Maybe he'd embraced and kissed Mina at the Heathrow Airport before leaving London. I didn't know why I did this crazy thing. What would've been proved, or I'd done, if I'd smelled Nina Ricci on him or if I'd only imagined it? Maybe I was merely trying to test Narges's theory about the reason Mina had stayed in London. Could it all have been only a big coincidence? Have they been meeting in London? Was Mina still wearing Nina Ricci?

5

Daphne went to school the following day, maybe only for leaving us alone. She'd already given me big instructions about handling myself and how to take care of Father in her absence. Always, when Daphne gave me her stern instructions about my behaviour and psychological issues, I wondered whether she'd forgotten that we've been taking the same courses together all along, all those years. I was also surprised, and pissed off, how quickly she ignored that I usually got higher marks than she did in almost all courses. What was she thinking? What a weird world! Was all this by any chance a feminine tendency or mere racism, or some other bizarre phenomenon altogether?

I prepared Father's breakfast and our communication felt natural after a while. Our initial timidity for opening a dialogue faded soon. We chatted about general stuff and he reported that the whole family was in good health despite the chaos in Iran. Grandma was upset with Jamal, according to Father, who himself wasn't too happy about Jamal, either.

"What's the problem?" I asked.

"He doesn't want to grow up, as if he has no brain at all. He's still irresponsible, with no plan for his future. He spends all his money on women and gambling. He makes good money, but he's always broke. He often comes to me to borrow money. I've decided to stop helping him so that he can possibly smarten up and put his life in order."

"Is he still fooling around with women?" I asked giddily.

"Yes. Nothing is going to stop him. There's no light at the end of the tunnel for your Uncle Jamal the way I see it."

"Isn't it dangerous to chase women in the new regime?"

"It is. Especially when he keeps dating married women."

"He is? Is he trying to commit suicide?"

"The ironic problem is that married women are easier to find, lure, and dump these days."

"The sad problem, you mean, I guess…"

"Yes, it is sad the way married women are losing their loyalty, especially out of spite for religious and radical rules.

"Uncle Jamal has always seemed to be too horny, anyway, beyond normal perhaps. Am I right?" I asked with a chuckle.

"Yes, you're exactly right. Sex and women are the only things he is willing to spend his brain and time on," Father replied.

"Although it could be some kind of psychological insecurity he's trying to hide or fight through sex and women," I said.

"Maybe... You're the expert now... Maybe you can go help him a little when you get a chance," Father replied with a giggle.

"Many people in our family can use help, including myself."

"But please put Jamal at the top of your list," Father said.

"Okay... These women are really brave, too, aren't they?"

"In fact, the more restricted they feel—due to religion or whatever—the wilder and braver they get," Father said.

"So, Uncle Jamal is having a ball...," I said with a giggle.

"Yes, but he's also playing with fire."

"Yes, and that's stupid," I said with concern.

"It is! He is a total fool... He's simply a helpless addict when it comes to women."

"Maybe it runs in our family's blood!" I said with a smirk.

Father kept quiet, pondering, weighing the meaning of my words. If he'd noticed my sarcasm, he'd preferred to ignore it, instead of opening the can of worms and giving me a chance to start an argument already.

"The most important thing to remember is that we must never let a woman stand between us; not even your mother. We must be smart enough to never let anything or anybody make us feel bad about ourselves or each other. Nothing and nobody is worth even a small grudge between a father and a son. Do you agree?"

"I agree. But when we're young and passionate we often can't control ourselves. We don't have enough maturity and willpower to handle our emotions."

"That's true. We learn from our experiences. However, you must remember something very important," he said in a soft tone. "I thought you already knew that!"

"What's that?"

"That you're the light of my life and I'd never do anything by purpose to harm you. You're everything I have in this world.

Everything else I do is just for amusing myself, because I don't know what else to do."

His comments showed he'd known the reason for my bizarre behaviour all along. I always had a tiny doubt about this matter. It sounded as if he and Mina had seen me running away in the car's headlights. Or, at least, my subsequent reactions had made it clear for them. Anyhow, he hadn't tried to lie about it. He'd accepted his share of guilt by humouring me for as long as I'd desired. He'd been only respecting my wish, most likely against his own preference, while hurting all along. Even then, he'd taken my side for occupying Grandma's house and ignoring her whining and ultimatums. But that whore, Mina Afzali, had pretended she didn't know what I was asking her as much as I'd begged her to confess. She'd just insisted on making a fool out of me. That was the kind of arrogance Father didn't have toward me. He sounded sincere.

"I know. I had a bad childhood," I said.

"Everybody does, I believe… It's all part of growing up for everybody. Is that why you're studying psychology?"

"It must be one reason, I guess, because I've found out there's no Minister of Psychology even in America," I said with a giggle.

"So, you stuck to your gun and chose psychology, anyway, even though we both knew this fact," he replied with a chuckle.

"Yup, I believe I'm a stubborn human, too, like my family."

"Daphne is also studying psychology, I gather?"

"Yes. She's very good at it, I should say."

"She sounds like a smart girl," Father said.

"She is."

"Are you two planning to marry?"

"I don't know. I'm afraid of marriage and commitment."

"All men are," he replied.

"But my problem is much deeper. I just don't trust women."

"Don't you even trust Daphne?"

"Sometimes I don't. I don't know why I feel jealous when she has a simple conversation with other guys."

"It's natural. You're jealous because you like her. She's a charming woman. So her tiniest attention to another man upsets you. I like her." A jolt of jealousy agitated me.

"But my jealousy and mistrust feel too drastic sometimes," I said. "I know something about psychology, too."

"Fortunately, she knows you aren't responsible for the way you feel or behave sometimes. She can help you fight your flaws. That's another advantage of marrying someone like Daphne."

"You're right. I need a resident shrink watching over me all the time. Daphne is my best bet to keep my sanity and have a relationship, too."

"Do you think you love her, if you don't mind my asking?"

"I don't know what love is anymore, especially without trust. That's the problem."

"At such a young age, losing your faith! That's sad."

"You compare love with faith?" I asked.

"Yes. Love is a precious thing in this shallow world."

"Simply because it is scarce and almost impossible to find or keep," I added with my juvenile wisdom and normal cynicism.

"True. Most love affairs nowadays are shaky. They're often even phonier than our lives."

"Have you ever loved a woman truly?" I asked after long hesitation and mental struggle for posing such a direct, personal question. But the topic and timing was too perfect to pass up.

"Yes. A few times. I'm sure you'll have your opportunities and disappointments, too."

"It is not worth the hassles then, ha?"

"I agree. Still, you must stop being so critical of the whole world and yourself, anyway. You must relax a little."

"A few other people have also said so…"

He was starting to sound a lot like Daphne, as though they were conspiring against me.

"So maybe you should look into this matter," he said.

"But I can't help myself, can I?"

"About what exactly?" he asked.

"About my outlook and people, especially women."

"Maybe it runs in our genes, after all, as you said yourself."

"What runs in our genes?" I asked wittily. Although I hadn't quite got his point, he'd sounded mocking, like a fair response to my earlier sarcasm when discussing Jamal. Was he using my own words a minute earlier to both tease and outdo me?

"Our lack of trust in women," he said with stress. He sounded as if we'd been cursed. "Could it be genetic, Dr. Kian Noori?"

"I really don't know," I said, wondering if it was a good topic for my doctorate dissertation. "Maybe I'll do some research."

"Maybe we're cursed!" He sighed.

"But in my case, there has been a direct cause, too," I said with sarcasm again but felt sorry right away. As much as I tried to be nice to Father and forgive him, these sneering remarks just kept skipping my mouth. My cynicism was most likely another genetic defect.

"So what happened to the girl you insisted you must marry for love? The one whose father had a big tire factory, if I remember correctly?" Father asked with a smirk.

I felt he was again sarcastic and fooling with me now that he knew I'd actually been in love with Mina and not Goli. He was really pushing it, I thought.

"I lost her too. I cannot hold on to anything."

"That's okay. But I hope you don't follow Jamal's footsteps. I know you two have been very close. I hope he hasn't been a bad role model for you."

"Are you worried about the way he's living?"

"Very much. I'm worried about him getting into a big trouble, but mostly for his childish attitude and focusing only on women. I don't think he's capable of ever settling down and having a normal life, with a family perhaps."

"Yeah, he's too obsessed with sex and drinking and gambling. He's sick in a way, I guess."

"He's now turned against me after I refused to give him more money like before when he'd kept coming to me like a beggar and asked for another handout. Now he's mad at me and acts like a jerk. He's losing his senses…"

It occurred to me that Father would've most likely had a shoddy life similar to Jamal's if he hadn't been forced to marry Narges and build a good career with Mr. Taibi's help. These two brothers had almost everything in common—like identical twins. So, either way, Father's life had been doomed from the beginning regardless of the option he might've chosen. More frightening, my destiny would probably be similar to his and Jamal's, too, unless Daphne could find a cure for my genetic defects. I wished I were a little braver and dared ask him about the women he'd confessed a few minutes earlier to have loved. Then I thought that would be a rude thing to do, especially today. Maybe I'd ask him about his true loves later, once we felt more comfortable with each other again and I could stop being too sarcastic with every word I uttered. He probably wouldn't mention any of his lovers' names, especially Mina, even if she'd been one.

On the other hand, he might! He might confess to everything, since I'd noticed, in such a short time, he viewed me in a different light now, with lots of respect like I was a prominent psychiatrist already. I felt he liked to relax and confess to all his sins in hopes of finding salvation at this stage of his life. He looked broken… He'd probably found me a reliable venue to do that, unless I'd misread his mind, which meant I wasn't a good doctor yet!

I thought I should change the subject. "What're you going to do in Iran now that you don't have a job?"

"I don't know. Maybe some kind of business."

"Do you think you can live in that environment?"

"It'll be difficult for me."

"I'm sure it'll be."

"It'll impossible for me to live there if you're not coming back to Iran. Did you say that to Uncle Mustafa?"

"Yes, I did… But where're you going to live then?"

"I haven't made up my mind, but I think I'll prefer to live in London then. I bought a flat in London."

"A flat? What's that?"

"A condominium. That's what English call it."

"To live alone?" I asked before realizing the subtle sarcasm in my question. I wasn't very curious about his plans with Mina or another woman. But, somehow, the words jumped out of my loose mouth. I could already guess he wouldn't want Narges to live in London with him. She wouldn't like to live outside Iran or learn a foreign language, anyway. Besides, her obligation towards Ozra Banu wouldn't allow her to consider the option of living abroad. That old witch, Ozra Banu, seemed to have a special deal with Azrael, refusing to set Narges free. Maybe she'd take Ozra Banu with her to London! The idea felt hilarious in my head and my loud laughter startled and confused Father.

"Yes. I must live alone for a while to decide about the next phase of my life," he replied cautiously as though annoyed by my childish laughter.

"What do you think will happen in Iran now?" I changed the subject fast, again.

"The situation will be chaotic for a long time to come. It wouldn't be the kind of place for us to live in."

"Many of your important friends are in prison, right?"

"Yes. Many of them are. They'll probably rot in prison."

"Or even get executed if these bogus courts convict them. They've already accused Hoveyda of all kinds of treasons."

"Yes, I know. Poor Hoveyda!"

"They'd probably execute him, right?"

"Nah! They won't dare," he said with confidence.

"Well, I hope you're right," I said. I didn't want to argue with him. I didn't want to be too negative with him considering his depleted state of mind nowadays. But I thought he was still too naive about the situation. He was underestimating the radicalism of the new regime. 'They won't dare,' he believed. It sounded rather arrogant in fact, a residue of the old regime's mentality.

6

Father and I spent a good part of the day strolling in Hollywood Boulevard and the Sunset Strip. We covered lots of topics, as though we were back in the old times when I was at high school. As if the incident with Mina had never happened and we hadn't pained each other for five years for nothing. I remembered our discussions when commuting in the mornings and evenings. I recalled the day he suggested I use my grandparents' house as my city residence. How happy I'd felt that day. I remembered our conversations about Genghis Khan's picture in my history book and his promise to get someone to contact the publisher and find out about the source of that picture. I recalled the way he always opened his wallet and let me take as much money as I needed. But that particular day, he was my esteemed guest in the new world. I'd decided to pay for everything that day—although I hadn't still earned a single penny of my own all my life. I paid for our expensive late lunch at a fancy restaurant, too. Early in the evening, I suggested we head home as I'd promised Daphne to return on time for dinner. On the way home, I thought I should ask him about the old matter we'd laughed together about many years back, just for fun and breaking the silence.

"Did you ever find out about the Genghis' picture?"

"Oh, yes. I actually did. I'm glad you asked," Father replied with a chuckle.

"So what did you find out?" I chuckled too.

"I sent someone to probe the publisher without mentioning our reason, because I didn't want anybody know it was merely a personal curiosity. They got sort of nervous about the purpose of my investigation, imagining it was an official matter. They told my guy they'd look into it and get back to us in a few days. About ten days later, the chief editor came to visit me in distress. He again tried to find the reason for my inquiry and I told him it was related to a simple review of textbooks and nothing to worry about. But he still looked quite agitated. I tried to put him at ease, but couldn't say I was only trying to satisfy my son's curiosity. Anyway, he apologized for half an hour for not having yet found the sources of Genghis' and other pictures. They've been simply printing those pictures for over sixty years and by now nobody knew where they'd originally come from, nor could they find some documents about the initial use of those pictures. But he promised again to assign a couple of guys to do more research. He kept apologizing on his way out. This was about five years ago, a few months after you brought up this odd subject with me. Anyway, he promised to return with more information as soon as they had the answers, but he never did. They probably couldn't find anything and were embarrassed to confess. I didn't want to push or embarrass them any more, either. So I didn't follow it up, especially since you'd already left Iran *in such a hurry*."

"I wonder if they're still using those, or any, pictures at all, in history books these days after your inquiry," I said with a giggle.

"That'd be interesting to find out!" he said and we laughed.

"Pictureless Persian history texts!" I tittered. "It's all my fault."

We joked and laughed for a long time about the whole thing and how I'd started a major concern and chaos for a publisher for no goddamn good reason. Yet I recalled how serious I'd been about this matter some ten years before. *How we change!*

"Most troublesome, of course, is that we still can't establish if Narges is related to Genghis Khan?" he said with a chuckle.

"Yes, I guess we can never solve this mystery," I said and we laughed. "Plus another mystery I asked Narges about uselessly..."

"What'd you ask her?" he asked with concern and cynicism.

"I asked her why all fortune-tellers are women and she said it was because men are stupid and have no foresight," I replied.

"No, it's because women are way crazier than men..."

Now I'd successfully proved my suspicion about Narges and Father's marriage having also messed up their images of opposite sexes. Their opposing, hostile responses to my cunning question had done that, although the mystery about fortune-telling sexual orientation remained unsolved as well!

Daphne welcomed us with a big smile and kissed both Father and me. She'd prepared meatloaf for dinner, which smelled very good and garlicky. The dining table looked inviting with the flowery dishes and a bouquet of roses. She remembered that both Father and I loved roses, but didn't know about Father's allergy. Father peeped at the roses with a hint of concern, but didn't say anything. I smelled the flowers and they didn't smell too strong anywhere close to the roses in Iran. So I didn't mention or make a fuss about Father's allergy. Daphne looked happy, though I could detect her subtle edginess. I was becoming a shrink, too, after all.

"What's wrong?" I whispered to her in private.

She peered at me and then peeped at Father who had noticed our quiet conversation. She was silent for ten seconds.

"What's wrong, Daphne? Why don't you answer me?"

"I heard something on the news," she said at last.

I turned toward the TV. It was off. She chased my probing stare toward the TV and back to her.

"What was on the news?" I asked, agitated.

"They executed your past Prime Minister with a bunch of other convicted officials."

I peeped at Father who was in total shock. He was pale and soon started trembling. I remembered our chat only a few hours earlier: "Nah! They won't dare," he'd said with full confidence.

He glanced at me with apprehension and then plummeted onto the chair while Daphne and I gazed at him. I poured a glass of whisky for him. He sipped the whisky, then forced himself to grin at us. He looked so helpless and innocent despite his lifelong experience with harsh politics.

"When should I serve the dinner?" Daphne asked, looking at Father and hoping to restore some air in the room.

"Any time. I'm not hungry anyway. I had a big late lunch," Father replied, trying to hide the sudden blow.

We had our supper in a sombre mood. Daphne and I glanced at each other now and then with distress. After dinner, Father said he was tired and preferred to retire. He refused to drink a cup of tea with us, so we said goodnight to him and watched him go to the bedroom and close the door behind him.

"Did you tell him that you love him?" Daphne asked me as soon as we were alone.

"No."

"Why not? Didn't I say you must tell him that you love him?"

"Yes, doctor. I remember what you said. But I couldn't bring myself to say it. This isn't something common in our culture."

"This has nothing to do with your culture. It's just a part of the healing process for both of you."

"Yes, doctor," I said. I'd been a real jerk, I realized, throwing sarcastic remarks at Father and Daphne all day.

"Are you going to say it tomorrow?"

"Maybe. If I feel like saying it, I would. Don't push me too much, Daphne."

Daphne and I tried very hard all night to stay as far away from each other as possible on our corners on the narrow sofa bed and did not even cuddle.

7

Early next morning, Uncle Mustafa called. We chatted for a few minutes, then he spoke with Father for a long time, arguing about something, but I couldn't quite understand the topic.

In the afternoon, Daphne went to school while Father and I strolled around the Rodeo Drive and Westwood areas. We visited some of the fancy boutiques Daphne took me to for shopping. Father bought two shirts for himself, one for me, and one for Daphne. I helped him in terms of style and size for Daphne.

"Did Uncle Mustafa have any special news?" I asked.

"No," Father replied.

"But you two were arguing about something."

"He was advising me not to return to Iran."

"Why?" I asked.

"He was worried about the situation and ongoing executions."

"He's right. You shouldn't go. Uncle Mustafa is a smart man."

"I haven't done anything wrong? I wasn't even a minister."

"Thank God. But you were a deputy minister. Why risk?"

"Because my business is there. I must return sooner or later to take care of my properties. If I don't go back, people will start to spread rumours that I've fled the country. It'll give the regime an excuse to confiscate my assets."

"To hell with your assets. Your life is more important. Dad, please don't go back," I pleaded with passion. It felt like a good opportunity to tell him that I loved him, but the words just wouldn't come out of my mouth. What was wrong with me? Why couldn't I even say it to Daphne? All of a sudden, I realized that Daphne's insistence about this matter might've been more self-serving than anything else. She wanted to cure me, of course, but it was quite possible she wanted me to learn to say 'I love you' to her, too. All those years we'd been together, I'd never told her that I loved her. I imagined how insecure she must've felt, waiting for me all along to tell her that I loved her. I couldn't even reciprocate on many occasions when Daphne had told me that she loved me. Poor Daphne. How patient she'd been with me all those years!

"Those assets may be helpful to you someday," Father said.

"I don't care about money. Forget it," I said.

"It's probably because you haven't still worked to realize how difficult making and saving money is," he said matter-of-factly.

"You're right... But it's still not worth your life..."

"If I feel any danger, I won't go; I promise."

"But it's difficult to estimate the level of risk in the present situation. There're no laws in Iran nowadays. Do you remember telling me they won't dare execute Hoveyda? They probably did it at the exact moment you were saying they won't dare."

"I'll be careful," he said with a grin.

He looked pleased to see my genuine concern for him, while probably thinking, like myself, why both of us had been such idiots to let a small incident ruin our relationship for five years.

How could we let our pride or prejudice blind our senses in vain.
He was also falling more in love with America every minute. It
was easy because we'd all along strolled mostly in Westwood
and Beverly Hills. I thought about showing him the hotel near
downtown where I'd stayed for two months upon my arrival in
L.A. I suggested that maybe he'd like to consider coming to live
in L.A. near Daphne and me. He said the idea was tempting, but
L.A. was a little far for his frequent travels to Iran. He promised
L.A. would be one of his options to consider.

Later that night, I told Daphne about my conversations with
Father. With great enthusiasm, I told her I believed he'd felt my
deep affection for him and my concern for him to go to Iran.

"But did you actually open your damn mouth and say you
love him?" she asked.

"No. But I'm sure he realized it," I replied.

"This isn't good enough. You have to say it aloud. Please do it
tomorrow."

That night we made passionate love with lots of torture to stay
quiet. *She was now merely tackling my psychosis from a different
angle.* Yet, I suffered throughout our sex, pondering what she was
thinking all along, pushing the envelope tonight with her pungent
expressions of love for me, *What's wrong with you, asshole Kian.
You haven't told me even once that you love me, not even when
you're making love to me so zealously like this minute!*

When we were done, she stressed with a tender tone: "Please
tell him tomorrow that you love him. You must say it a few times
actually, before he leaves Los Angeles. Okay?"

But I never got a chance to tell Father that I loved him.

CHAPTER TWENTY
The Fiend on Earth

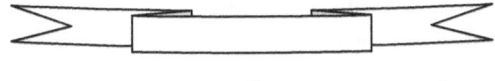

1

Uncle Mustafa sounded nervous when he called me four days after Father left L.A. He said he'd tried to contact Father at the same hotel he'd stayed before, but he wasn't there anymore. He asked me whether I had a number to reach him. I said I didn't.

"What's the urgent matter you need to talk to him about?" I asked.

"Hmm... I'll tell you later."

"Can't you tell me now?"

"It's about his travelling plans."

"You mean, about going back to Iran?"

"Yes. Did he talk to you about it?"

"Yes, he did. He told me he'll go to Tehran soon and not to worry about him."

"He's such a fool sometimes!"

"What's wrong? Please tell me," I asked.

"Nothing. Don't worry. I'll take care of everything."

"Take care of what? Why are you so secretive today?"

"Listen. You just concentrate on your studies and don't worry about anything. I'll talk to you soon."

"But, Uncle Mustafa. Is everything okay? Is Narges okay?"

"Yes," he said with a sigh. "As good as she'll ever be."

"What do you mean?"

There was a long pause. Finally, he said, "Listen, Kian. If you hear from your dad, tell him to call me right away. It's very very important. You understand?"

"Okay. But can you tell me what's going on there?" I begged.

"I can't right now. I'll call you soon to update you. Just ask him to call me if he contacts you."

The way Uncle Mustafa had sounded worried me, but I also felt grateful for having him in our lives. Especially, his devotion felt so surreal in our family whose members have been so aloof and self-absorbed. I suddenly felt a world of difference between the kind of passion and humanity that Uncle Mustafa emanated compared with all that superficial, antagonistic communication that Uncle Jamal had shown towards Father—his own brother— even after everything Father had already done for him.

I didn't hear from Father. He'd called to thank Daphne and me the day after he'd left L.A. He didn't mention where he was staying in London and it didn't occur to me to ask him, either. He mentioned he'd give me his phone number as soon as he moved to his new flat in London. Anyway, I was worried after Uncle Mustafa's peculiar phone call. But Daphne insisted no cause for alarm existed. Father was an intelligent man and knew what he was doing, she argued.

"Besides, your Uncle Mustafa has promised to take care of everything," she continued.

"Take care of what?" I asked her with tension.

I recalled my last words with Father at the airport in L.A. He asked me whether I wanted him to repay Uncle Mustafa's loan to me during the last five years. I thanked him and asked him to discuss it with Uncle Mustafa.

"Let's make another plan to meet soon," he said.

I nodded with a smile, but my throat was clogged from sad emotions and I couldn't speak. We kissed on the cheek and he stepped into the boarding area.

I didn't hear from Uncle Mustafa for two weeks, so I called Narges. She said Father had arrived in Tehran a few days earlier and Uncle Mustafa had taken him to Isfahan. And now she was angry with both of them. I felt anxious and called Uncle Mustafa.

"Kian, I can't talk to you today," Uncle Mustafa said. "I'll call you tomorrow at this time. Is that okay?"

"Can I talk to Father at least?" I asked.

"No. He's not here. I'll call you tomorrow," he said with haste and we hung up.

I felt Narges, Uncle Mustafa, and Father were playing a game or something among them and didn't want to include me. Daphne looked a bit nervous, too, for the first time. So, at least, I didn't have to listen to her positive thinking lectures, on which she'd become a fanatical expert. Especially considering my mood these days, I felt sick and tired of all that crap she'd been trying to force-feed me in recent years. I appreciated her good intentions. But sometimes when she talked to me, she sounded like a kindergarten teacher talking to a toddler. She still does, sometimes. I don't mind her making a note about this point as she reads these pages. How silly we shrinks sound sometimes and Daphne is no exception!

The following day Uncle Mustafa called me as promised.

"Listen, Kian." He sounded agitated and serious.

"Yes, Uncle?"

"I can't talk on my home phone. So I've come to the phone centre to use a public line to call you."

"Why?"

"I'm a little concerned about privacy."

"You think your phone is bugged?"

"Maybe... I don't know"

"What's going on, Uncle Mustafa?"

"Your father is safe in another house. So don't worry."

"Don't worry about what?"

"Listen, Kian. I guess you're a grownup man now and you deserve to know all the details."

"Thank you. It's time everybody starts being honest with me," I said, irritated. I peered at Daphne who sat across the room from me. She looked worried, too, watching my anguish the way I was sweating on the phone.

"I picked up your father at Tehran airport and brought him to Isfahan with me to avoid possible problems."

"What kind of problems?"

"Your mother mentioned something by accident on the phone. So I thought I must do something about it."

"What'd she tell you?"

"When I asked her if she knew when Jalal is returning, she said yes, and then added that the Komiteh had come around to arrest him. I asked her why and eventually dragged some odd information out of her."

"What odd information?" I asked.

"She'd told Dr. Afzali that maybe the reason Mina had stayed back in London was because she was seeing your father. Then, under pressure, she confesses to him that she'd suspected a long affair between Mina and your father for many years. Dr. Afzali is quite furious these days."

"I can imagine how he might've gone totally mad now. She's really done it this time," I exclaimed.

"I'm sure you know how she is sometimes."

"Of course… If only you heard some of my stories!"

"But this Dr. Afzali has been under a lot of pressure recently."

"He's always been under a lot of pressure."

"But it's different this time."

"Why?" I asked.

"Because Mina has kept postponing her return to Tehran. Now she says she doesn't know when she'll come back."

"I don't blame her. She knows she might be stoned to death for adultery if she comes to Iran."

"They don't do those stupid things in Iran, but she'll be in trouble somehow. Mina hasn't confessed to any wrongdoing, but Dr. Afzali has promised to forgive her, too, according to Narges. But she says she's still not ready to return to Tehran," he said in a sombre tone.

"Of course… She's not crazy," I said. I couldn't help feeling some kind of respect or pity for Mina. She'd finally found a way to gain her freedom away from Hassan. "She's smart."

"But that has made Dr. Afzali really mad. He's gone to the Komiteh and told them about your father. He's told them Jalal is the reason Mina is refusing to return to Iran. So now the Komiteh is looking for your father. They sort of assume that by arresting Jalal Mina might return to Tehran to save him."

"Doesn't the Komiteh have anything more urgent to do?"

"That's exactly why I'm worried, too. It seems this Dr. Afzali has some friends and influence in the Komiteh."

"Oh, my God!" I cried with rage and desperation. How could Narges cause this crap? I would've really used Father's handgun this time to kill her if I was in Tehran. I should've done this holy mission many years ago and prevented all these needless agonies. I wondered if Father had actually been the main subject of Dr. Afzali's subtle threat the night he asked me to return his dagger in front of Mina and my parents. Poor bastard had tried his best to stop things from getting out of control, like what was happening right now! And still that poor sullied soul had failed miserably…

"So, when your mother bragged about what she'd done, and the Komiteh looking for him, I got concerned. I decided to do something before it was too late. She thought I'd be happy for her, to witness her revenge. Your mother is nuts, you know!"

"Now you're catching up… Is Father okay?" I asked with tears in my eyes. Daphne's eyes were filled with worry, too.

"Yes. I'm keeping him safe in a friend's house."

"What's gonna happen now?"

"We're trying to get him out of Iran quietly."

"How?"

"Through Pakistan or Turkish border."

"How can I get the news?" I asked.

"I'll contact you anytime I can use the public phone. Don't call me at home, but if you must talk to me, be careful what you say. No mention of your father and things like that. Understand?"

As I hung up, Daphne ran to me and hugged me. I couldn't say how she could've figured the severity of the situation only from the stress on my face. She'd learned a few Persian words, but not enough to understand my murky conversation with Uncle Mustafa. I suppose my face showed my deep anguish. But I also believed she was a psychic as well. She was bound to become a natural psychiatrist. I told her about the sequence of events and Father's hiding somewhere in Isfahan. I bet she already knew all that. Again, she tried to calm me down, promising that everything would work out fine. She promised the phone would ring very soon and when I answered it, I'd hear Father calling me from his flat in London. For once, after all the years of killing me with her positive thinking lectures, I really liked the sound of her promise. I wanted to believe her totally. Aside from her half-assed logic, her ability to calm my nerves has always been precious, anyway. Without her in my life, I would've gone totally mad years ago. She suggested we go visit him in London as soon as he got there.

"We'll both tell him that we love him, okay?" she stressed. "We'll go even if it has to be for just a few days."

I nodded. Her compassion and sincere efforts to calm me were invaluable. I loved her for all this and lots more, but I missed the opportunity to tell her as much. Another weird puzzle was how could a person who was so worried about his dad these days had been so careless about him for five years for nothing? Maybe my deprived psyche was now making up for all those years I had restrained or confused my feelings!?

For three weeks, I leaped out of the couch to answer the phone every time it rang. But Uncle Mustafa didn't call. I was upset with him and Narges. Calling Narges wasn't wise, either, considering my mood. I would've screamed at her so loud all the phone lines would've burned and melted. Even Daphne agreed I shouldn't call her at this time. Calling Uncle Mustafa at home couldn't help, either. So I just sat near the phone and waited for some news from Iran. Thank God, Daphne stayed around to keep me engaged as much as she could. She forced me to go out with her to the movies or for a stroll in Westwood streets in order to be away from the phone for a while, especially during the sleeping hours in Iran.

2

Another week went by and Uncle Mustafa didn't call, so I called him. I hoped to gather some hints at least about the situation without mentioning Father on the phone. But for almost a week, I couldn't find him any time I called his house. Even when I called late in the evening at Isfahan's time, his wife or children said he wasn't home. But I was starting to feel he was avoiding me.

A few days later, Daphne suggested calling Narges. She might have some information, anyway, which would be better than waiting for Uncle Mustafa so much. I was hesitant, but Daphne dialled all the numbers to contact Iran. When Narges was on the phone, she passed on the receiver to me and whispered, "Call her 'Mother' right now."

I took the receiver testily. "*Salam, Maman*," I said to Narges.

For the last few months Daphne had been bugging me to call Narges 'Mother' to let my subconscious accept she was still my mother, after all, no matter how evil she was sometimes. What pure garbage! Daphne was already angry with me for not telling Father that I loved him before he left. She made a big fuss about my lack of sensitivity and scorned me for not following her therapeutic instructions. I was really fed up with her for pushing me around so much with her psychotherapy. Yet, I didn't have the heart to tell her to shut up. I wanted to improve my relationships, too, with Daphne and also with Narges, if at all possible. So I felt obliged to follow her stern instruction this once, which showed my ultimate desperation to suck up to Daphne. I really needed her at my side at that critical point in my life—even at the cost of calling Narges, *'Maman'*.

"I have good news, Kian," Narges said with a glee in her voice. She was not moved or surprised about my sudden affinity and calling her 'Maman' for the first time. She simply ignored it, I guessed, or maybe was even bothered by it.

"Oh? What good news?" I asked, sceptical.

"They caught him," she said. "They caught him."

"Who caught who?"

"The Komiteh caught Noori in Isfahan," she said with joy.

"They caught Father? This is your good news?" I screamed in absolute disbelief.

"Yes. I knew you'd be happy, too, deep down... Aren't you happy?"

"Happy about what? Have you now totally lost your brain?"

"After everything he's done to you!" she said. "He deserves to rot in prison."

"What do you mean?" I yelled. "What has he done to me? Are you crazy? Why don't you go to a madhouse?"

"Kian, I know everything. You don't need to deny it. I know how much he hurt you."

"God, please help me. You're a crazy witch. How can you be happy to see my father rot in prison?" I yelled at her in English and hung up the phone.

After all those excruciating years of knowing Narges, still I couldn't believe the depth of her wickedness, not to mention her unprecedented stupidity in this particular case. I realized her thrill from Father's arrest wasn't only out of spite, but also the fear that he was about to abandon her and go live in London. Father in a Tehran prison was surely closer to her—thus more acceptable to her—than living in London with Mina or another bitch, totally out of her reach! But how could she assume I'd be happy, too? How could she imagine I'd never forgive Father, not even after Uncle Mustafa's efforts to mend the situation and Father's trip to L.A. to see me? I was amazed of her mentality then, but not now. As a psychiatrist, I've noticed many individuals are merely too damn spiteful to understand the possibility of people forgiving one another. Many of my patients are inherently just incapable of forgiving others. Therefore, now I can imagine why Narges had assumed that I, too, would be thrilled to see Father punished. A spiteful person like Narges always makes these kinds of gross misjudgments about some people's ability to forgive others. She'd proven not clever at all about this matter. That's why she was in fact surprised by my reaction on the phone. Silly Narges!

On the other hand, I wonder if I would've actually forgiven Father if Daphne hadn't pushed me to do so. Without Daphne in my life, Narges's assumptions would've probably been accurate, especially after agitating me with the news about Father and Mina reuniting in London. What if I hadn't forgiven Father? I believe I would've been much more miserable today. I really would. I must be grateful to both Uncle Mustafa and Daphne for pushing me to meet Father and make amends with him. They were the only reasons Narges had failed in her judgment about my ability to forgive Father.

I called Uncle Mustafa right away. His wife answered again.

"It's urgent that I speak with him. Please ask him to come to the phone," I begged her.

"He's not home, Kian," she replied.

"It's midnight there. When is he coming home then?"

"I don't know, Kian."

"Please ask him to call me tonight, as soon as he gets home."

"If I'm awake, I'll tell him."

"Leave him a note. Tell him that I know everything."

"You know everything about what?" she asked.

"I know about Father's arrest. Ask him to call me."

There was a long pause on the phone. "Hold on Kian, Mustafa just arrived."

"*Salam*, Kian... How're you?" Uncle Mustafa asked with tension. I tried to keep my cool even though he'd obviously been avoiding me for almost one month.

"Uncle Mustafa, is it true? Narges just told me Father is..." I couldn't bring myself to finish the sentence.

"Yes, Kian. Unfortunately it is true."

"Oh, god! What happened?" I asked.

"The same old story."

"What do you mean?"

"Your mother and father. Their silly grudges and games."

"What happened?"

"Your stupid mother again couldn't keep her big mouth shut."

I couldn't believe Uncle Mustafa calling Narges stupid. He must've been really mad at her to lose his normal serenity. She was destroying his life, too.

"What garbage she let out of her big mouth this time?"

"She told Dr. Afzali that your father was in Isfahan. She told him I knew where he was in Isfahan. This time she did it not only out of spite for Jalal, but to hurt me, too, for helping him. Then, Dr. Afzali had informed the Komiteh. They came to my house. They kicked the door. They threatened to take me and the rest of my family to prison if I didn't tell them where Jalal was. I said I didn't know. They clubbed me and took all of us to the Komiteh for interrogation. Sorry, Kian."

"Sorry for what...? I'm the one who should apologize for Narges's wickedness and putting your family in this position."

"After six hours, I couldn't bear watching my family put through such an ordeal. They forced the kids to confess they'd seen your father in Isfahan recently. My young kids were terrified and crying. I realized Komiteh just wouldn't give up. So, I had no choice but to take them to Jalal right away. I gave them Jalal with my own hands. I couldn't even inform him to escape. My friends may also get into trouble for hiding him. We're all still in a mess. I simply can't imagine my crazy sister could do such a thing to me and my family. But the worst part was telling you that I failed to protect Jalal. I couldn't bear the idea of bringing you the bad news—especially about giving them your father personally. I was hoping to find a way to tell you everything on the phone or get him out of the prison without causing you unnecessary worries."

"It's not your fault, Uncle Mustafa. You did your best."

"I tried, Kian. I really tried."

"I know you did, Uncle Mustafa."

"Sorry... I don't understand how your mother can be so cruel with all of us?"

"I'm familiar with her malice. I don't know what Ozra Banu has done to her."

"I wish I knew."

"When did they arrest him?" I asked.

"Ten days ago. But they took him to Tehran last week."

"Is anybody following his case in Tehran?"

"I've found some people to follow the case seriously. But I'm not sure anybody can tell us what is going on or what kind of charges will be brought against him."

"Please keep me in the loop if you find out anything."

"I will. I'll let you know everything."

I told Daphne what had happened. She looked dumbfounded listening to such a bizarre story. I told her to never ask me again to call Narges or address her as 'Mother.' She was quiet, not even daring to peep. She was probably thinking 'What a family!' She might've even worried about her expertise as a psychiatrist after all her suggestions failing so miserably. I hoped she'd learned a lesson! But, of course, I'm sure she'd actually continue to blame me for not following her instructions ever or on a timely manner; especially refusing to call Narges 'Mother', be nicer to her, and telling Father that I loved him, among many other stuff she'd wanted me to do all those years. Maybe everything was my fault, after all, at least according to Daphne!

I pondered going to Tehran to help Father somehow. Nobody was there to help him, other than possibly Uncle Mustafa. But he had his own family and business, and he was living in Isfahan. I discussed my plan with Daphne and she rejected it right away. She asked me whether I knew how I could help. How could I deal with the chaotic bureaucracy in Iran, especially in the hectic justice system of a revolutionary government? She insisted I must focus on my final exams. She insisted we must have faith in God. The way she said it sounded silly, "Leave it in His hand *for now!*" As if I could go and take over from Him later, if necessary!—in case God failed to do the job! As if I could handle the mullahs better than God could direct His disciples—a bunch of radicals He had now put in charge of running my country and its courts under the name of Islam! Again, Daphne insisted I must focus on school, since I hadn't been studying enough throughout the year.

"Okay... Let me think if it's wise to I leave it in His hand for now since you insist," I told Daphne. Then, a few days later, after some thinking, I added. "Okay, I've decided to give Him His last chance to prove Himself."

"That's the right thing to do...," Daphne replied with a smirk. "I bet He was also hoping you'd give Him another chance!"

"Do you think He can handle it?" I asked with a chuckle.

"If He can't, nobody can, especially you," she replied.

God was my best bet under the circumstances, I thought then. I also decided there was no point staying mad at Him forever. He was definitely surprised and frustrated Himself about the way humans had turned out against His initial design. Things happen and things could go wrong for Him, too, the way humans' regular scientific experiments go wrong. He was probably most amazed about humans' weird imaginations about Him, heaven, hell, and all the stuff we've made up about Him, especially His special love for humans. He is probably most furious about the kind of silly humanly words that all prophets have attributed to Him! Anyway, I begged Him to save Father *at least* and let me hear from him in London, out of the mess he was in in Tehran. I really believed in Him and His silent promise to save Father. I promised Him, as another Nazr-o-Niaz, to go to London with Daphne right away and tell Father loudly, right there and then in front of her, that I loved him! To make the deal even sweeter, I promised Him to also tell Daphne, right away, that I loved her too, right in front of Father. Maybe I'd even ask Daphne to marry me right there and then with Father as our legal witness.

But now I often question my wisdom then to listen to Daphne or depend on God. Sometimes, I actually curse myself for being so trusting and gullible. Maybe I should've flown to Iran right away and hired some lawyers or done something directly myself. My sense of guilt for not getting involved fast personally has been another source of my stress in recent years. It possibly also tainted my relationship with Daphne amongst a few other things.

3

For three months, I called Uncle Mustafa regularly and asked about the situation. He said he had no news rather timidly. He couldn't even visit Father in Evin. Nobody knew anything about his status, but Uncle Mustafa consoled me on the phone. He promised things would work out fine sooner or later. He tried to help me stay calm and focus on my education. I tried. He asked me every time whether I'd talked with Narges, and I always said no—the truth. I couldn't even bear her voice on the phone.

Then it dawned on me that perhaps Uncle Mustafa's repeated inquiry had another reason. Maybe Narges had some information that Uncle Mustafa was again hiding from me. I was dying to know what was going on, but calling Narges was simply beyond my capacity. She hadn't called me either for such a long time, which was sort of expected. She was now either too embarrassed or timid to talk to me. But I also tried to find relief in the chance of nothing hurtful she knew to share. Otherwise, she would've probably not hesitated to call regardless of my attitude. So maybe things were under control, after all. Still I tested Uncle Mustafa. I asked him if Narges knew something he wasn't sharing with me. His stutter and tone of voice on the phone alarmed me and I felt he was most likely lying again. But, of course, he didn't confess to anything. My life felt like hell for three more months, while I remained in dark and helpless about my father's dire situation in the notorious Evin. I wondered what was happening in Tehran and what was going to happen to him.

Near the end of the summer, I was just too restless. With no news about Father and my school starting in a month, I pondered skipping school for a while until the situation was settled. How could I focus and study under the present circumstance? Then I decided to go to Iran to do something for him. But again, Daphne was against my dropping out even for one term. She asked me what I was hoping to achieve by going to Iran. I had no rational answer for her sensible question. Besides, I had to go live alone in a hotel, God knew for how long, because living in the same house with Narges or even Grandma felt awkward. Without knowing anybody important in the new regime, how could I really do anything for my poor father in that chaotic city? Yet, in my condition, nothing could convince me not to go. Logic meant nothing. One day, I told Daphne I was going to Tehran regardless of the prospects. I felt I must act. We had an argument, but I was determined to go.

"It seems time has come to take over from God according to your previous suggestion," I told Daphne hoping to sell my plan to her by teasing and amusing her.

"No, not yet… You still shouldn't go…," she replied sternly and left with a grudge.

I called Uncle Mustafa. "I'm going to Tehran for a visit."

"No, no. It's not a good idea."

"Why not? I'm going nuts sitting here doing nothing."

"I understand, but don't come."

"Why?"

"Because there's nothing you or anybody else can do."

"I must try, anyway… I'm coming next week… I was just wondering whether you can come to Tehran, too."

"No, I can't. And I don't want you to come, either. Just listen to me, *pesaram*."

"Sorry… I can't. Not anymore."

"Listen… What if I come to see you? There're some matters we need to discuss. But it's better if I go there."

"Uncle Mustafa! What matters you want to discuss with me?"

"Just wait there. I'll be there in a week. Would you listen to me please?"

"You'll be here in a week?"

"Yes. I have the visa and everything else. I was planning to go and see you, anyway. I'm on my way."

"Okay, I'll wait for you," I said, confused about his comments and his rush to visit me.

"Good boy."

"I'll go back to Iran with you," I said.

"We'll discuss it when I'm there," he said.

Again, I explained everything to Daphne. She was surprised, but also relieved I wasn't going to Iran, at least not in such a hurry. She said Uncle Mustafa was a smart man. Her comment worried me because that was exactly the same crap she'd said about Father, too. But then he'd returned to Tehran like a fool and brought this mayhem upon all of us. I started to count the days for Uncle Mustafa's arrival, hoping he'd be a good moral support for me for a while at least. Of course, poor Daphne tried to be helpful, too, but I needed someone to help me make a plan to save Father. The idea of him rotting in prison, maybe for the rest of his life, as Narges had prayed for, was driving me crazy

The night before Mustafa's arrival, the phone rang and Daphne answered it. She said it was for me.

"Kian?"

"Speaking. Who's this?" I asked.

"*Salam*, Kian. This is Ahmad Javid. How're you?"

"*Salam*, Ahmad," I replied.

"I'm very sorry. I just found out," he said.

"About what?"

"About your father. I'm sorry," he said.

"About my father?" I asked like an idiot, but then blood rushed through my veins. I shuddered.

"My father told me on the phone just now. He had seen your father's name on the long list in papers ten days ago."

"What list are you talking about?" I yelled at him.

"Those who got execu...," he mumbled timidly, realizing only then perhaps that I didn't know anything about the execution.

"What're telling me, Ahmad? Are you sure?"

"I'm sorry. I thought you knew. Sorry… Sorry."

I dropped the phone and began screaming. Daphne ran to me and hugged me. I kept her in my arms for a few seconds, but I was about to suffocate. I began running around the apartment and cursing Ahmad Javid and his creators. I tore off my shirt. I was overwhelmed with the same kind of panic attack and madness I remembered from the night I broke the front door of Grandma's house. Daphne ran after me and tried to catch me, but I pushed her away anytime she got near me. At one point, I slapped her by accident when I tried to elude her. After running around for ten minutes, I fainted on the sofa. Daphne brought me water. I sipped it before calling Uncle Mustafa's house. I knew he was on the plane somewhere by then. His wife answered the phone.

"Is it true Father is dead? I already know," I asked with a loud voice without patience.

"Yes, Kian. I'm sorry. Hasn't Mustafa arrived yet?"

"No. Sorry to have bothered you."

"It's no bother. My condolences, Kian," she said.

"Thank you. I'll have to go now."

I was badly bewildered and didn't know what to do. I just walked in circles and drank a half bottle of whisky in about two hours. Daphne stayed up and watched over me. She drank a little bit whisky, too, to calm her own nerves. She was getting really fed up with me, my family, and my madness, I imagined. So many thoughts turned in my head while I drank whisky, but for a moment, I wondered about the way I always ran and shouted during a catastrophe. What was that all about? Everybody reacts differently, of course, but mine was too loud and involved a lot of sprinting. Pondering my rather comical reaction distracted me for a second and it helped.

"I'm glad I got a chance to see him once at least," I told Daphne near dawn, totally worn out and drunk.

"Yes. It was great that you two reconciled at the end."

"I know," I said. I burst out howling. She hugged me while I bawled for two minutes. "I'm really glad we forgave each other."

"Yes, for sure… I just wished you'd told him that you loved him, too," she said. The poor girl probably didn't mean to torture me, but her comment felt too insensitive. It had probably just slipped her tongue. I realized she was trying to console me, but sadly, she'd goofed in a bad way. For a soon-to-be psychiatrist, she'd really blundered.

"I tried, Daphne. I tried, for God's sake!" I screamed and ran to the washroom. "How long are you going to torture me with your nonsense? You crazy shrink!"

I hid there and wept for half an hour. Daphne kept knocking on the washroom door and begging me to open it and forgive her, but I ignored her. I was drunk. I lay on the floor in the washroom for over two hours and finally fell asleep.

4

There was daylight when I heard Daphne leaving the apartment. I got out of the washroom in a haze. As I walked into the kitchen, she leaped and embraced me. She giggled for tricking me out of the washroom while helping me dress. We went to Pancake House for breakfast, but I could hardly eat anything. I sipped a little bit of orange juice and ate a small piece of pancake. Later, we walked in the neighbourhood's main shopping areas for three hours and stopped at a café.

In the afternoon, we took a nap in the apartment before going to the airport to pick up Uncle Mustafa. Daphne drove, of course, despite my insistence to drive. She'd suspected my mood might kill the both of us and the Celica with my suicidal driving. Uncle Mustafa appeared in the luggage area at last and we hugged. I started sobbing and he began to cry, too. At first, he probably thought my emotion was from the joy of seeing him and all the pressure I'd been under in recent months. But my heavy howling soon told him that I knew everything.

"My poor dad," I blurted.

"Oh, my dear, Kian. *Pesaram*, I'm sorry."

Uncle Mustafa stayed with us for a week and we discussed lots of family issues; mainly my late father, of course. He said he had very fond memories of him, too. He was a real gentleman, he said. Then he confessed about his guilty conscience.

"What guilty conscience, Uncle Mustafa?"

"I get anxious sometimes when I wonder if Jalal realized I was really forced to hand him over to the Komiteh. I'd told his lawyers to make sure he understood I had no other choice, but they could not get any reaction from your dad about forgiving me or even believing my story. I just hope he didn't think I'd actually betrayed him by handing him over to the Komiteh deliberately or easily, especially for Narges's sake. I'm upset about this matter and my failure to clarify my situation for him before he died."

"Oh, Uncle Mustafa, I'm sure he knew you wouldn't betray him."

"I don't know; I hope so… But still I feel terrible sometimes thinking he might not have realized the severity of the pressure the Komiteh had put on me and my family before I finally couldn't take the torture anymore. I failed him and you. I hope you two forgive me."

"I understand and forgive you totally," I said while feeling disturbed by his confession somewhat, anyhow. Suddenly, I couldn't stop thinking whether he'd really done his best and truly born enough torture before giving up Father!

"Now, I also feel guilty for taking him to Isfahan in the first place. I thought I was doing a very smart thing to hide him and try to get him out of the country," Uncle Mustafa said with tears sluicing down his face and shaking his head in despair.

"Now you think that had been a mistake, too?" I asked with surprise, but also thinking that his point might be valid.

"Yes, maybe if the Komiteh had talked to him right away when he arrived in Tehran, they might've focused only on family quarrels. Maybe all these hiding and secrecy agitated Komiteh, but also caused so many other issues come to surface as well…"

"You think so?" I asked.

"I don't know for sure, but cannot stop feeling guilty about my interfering and possibly becoming responsible for Jalal's case getting totally out of control. Oh, God, forgive me if I've caused your father's demise. I'd hoped to do something decent to avoid a catastrophe, but might've in fact made the matter much worse and committed a crime."

"Your intentions were honest and prudent," I said with a new round of grief for the way things had gotten out of hand.

"Perhaps if I had not agitated Narges unintentionally with my interference, she would've not gone to that extreme and telling so much stuff to Dr. Afzali and the Komiteh. I'm just going crazy with all these 'what if' thoughts, Kian."

Uncle Mustafa's points made absolute sense and stirred a new wave of commotions in my head now as well. He'd found out about the execution the same way everybody else had, through newspapers. While fighting with his conscience about his likely initial guilt for giving up Father to the Komiteh, he'd been hoping to take care of some issues before coming to see me. He said he didn't have the heart to tell me about Father's death on the phone, so he'd just been planning to come to see me and hug me before revealing the sad news. He hadn't seen Narges lately and wasn't in a hurry to see her, he emphasized with unprecedented rage. He assured me that he and my uncles would take care of the funeral arrangement most decently. My presence wouldn't be necessary. Together with Daphne, they tried to convince me to forget about going to Tehran. At last, I submitted again. According to the court ruling, Father's assets would be confiscated, too. Uncle Mustafa wasn't sure what would happen to my parents' main residence in the subdivision, but it was possible they would even evict Narges because the house was under Father's name.

"Were you hiding something when you kept asking me if I'd spoken with Narges?" I once asked Uncle Mustafa.

"You have a good intuition," he replied. "A lot was going on actually during the last three months. I hoped to spare you from all those hectic and embarrassing proceedings."

"Well, you can tell me everything now that poor Father is dead."

"Everything simply got out of control for so many reasons within a few months. Too many people came forward and caused added problems and your father was not helping the situation with his normal simple-mindedness, either, always assuming and stressing he hadn't done anything wrong."

"Yes, I'd noticed that attitude in him, too. He was stupid and stubborn in that regard, like his younger brother, Jamal."

"But let me emphasize again I could've never imagined the whole thing would get out of hand so fast. Otherwise, I would've probably died before giving up your father."

"Nobody could've imagined any of this," I said with a sigh.

"I couldn't bear my family's torture mostly, but who could imagine this outcome for some silly accusations."

"So what happened," I asked with cynicism.

"I guess I'd better give you this last piece of information, too, to relieve my conscience just a bit perhaps."

"Thanks…"

"Well… A trial proceeded off and on, during the last few months. Some work and business related evidences were brought against him. His close friendship with Hoveyda and many special services he'd apparently done for him were also raised in the trial. But his personal life was under great scrutiny the most. Dr. Afzali and your mother were among the main witnesses against him."

"Narges testified against him?" I asked, dumbfounded.

"Yes, they gave the court all the information they needed to declare your father a 'Fiend on Earth.' I'd like to believe your mother was forced to testify. After confessing everything she knew to Dr. Afzali, the Komiteh interrogated her and forced her to repeat all the facts again in the court. Maybe they convinced her that telling the whole truth would save her husband."

"You think so?" I asked Uncle Mustafa with cynicism.

He looked at me with desperation and whispered, "That's the best I can hope for…"

CHAPTER TWENTY-ONE
Farewell to Narges

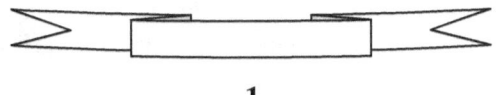

1

I'd imagined I'd never see Narges again. I had no interest to see her. I had no reason to return to Iran either. I had no business with the people who'd killed my father for no goddamn good reason. I had no idea regarding the other charges before the court against Father other than Dr. Afzali's complaint and Narges's testimony about Father's colourful past. Only God knew what other stories the spies and Father's enemies had sworn to in that bogus court. Maybe Uncle Mustafa knew more about those charges beyond the overall points he'd mentioned to me briefly. But neither of us saw any point discussing them now that Father was dead. The bottomline was that the new Iran had taken away Father from me just as I'd gained my sanity, realized my own crime towards him for five years, and we'd begun our new promising relationship. His naïve comment, "Nah, they won't dare" rang in my ears for many weeks. All his assets were confiscated, too.

Yet, in the following years, Uncle Mustafa insisted that I go visit Narges. He said she needed help, but I couldn't imagine how I could help her, especially after what she'd done to all of us. Over the years, before she betrayed Father in the worst manner of retaliation, I'd tried to help her, all in vain. I recalled her vengeful stares at Father after he'd returned from Europe and left piles of pictures with other women during his trip around the house so casually. I'd felt her dire determination at that moment to retaliate in a horrific manner; way worse than what she believed he'd done to her. Now she'd succeeded beyond anyone's imagination.

Daphne had also been pushing me all along to forgive Narges, anyway, and repair my relationship with her. She'd insisted that Narges would change if I started to be nice to her. I was really sceptical, but tried, anyway, just to keep Daphne happy with me. All along, I pondered Saadi's famous quote: "Educating a shrew is like trying to balance any round object on a dome." I recited the poem to Daphne once, but she didn't get the gist of it. Surely, my translation of the poem could never convey the poet's delicate meaning and fluent lyrics. So I only explained to her that 'trying to keep any round object on a curvy dome is simply useless.'

In my letters to Narges, I'd tried to explain how I'd felt about our relationship. I'd tried to explain some of the ways she'd hurt others, especially Father and me. In the end, all those efforts had proved futile, too. So I could really see no reason to go to Iran. It was a pity, and a cause for my shame, I couldn't help her even when I became an accredited psychiatrist. I believed nobody could help her. Period. But Daphne disagreed while pushing me with her psychotherapeutic gimmicks any chance she got. She'd never give up, I knew. It seemed amazing how one psychiatrist could be so much more optimistic than the other about the effects of psychotherapy, although we'd taken the exact same courses from the same professors. There was something special in her genes apparently, but then could a psychiatrist's personality affect the outcome and value of psychotherapy? If yes, then maybe I or she wasn't suited for this profession. That was a new dilemma for me now suddenly. Anyway, she insisted that I should go to Iran and forgive her at least for helping myself. I said I couldn't. Then one time, she did the stupidest thing in the world. She gave me a kind of ultimatum.

"Kian, you have many issues you don't want to address."

"What're you saying?" I asked her, while trying to read her mind. I bet she was thinking, *For one thing, you've still not told me, even once, that you love me!*

"I'm saying that unless you get down to business to solve your problems, we'll never be able to build a real relationship," Daphne stressed with a grimace.

"How do you expect me get down to business, dear doctor?"

"Stop being sarcastic for one thing."

"I'm not sarcastic," I said. But I imagined my paranoia and sarcasm would ruin my life eventually.

"I'm saying all this for your own sake and our relationship."

"I know and I appreciate that," I replied with sincerity.

"I'm really worried about you, to tell you the truth."

"What do you really expect me to do?"

"As a start, go see your mother and make peace with her. If you want, I'll go with you."

"No. Any other suggestion?"

"No. Sorry, Kian. The bottomline is that until you fix yourself you can't be of any use to anybody else."

"I'm of no use to you, then?"

"Not until you resolve your issues," Daphne said.

"I won't be of use to my patients, either?" I asked teasingly.

"I doubt it," she replied so seriously my pride and poise broke.

So, Narges also caused the collapse of a *perfect* relationship between Daphne and me. Daphne completed the accreditation requirements one year before me and opened her private clinic in 1983. She rented a new suite close to her clinic near Orange County. I stayed in the same suite in Westwood. We continued to see each other off and on. But the harsh circumstances of my life and my personality flaws had ruined our chance of building a lasting relationship. A month later, she told me she'd met another guy and renewed her ultimatum. She asked me whether I was willing to change my position.

"In what way?" I asked her.

"You must listen to *all* my suggestions."

"All your suggestions?!" I yelled with surprise.

"Yes."

"Like what?"

"We must go meet your mother, for example."

"And then?"

"Then we must work on your childhood traumas."

"Otherwise you can't like me?" I asked.

"Otherwise we'll be fighting all the time. Liking or loving each other wouldn't solve anything."

I couldn't grasp the wisdom of her suggestion then, so I said no. But the way she saw me so useless had singed my pride, too. She started a relationship with the new guy and married him six months later. When I completed the academic requirements, I opened my clinic in Woodland Hills and repaid Uncle Mustafa's loans in four years. I also married one of my depressed patients for no goddamn good reason. So dejected and lonely, I didn't realize my stupidity until it was too late. I probably married her out of pity. I couldn't take her constant sobbing in my office and whining about life anymore. My clinical treatment just wasn't working, so I married her instead.

It seems everything the gypsy woman had predicted about my life has come true except for one crucial thing. Her promise that I'd meet a nice girl and have four cute children had been rubbish. My present wife, Katherine, has been nasty—too far from nice. My three children are cocky at such young ages already—too far from cute. Sometimes, I want to kick their asses if I weren't so afraid of their mother kicking mine.

Often I wonder whether the gypsy woman had meant Daphne as my wife. Had I sabotaged destiny with my stubborn refusal to keep Daphne happy. Can fate be interfered with, the way I think I might have? It doesn't make sense. But I've done so many things wrong in my life. So perhaps things would've changed if I'd done just one of them right. For instance, if only I'd gone to see Narges for a couple of weeks, I wouldn't have been in the mess I am today. Daphne would've become my wife and my lifelong psychotherapist. In fact, my entire life would've been completely different if only I hadn't stuck my head out the door thirty years ago and let the gypsy woman see me. I would've most likely married Goli and had a comfortable life in Tehran with her. She would've probably forced me to become a regular medical doctor from Tehran University, too. *We always regret our stupidity only later, when we cannot do a damn thing about our past decisions.* Remember these words of wisdom to avoid feeling stupid like me later!

Uncle Mustafa kept me abreast of Narges's general health and condition. He said she was getting weak and old. Daphne asked me about Narges regularly, too, whenever we happened to meet. She has always remained concerned about her, but probably thinking of her also for two other reasons: First, as a challenging subject she'd aspired to take on. Maybe she craved a chance to meet her and prove me wrong! Second, as the main cause of our separation. Daphne's family and mine have kept in touch, even though Daphne and Katherine don't like each other at all.

2

The irony is that I went to Iran to see Narges at last, seventeen years after Father's death. But it was too late in many ways— mostly because Daphne had already married another man and had a couple of kids. I told her one day I was considering going to Tehran to see Narges and she got happy. Then I gave her a corny ultimatum of my own! I told her jokingly that I'd go only if she promised to help me with my old traumas when I returned, and she agreed. By then we both knew I needed her help. To be honest, I thought she needed my help to get over her growing problems, too. She had major issues herself, including with her marriage. But I decided not to bring up her problems at that point, so that we could focus on mine. Daphne also agreed to look after my patients in my absence. I was worried that some of them might decide not to come back to me after discovering what an excellent and compassionate psychiatrist she was. Most of them must drive a long distance to her office instead of mine, but they'd probably think that it'd be quite worth it.

Uncle Mustafa said he'd travel to Tehran to pick me up from the airport. He insisted it was necessary for us to meet right away. I didn't understand why until we met. He'd booked a room for me at Bahar Hotel, his usual quarters in Tehran. He explained Narges's tough life after Father was executed and his assets were confiscated. Uncle Mustafa had offered to buy a condominium or a house for Narges and hire a maid for her, but she'd refused his offers. I knew she would. Such a proud woman she was, she'd never accept charity from anybody, not even her brother or son. Ozra Banu had died, too, two months after Father. So Narges had moved into the tiny suite Ozra Banu had rented from Mr. Nozari for many years. Other than two of Narges's faithful colleagues at elementary school, none of her aristocrat friends had bothered to come around and visit her or invite her to their houses. She'd been living a life of seclusion, the same way Ozra Banu had been in the last decades of her existence. Uncle Mustafa prepared me to see an old woman living in a depressing suite after having lived in luxury all her life. *She brought it upon herself*, I thought with cynicism, while Uncle Mustafa explained Narges's gloomy situation. Even if she'd inherited lots of money, she would've lost it all by now, anyway, the same way Ozra Banu had.

Narges recognized me promptly and smiled as I entered her living room unexpectedly without Uncle Mustafa. In fact, she quickly realized I was tricking her again like the good old times and asked if Uncle Mustafa had brought me. I hugged her and kissed her on the cheeks before Uncle Mustafa came out of his hiding corner. I did everything according to Daphne's meticulous instructions. I smiled at her time and again. She looked frail, but at least she recognized me and could still limp on her feet. She whined about her heart condition, arthritis, acid reflex, digestion disorder, and a bunch of other health issues. Nobody mentioned Father the entire time I spent with her. She looked happy to see me. And I sort of felt happy to do something that was right to do, according to Daphne at least. It didn't matter what I felt and how deep my wounds might have been, I tried to remember.

Uncle Mustafa took me to Father's grave in Behesht-Zahra. I placed a bouquet of red roses on his grave, and Uncle Mustafa recited some religious verses. Grandma had passed away too. Uncle Jamal said the shock of Dadash Jalal's execution killed her within six months. Uncle Jamal looked old and gloomy himself. He was still a bachelor and broke. I met my other uncles and aunt briefly in my aunt's house.

The following week Uncle Mustafa suggested that we go to Isfahan together so that I could meet his family for the first time. On the road, as Uncle Mustafa drove in silence, I couldn't get the image of Father's rotten body at the bottom of that cold, damp grave out of my mind. His name on the gravestone had looked so surreal and unacceptable. All my mental quarrels about Azrael's cruelty and the unfairness of death in the past hadn't still prepared me to see my energetic Father turned into only a name on a gravestone. Hardly anyone visited his resting place to even read that long, traditional name—Jalaleddin Noori Tabrizi. All his loud chatter and laughter on the dance floor of Royal Club still echoed in my ears. All that charm and vigour had now become only dust and bones. Nobody would call his name again.

Suddenly, the sound of Narges calling Father rang in my ears and the memories made me chuckle. Another funny thing about their relationship was that she addressed Father only by his last name all those years. "Noori, *your son* is driving me crazy," she told him often. "Noori is probably having a new affair," she told her close friends too often. "I guess Noori is planning to go to Europe without me." When she was really mad at him or meant to offend him, she used his secondary last name, which denotes the people related to the city of Tabriz and grown a reputation for being slow in social skills—maybe even a rather dumb person. "Tabrizi, tell *your son* to be polite."

"He was barely fifty years old," I murmured unconsciously.

"I'm sorry, what'd you say?" Uncle Mustafa asked.

"Oh, I was thinking about Father. He was too young to die."

"I know, Kian. I'm very sorry. I know how you feel."

"Well, I'd always feel, for the rest of my life, that maybe I could've done something more. Maybe a better lawyer could've saved his life at least," I said.

"Believe me, Kian. I'd hired the best lawyer in town for him and I bribed so many people who could possibly influence the outcome of the court's decision. We did everything that anybody could think of."

"So what happened? Why this outcome?"

"Only one thing could've changed his destiny, but at the end we couldn't do it," Uncle Mustafa said with a big sigh.

"Oh...? What was that?"

"His lawyer told me that, according to the prosecutor, the charges against him would be reduced if he or somebody could convince Mina to return to Iran. Dr. Afzali had promised to drop his charges against your father if Mina returned to Iran."

"Did you really believe that returning Mina to Iran would've saved his life, just by dropping one person's charges?"

"Yes, we believed the prosecutor had the authority to reduce the charges and he was apparently Dr. Afzali's close friend or something like that. If at least this 'fiend on earth' charge had been dropped, it would've really helped your father a lot."

"But how could he ask Mina to return, especially since he was in the prison and Mina was having fun in London?"

"His lawyer told me he'd tried to convince your father to give him Mina's address or phone number in London and let him speak to her on your father's behalf. He could give her the details of your father's case and clarify that without her assistance your father's fate was quite grim. He wanted your father's permission to contact Mina somehow. But your father refused. So, his lawyer asked me to try to contact and convince Dr. Afzali to give us Mina's telephone number. I agreed to do it. I got Dr. Afzali's number from Narges with some difficulty and finally found Dr. Afzali. We met the next day and discussed the matter.

'I heard you've agreed to drop your charges against Mr. Noori if your wife returns to Iran. Is that correct?' I asked Dr. Afzali.

'Yes, I promise to do that the minute Mina arrives in Tehran. I'll write it down if you want and I've already told the same thing to the prosecutor as well.'

'His lawyer told me that too. Is the prosecutor your friend?'

'Yes… The bottom line is that my children want their mother and I need her, too. I'll do anything to bring her home.'

'Does she know what is going on here? Does she realize her absence might jeopardize an innocent man's life? Doesn't she miss her own children?'

'I don't know. She doesn't talk to me.'

'Then you should show some mercy and drop your charges, anyway,' I said.

'Why is that?'

'Because it is your wife who's making you angry and not Mr. Noori. You're probably not even sure he's guilty. You're making your judgment only based on Narges's words and circumstantial evidences. You know that Narges talks a lot of nonsense all the time. I know my sister.'

'Let's drop this bullshit. We all know he's guilty. There're also many private issues I do not wish to discuss with you, but he's terribly guilty of so many things.'

'But maybe you can still show some mercy,' I pleaded.

'Why should I do that? Did he show any mercy when he was ruining other people's lives? He's stubborn and selfish even now.' Dr. Afzali said with fury.

'Why?'

'Because he refuses to convince Mina to come back. Why don't you ask him to talk to Mina and tell her that he'd get into big trouble if she doesn't return to Iran?'

'His lawyer has asked him to do that, but he says he does not or cannot interfere in other people's lives.'

'He's just trying to protect Mina. He thinks he'd get away by denying everything and going back to her. He thinks he's smart.'

'Can you give me your wife's address and phone number, so I can personally contact her and tell her how bad the situation is here for Mr. Noori?'" Uncle Mustafa said and paused. I noticed tears sliding down his cheek.

"So Father could've actually helped himself if he'd talked to Mina at least?" I asked.

"Yes, but he didn't listen to any of us."

Uncle Mustafa delved into deep thoughts again and stayed quiet for a long time. I didn't say anything either. I wondered whether Father had refused to ask Mina to return merely out of sheer arrogance, sacrifice for Mina, or merely knew that Mina would not listen to him, either! He'd sure been in a tight spot, too —that poor, helpless Casanova!

At last, Uncle Mustafa regained his composure and started speaking again. "I called Mina in London and she talked to me after I said I had news about Jalal. I gave her all the details about Jalal's trial and told her that his life was hanging in her hands. She understood everything perfectly, but didn't say a word. I told her that no crime against her had been proven other than some rumours that Narges and Dr. Afzali had spread around. Again, she didn't say anything and we just said goodbye."

"But she knew her own life was in danger," I said. "She also knew she'd never get a chance to leave Iran again even if she wasn't stoned to death or something for adultery. Without her husband's permission she'd never get an exist visa again. Did you really expect her to do such a silly thing?"

"If she loved your father she should have, I thought," Uncle Mustafa said. "Isn't that what love is all about?"

"Love...! Ha!" I groaned and he peeped at me with surprise.

How naïve Uncle Mustafa appeared to me in that moment about the meaning of love! I imagined how little he probably knew about this matter and how shocking my story with Mina would be for him. I also recalled Mina's words the night she said she loved me more than her kids and I'd imagined it'd been a big deal. Now hearing about her careless attitude about seeing even her own kids ever again, my astonishment of her words and love that special night felt so silly! Suddenly I realized I'd actually been lucky Mina had not confessed to me about her affair with Father. I would've most likely bought her excuses, forgiven her, and pursued a life with catastrophic outcome. God had indeed done me another favour by pushing me to leave her instead of fooling or forcing myself to love her. I must thank God and the gypsy woman, although I'd preferred a different outcome for my affair with Mina then. That luck thingy again! It had somehow saved me from getting trapped even deeper within Mina's grip and maybe even forcing her to marry me. Maybe that's a crucial point to remember, especially now that I should really count my blessings and stop whining so much about my present doomed destiny with Katherine and our cocky kids.

3

After two days in Isfahan, Mr. Nozari called Uncle Mustafa and told him that Narges wasn't feeling well. So, Uncle Mustafa and I departed for Tehran and arrived at her suite ten hours later.

Mr. Nozari had called her doctor. He'd visited her already and installed an oxygen capsule to help her breathing. I held her hand often, as I recalled Daphne's instruction. Her eyes were narrower than ever and filled with tears. Her breath was short and shallow. Her dentures sounded loose in her mouth and it was hindering her occasional attempt to speak. Her hair—just a few faithful strands—was partly white and partly red from henna. I recalled how sternly she blamed and cursed Father for every strand of hair she lost and for every gram of fat she gained. "I was thin and had a head full of hair before marrying Noori," she emphasized often with pride to whine about the stress Father caused her.

"I will stay in Tehran as long as you want me to," I told her. I wasn't sure she could hear me, but she nodded with a faint grin, which I took as a positive sign. I kissed her cheek again and hugged her. Mustafa and I sat there all night and talked about past memories and life in general. We pushed her to drink water and juice, but she wanted us to let her rest. We respected her wish, yet

worried about her possible dehydration. I suggested taking her to
a hospital, but she refused to go. She was conscious enough to
stop us from doing things she didn't want to do. I felt she was
seeking death, maybe partly due to her pride, to end my torture of
sticking around perhaps. But I was happy to stay with her for as
long as she wanted me to. I had nothing exciting waiting for me
in L.A., anyway. In fact, I was happy to stay away from my crazy
patients and family as long as possible. They were getting nuttier
every week! Hearing their bizarre, cruel life sagas was ruining the
last grains of my own sanity.

I couldn't believe my own eyes, holding Narges's hands with
compassion. Maybe I was learning to be a real, caring doctor,
after all. In the past, even thinking about touching or hugging her
would've revolted me. Kissing both her cheeks on New Year was
torturous enough, but it was an obligation once a year. Such a
domineering woman now looked so helpless and resigned. She
looked innocent, although some hints of her malice toward me
and Father still rolled in my head. I just caressed her hands with
passion. I was delighted with my sudden enlightenment, a divine
sensation probably caused by my sincere intention to forgive her.
It was no longer only for Daphne's sake, either. Uncle Mustafa
looked pleased with my unexpected adjustment as well. Daphne
would've been ecstatic about my maturing and learning *at last* to
express affection, especially toward the least likely candidate for
my attention. I was proud of myself too.

Uncle Mustafa begged Narges to eat a little bit soup and she
declined again. He insisted it was good for her, but she only
frowned as if repelled by the sight of food or even hearing the
word 'soup.' Her resistance reminded me of the times she'd done
the same thing to me: forcing me eat the food—especially soup
—she knew I resented. I hated cooked carrot, spinach, egg-plant,
eggs, cabbage, lentil, tomato, green bean, egg, fish, and many
other things. I felt like puking even by the smell or a small taste
of these foods and Narges was well aware of my 'condition.' I
call it a 'condition' because it was beyond my control and any

intelligent parent should've realized that. Still our meals were filled with all these vitamin-loaded ingredients and Narges nagged at me to eat them. Often I forced myself to eat a little bit just to please Father. Still, he looked quite disappointed in me as he saw my hesitance, while Narges just kept insisting that it was absolutely necessary for my health and growth. I remembered his face, watching me with concern, as if I were going to die soon the way I looked so thin—which probably related to the kind of milk they'd fed me as a baby. We all knew that Narges liked to bug me more than she was concerned about my health. Father knew it very well indeed, yet grimaced when I refused to eat—weird! By the way, now I like all these foods. I'm surprised at my fussiness, then, about all these fine foods, especially vegetables. Maybe my taste buds have improved so much. But maybe my 'condition' at the time was merely the symptom of my subconscious resistance toward anything Narges insisted was good for me? I've made a note to discuss this topic with Daphne later among a few million other stuff. Most significantly, while my parents' behaviour had felt odd and annoying during my childhood, it felt only funny and natural now.

"Eat your soup... It is good for you," I said to Narges a few times myself. And I also asked Uncle Mustafa a dozen times to try to make her eat her soup. But Narges didn't budge. She only glared at me the same way I remembered from the good old days. Maybe she realized I still enjoyed teasing her, even on her deathbed.

Near dawn, I was still holding Narges's hands and staring at her. She didn't look too ugly. She actually had some kind of a divine glow on her face. Uncle Mustafa saw it too and told me so later. Then she was gone. Uncle Mustafa and I hugged each other and cried a little. But I didn't scream or run around the room like the case had been in the previous catastrophes.

"Do you know her real name was Golbesar Khodadadeh?" I asked Uncle Mustafa.

"No, I didn't know... What a weird name!"

"That's probably what happens when an angry, desperate mother or some strangers in an orphanage chose a name for a fatherless child to get a birth certificate for her."

"Why did everybody call her 'Narges' then?"

"She'd asked her adoptive parents to call her by a nickname she had chosen and liked very much," I replied.

"I suppose she had a tough life, my poor sister!"

"Did your mother also confess why she'd abandoned her? Did she show any remorse for what she'd done?" I asked.

"No," Uncle Mustafa said with gloom.

I didn't have the guts to ask him whether he thought their mother had been too cruel like Ozra Banu and Narges—or maybe even a slut, too. On the other hand, the answer was there already in front us, finally dead—another poor victim of her mother's cruelty. She was with God now, I hoped. Finally rid of a lifetime of misery, disappointments, and nagging questions in her head—about her natural mother, adoptive mother, husband, son, friends, a half-brother, and a phantom father she never met or knew anything about. *What a life my poor mom lived!*

4

I returned to Los Angeles three days after Narges's funeral and recounted all the details to Daphne, in particular my abnormal, passionate feelings at Narges's deathbed. She was happy with me after such a long time. She was truly proud of me for the first time. I felt all this from the way she kissed me on the lips with great warmth, like the good old days, but I knew she meant well. Nothing that her husband should worry about—I hope, or not? We're only good friends, if you like to believe me. Now that I had finally matured and gotten over my phobia to say 'I love you' to Daphne, I didn't have a right or guts to say it. Yet I wondered how she'd react if I did!

Even sadder, now that I've finally learned to say 'I love you' to somebody, I have nobody deserving my affection. What a life!

EPILOGUE
Daphne's Document

Another Heads-up

1

This is it… This is what you may call Daphne's Document, because she was the one who asked me to write it.

Yes, revealing my obsession for a gypsy thirty years ago and recounting my life story after her visit, including my deepening sense of guilt for so many things, were Daphne's idea as a first step to psychoanalyze me. I'm so fortunate she's still in my life. Aside from our *special* friendship, we're good colleagues and I trust her judgment. She's promised to help me study the events that set off my life on a wrong path. It's odd that two psychiatrists are trying to cure each other, although she hasn't actually asked for my help yet. But, trust me, she needs help, too, despite all the optimism she tries to emanate for my and her patients' benefit. I'm probably a bit responsible for her mood after eight years of torturing her innocently, while we tried to keep our relationship going. I guess I must feel guilty and ask for Daphne's and her parents' forgiveness, too. I owe the whole world a goddamn big apology for my existence! And, no, believe me, I'm surely not trying to be overdramatic! Daphne and I are probably crazier than half of our patients due to our own traumas and demented fates.

Speaking for myself, I really need Daphne, at least for helping me make a few crucial decisions. For one thing, I believe more every day that psychiatry has been a wrong choice of career for me. It hasn't helped me cure even my own quirks, which had been a main reason for choosing this profession. This also makes me wonder about the value of all that education, and even more significantly, my suitability nowadays to help my patients. This thought alone is ruining my spirit quite often. How can I preach others if I cannot convince and cure myself? Such a trusting bunch of people they are! They expect me help them with their relationships, unaware that my own marriage is doomed. They expect me guide them overcome their depression, unaware that even the strongest anti-depressants are failing my own growing melancholy. They expect me aid them deal with their repressed hurts and broken hearts, unaware that I'm still wrestling with my own childhood traumas. So, the new patients are probably better off remaining longer on the damn waiting list than visiting me under the present circumstance. Some of them might luckily stumble upon a natural, holistic cure to avoid my superficial clinical solutions. Besides, I'm tired of keeping a straight face when advising my patients with conviction. In fact, I may burst into loud laughter one of these days in the middle of one of my silly lectures to these poor souls who're relying on my expertise.

2

Daphne was surprised when I asked for her professional opinion about four months ago. I only grinned with embarrassment while she basked in my final defeat and unbelievable change of heart. The poor girl had really tried to cure me, while I'd resisted with my stubborn attitude. Anyway, we met a few days later for coffee and an initial consultation in a café near her office. This was just before my trip to Iran and Narges's death.

"It's about time you came to your senses and let someone help you," Daphne said. "It is also wonderful that you're going to see your mother. I'm so proud of you."

"I should've listened to you," I said with distress. "Maybe you would've not left me if I'd let you psychoanalyze me?"

"Yes… Things could've been different. I really loved you."

"I know. I cared a lot about you too," I said, curbing my desire to tell her that I loved her then, too—the neglected truth—simply because she was married now. I still loved her in my weird way. Not having the right to say, 'I love you' to Daphne after years of ignoring her right and need to hear it from me was maddening. What a twisted, cruel life! I wished I dared ask her if she still loved me, too. Ironically, I believed, as a psychiatrist and a torn lover, Daphne would've been thrilled to hear me say I loved her, not for rekindling any kind of romance, but just to ascertain my defeat. I was sure, she'd be happy to hear the truth she'd failed to drag out of me for years, at least as a show of her power to make me admit at last what she'd been hoping to prove for years. Only social norms and tact stopped me make her happy!

"But I'll be glad to help you now, anyway," she said with pride. "Try to summarize your major childhood experiences and I'll review them before we start to talk one on one. Jotting them down will save a lot of my time and it'll help you dig into details and your subconscious better."

"Maybe I get cured automatically, anyway, if I do that?"

"That's the idea... You may not need me, after all, if you write everything down and live through those years in your head again. Make a list of everything you feel guilty about, too."

"This summary may turn into a big novel if you want me put all these details on paper."

"That's okay. Take your time. I like reading novels."

"Fine. I'll start right away. It may also be a good distraction for me these days," I said.

"Good... But let me ask you a question today."

"Okay, shoot."

"Do you see the glass of water half-full or half-empty these days?"

Here we go again, I despaired. Just the old cliché, I thought. Yet, I couldn't blame her for gauging my mood and the difficulty of handling me again. I could lie to keep her happy. But she could possibly help me better by knowing the whole truth.

"I'm going to tell you the truth. But promise not to get angry."

"If you're serious and want my help, you'd better be honest about all your stories and feelings. Do you think you can do it?" she asked with a tone of ultimatum. I knew I had to do exactly as she said. The old Daphne, always giving me tons of ultimatums.

"Yes, please… I want you to help me."

"So how do you see it these days: half-full or half-empty?"

"I see it completely empty, in fact," I said with a grin, but I wasn't lying or joking.

Daphne shrieked, "Are you jerking me around already?"

"Of course, not… I've just answered you truthfully."

"But how is it possible? How can it be empty?" she yelled.

"Well, I can't stop imagining what'll happen to that water soon: Either somebody's going to drink the other half if I turn my head for a second or it'd evaporate in a few days when everybody ignored it. It'll be empty soon enough. That's the way I see the world. We're doomed whether we like it or not. There's not even a smidgen of hope, the way a pessimist sees a half-empty glass," I said. I could go on for hours to explain why I felt that way.

Thank God, she stopped me. "Kian, Kian! What can I do with you? What can I do for you?"

"Please, Daphne. I promise not to argue with you."

"But, Kian, I doubt I can help you."

"Let's give it a try anyway. For the good-old-time's sake."

"From everything you've told me about your childhood, I'd say your problems relate to your mother's way of treating you."

"Some of it is, I guess. Probably thirty percent of it is her fault. The rest of it relates to other women breaking my heart. In the end, it's all women's fault any way you look at it; you know!"

"Yes, I know. I'm familiar with your heartbreaking affairs."

"Including the one with you. Why did you leave me?"

"Including the one with me…," she mimicked me with stress.

"And then this damn marriage. Why did I marry Katherine?"

"It was a rash decision. You didn't even discuss it with me."

"I'm sorry... I should've seen you before agreeing to marry her," I replied. She didn't notice or ignored my mocking tone.

"Choosing Katherine might've had something to do with your background with your mother, too," Daphne said.

"In what way?"

"The classical theory. Marrying someone like your mother."

"Maybe... I don't know... There must be other reasons, too, for my hasty decision to marry Katherine."

"I think you felt guilty for being unable to cure her after so many long sessions you spent on her. You felt sorry for her and thought by giving her love and security she might be cured."

"I guess! My sense of guilt for so many things is ridiculous."

"You had probably become obsessed about curing Katherine, too, and you wanted to succeed at any cost."

"You're right..."

"You'll go nuts if you don't stop feeling guilty all the time. Katherine sounds very much like your mother and you feel sorry for both of them. Maybe you think you've been hard on your mother or even neglected her."

"Then you better cure me before I marry all my patients just for curing them!"

"Though it'd only make them and you even sicker. Now you should know that at least!" Daphne replied with a smirk.

"I cannot help anybody in any way," I said with gloom.

"Going to Iran finally to see your mother might help you treat your old traumas and maybe solve your marriage issues, too! I'm really happy about it."

"I'm also hoping to get you and Uncle Mustafa to like me again. Maybe you like to tell me what to do when I go there."

"Okay, I will. I'm sure this trip will change you."

"Maybe! There's something else Narges has done to me."

"What?"

"The last couple of years I've had a lot of pain in my right wrist. Sometimes it hurts so much I cannot move my hand or even write a prescription for a patient. So my doctor sent me for x-ray and I visited a specialist, too. He says the pain is from some old injuries. Maybe an operation fixes the problem a little."

"Old injuries? What kind of injuries?" Daphne asked.

"That's the funny part. I couldn't figure out what injuries I could've had in the past. I hadn't even done the military service in Iran. Then one day it dawned on me that it should be related to all that grinding of gum tragacanth for Narges."

"Are you gonna let them operate on your wrist?"

"I might have to eventually."

"Good luck. Get a second opinion first, though."

"Thanks. But more painful than my wrist is the pain in my head. Please promise to help me when I return from Iran."

"Okay, Kian. I don't know what I'm getting myself into. But I'll give it a try for the good-old-time's sake."

"Your promise gives me a lot of courage," I said tenderly.

"When you come back from Iran you must think about your life and options seriously. Maybe you should divorce Katherine if things cannot be improved," she said with affection.

"Divorce Katherine?"

"Yeah…"

"And then what?"

"Maybe better things happen for you, you never know."

"Thanks, Daphne. I promise to help you, too."

"Help me? How?" Daphne stared at me with her old charm— a cute mix of surprise and suspicion.

"Any way you like," I said.

She rolled her eyes and grinned. "Let's start with the main document I asked you to prepare. I'll read it first and then decide whether there's anything I can do for you or not."

"It's a fair proposal. I accept."

3

Daphne's job to help me sort out my hang-ups, career, and sense of guilt would be tough, I admit. Feeling sorry for my patients is sort of understandable. Feeling guilty for not forgiving Father sooner and telling him that I loved him makes sense. Ignoring Daphne's various suggestions, for so long, had been a mistake as well. I feel guilty for bugging Narges so much. But my inability to help her, not even after I'd became an alleged psychiatrist, is probably most embarrassing. I couldn't help her deal with her severe conflicts, nor could I stop her evil acts that destroyed the whole family. Sometimes, I believe I'd tried my best to help her, even when I'd been a child, but maybe not enough. Most of all, I feel ashamed and guilty right now when I consider the possibility of meeting Narges in heaven or hell and having to explain myself for saying some nasty things about her appearance and character in this document. I don't feel good about it at all. But Daphne had asked me to be honest about the facts and my feelings during those sad years. I've copied everything from my diaries, anyway, even the words I used then, in order to remain as objective about my feelings then as possible. I beg for Narges's forgiveness, even though I've only told the truth and still cannot forget some of the things she did to me. My sense of guilt toward her, while writing Daphne's Document, actually brought me nightmares a few times about my horrific encounter with Narges in heaven. We instantly started to bug and curse each other all over again. Are we both too stubborn or what?! I'd always imagined that nobody fights in heaven, so our squabble before God Himself was funny and embarrassing. In my dreams, I wondered what had happened to all that forgiving, compassion, and caressing at her deathbed.

I'll always remember the morning she died in front of my eyes, while I held her hands and prayed for her soul sincerely from the bottom of my heart. I begged God to bless her and give her a peaceful place in heaven. I asked Him to make up for His big goof-off about the way He had created and treated her. I told Him He must make up for giving her the destiny of living with Ozra Banu and Father in such humiliating conditions, plus the agony of bearing a mischievous son like me. His divine refusal to give her a pleasant, pretty daughter at least, instead of a brat like me, when knowing her heartfelt hatred for boys, is unforgivable and unbecoming for a supposedly kind God the most, though! Yet, I'm surely the only one feeling guilty about this matter, too, since even He seems adamant to do everything any way He likes with no recourse or a simple sense of remorse, so unlike me!

My inability to forget all the problems I'd caused Grandma brings me another big wave of guilt and shame. Recalling the ways I'd disrupted her normal life, not to mention the disrepute I'd caused her, saddens my spirit. More troublesome than feeling guilty for bugging Grandma so much is my feeling of shame and guilt for awakening her dormant need for attention, love, and sex. I sort of believed that if I had been a stranger,—a professional and persistent photographer perhaps—Grandma would've most likely agreed to taking even a few nude pictures, too. I feel guilty for thinking and saying this as well! She might've even slept with the guy—that's how rejuvenated she was feeling after God knew how many decades of neglect. These bizarre but basic facts also show how hypocritical and useless some religions' efforts are to curb humans' instincts and spirits by forcing hijab or similar guidelines, and believing that such gimmicks can withstand the power of humans' drives for attention, love, and sex.

I also feel guilty for breaking Goli's heart and leaving her so selfishly just for going to the new world—another stupid decision perhaps. Indeed, I feel guilty for making so many bad decisions in my life. I wonder whether my life would've been way simpler if I'd never left Iran or if I'd at least returned after my major shock during the first few months in L.A. and realizing my big mistake. Maybe I must find Goli and beg for her forgiveness. On the other hand, my travel to the new world has perhaps been the best decision of my life judging by the present situation in Iran and the world's animosity towards the new regime.

Even in the hindsight, I just don't know what would've been the best decision for me. So, now I try to count my blessings for my relatively comfortable life away from the chaos in Iran. In particular, the regime's determination to fight America, my new country, is creating such havoc on the international scene and causing mayhem in my heart. To be honest, I can't say, for the life of mine, whether I'd like to take side with my old country or the new one. I know both countries are doing so many things wrong, but mostly I hate the way my new country has been exploiting the world for centuries. I feel ashamed and guilty to become, or already being, an alien American. Anyway, I've decided not to dwell too much on these political issues. I have enough personal problems and sense of guilt already without getting into politics, too. I never liked politics anyway—the notion I had to repeat to Father often when he strived to make me follow his footsteps. Politics is such a cheap profession when people in charge are so power-thirsty and look only after their personal interests and then the interests of oil companies and other conglomerates. Me, I feel like an old veteran still suffering from post-war syndrome. I can't shake off my haunting past in Iran, which is now augmented by many sad experiences since I arrived in L.A. Often, I feel useless indeed, exactly as Daphne had suggested many years ago when she gave me her ultimatum. Writing this document hasn't helped much either, despite Daphne's promise that it would.

Actually, all these refreshed memories of old incidents and my guilty conscience are raising my edginess these days. It is quite absurd to feel guilty for million other silly stuff, even old incidents, such as ignoring my neighbourhood friends, who were waiting for me to bring them water. I know I neglected them while gulping water myself like a madman in the kitchen and watching the gypsy foretelling Narges's fortune. Carrying a bottle of water for them would've been easier and nicer than rushing out and cursing them. But no one expects a child to have a better conscience and presence of mind. Trying to fathom even my past perturbing decisions and actions all my life is stupid. Yet, my chronic nastiness during adolescence feels absurd and hurtful.

I never hurt anybody by purpose, I believe; in particular my patients. Well, almost never! You see, my wife, the darling I'm still living with, often makes me lose my temper and we say nasty things to each other. Why did I marry a depressed patient and how did I fall into her trap? I guess I'd already lost my mind, partly due to my background and crooked genetics, before many bad relationships with women destroyed my sense of judgment altogether. How absurdly I'd imagined that escaping my parents would bring me freedom and happiness! How stupidly I'd thought that life in the New World would be so heavenly and democratic. How naively I'd assumed that marrying Katherine would help her relax and turn into a better person! How foolish we feel when we get old and realize the sheer vanity of our youthful imaginations! Only now I realize that freedom is never possible for any of us naïve humans with so many obsessions, sexual drives, shallow needs, and social attachments, even if a free world could ever exist. Anyhow, my guilty conscience and tension are major hurdles now that I need my objectivity to at least cure myself or go find a more sensible profession. I'm glad Daphne has agreed to psychoanalyze me.

4

I'm ready for Daphne now after putting this document together in the last three months by using my scrupulous diaries compiled during adolescence. In fifteen large notebooks, I'd amassed a great deal of information over the years with unbelievable details. Maybe I'd anticipated I'd need them so much when I grew up, though I could've never assumed they'd be used for therapeutic purposes. Reading all those old writings and remembering how much time and effort I had put into my analyses and thinking, mostly for figuring out those weird adults in Royal Club, was both amazing and depressing. *How sadly my youth was wasted!*

When I started to review and organize my notes, I noticed I'd jotted down not only the details of *events*, but also the related *thoughts* and *feelings* of myself and people around me. Oddly, I'd realized at such young age that events, thoughts, and feelings go together often and trigger one another endlessly. We easily get entangled in their mix and hope to keep our sanity, while they spin in many bizarre directions and create many other hurtful thoughts or memorable experiences.

Anyway, I'm really looking forward to spend some time with Daphne during this psychoanalysis at least. It seems the more I live with Katherine, the more I want Daphne. This condition (missing Daphne in my life) might be another cause of my stress nowadays, too. But this is a secret I must keep to myself. I cannot tell Daphne anything that might screw up her life or our great friendship. I still love her. But what can I do? I must stay practical and focus on gaining my confidence first. My feelings for Daphne also reminds me of Father's comment in Los Angeles when I asked him whether he'd ever loved somebody and he said, "Yes. A few times. I'm sure you'll have your chances and disappointments, too."

"It is not worth the hassles then!?" I'd replied so wisely.

Now, all I can do is to just wait and hope Daphne can help me get hold of my skidding life and cure my freaking head. The best solution is to convince her to elope with me, of course. It'd be really nice if the two of us could go hide somewhere and forget everything and everybody else. That same old running-away urge seems to be still haunting me except that I want to do it with Daphne now, instead of the gypsy woman. You never know… it may happen this time! Meanwhile, the only positive point these days in my life is the great sensation I feel anytime I remember my last hours with Father and Narges. I feel proud of myself for forgiving them. Thanks Uncle Mustafa. Thanks Daphne.

I hope my parents accept this novel as my sincere tribute to their good hearts and to express both my gratitude and apology. I'm proud even for being their midnight gate-opener for so many years even during those cold winters. I'll always remember and regret my neglect towards them the most.

Meanwhile, I can never thank God enough for sending Uncle Mustafa to help me and my family so much. He's been especially responsible for my relative sanity and mere existence nowadays.

I would've been in a much bigger mess, if alive, without Uncle Mustafa in my life. He's always been funny too. But last night, especially, he made us laugh for a long time on the phone with his hilarious suggestion. He said all new graves in Behesht Zahra, including Narges's, would be in two levels due to space shortage and the exploding Tehran population. For now, Uncle Mustafa has paid for both levels of Narges's resting place. But he believed he might be forced to use the other level in the near future or let somebody else use it.

"So Narges cannot be left alone in peace even in her grave?" I asked him with distress.

"No. That's going to be the rule now for all Tehrani citizens."

"How about Father's grave?"

"He is in an old section a few kilometres away. The new rule doesn't apply to those graves, for now at least."

"So, what's gone happen to Narges?"

"We'll have to put somebody on top of her someday. Nothing urgent. But eventually there must be another body. We need a corpse soon!"

"I'm sorry… I wish there were a way around it. I hate to see a stranger in the same grave with my mom."

"Yeah, I know. Only one solution exists, if you agree…"

"What solution?"

"We can move your father and put him in the same grave with Narges."

Uncle Mustafa's hilarious suggestion made us laugh together for two minutes before I said, "Wouldn't that be both Narges's and Father's dreams coming true! To be together for eternity!"

I'm thinking about his suggestion seriously though! Maybe they deserve to rot together for so many good and bad reasons!

5

The phrase 'history repeats itself' is just another thought I'd like to share with you before ending this document. Obviously, it's only an old cliché that some people believe in, while most of us consider it an anecdote or superstition. But I'm starting to think that maybe I should change my position. Perhaps history does actually repeat itself, after all! Maybe our genes, and growing-up experiences, foster our brain and spirit to behave in certain ways. They might force us do all the stupid things necessary to write a particular story for our lives, usually akin to our families' past histories. It sounds silly, I know, but so many events in my life make me wonder. For example, it appears Narges did everything in her power to end with the same kind of dismal destiny that Ozra Banu was forced to endure at the end of her life. Another example: I married a woman who is also ugly, balding, and nasty. Sounds familiar? That was exactly what Father had done for no goddamn good reason. I did it out of pity too! The same way he had. And I'm paying the price for it, as well. I married Katherine also based on wrong assumptions. I'd imagined she was at least intelligent; the same way Father had thought about Narges. And then I was proven wrong on that ground as well. She is actually a big moron at so many levels, and also as spiteful as Narges had been when she'd assumed I'd never forgive Father.

It really hurts when Katherine often tells me that I am a lousy shrink, especially in front of the kids. The nerve of this woman! All along, I'd imagined I'd saved her life. Now, as my reward, she's killing me with her arrogance! I married her purely out of compassion and now it really hurts when she shows only malice in return. I guess she's probably right about my being a lousy psychiatrist, after all. The gross mistakes I've made are excellent evidences. How could I have not anticipated the consequences of marrying her? How could I have not diagnosed the depth of her incurable wickedness? I should've known that people like Narges and Katherine are just too mean to be cured.

My kids have turned even ruder than Katherine. When I recall my deep affection for Father, I feel sick to my bones witnessing my kids' cockiness. I just go nuts. In the old times, respect was instilled deep in our genes and culture. We couldn't imagine youngsters, or even grownups, talk so idiotically to their parents. It's amazing how these kids call their fathers by the first name and talk to them as foolishly as they wish. They even insist on their silly opinions about life as if they were born a philosopher. At least I'd kept my mouth shut all those years I'd felt the same way myself during my fidgety youth. On those creepy occasions, every time an adult asked me what I was thinking, I only said, 'Nothing." It made them madder at me, though!

The story of my marital mess and whether Daphne Cox can help me save my soul deserves another book. I may tell you all about that later depending on how things go and how I feel. Things don't look so great at the present time though, as you have surely guessed after reading this gloomy novel—the Daphne's Document. Exhaustion and Katherine's nagging are making me sick. Now what can I do? I just wonder about the next chapter of my life and a chance to put it in a happier document for, or with, Daphne.

My relationship with God is a bit sore again as well, after His failure to save Father, then sending me Katherine and letting Daphne slip away! Sometimes, I wish I were a blind believer or an arrogant atheist, instead of still wondering about God's real nature or mercy, while admiring His mastery in creating such an intricate Nature and enjoying all this beauty with every breath.

Still, my life remains rickety, as if a quicksand gulping me now, although a bizarre event is keeping me somewhat amused these days, while the points I made about 'history repeating itself' also roll in my head. Two weeks ago, I received a letter from a woman who lives in London and claims to be my sister. She's asked me to contact her so that we could possibly meet. I'm kind of hesitant to open a new can of worms, though, especially in my present state of mind! What do you think? Who could she be?

Kian Noori, M.D.
Los Angeles, July 1997